The Abundant Dreamer

ALSO BY HAROLD BRODKEY

First Love and Other Sorrows

The
Abundant Dreamer

HAROLD BRODKEY

JONATHAN CAPE
THIRTY-TWO BEDFORD SQUARE LONDON

For Ellen and Elena and my Ann Emily

First published in Great Britain 1989
Jonathan Cape Ltd, 32 Bedford Square, London WC1B 3SG
© Harold Brodkey 1963, 1965, 1968, 1969, 1973, 1975

A CIP catalogue record for this book
is available from the British Library

ISBN 0-224-02687-9

Printed in Great Britain by
Mackays of Chatham PLC

Contents

The Abundant
Dreamer

MARCUS WEILL has said he is chiefly concerned with virtue and death in the movies he makes, but the truth is that his usual theme is that we are not capable of much virtue because we are afraid of death. He would have us believe that we flee from logic and order because they remind us that we must die, while illogic and disorder soothe us by proving that nothing makes sense, that nothing is certain, not even death. In his movie *La Nouvelle Cléopâtre en Avignon*, the narrator says, "Do not be cross because our characters do not always have the same faces; they are being true to life and death." The narrator says, "We hope to demonstrate not Euclidean but mortal geometry, the grand trickery of theorems we place in nature and find there for our own delight." So the image exists for Marcus. In *La Nouvelle Cléopâtre en Avignon*, the heroine bends over her lover. One hears a clock and the heroine's breath; one sees the drowsy pulse, the lecherous tic beside her lover's eye and the heroine's finger stealing out to touch it. The narrator says, "Is it not time for her to guess that the flesh is a clock, an unrenewable clock?" The narrator says, "It is an axiom in the mortal geometry that the noise of a quarrel will drown the sound of all the clocks in a room." When the lovers quarrel, we are not permitted to hear what they say; we see their faces change and we see that from moment to moment they are different people. The narrator says, "Uncertainty increases their passion," and the scene of reconciliation is the most passionate in the movie. The hero lies asleep. The heroine enters his room and wakes

him with her kisses and her tears. He opens his eyes and abruptly she
ceases to cry and moves her head until she and her lover are face to face;
then she assumes a dizzying, not quite convincing—so bright is it—
smile. The camera is suddenly a great distance from the bed; the lovers
embrace in a room with melting walls. Trees appear, their branches
agitated as in a summer storm. Among the trees, lions and monkeys and
snakes and tigers glide and prowl or sit or crouch or sleep. Shadows are
flung back and forth; in the room, the shadows have the fish shapes of
terror. The lovers on their bed are figurines inside a cracked glass bell,
a thin, cracked glass arbor in the middle of a wind-torn, window-
haunted garden. The heroine cries out, "Ah, God, I am so happy," and
the scene ends.

Marcus is thickset, temperamental, good-looking. He has made five
movies in France, one in Belgium, two in Italy, one in Greece. Four of
his movies have been shown in this country with considerable critical
and public acclaim, one with no acclaim. Exhibitors would like to show
the others, but Marcus is careless and somewhat grasping about money,
and he has signed too many contracts: who is privileged to sell what,
who is to receive what is under litigation in three countries. He was
born in New York and often uses as backgrounds vistas of a city—
distant, seen through windows, light-struck, overexposed, resembling
the sun-washed backgrounds, pale and geometrical, of early Renaissance
paintings: Piero della Francesca and Botticelli; against such backgrounds his people move in simplified costumes, linear, eyes and mouths
like pebbles, and dominant. He is a Jew. He avoids dialogue in his
movies if he can. In life, he experiences very little simply and directly;
nothing is merely itself. "For me," he has said, "it is like the glass walls
in that place in Proust—the restaurant reflected in its own walls, and
the diners, and through the glass the flowers outside." A kiss is a moment—heavy, round, a melon; the sharp abridgment of isolation is a
knife into the melon, parting the tough skin; the soft pastel interior
appears. Lo, it is hollow. In the hollow, seeds. His emotion for a woman
tends in the early stages to be formal and dark. It is as if he were
practicing one of the early religions with superstition and awe. But later
she becomes a girl (or two of them) he used to know, or a bucket too
small for the live fish in it, or the Rond Point: tourists, garishness, *art
moderne*, flowers, fountains, all of it. He cannot evade this elaboration
of the sensual event; it is a circumstance of his existence.

A movie is to him primarily an arrangement of recognitions, an *allée* laid out so that at every step what is being seen alters the sense of what has been seen. The audience must be paradoxically surprised by logic, as if logic were unpredictable. Success is to have the audience accept the conclusion in the full pride of having recognized the geometry that caused it. At the end of the film comes a recognition that the *allée* could lead nowhere but to this. In Rome, about to commence shooting on *Rencontre du Voyage*, he says, "The beginning will be very simple. She is in the Sistine Chapel, in a crowd of tourists, looking up at the ceiling. She is sad and restless and frightened in that crowd, looking at that ceiling. Then we know her. . . ." He speaks slowly, asthmatically breathing through his mouth, at breakfast on the terrace of the large villa outside Rome his backers have rented for him. The movie is to go before the cameras in an hour. Below the terrace lie a largely untended garden and a swimming pool, and, beyond an uneven hedge of oleanders, greenish-yellow fields (a sunburned golf course), and the hills leading to Rocca di Papa; in the middle distance are the ruins of the Claudian Aqueduct. It is not quite eight o'clock in the morning, and some coolness remains in the air from the night, but it is unsubstantial, wispy, and will soon disappear.

From the head of the table, he addresses his writer, Loesser; his cameraman, Alliat; and his stars, Jehane Duret and Oskar Haase. (Marcus's family—his children and his housekeeper-companion—are in Paris; he has brought only his valet.) Jehane Duret is his mistress, but the affair is dying. She is tall, with a taut body, a broad, self-assertive mouth. "You are both restless," he says to Jehane and Oskar—"Oskar le Beau" the French papers call him. "They— You must see this thing about them." He has trouble finding words. "They are *ordinary*—not in looks . . . not in soul . . . but in the guesses they make. . . ." His voice trails off. His auditors stare at him with incomprehension. He frowns. He says pleadingly, "One could photograph them anywhere. In front of a department-store window—they would look *suitable* there!" His audience stirs, sensing something performable; they wait for further instruction. Marcus jumps up. "Look. Look, I will *show* you." He is a poor actor; there was a time when he tried to act, but no matter what part he was assigned he was onstage merely an overintense, large-eyed young man anxious to be an actor. He embarks on a pantomime. His smile fades; he looks bored, distant; he wrinkles his mouth, knits his fingers.

A maid hurries out of the villa, her shoes loud on the stone pavement;

observing the pantomime, she tiptoes the last few feet, a finger to her lips signifying she does not intend to say a word, and she slips a cablegram into Marcus's hand. Marcus shrugs and resumes his pantomime, turning in a slow circle until he confronts the striking view—the slow, yellow-brown descent of the fields to the aqueduct and the skirts of the bluish hills rising to Rocca di Papa. He hopefully scowls, reaches out his arms, turns away, head drooping. It is a ludicrous performance. Loesser, the writer, says in a low voice, "Isolated—sensually and personally. Trapped. Unable to feel." Oskar Haase exclaims, "*Ja! Gut!*" He nods, but he looks eager to please rather than penetrated by understanding. Jehane's eyes are shut, probably with embarrassment at Marcus's performance.

Marcus says, "They feel this way in front of expensive automobiles and movie theaters. Their guesses are crooked." Oskar and Jehane sit up, actors' shrewdness and voracity in their eyes. The cablegram rustles in Marcus's hand. "So you are very restless," he instructs them, adding, "and cold. If there is no self-pity, you cannot pity others." He turns to the cablegram. It is from America, from his stepmother, and states: "NANNA DIED IN SLEEP LAST NIGHT FUNERAL TWO-THIRTY B'NAI SHOLOM BOSTON SEVENTH JUNE."

The sun lies heavily on Marcus's white shirt; dampness wells from the ocher walls of the villa.

"*Qu'est-ce que c'est?*" Jehane asks.

"*Ma grandmère est morte.*"

"*Oh, pauvre petit,*" Jehane says. Her actress's face plunges into sympathy, the muscles of the strong, self-assertive lips loosen, the eyes grow somber. It is a familiar sight; she has stayed up with him for long nights on lawns, in rooms: "I cannot sleep." "*Pauvre Marc.* Shall we play cards?" "I am too nervous for cards. The picture is not growing. *La mort vient et je suis nu.*" He is afraid of being tired the next day, but he fears death more and cannot sleep. "I've taken three Seconal, but they don't work." Jehane has walked with him for hours in the city, among lampposts: "Our orchard," Marcus calls them. He can always sleep after dawn.

Jehane is thin-shouldered, long-necked. Her hair is straight, an arras. The famous eyes ripen with emotion, and Marcus scowls, wanting to discourage her; shooting is about to begin. He has no intention of being upset because a cablegram has announced that Nanna is dead. He hears—it is imaginary—a metallic clang, a corrugated metal door sliding shut, rollers spinning in the curved tracks (he sees them); the door bangs. What was a doorway is as solid as a wall. Fingertips creep along the bottom edge of the door, work it up an inch or two; is this memory? Nanna's neatly waved, short gray hair, like ribs of grayish-brown sand.

"She is a rich woman," he says, careless of his tenses. "Perhaps she's left me her fortune."

His senses bucket uneasily on the tide of sunlight. Marcus rides their plunging momentum, legs braced, paunch distending his belt; the figures at the table are cut about with shadows. His eyes, his nose, the features of his face are full-formed, fleshy; nothing in his face is skimped or in short supply: not flesh, not shapeliness, not intelligence. The thick quarter-moons of his eyelids blink rapidly over the strained eyes. To control the blinking he squints. He does not want his actors to be distracted or alienated. Actors are sentimental, harshly ceremonial like children, and, like children, suspicious; should they be put off, they will disbelieve his judgment, they will evade his will, commit surprises in front of the camera. "She was not very kind to me. Or to my mother," he says sternly.

To his mother, no. Noreen was pretty, long-limbed; her hair was gold red. His mother, Noreen. A gay, laughing Irish girl—so she saw herself—bringing love and joy and religious truth into her husband's family. Pretty Noreen said, "I've always admired Jews, their close family life." She was taken by surprise. Her husband's rich German-French Jewish family looked askance at the gift of love and joy brought by religious truth—intensities and rivalries and everything ugly breathed out through the confessional as through a whale's spout. They practiced self-cultivation and seriousness and owned to a bewildering complexity of attitudes and rites. It seemed that they already had a religion. Noreen sat, laughed, displayed her jollity, showed off her full trousseau of beliefs on all matters, her acceptance of Jews, and her in-laws watched her politely, with good-natured patience, until they grew bored, and then they ignored her. The child Marcus looked on, and thought of a Maypole that danced and threw out streamers to dancers who would not move to pick them up. Noreen drank a good deal. "Oh, it's four o'clock! I'm in the mood for a drinkie. Anyone else want a drinkie, too?" Marcus, catching Nanna's eyes studying him, realized that in some lights he appeared ordinary, a doubtful quantity.

Marcus abruptly sits down at the table. The others, to soothe their uneasiness, talk of their grandmothers; Oskar mentions a *Grossmutter* killed in the bombing of Hamburg, Loesser a grandmother who played pinochle with her nurse between attacks of angina. Marcus listens. Nanna walked with her sons after dinner at Scantuate, in the garden, above the sea. The flag crackled blusteringly on the flagpole. The children in a crowd went out at dusk to lower it. Nanna was small, well formed, neat gray-brown—beside Noreen a thrush next to a flamingo. She wore dark floral-print dresses that had no particular style, and hair nets; she did not like to have her hair disarranged. Marcus sees her old-woman's hair, grown long during illness, blowing loose, unconstrained; her uncapturable minnow eyes (he had never as a child managed to control them, hold them, as he wished, to his will: One day when he was five, he knelt by the ornamental pool in the garden. "Are you trying to catch fish, Markie?" He shook his head. "I can't. They won't let me catch them") and her round cheeks, and the small almond chin that was the focus of her old-woman's prettiness, and the thin, always somewhat awry, intelligent lips are as constrained and without vivacity as if, in a game of turnabout, they have been netted and her hair has been set free. Her face—to him a creature, like a marmoset—has been extinguished. Jehane has told a story of her grandmother bidding her obey the nuns at school or risk hellfire, and now she leans her head on Marcus's shoulder; sweat breaks out on Marcus's skin. He does not want to be consoled. He is concerned with facts. A fact is, he is not grief-stricken. Another fact: Nanna will not again give her letters to Nils, the chauffeur, to mail. Nor write checks.

NANNA WROTE checks in such numbers that one could not see a checkbook without thinking of her. "Markie," Noreen said, "Nanna's sent you another check." Nanna's emanation arrived in the small apartment in New Rochelle where he lived with Noreen after her divorce from his father. They brought privileges: clothes and lessons—riding, tennis, piano—summer camp, books; a bicycle, a cashmere scarf, a globe of the world for Christmas. Nanna's checks made him special, separated him from the other children in the block of shabby apartments. Nanna wished her grandsons and granddaughters to pursue interests, hobbies, projects; hobbies, followed seriously, became distinctions. Nanna believed a Weill was, by definition, able. To go to see Nanna was to have a darkroom in the large cellar beneath the house at Scantuate, the walls of which thrummed when the waves broke on the bluff on a stormy day.

Was to have Nanna look at him again, reconsider him. "Would you like to go away to school?" He went to Andover on Nanna's checks like a north-woods boy on snowshoes. The doctors who tended him that spring, when the nervousness he'd suffered at school turned into pneumonia, said he must have sun, air, and untroubled rest. He spent the summer at Scantuate with Nanna. Nanna said, "I would like to buy you a present." He said, "I am very happy you could let me come. That's a present. I don't want anything else." He could not look at her directly; it seemed a hand that signed a check could circumscribe a heart. He absorbed calm from the brown, ugly house, the carpeted rooms, among the Chinese bronzes. "You should be outside—swimming." He said, "I thought maybe you wanted company." She said, "Later. You must have exercise, Marcus."

"Dear Mother," he wrote, "I am fine. I am well. I miss you." He wanted to be polite.

He made two comic books, lithographing the pictures. One comic book was "Madame Bovary"; one was "Wuthering Heights." He showed them to Nanna. "I like to tell stories with pictures," he said. "Would you like a movie camera?" Carefully, Marcus said, "I would like one, but I don't think I deserve one. I mean, it isn't my birthday. I haven't done anything to earn it." The chauffeur brought a movie camera from Boston, a model recommended by Nanna's lawyer, whom she telephoned for advice. "You must think about going to visit your mother sometime this summer. Perhaps after Labor Day," she said. Marcus said, "But you'll be alone then." The next day, she said, "Since you don't seem to want to leave me, I have written your mother and asked her to come and visit us here." Marcus was intent on making his first movie with Nils, the chauffeur, and with one of the Irish maids. "Now, you're a murderer. You come sn-sneaking," Marcus stammered to Nils. He had stammered when he was younger only at moments of high excitement, but lately—for the past year—he had begun to stammer more; he stammered almost all the time now. "You c-come around the garage door with the knife. . . ." He set the Irish maid running along the bluff, hair and skirts awhirl. "You are in mortal t-terror of your life." Noreen came, almost as pretty as ever. He showed her the darkroom, the comic books he'd lithographed. The comic books upset her; they were lewd. Noreen said she was seeing a man named Little, a hardware dealer. "We just may get married, Markie. You'll have another father— won't that be fine?" she asked hopefully.

Noreen drank quite a bit on that visit. Marcus watched—she filled herself with bubbles; the surface of her face bubbled like paint with air in it. Noreen asked, "Is it true you want to live with Nanna?" She let slide a glass tray of laughter. She said, a good sport, "After all, you have a right to all this. It's part of your heritage." Her gaiety was inflexible. "He can't make a decision. Poor Markie, he won't laugh." She tickled him with her forefinger, saying, "Stop being a sourpuss. Come on, Markie, let's be happy." She said to Nanna at the dinner table, "Markie's been disturbed; he ought to have some religious instruction. Religion is very stabilizing for a young boy." Nanna changed the subject. In the apartment in New Rochelle, when Noreen made breakfast, she sometimes sang in a tremulous, thin, weak, charmingly lyric voice—God, what charm there was in that tremulous voice—"Pack up your troubles in your old kit bag, and smile, smile, smile. . . ." Noreen said, "Markie, you must tell me how you feel. I'll help you think. I have to admit Nanna can do a lot for you." Noreen said, "What's best is what helps you to concentrate on your studies, to work hard and do well in school, Markie. Do you want to live with Nanna?" She turned her amusement-hungry, warm, and depthless face to him. The child Marcus saw a face bubbled like paint with air in it, saw noise and a party and someone shouting, saw a hillside with shepherds and shepherdesses—and Noreen singing—and a breeze ruffling the leaves of the chairs turned into roses of Sharon. Marcus said, "I don't know." Nanna and Noreen were closeted in the library for several hours. Noreen came out and kissed him goodbye. She said, "You work hard and do well in school, Markie." She went to live and drink in sunny California—Nanna's checks helped ease the strain of emigration—and Marcus made his home with his grandmother.

A FLY struts jerkily in the sunlight. Marcus says, "We were talking about the movie. Where was I?" "Self-pity," says Loesser. "Yes," says Marcus. Noreen still held legal custody. "A formality," Nanna said. Nanna said she was going to Florida for the winter; Marcus was to have Thanksgiving, Christmas, and Easter with his father and his father's second wife and the four children he had by that second wife. "You must get to know them better," Nanna said. Nanna said she had brought Marcus back to the family. "You are a Weill," Marcus's father said. "I want you to feel free to come to my house at any time." "Thank you,"

Marcus said. He was thirteen. Marcus says, "Yes. Well. These people have no self-pity. They go *at* things." He makes a gesture of someone grabbing. It crosses his mind to say that they are as bold as doctors, that what they want—their habit—is to fall in love. But instead he falls silent. His father said, "Marcus, I want to say I'm glad you're— Well, let me say a father and his son are not happily parted." "Thank you," Marcus said. His father said, "You never asked me about the divorce. You must have a good many questions." "No, sir. I mean, no, thank y-you, sir." His father said, "Marcus, I'm not doing this for *my* sake." He paused, he said, "Don't you want to talk anything over with me?" Marcus said, "It's up to y-you, sir. If you w-want to talk, s-sir." Marcus says, "You have any questions about the camera angles? Oskar? Jehane?" His father said, "Never mind. We'll try again later." Marcus was ashamed of his father. What did talk mean? Talk didn't mean anything. Jehane cries, *"Marc, c'est impossible!"* The day is *triste*, the city, Rome, is *triste*, unendurable on the occasion of a death. "How can we work?" she demands. She is insistent, bitter, contemptuous. "How can we be expected to work as if nothing has happened? A woman is dead. It is a terrible thing. A terrible omen. My God."

Nanna said, "Your allowance will be fifty dollars a month. I expect you to keep a record of your expenditures. Someday you will have money of your own, and you must start now to learn how to take care of it."

Oskar, eyeing Jehane curiously, strokes his long, muscular throat. Jehane is always unsettled before starting a movie; the geometry of old age and death appalls her. Marcus says, "Our work makes us monsters." Jehane says sadly, *"C'est vrai; tu as raison."* She lifts a sugar-encrusted roll to her mouth. Marcus thinks, That will stop the rathole . . . nothing can slither for a moment.

The maid announces the car is at the door. *"Bon!"* cries Marcus. *"Allons,* everyone." He chivies them along. The immense and dusty rooms swing up, float, descend behind him.

Two boats rode at mooring in front of Nanna's beach, which gardeners raked free of shells on Mondays and Thursdays. It was forbidden to swim or take out the boats on Sunday morning. Almost everyone in Scantuate went to church. "It is not polite to desecrate the Sabbath of others." To be late or unwashed at mealtimes meant eating in the kitchen. One wore a jacket to dinner during the week, and a jacket and tie on weekends. The only permissible way to dress was in the casual, local, escape-from-the-city style. A daughter-in-law foolish enough to attempt chic would be greeted with "I love red silk at the seashore. So suitable." Nanna's sarcasm, politely uttered, continued until the offender was submissive. Anger or sulkiness or a son's trying to persuade her—"Be more reasonable, Nanna"—would lead her to say, "It would seem I am not free to enjoy my own house." Her son then admitted he was wrong or gathered his wife and children and left—so the family joke went—on still another of the flights of the Jews. As her children grew older and more prosperous, they came to visit Nanna for shorter periods of time and more formally. The worst thing Nanna could say was, "This is boring. This is so boring."

Alliat, the cameraman, talking of emulsions, lenses, says, "In *Rashomon* . . ." Nanna's voice mocks: "Panchromatic! Emulsion! Egg tempera sounds so much nicer." "Not really, Nanna. Listen—*egg tempera* . . ." Nanna rarely went to movies. Oskar, Jehane, Loesser, and Alliat climb into the black Lancia; the sunlight beats down on the white stones of the driveway, the nearby bushes; the atmosphere, Marcus thinks, is exactly that of a funeral—the tension, the unease, the constraint. It is always the same before a movie begins.

Marcus has said in interviews and to disciples that a movie is a face. "People go to movies to spy on a face. If a movie gallops, only children are amused. A true film advances from gossip to weeping. In *Camille* you see Garbo first as a demimondaine, a very simple, very glamorous piece of gossip, but scene by scene the gossip becomes more complex, more details are added—she practices falsity, is ashamed of her body and herself, has a neurotic longing for honesty. Suddenly you get this breath, this sensation, My God, she really is a whore; she really does love that young man; he mustn't marry a whore; oh, my God, how awful. And then you cry."

W H A T   H E imagined Nanna's expectations of a boarder to be caught like cobwebs at Marcus's eyes and throat. (Marcus in the car traveling in the line of traffic on the Appia Antica places his hand on Jehane's thigh, near her stomach; he folds his large hand over her flesh.) Marcus suffered from a form of asthma and breathed noisily. Nanna made much of the manners of Marcus's half-brothers and half-sisters, who were soft-voiced and reserved, the children of the English Jewess his father had married two months after his divorce from Noreen. They were better-mannered than he was, but not as interested in pleasing Nanna. Doctors had said Marcus's breathing was a physical affliction. Marcus was careful. He learned. He breathed quietly. Nanna said, "You see, the child's not asthmatic." Nanna did not always look at him; sometimes it seemed to him she imagined he was someone else. The school had written, "Mark has the capacity for brilliance but is eccentric in execution." "In feeling, too," the teacher had added when he spoke to Marcus's father. At the moments when Marcus stammered, his mouth, awry with strain, resembled Nanna's. He said, indicating the wicker furniture, the heavy sideboards, the Chinese bronzes, Japanese chests, and Corots his grandfather had collected, "This room has the r-richness of the Orient." Nanna sighed. "Jews are often called Oriental. Do you know what fatalism is? It leaves out the will. I disapprove of that very much." The minnow eyes struggled with momentary confusion. "What was I saying? Oh, yes. I loathe fatalism." Marcus said, "The wind is rising. Look at the spray. The sea has crinkly, Jewish hair." "I dislike poetic conversation," Nanna said. Marcus asked, "What c-color were the P-Pyramids when you and Grandf-father were in E-Egypt? Was the sun very bright? Was the sand white or brown? Did your sit-upon h-hurt from riding on the camel?" Nanna said, "I did not know I remembered so clearly." Marcus, in his desire to please, tended to mimic the grownups he was speaking to. He was small for his age (but he grew twelve inches in his first sixteen months with Nanna), and his mimicry unsettled adults. He would say, "Have you licked the crabgrass problem this year, Dr. Poore?" His voice was changing, and he was excitable and nervous. He saw that at the dinner table others made straight-angled and orderly remarks that were like toy wooden blocks. But he could produce nothing so regular, geometric, and gay; his conversational throat was a cave, and what came out was an overgallant compliment from his reading—"I'd g-give the g-golden apple to you, Mrs. Tredwell," he said to one of Nanna's guests, and blushed—or he spoke and Nanna lifted a hand to her hair as if to protect it against a bat Marcus had released to flitter around the dinner table: "People not t-talking about money is like people not talking about sex. I bet they don't want to g-get excited in public." He blurted once, "Do all women go cuckoo at menopause?" Nanna's minnow eyes flickered and took refuge in distance. "Medical matters are not discussed at table, Marcus."

Outside the dining-room windows, Crimson Glory and Maréchal Niel and Peace roses (a staining of pink along the lips of their ivory petals) grew around a reflecting pool. Nanna ordered the roses thinned, ordered speech lessons for Marcus. The roses prospered. Marcus did not stammer anymore.

Charities. Reforms. The will to do. Improving Marcus. "Conversation should be light and pointless and yet have a point—but by surprise, like scent in a sweet and pretty flower." "Yes, Nanna." The minnow eyes moved in, away, not quite regarding him. "Like posies?" he asked, drawing the minnow eyes out of the shadows to laugh. "Like poesies," he said. "Poses." The minnow eyes moved away. He had gone too far.

The car pauses at the traffic light in front of the bastion gate of San Sebastiano. Its two towers guard a narrow gate set in the rose-pink walls, folded stiffly along a tussocked rise. Traffic moves through San Sebastiano one way, out of the city. The Lancia turns left, past a row of suburban apartment houses, beyond which appear distant fields. The country, *le paysage,* passage everywhere; a city is precise about passage. Reasonably safe. Nanna was never drunk.

Guests at Nanna's table were honored by her invitation and worked to be amusing. She was well served by her tradespeople and her servants; the dowagers of Scantuate treated her with respect. Marcus sat, taking care not to slouch, and reported his progress with his boxing lessons; Nanna admired the ability to protect oneself. Nanna listened. Her minnow eyes swam over his face, his posture. She was lonely. She did not get along well with her children. Her friends were ill or dying. Arthritis clenched her fingers. She was old.

Through a modern gateway (two croquet wickets, one twice the size of the other) cut into the wall, the car enters Rome.

Marcus's father said to Nanna, "It must be difficult for you." Nanna was a chauvinist. She said, "Marcus is a genius." Marcus walked with Nanna before dinner on the bluff above the harbor. Nanna spoke of Europe; the children of the family usually went to Europe before they came of college age. Marcus, pretending to be unshaken, said Europe sounded very interesting. Nanna said they would think about Europe; he was becoming very gentlemanly; he was a dear boy. Marcus burst out into his imitations. Formerly, he had done imitations of animals— lions, roosters, rabbits—the wit of which had resided largely in the abjectness of his performance. He had adapted his repertoire to doing people as animals—Franklin Roosevelt as an otter, Ethel Barrymore as a lemur, Gamma Foster of Scantuate as an elk in the rain forest; his imitations sometimes jolted with a queer penetration and induced painful, unhappy laughter. Nanna did not approve. She laughed and changed the subject; she spoke slightingly of certain Massachusetts politicians. Marcus, beside her, glanced out over the harbor, the silken water of high tide, moored boats with masts like splinters rising into the quivering, yellow-powdered air, the uneven bluffs and wandering frame houses across the pipe bowl of the bay, neatly pretty and calm, peaceful, a scene glazed on a plate; he walked beside an almond-chinned Manchu empress; he wore a Chinese court costume of brilliant red and blue; the frame houses were pagodas.

"It is interesting," Oskar says, "that the trees in Rome are not so many or so tall as in Paris. I think the average rainfall here must be less. I think this is truly a more tropical climatological region."

The pedantry in Oskar's voice belongs to Willi—the German tourist who has an affair with Jehane in *Rencontre du Voyage*. Since rehearsals began, Oskar has become less certainly Oskar; he has become Oskar-Willi; it is difficult to make out when Oskar is Oskar and not Willi. Oskar himself no longer clearly knows. If an actor holds too strongly to his image of himself, he will seem sly to his audience, clearly an imposter; the audience will think they do not want to have anything put over on them, and they will not be amused. Oskar is in earnest about his art and deludes himself.

But he is afraid of not winning the love of the audience, and his voice as Oskar-Willi is wan, and sorrowful as if to say that he is not the man that he should be and might he not be pitied and understood. Oskar is self-exculpatory. Oskar as Willi has the moving sweetness of Oskar's view of himself. Marcus thinks that Oskar conceives of time and the world as a story in which he is the hero, that Oskar is not convinced that other people are as real as he is. For the part of Willi, Oskar the man is quite right. It is Oskar the actor trying to improve on Oskar the man who does not suit the part.

Marcus wants Willi to be savagely alive, more lifelike than Oskar's acting allows him to be. But if Marcus goes to Oskar and says, "Oskar, look, I want you to see your own fatuity and your habits of self-delusion and use them for Willi," Oskar will grow depressed and look for a philosophy or to psychiatry to set himself right, and since acting to Oskar means a chance to improve on himself, he will be denied access to his talent and give a wooden performance in front of the camera. Marcus must be devious with Oskar to get what he wants. He has a scheme ready to limit Oskar's fancying up his image too much; he will let Oskar be simple and charming and then he will catch Oskar out—he hopes to have Willi, Willi as he wishes to be, Willi perhaps so real that the audience will be torn with pity and fear.

Marcus eyes Oskar's hands. Oskar's hands are Willi—sinewy, ready, recognizably male; they are versatile machines. Marcus reaches out and takes Oskar's wrist. Oskar jerks, then relaxes, as if to say, "Do with me as you will." He is being seductive. Marcus murmurs, "Sh-h-h." With a dry rudeness, he lifts Oskar's hand into the light and turns it this way and that, examining it as if it were an objet d'art someone was willing to sell cheaply. He sees in the shape of the side of the palm and its continuation into the little finger the shell of a dog whelk. The gulls hunted them at Scantuate. A shell, he thinks. Marcus the psalmist. Marcus sighs at the beauty of Oskar's hands. He looks like a Jewish peddler.

When had he ever held Nanna's hand? Not often, since Nanna was not demonstrative and did not like demonstrativeness in the people near her. When he was very little, five or six—his affections came quickly and powerfully as a child (and did so still, but in another context)—he'd held one of her hands with both of his, sitting on her lap while she told him a story; and once, when his Uncle David died, he was scared and wanted to be with her in her remoteness; he pretended grief and held her hand; and when he was seventeen, lying in front of the fire in the fireplace at Scantuate (September, time to go back to school), he told her boastfully, to compliment her for her labor to make him well and strong (he was not deaf to her requirements), that he was in love. He did not tell her how happy he was, or what love was like. Whenever he closed his eyes, a myriad-pointed light exploded; it was unbelievable—this girl, this pretty girl cared for him. Nanna was not amused by sex in the young. He was very careful in what he said. Nanna talked about "grace" in people; those who had it were like falcons in the air, chamois on a rock; love and grace were cousins, she said, joining him in admiration for Sukie Tredwell. He reached for Nanna's hand and she let him hold it. "I can tell people's character from their hands," Noreen had always said. Nanna's hands were round and firm. White. Ringless. Now dead.

"L o o k," he said, "as white as the flesh of dead hostesses," and held up the note. After eleven years of silence, Nanna (aged seventy-eight) announced that she was in Paris at the Lotti and would like to see Marcus. Marcus was thirty-one then, a celebrity of sorts, a thickening, heavy-lidded young man. In a white suit that needed pressing, Marcus sat in her suite at the Lotti while she prattled—she was so oblique, the impression was of wit—about doctors, travel, the condition of Paris, indicating that she was ignoring the past, he could do as he wished. It disconcerted her whenever he looked at her; he studied the gloss of the wooden floor. He listened to her voice. It was tired and broken by little clicks. Her sense of grammar was intact. He could not remember if she had always talked so much. He heard in her light, old-woman's sarcasm the stumbling chords of a vast boredom. She was at odds with the family. "I don't, however, tamper with my will. Perhaps you'd like the house in Scantuate?" She was not as clever as before. Marcus saw a crooked rick of thin quartz rods, largely cracked, peeling, and broken, supporting the weight of a large rock that half rested on them. He was touched by the sight of her almond chin. She rested or slept for long hours in order to be fresh and "able" when she was with people. He introduced her—"My grandmother"—as if she had been a charwoman who had scrubbed floors to send him to college. He took her to Rubinstein's, Braque's, and Colette's.

"My new movie is a comedy," he told her. The Comic Spirit—he had reasoned it out; he saw—was a total thing. Every action had to have a comic cast—cast of characters, tone, and deformity of vision. To see the comic side one had only to refuse indulgence to the tragic; what was left was comic. Marcus spoke gravely; he was obviously deeply immersed in his movie. The rhetoric of tragedy was that the characters were under the pressure of death and of their lives and were bereft of choice. The tragic imbecile cared and suffered and forgave. The Comic Spirit took everything for granted, ordained that one suffered little and found little to forgive. His movie was to be about the lives—that is, the businesses and love affairs—of certain Parisians. Each of the characters professed a belief: "It's all psychological. It's all in my mind (or yours)," and "This is a troubled age," and "Religion is utterly necessary to mankind," and "As the good Russian Chekhov said, 'Man finds happiness in work.' "

"You see how funny that is," Marcus said. "Take almost anything—cutting yourself shaving. A c-character can cut himself and say any one of those things—'This is a troubled age'—and it's funny, you know. We are going to have only simple happenings, you see. It is a sincere movie. A little cruel. One is sincere on so many levels." He began to talk very fast. "And, of course, sometimes it will be sad enough that you can cry.

The pet dachshund of the woman who holds that religion is utterly necessary to mankind is run over and killed. The woman is basically a very kind woman, but she was her dog's religion and now she can't say anything. She does not know what she can say about her dog."

"I am not certain I would cry," Nanna said.

"Yes. But it goes on. She recovers. Her grief has made her self-centered; she still says that religion is necessary for mankind; she says she could not have managed without it; she has a new dachshund she doesn't like very much. She says that good dachshunds who do well in obedience school and are faithful to their mistresses go to Heaven. She says, 'Religion is utterly necessary to mankind.' She is very consistent, but basically, by then, she is a broken woman. Wait until it is in the movie and you can *see* it."

"Yes," Nanna said. "I'm certain it will be good."

. At Orly, Marcus kissed her goodbye. Nanna said, "Perhaps you will come see me at Scantuate." Her smile was small, and wry; he saw a paper airplane hanging in the branches of a tree.

"I need so much in the way of comfort. I am not a good traveler," Marcus said. He broke off. Very little could be said without lying. He pressed her hand to his cheek. Orly; the noise of jets. A departure is like a funeral.

Jehane says, "The Ardeatine Gate opens onto the Avenue of the Baths of Caracalla." She is jealous of Oskar, and Marcus's mood oppresses her, and she does not look forward to the movie. She pushes the hair back from her face with one hand and imitates Oskar-Willi's voice: "I wonder that in this part of Rome there are so few structures." She is making fun of the movie. Loesser and Alliat smile. Oskar says, "Ah," and continues the line: "Does it say nothing in the guidebook?" Jehane plucks at her lip and pretends to squint at a peculiarly worded paragraph: "It says a pope was besieged and asked the Normans who at that time held Naples to come to his aid, and they came; they rode in armor, and arrived at the city walls at night, and the leader of the Normans ordered this part of Rome set on fire to make light and clear away the defenders and open the narrow streets so that he and his troops could make their way to the center of the city. Ever after, this part of Rome has remained vineyards, gardens, and farmland. No one has lived here."

Nanna said, "Fools think nothing is serious, but only a fool makes a show of how serious he is." What one valued showed in one's manners. One trusted people whose manners were like one's own. After a dinner party once, when he was fifteen, Marcus said, "Nanna, did I do all right?

Did those people like me?" Nanna replied somewhat angrily that it was impermissible to ask such a question; it was always clear—common sense always indicated quite clearly—our situation vis-à-vis others. He was being self-centered and eager for flattery and was not being nearly clever enough. He said, "Nanna, I thought Cook outdid herself tonight. And, God, how you handled Gamma Foster. Like a master." Nanna smiled and said, "You were very amusing. You're always amusing when you try."

Oskar in a falsetto does Jehane's next line: "The Normans in Normandy are terrible people." Loesser recites with him: "Once, on a vacation, I went to a Norman farmhouse and the farmer made ugly overtures to me." Jehane says in her best Germanic baritone, "My father was killed in Normandy. He was a lieutenant in the Luftwaffe." Marcus says suddenly, "Did you know there was a Jewish pope? A Jew named Pierleoni, a butcher, was the strongest man in Rome. He gained control of the Castel Sant'Angelo and the island in the Tiber and served the Pope. He had his second son baptized, and when the old Pope died, Pierleoni saw to it his son was elected Pope." Oskar says, "That is very interesting." Marcus continues, "However, the bishops outside of Italy refused to recognize him. They did not take baptism seriously enough; they still considered Anacletus the Second a Jew." "The history of Rome is very rich in incident," Oskar says, lapsing into Oskar-Willi. "Yes," says Jehane, taking up her part. Oskar says, "Every people is forgiven its war crimes. The British are forgiven their terror raids, the Americans are forgiven Hiroshima. Only the Germans are not forgiven. I am certain even you, being French, are prejudiced against us." "Not enough," says Jehane.

The psychiatrist said, "Don't take yourself so seriously, boy." Marcus's father said, "We do like you. You know you're always welcome here." Noreen said, "A little bit of humor is a big, big help." Marcus's roommate said, "Take it easy, fella." Marcus at fifteen said at the dinner table, "I can't go along with *King Lear*—I don't believe in tragedy. When people start to take themselves that seriously, I get very uncomfortable." He spoke with a convert's snobbery. "He's only one man. Is it fair to ask an audience to take anyone that seriously? Why doesn't Lear develop a sense of humor and sit down and laugh awhile?"

IN THE Piazzale Numa Pompilio, an immense green bus cuts diagonally across traffic toward the Lancia. The light is blotted from the

Lancia, and green shadows appear on the back of the chauffeur's neck and Loesser's hair. Marcus's work requires that his nerves be uncovered; the nakedness of his nerves is the reach of a pianist's fingers. The possibility of an accident rends him with anguish. Abruptly and passionately, he lifts his hand to shield Jehane's face. The speed with which his mind moves is very great, because it has no stillness to be aroused from. It pictures the disorder on the faces of his two sons and his daughter if he should be killed. (By the well-being of his children Marcus measures the goodness of reality.) They will be convinced of their bad luck; nor will there be enough money for them and for their mother—in a sanitarium in the Vosges, her peculiar and private gaiety soars like a balloon, and forgets to return. Marcus hears the rain of sounds of an accident; experiences despair at the waste, and astonishment at the softness of metal, which wrinkles as easily as a flower. He sees time wadded, crumpled, tossed into a fire, thinks Scotland's burning, and grieves for his children.

He is pressed back against the seat as the Lancia, accelerating, moves left, eludes the bus, faces oncoming traffic, hurtles to the right, slows to a more reasonable speed. He has been misled. Sunlight floods his eyes. Alliat's hair stirs slightly in the wind. The chauffeur expostulates, *"Imbecille! Omicidio!"*

Marcus snorts, chokes, then snorts again—he is a fool. He wants to make a noise. Loesser and Oskar turn and look at him. Loesser demands, "What is so funny." Between spurts of laughter, Marcus says, "We were not killed." Oskar, eyeing him, tentatively begins to laugh, like someone who parts the branches of a bush to start a rabbit—he hopes to discover the nature of the joke. Jehane says, *"Nous étions presque tués!"* Marcus gasps and says, "All's well that ends well." Jehane cries out that this shows the effects of a reactionary government; an oppressed people reverts to savagery. Loesser cuts in in his high, clear voice: The Romans are not a people, they are a history. Their history has made them megalomaniac and simplified their desires: they want power, life after death, and the pleasures of the body and of art.

Alliat exclaims, "Ah!" and Marcus sits up, shoves aside his laughter. The Arch of Constantine is written into the movie; the lovers are to shelter under it from the sun and speak there for the first time of their love. The movie is to be ironic but not a comedy; the lovers are without choice, sensualists in the Greek tradition, in the tradition of the moment uninflected by the presence of God. The Arch, hardly more than an interference, draws near, metamorphoses into a stream of sunlight. Marcus thinks of wings carved in stone, of things become their opposites, of the mood of music striving to be architecture. The jamb of the Arch is out of true from age, and whatever boast it had once been meant to make has been obscured by its lapse from geometry. Oskar will stand beneath it, his arm around Jehane, and point across the street to the rows of evenly spaced cypresses clipped flat on top and cylindrically at the sides to mimic columns, and say, "That was a Temple of Venus."

The Arch is suddenly near: a door without walls; no one need pass through it. But the Colosseum, which rises to the right, is an immense circle, with a multitude of doors that one must pass through to enter or to leave. Marcus breaks into a sweat, and exclaims, "Loesser, we have the symbolism all wrong!"

"What?" says Loesser, frowning. He is satisfied with his script. If Marcus deviates too much from it, then what is filmed will not be Loesser's work; he does not feel he is a pensioner of Marcus's.

Marcus, wordless, points. Outside the car windows wheel the barrel vaults of the Colosseum, tier on tier.

Loesser says in confusion, "The Colosseum, Marcus? You said you thought it was a cliché."

"The Colosseum is a wall," Marcus says. "If the lovers . . ." The car has entered the Piazza del Colosseo. Directly ahead, in the side of a hill, is the entrance to the remains of the Domus Aurea, Nero's house, the Golden House. Underground, a cave; the word "grotesque" comes from the figures in its wall paintings—*grotteschi*, things in a grotto. The image grows. The Colosseum. Nero's house. Marcus never claimed to know, only to see. On the topmost rim of the Colosseum is a place— there—visible as the car passes, where the stones have started to fall; the courses waver, large cracks, uneven V's, are kept from growing by a modern brick wall that rises in a smooth sweep to hold the stones in place.

Marcus says excitedly, "The lovers come out of the Domus Aurea; they will see the Colosseum falling. No. We'll start when they go into Nero's house. No. She refuses to go in. At first. '*Lui, il était fou . . .*' Nero the madman, do you see it? She's afraid. I mean, she doesn't know the person she's fallen in love with. What will he do to her? . . . He insists. They go in. She says, '*Comme un tombeau ici.*' "

"*Naturellement,*" Loesser mutters. He says, "Marcus, we planned this episode to—" but he is interrupted.

Marcus says, "No, no, listen to me. It's dark in the Golden House, and he says 'Boo!' to scare her—my God, as if she needed it! He wants her to embrace him. She does. She clutches at him. Then we cut to— They are walking out—out into the sunlight, and he whispers in her ear, *'Je t'aime, je t'aimerai toujours,'* and she sees the Colosseum falling. These will be real lovers," Marcus exults. "They go into the Colosseum; they pick their way among ruins, and Oskar can whisper, *'Tu es belle, tu es belle, belle, belle.'*" Marcus presses his hands together. He says sentimentally, "They kiss in one of the archways, little figures in an archway. *Then* Oskar can point to the Temple of Venus."

"It won't mock anything in that context, Marcus," Loesser says. "You said when we were doing the script that you didn't want to do *Wuthering Heights on the Seven Hills.*"

"Good God, you're stupid, you don't see anything!" Marcus bursts out. He adds, "For Christ's sake, leave me alone. I have a day's shooting ahead of me." Jehane peeks at Loesser in the rearview mirror, and Loesser, meeting her glance, raises his eyebrows as if to say, "I don't understand a word. What am I supposed to do?" Marcus sits, his hand over his eyes. The image, if captured, is a landfall, a mooring, the transfiguration of danger into safety, his life's work. The Golden House that is a cave, the Colosseum falling, half fallen. *"Tu es belle, belle, belle!"* is a harbor, is a spasmodic twinkling of the hypnotist's mirror, is a blank white concavity in which Marcus's mind rolls like a metal ball helplessly, obstinately, noisily. His forehead dampens. He cannot let this obsession with a half-glimpsed image interfere with the day's shooting any more than he can the news of Nanna's death or the rearoused wonder at her meaning in his life.

At prep school, he told the doctor, "It scares me when I make up my mind. My mind seems to have a mind of its own . . . I guess; that's a joke." He said, "Tell me, do you inherit your mind? I'm very quiet or else I'm a fanatic. Do you think it's because I'm Irish and Jewish, and a lot of Spanish, if you go back far enough?" He promises himself he will get to Loesser later, seduce, cajole, nag him—bend him to the image and see that it is captured. He tells himself he does not need the image for the movie. But he cannot be consoled. Delay is dangerous, suspense beyond him. He tells himself, *"It doesn't matter."* His method for calming himself at such moments, the only one that works, is to abandon caring; he subsides into what he calls his Christian mood. He grows calmer, abandoning for the moment his enormous and inchoate hopes,

like a Christian assigning the spiritual portion of existence to the care
of the vicars of God and modestly resigning himself to the sensual
remnant, which is transient, sun-brittle on a summer's day, and sour to
the tongue like grass.

NANNA TOOK him in at the suggestion of the doctor at Andover.
The doctor said, "He suffers from having no sense of belonging." He
said to Marcus, "Your mother wants you to be happy here or she
wouldn't have sent you to Andover."

"She doesn't send me. My grandmother pays for it."

"But your mother agrees. She signs the reports and so on."

"She wouldn't approve of this school if she knew more about it. She
wouldn't like it if I changed."

"Would she want you to be rude to the teachers, to most of the
students?"

Marcus said, "If I ever got to be like them, I'd shoot myself. My
mother would shoot me. I study. I mostly use my memory. I show I can
do it, and then I *despise* it."

The doctor said, "You seem to have a great interest in moral questions."

Marcus said, without self-consciousness, "Thank you. It comes from
traveling around in different houses. You get to thinking about what's
right in one house and not in another."

The doctor said to Marcus's father that Marcus could not handle the
conflict between his loyalty to his mother and the education offered by
the school, and that Marcus would not betray his mother by going to
live with his father. ("I have no problems," Marcus had said. "My
mother is wonderful. She takes good care of me.") Nanna took him in
and gave him a camera.

In Nanna's house he found himself stilled. In the new silence he
read, at once a little in love with other people's minds and with his
own; in the stillness he could have these mental affections. His
strength no longer went so much into survival. Nanna said he was
a genius; he thought himself to be stunningly ordinary, the world's
guest, on sufferance, someone bluffing, a common boy. The genius Nanna referred to he took to be a social thing that earned the admiration of
outsiders and did not extend into the house, where Nanna frowned
on and discountenanced temperament, wild talk, rude behavior,

burning eyes, uncombed hair, and flushed and nervous mannerisms.

Nanna's intelligence awed him. She had known and admired Maeterlinck. With the camera she gave him, Marcus made a movie, a sea-and-harbor étude to be set to Debussy's "La Mer." Nanna thought it very dear, excellent, quite beautiful in its way. (But it was mannered and incoherent, because Marcus's understanding of Nanna's taste was fitful.)

Nervy and alert and quick-eyed, Marcus at fourteen, as later, loved frequently; he loved secretly and from afar a girl named Sukie Tredwell (the granddaughter of old Gamma Foster, the bishop's widow). For companionship he relied on the gardener's son, who came and went at Marcus's (and Nanna's) convenience. He had friends of a sort, boys from the Yacht Club or from school, but somehow friendship never grew. Something would occur in the course of an afternoon—loneliness in their company, or one or the other caring too much, or boredom— and nothing took. Nanna became irritated at his isolation. Nanna called Gamma Foster, who had staying with her a grandson two years older than Marcus; the boy had grown up in Paris (his father was in the Foreign Service and about to be sent to Tokyo), and was to start at Andover in the fall and be Americanized. "We think," Nanna said, "you and Robin might have something in common. Robin is intelligent. Gamma says her grandson is artistic."

Marcus drove with Nanna in her black Packard, Nils, the chauffeur, up front, down the shore road to Gamma Foster's immense, beporched, and undistinguished house. He and Gamma Foster's grandson Robin stole glances at each other across the luncheon table. Robin was as thin as string, and fair, with dark, opaque eyes and enormous, nervous, graceful hands. He was Europeanly precise in his movements, and Nanna smiled at him. Robin showed up the next afternoon at Nanna's with a portfolio under his arm of several of his large, Bérard-like ink and watercolor sketches of theatrical *mises en scène*. He said to Marcus that he intended to go into the theater, that he was something of a genius. Marcus asked him, "Does your family harp on that, too?" Robin said, "No. You're lucky you're a Jew. Jews have a real appreciation of the arts." He confided to Marcus that he was lonely. Gamma Foster was impressive, but not European—not like Nanna, who was clearly very cultivated. He gestured with his large hands while he talked. He came the following day, and the one after. The two boys lay on wicker couches on the south porch and talked. He told Marcus, "I am deeply French. I do not care what you say as long as you say it with distinction."

"My friend, my friend," Marcus said to himself, lying in bed at night. He was cautious and did not reveal the extent of his affection. He did not trust Robin, because he could not see that Robin had a moral nature, but he blamed himself for his lack of trust. He had not yet been told the tenets of that particular Jewish hagiology—Jews are saints (Noreen did not know of it, and Nanna never spoke of it) and Gentiles are a cross they bear. When Gentiles pursue the company of Jews, the hagiology states, they do so because they are rejected by their own kind and feel they will be welcomed by Jews, who are, of necessity, flattered by the attentions of a Gentile. These Gentiles are not to be trusted. A Jew who takes Gentile friends must expect to be exploited, lacks pride, and is a fool.

Robin talked of Jewish understanding and Jewish warmth and Jewish intellect. Robin was sweetly-smiled and a petty thief (loose change, bibelots, fountain pens). Robin was experienced with whores and well read. Robin told Marcus he had talent but that he was pedantic, heavy-handed, rather old-fashioned and ignorant in style. (When Marcus imitated Robin's manners, the results pleased Nanna.) Robin introduced him to symbolism, to Mallarmé, to Rimbaud. He said he admired vitality and earthiness, and that no one should refine his mind and tastes too much and become effete; he should remain a little clumsy, because clumsiness was strength. Marcus began to make another movie, one never finished, with Robin as protagonist. Robin said all titles sounded better in French, and the movie was called *Les Yeux d'un Poète*.

Marcus thought as a child that people were speeches, delivered with sincerity in incomprehensible languages, and one had to learn those languages. (Death was that people grew silent. The end of a conversation was death, and he was left alone. His terror of death at that age was terror at the breaking off of a dialogue.) Before he learned someone's language and knew how to translate into it, he hid himself in eagerness to be agreeable: "What would you like to do? What kind of mood are you in?" He'd known Robin five months before he risked showing one of his images; it was after Thanksgiving, which Marcus spent in New York at his father's. When he was back at school, he said, "Do you know what I think at family dinners? I'm at the Wars of the Roses. There are people in a living room and they throw white and red roses at each other, with thorns on them. There's blood on the carpet. They squawk; it sounds like 'York, York, York.' But if everybody's peaceful it sounds like a fire in the fireplace: 'Lancaster . . . Lancaster . . . Lancaster.' "

"That's rather farfetched," Robin said. "Frankly, I think it's overdone. Anyway, I don't get it. Family life is much more psychological. Freud appears with the hors d'oeuvres and stays through the tapioca—that's my opinion."

"Yes, you're right," Marcus said. Robin's difficulty in getting grades (except in English, where he wrote a superbly terse and grammatical prose, more French than English in spirit) proved he was intelligent and thought for himself. Marcus tried to think with Robin's thoughts. He began to erupt in scenes without understanding why he was making them. "I have a terrible temper," Marcus kept saying. Robin admitted that Marcus was violent and deep. He admitted it with pleasure and with proprietary conviction.

MARCUS LEANS forward as the Lancia enters the Piazza di Spagna. He thinks, Yes, yes, yes—he wants the two shoals of parked cars on either side of the open channel in which traffic moves. He wants for the movie the tourists in shorts and sunglasses, the Peugeot with bedding rolls strapped to the rear, and the four dust-coated taxi drivers smoking as they sit at the foot of the obelisk. The urban jumble will explain the lines in Jehane's forehead above the bridge of her sunglasses when she crosses the piazza.

The car halts behind the costume-and-makeup trailer and an orange generator truck from which spill out black electric cables; up and down the travertine curl of the Spanish Steps, extras and passersby hurry or stand. The workmen turn with an air of expectancy as Marcus climbs out of the car—a wooden-faced episcopal figure in the stillness at the altar beneath the dome. A bystander, a woman, cries out, "*Je vous ai toujours adorée, Jehane!*" Jehane smiles at the ground, somber-faced. She and Oskar are hurried off to the costume trailer by the makeup man. Marcus waves to the electricians. "*Noi cominciamo, sì?*" They call "*Sì*" and smile. The lighting man, brought from Paris, points to the lights already in place on the second landing, where Jehane will meet Oskar going down. There is to be a close-up of their faces, and Marcus wants the faces to be without shadow. "*Bon,*" Marcus says, gripping the man's shoulder. "*Nous commençons.*" Marcus greets the script girl and the Italian workmen and the Italian translators: "*Nous commençons. . . . Noi cominciamo.*" And he smiles and pauses to shake hands. "*Un buon momento, non?*" He has charm; he finds it easy to be charming whenever he is certain people are listening.

He greets Whitehart, the assistant director, with overt affection, as if it has been months instead of hours since he saw him last. He puts his arm around Whitehart's shoulder, and Whitehart returns the gesture. Whitehart tells him that Liselotte (the Munich stripteaser who is to play Oskar's middle-class, self-conscious, sexual-looking wife; Oskar will describe her to Jehane as cold. *"Und du, du bist . . . Ich kann nicht sagen. . . ."* The audience will not know if he is lying) has had a broken filling, has been to the dentist, is a little shaken but otherwise all right. Marcus nods. We are all breakable, he thinks. Whitehart goes over the order of the takes to be shot that day. Marcus listens; details are commands of conscience. The sunlight touches him. He is seized by a nervous desire to begin to hunt down in the sunlight and in the faces of the actors the shadows of meaning in his movie. He wants to ask Whitehart if the camera boom is in place atop the Spanish Steps for the first scene, but he cannot think of the word "boom," and he points and says, "The thing—the thing." Whitehart says, "The boom? It's there. Ready," and Marcus smiles at him and says, "Thank you."

R o b i n t o o k him to Boston and introduced him to Sukie Tredwell, his cousin. Sukie was getting over a crush on Robin. Sukie said she was in love with Marcus and acted as if she were. She was short, thin, and her face was porcelain white and sunrise pink, her hair ash blond; her hips were wide, her shoulders high. She chain-smoked, and spoke in a small, nasal, high-pitched flat-in-tone voice, very directly and simply. Sukie was a prism in which sunlight broke up into a rainbow. Marcus's happiness was vertiginous, steep-sided like a cliff.

Summer came. At Scantuate, Robin sprawled in a wicker chair and picked at strips of skin peeling from the sunburn on his arms while he hummed and grimaced to a recording of *Don Giovanni* on the radio. Night made mirrors of the windows of the porch, the sea soughed, and the soughing curled the night outside into a shell. "Sukie," Marcus said, "I want to tell you something, something very strange."

"May I listen?" Robin asked.

"Well, you're here," Marcus said. "Sukie, I have a very strange mind. Listen, I'm just sitting here just now, and it was like—well, a man in armor walked in," he said quickly, interpolating, improvising to soften what was really in his mind. "He walked in through that door. I could see the straw mat through his feet, and he struck me on the arm with his sword. I have a big wound on my arm. I have a wound but not on my arm. My wound is your mouth. I look at you and it changes; then it's your mouth is my wound. And I'm going to die. But I can close this wound if I kiss you."

"Good God, Pony!" Marcus was called Polo (Marco Polo) and Pony (Polo pony) and sometimes Pony Boy. Robin, his large gray eyes fogged from listening to music, exclaimed, waving one large hand irritably in the air, "Kiss my cousin if you want, take her out in the garden if you want, but cut out the Hebrew poetry. Mozart is being played."

"Shut up, Redbreast," Marcus said, blushing. "Come on, Sukie." He and Sukie stepped outside. The night widened around them. They walked through the squares of orange light that fell on the path from the porch windows (inside, Robin, his legs over the arm of his chair, jiggled one foot high in the air to "Il mio tesoro") and then in the dark made their way to the rim of the bluff. There was no moon, only a vast dusting of stars, and the lights in houses across the bay sparkling fireworks trails on the water, and occasional headlights of cars driving along the shore road.

Marcus said he didn't mean to be boring but he really wanted to know what Sukie thought of his mind. "Wait: you know what I was just thinking? We're all death. We're little envelopes around death, and everywhere we walk we arrive like the mail, and people approach us with hope, with letter openers in their hand to open their mail—that's what I was just thinking. . . ."

Sukie said, "Everybody gets strange thoughts. I have very strange thoughts, too. Like I'm going to die any minute—things like that."

Marcus thought abruptly it was true (it sounded true); everyone had strange thoughts, and he was callow and inexperienced to have thought it odd in himself. He laughed suddenly. "Letter openers—ha-ha."

"I don't mind the way you talk," Sukie said. "I think you're very, very sensitive. I help make you secure, don't I?"

"Yes," he said. "You do."

Marcus told no one (except Nanna, later), discussed with no one (except Robin) that he loved Sukie. He wanted no one's opinions, no one's breath, to touch his love. A second Adam, he saw that all leaved plants were beautiful, and that on windowsills sunbeams slowly seesawed once each day. Sukie held a cigarette between the tips of her short, square fingers. She lay supine on a towel at the beach, and said, "It's a perfectly beautiful day, isn't it, Marco? Isn't it the most beautiful day?" He had been wrong ever to doubt himself. Such errors were conceived in the vagaries of manners (like light dancing on something bright and obscuring what lay beneath); people when upset invented faults, but there were no faults, only bad habits. People were achingly akin. He was sixteen.

He waited on Sukie's pleasure with the care and attention with which he waited on Nanna's, and he was grateful and flattered when she was pleased by his devotion. He was circumspect and watchful of the decencies. He was half in love with Sukie's mother, whose breasts bobbled, and whose eyes were electric and dark, and who spoke in a baritone register when she wanted to be funny: "My God, here comes Sukie's lov-err," the "err" of "lov-err" dropping to C below middle C. Or she'd say, "Here comes Sukie's swarthy, handsome lov-err," and offer him a drink. She radiated an intense awareness of him, of what was happening; she had an air of caprice, of serious devotion to the idea and practice of love.

Sukie said, "No, don't go photographing. Lie on the beach with me." Sukie said, "Robin is more sensitive than you are, but you're a more complete person." Sukie said, "Everybody knows Jews make the best lovers and husbands." Lying on the beach, she permitted him to kiss her arm, her leg, the small of her back. She never touched him. She would lie still, growing more and more rigid while he slowly kissed her, and then she would sit up, pushing her hair back, a heroine, and say, "Oh, Pony, I'm *mad* about you. It's inevitable, isn't it? We will—all that, I suppose. It's inevitable, don't you feel that, Pony?"

OSKAR STANDS at the top railing, looking out over Rome; the Spanish Steps fall away beneath him. A young workman guards an electric fan that stands on the railing and blows Oskar's hair. Oskar looks unconscionably noble, even in his sunglasses. "Look up higher in the sky," Marcus instructs him. "Oskar, *mein Lieber,* this is the City of the Popes." Marcus leans precariously over the railing and sights through a portable camera at Oskar's face. "It must be overexposed," he says to Alliat; he wants Oskar's face to be like a pencil drawing—a few lines, and the darkness of his sunglasses, and the reflection of the view in them, and Oskar's mouth. Oskar's mouth, if he can lead Oskar into the right mood, will be alive and dangerous: an artful shape, the instrument of the most human music.

Oskar, determinedly holding his pose, remarks, "That one is the Keats House, *ja?* He is your great poet. 'Truth is beauty and beauty truth'—*ja?*"

"*Mein Schatz,*" Marcus says, "lower your chin perhaps one inch." Marcus minutely and slowly inches the camera this way and that. Oskar's mouth grows bedraggled but dutiful. Marcus says, "When I was a child, I spoke as a child and acted like a man, with bows and arrows and guns, but now I'm a man and spend my time doing childish things." Oskar smiles vacantly. Marcus says, "Willi, imagine a naked woman in the shower, completely unselfconscious; she does not know you're watching." Oskar's lips thin sensually. Marcus beckons and Alliat leans over him, observes the position of the camera, takes it from him while Marcus scrambles free. Marcus holds a small mirror in front of the camera and studies Oskar's reflection in it, and says, "To the right. Up. A bit m— Yes."

Nanna was alert and watchful, but not as alert and watchful as a moment to be placed on film. In the mirror, Oskar's face flickers. The mirror is an eye; and the pupil, the tunnel to perception and the capture by memory, is Marcus. On the glassy lids of the large, silvered, metal-rimmed sunglasses Oskar wears float twin reflections of a swarm of roofs, sweetened by the rising in their midst of grayish, high-arched domes. Oskar's hair moves. Marcus says, "Oskar, *mein Schatz,* what would it be like if they put up a statue to you in the Villa Borghese as the most talented German since Goethe?" Oskar takes a deep, simmering breath. An internal shift occurs within the oval of Oskar's face—a queer light, an illumination. He looks Olympian. He waits, unattached and daydreaming, and Marcus touches Alliat's knee and the camera starts up, stops, starts up again. The camera whirs a third time.

"That's it for the moment," Marcus says. He touches Oskar's shoulder. The actor has grown into the railing, the sunlight, the daydream, and must be summoned back.

MARCUS SAT in the classroom unprotected, his feet on the floor, his head and eyes lowered as if a wind blew. In the shower room, he exclaimed inwardly, "I love you, Sukie." He wrote her, "I love you." His roommate bumped into him and Marcus lashed out, "Don't you touch me!" Marcus cried out in his sleep, "Sukie!" He wrote her, "I miss you crazily."

Robin played the pander. He asked, "When are you two going to sleep together?"

Marcus shouted, "I don't want to hurt her! I don't want to do any harm!"

Robin said, "Don't tell me you think sex is wicked, Pony. Haven't you ever read a book? Haven't you read D. H. Lawrence?" Robin said, "There's a real beauty when a woman becomes a woman." He said, "Jewish morality has crushed everything in Western culture that's beautiful and natural. If our own sense that it is necessary to sin—and Freud, of course—hadn't come along, we'd all be neurotic Calvinists. Tell me, Pony, do you believe in the Old Testament?"

Beneath the springs of the upper bunk distended with the weight of his roommate's sleeping body (whose breaths made runners of sound in the darkness), Marcus lay in a tangle of imaginings. He yearned to tell Nanna, far away, in Florida, that he was about to become transfigured. He said to Sukie over the phone, "Sukie, I want— Listen, I don't mean to be a bastard, but I— Sukie, please just tell me *when.*"

"Oh, Pony," Sukie said in a small voice. "Whenever you want. I'm helpless in your hands, Marco."

Robin made a reservation at a hotel in Boston and drove Marcus up the afternoon the Thanksgiving holidays began. Sukie came by train from her school in Connecticut. Robin said, "You have two hours before I have to get Sukie home," and he said he would wait in the coffee shop.

In the hotel room, the pleasure was brusque, simple, and heart-stopping. When it was over, Sukie said, "You control all our lives, mine and Robin's and my parents'! You're incredibly powerful." She said, "You're beautiful and very sexy and have a much nicer body than Robin's." She said she'd slept with Robin but it hadn't meant anything, not like this; and once with a boy in Maine, but that hadn't meant anything, either. "Pony, I'm embarrassed. Everyone will see the change in me. I know I'm going to blossom." She said, "Are you one of those men who only want what they can't have?" She said, "I wish you weren't going to New York. I don't know what I'll do without you." She said she hated her mother and her mother hated her. She said boys never liked her. She said the girls at her school avoided her. She said she wanted to kill herself. She said, "I know you'll bring me happiness. Everybody knows that Jews make the best husbands and lovers."

At Christmastime, Marcus told his father he had to return to Boston

Saturday morning to see Robin about the school play. In Boston, snow was coming on. He arrived bone-broken and askew with longing for the sensation—very like the assurance of being wanted—that had come when Sukie had undressed and let him hold her. He was dull with a sense of humiliation he couldn't identify. He thought, She needs me. He was racked by astonishment as much as by desire. From the hotel, he called Sukie; she said she would come as soon as she could. He waited, and the moments seemed to him to lack walls, roofs, and floors. Never since had he experienced anticipation so violently.

At four o'clock, Robin and Sukie arrived—together. Marcus told Robin, "Please go away," and when Robin left, without a word, Marcus began to undress Sukie. In the silence, it was as if certain sounds that had been curtained by a rush of noise became audible. Sukie grew nervous. Marcus told her to hold still. She said, "You don't know what you're doing; this is creepy," and began to cry.

Marcus said, "Sukie, what did I do wrong?"

"You don't act as if you like me."

Red-faced and taut, Marcus assured her that he liked her, swore that he did; he swore it on his soul.

Sukie blinked, then said submissively, "All right."

After that they made love.

When Robin came back, Marcus went to the door, wrapped in a blanket, and said, "Give us five minutes and we'll get dressed."

Robin said, "No, let me in. I won't peek," and he came in and sat on the foot of the bed. He leaned across Sukie's ankles and talked rapidly—chattered about what an ugly town Boston was, how dreary winter was. Sukie and Marcus lay as quietly as corpses. Robin turned his head away while Sukie got dressed. (He'd said like a gym instructor, "It's time we got going.") Marcus remained in bed, propped against the headboard, the blanket up to his shoulders. Robin's weight hurt his ankles. Stiff-necked with excitement, Robin said, "I'll bring her back whenever I can."

Marcus returned to school and told himself that people were all alike. Sukie would soon change for him, as he had changed for Nanna's sake. She would become a warm, responsive, trustworthy girl. He would help her and be strong. At the same time, he longed to escape from her. But he wanted her, too. He wrote Sukie twice a day. He was tired and could not sleep. He toppled into periods of nervous exhaustion and lay staring at the wall, drenched with sweat. He'd lock the door of his room at such times; he wanted no one to see him. Feelings that he could not put a name to, incomprehensible but powerful feelings, like abstract paintings—a blue one, a blue-and-black one, a gray one shot through with viridian—filled his head and chest. The recollection of the texture of the skin on Sukie's back drove him from the lunch table to walk slack-jawed, both exalted and wretched, in the snow. He began to avoid his mind. (When he grew older, he found he could avoid his mind easily whenever he wanted except when trying to fall asleep; to quiet his mind then, he would drink two shots of brandy and take a Seconal, and wander around his bedroom until he entered a state of near idiocy; only then, when he fell on his bed, would he find unconsciousness within reach.)

Sukie's letters burned like dry ice; in them she complained of her classmates, described her feelings—"Everybody looks at me; I think I'm blossoming"—begged him to arrange with Robin to drive down to her school: "I'm going out of my mind. I'm suicidal. I'm so bored, Marco. I must see you. I love you."

He'd make arrangements to go with Robin to Boston to stay in Gamma Foster's house on Saturday night, and then, Robin telling Gamma Foster he and Marcus were going to the movies, they'd drive to Connecticut, both boys sitting hunched forward as if to hurry the car on. Sometimes he felt Sukie's presence was unpleasant and he would tell himself passionately that she was stubborn, insisted on being unlovable, did not care if she alienated him or not; she was spoiled. He watched her face always. He knew its lineaments. He saw apparitions in it, landscapes, the hues of flowers. When his will faltered, he saw it as something associated with pain, a bandage. Sometimes a mood would warm that porcelain-white face and him, and he would begin again the fall of falling in love. On his way to see her, not knowing what he would find, his heart and nerves went rackatty-clack like a half-empty train rushing through a countryside at night. He'd arrive and his eyes would fly to that face. ("Don't, Pony. It makes me so nervous when you stare at me.") If her face was trampled or muddied, he would grow distant and emotionless, like a doctor; he was anxious to help her, not to be bad for her. He tried to be a proper lover, like one in books, and he told her—remembering another moment when he had been unable to speak—that she was the sun and wind and clouds and a rosebush. Sukie brightened and said, "Oh, that's lovely." He continued with increasing sincerity, and compared her to the craziness of dreams, to a beach, to warm sand and the sun making you dizzy, and sand fleas making your legs twitch. She said, "I don't think I like that. No, it's nasty." She looked uneasy. He said he hadn't meant anything, a beach was a force of nature—he'd only meant to compare her to a force of nature.

She was most peaceful when he was tired, half asleep (although in his pride he did not like admitting to her that he was tired). Then, sometimes, she'd touch him or smile in a warm way. It excited and exhilarated her when the three of them—Sukie, Robin, and Marcus—went out together in Robin's car. Bars wouldn't serve Sukie; in the car, Robin, Marcus, and Sukie passed a pint of bourbon back and forth. They drove on back roads, safe from observation in their world inside the car. They often went at ninety, the automobile swaying, with only the loosest connection to the road, the earth, to fixed locations. The air inside the car was dry and warmed by the heater and chilled by cold leaking in at the windows, and faintly visible with their breaths, and sweetish with the smell of whiskey. Sukie's excitement affected Marcus as if she were a flag.

She cried, "A ciggy-boo, I must have a ciggy-boo. Did you remember my Sen-Sen?" She said, "That school's a tomb!"

Robin said, " 'The grave's a fine and private place, / But none, I think, do there embrace.' "

Sukie said, "I love you, Marco."

Outside the car, moonlight lay tremulously on the thin fields. Marcus said, "The world is coming to an end tonight."

Sukie said, "Don't be gloomy. Let yourself go on the Happiness Swings." Happiness Swings were the opposite of Bad Weeks. "It's a Bad Week," Sukie sometimes said.

Marcus said, "I am on it."

But Sukie said, "No, you're not." She turned to Robin. "Isn't Marcus difficult? He scares me."

Robin agreed. Marcus was awesome.

Marcus didn't see it. Robin's tongue was more cutting than his—Robin said Gamma Foster had a face like the Bible. Sukie and Robin were less sentimental, less eager to please, too, than he was. "Do I seem to you abnormal? Maybe what bothers you is that I'm Jewish."

"But you're not all Jewish," Robin said.

Sukie said, "It isn't being Jewish that makes you so difficult."

Marcus was accustomed to women approving of him most when he was happy. "Oh, God, I'm happy!" he exclaimed. "You just don't know. I used to think when I was a kid nothing would ever happen."

"All kids think that," Robin said, one arm on Sukie's shoulder.

Sukie said, "I did. Do you want to hear a joke? Knock, knock. Who's there? Abie. Abie who? A.B.C." She giggled and leaned her head on Marcus's shoulder, then on Robin's.

They stopped and walked barefoot in the snowy field, shouting and laughing. Marcus threw himself down on the snow and stretched his arms out and said, "I am ready for Easter." Sukie circled, turned round and around in the field, her shadow hopping behind her, then in front of her. Marcus said, "She's dancing with crows."

Robin went for a walk while Marcus and Sukie lay in the car, their breaths feathery, their eyes shining in the dark. Robin returned, and then they drove to the door of Sukie's school. The girl Marcus held was muffled in a coat, was warm, and smelled faintly of gardenia soap. "Oh, Pony, I have to go back to the tomb. I love you."

Robin said, "Wait, Suke! Better have some Sen-Sen."

Sukie said, "Oops, stupid me!" Smiling secretively, she put her arms around Robin's neck and Robin kissed her ear.

On the way back to Boston, Marcus said, "I don't like the way you kiss Sukie. I'd like to smash your teeth in."

"Look, Pony. She happens to be my cousin. I—"

"Shut up! Shut the hell up!" After a minute or so, Marcus said, "Oh, God, I'm sorry. I'm sorry, Redbreast. You know I'm crazy. I'm so much in love, you know." He sat slouched in his seat, tired, nervous, in an agony of fatigue. The dark, now stale air in the car seemed to him a fit setting for himself.

In the movie, Jehane, after coming to understand that Oskar does not intend to divorce his wife, returns to her *pensione*, opens the door of the room, and steps inside without turning on the light. At first, she simply sits in the darkness; then she begins to sob, reaching into her purse on the bureau for a handkerchief to stuff between her lips to prevent herself from making a noise and disturbing the other tenants in the *pensione*. She falls on the floor and cries without a sound, accepting almost with relief the humiliation. She does not move, but continues to cry silently on the floor.

Earlier in the movie, before she meets Oskar, she walks along the Via Condotti, past the store windows, the reflections, the things for sale. (The camera will be low, at waist height, because Marcus thinks one of the secrets of the beauty and credibility of Italian Renaissance frescoes is that the figures seem to be taller or on higher ground than we are and we have to look up at them; this helps persuade us of their reality, because we remain children and continue all our lives to crane our necks to see the expressions on the grownups' faces.) And she will walk past a young man in sunglasses similar to hers; she will slightly hesitate, as if amused that he is wearing similar sunglasses, but then, because the young man does not smile at her, she hurries on in an access of memory of what she expects for herself, ending what Marcus calls a masked moment, like the one when Robin told him, "I don't see why it matters in what way I take my pleasure. I don't see that it matters in what way anyone takes his pleasure." She prefers flight to self-knowledge. She careers on, grandiose and virginal. Between the Jehane of the Via Condotti and the Jehane of the *pensione* lies the death of the hardness of her self-regard.

Oskar intervenes between the two Jehanes. Marcus says to him, "It is your second day in Rome. You have left your hotel and walked through the Villa Borghese. Trees and children. The Latin sense of design. Your wife hangs heavily on your arm; you walk a little too fast for her. You made a mistake marrying her. She asks questions: 'What is that? What is that?' And 'that' is only the water clock. Yesterday with her was dull. Today seems it will be dull, too. But you don't show irritation; you are good-natured. Always. You are clean in the sense that you never rebuke yourself. You have a very fine sense of life. Do you understand?" Oskar nods, his face slipping into lines of ease, intensely good-natured and impenetrable; his face looks scrubbed. Marcus gazes at him and says, "Good."

He glances over Oskar's shoulder at Liselotte, the Munich stripteaser who is to play Oskar-Willi's wife. She sits in a canvas chair beneath a tree, in speckled light and shadow, hands folded in her lap, eyes closed. Marcus thinks, Her tooth still hurts. Oh, does she feel self-pity! And he grows cold, froglike. He beckons to Whitehart. "Tell her just to play she is in a strange city. Tell her not to try to act. I don't want to touch her mood." Whitehart winks, and hurries off. Marcus stands, measuring the two realities of Liselotte with the fingers of his mind. Her real inexperience and nervousness, her attempt to deceive the camera and to appear not like a striptease artist from Munich, will become on film the unhappy manner of a middle-class lady whose manners are all at sea with her pretenses. Her heavy breasts will be the lure and misinformation that caught Oskar-Willi. (Marcus thinks with amusement of Oskar-Willi's illusions, and how easily he is fooled.) The audience, Marcus hopes, will recognize in Liselotte's two realities the same blur of identity that obscures the people they know.

MARCUS TOOK refuge in principle (his determination strengthened by a Gary Cooper film; the theater was dark, like chaos—the images on the screen clear and large, light-filled) when his trying to figure out what he felt, or what Robin was like, or Sukie, led him to the admission that he was guessing, that he did not *know*. He went to the school doctor and asked for a sedative, giving as the reason that he was studying too hard. He told Sukie he couldn't see her in Boston over Easter vacation. "Nanna's come up from Florida. I owe it to her—I want to see her. It's not that I don't want to see you, but I owe it to her."

But then Sukie followed him to Scantuate with her mother, Robin, and Gamma Foster; Gamma Foster wanted to smell the lilacs and the sea, and sat all morning on an open porch, wrapped in a blanket, not reading, not sleeping. (She fell the following winter and broke her hip and became an invalid until her death four years later.) The children roosted in the light damp chill of an upstairs porch. The wicker couch creaked when Robin stretched out and laid his head in Sukie's lap.

Marcus stood up and said, "I want to go photographing at Miller's Pond."

"What a dreary idea," Robin said.

"I don't feel energetic," Sukie said.

Marcus looked at Sukie and saw a short, square-shouldered, moon-bodied girl. He bit his thumbnail. "I'm going," he said.

"All right, all right," Robin said. "What a bore. Our master's voice."

"Where was Moses when the lights went out?" Sukie asked, with a giggle.

"If you don't want to come, don't!" Marcus shouted, holding to his principles like a monk to a cross, exorcising demons.

"We're coming. We're coming."

He did not get back to Nanna's in time for lunch, and Nanna complained he had given her no warning he would miss the meal: "I didn't know if you were stricken with illness. Or perhaps in a highway accident."

He apologized—"I'm sorry. I was photographing. There wasn't a phone"—but he wasn't humble.

"Please don't do it again. You know how easily Cook is unsettled."

"Oh. Well, I'd better warn you I might miss lunch the next few days. I'll be out photographing." He was distracted by a sensation that he was being rude, yet he did not back down.

The next evening, Nanna said dryly, "I do not want to monopolize your time, but I had hoped to see something of you during your spring vacation, because I thought I might send you to Europe this summer."

Marcus said, "Oh," and stopped photographing, and told Sukie he was going to Europe.

He went to Europe with Mrs. Tredwell, Sukie, and Robin; Robin arranged the party. Europe made Marcus uneasy; it was an old prostitute armed with devices to catch the eye and the absence of principles. He told himself that he must be careful not to turn into a shallow person. He wrote Nanna every day, and the salutation, "Dearest Nanna," evoked in him a spasm of sorrow. Europe had the strangeness of a carnival on the edge of town under a night sky, the lights of the Ferris wheel lifting and falling, and the shouts of the exiles echoing from behind the rim of colored lights.

"They made their cathedrals like movie theaters!" he protested. Robin said, "*Voilà*, Moses!" Mrs. Tredwell looked at Marcus curiously.

Sukie complained he was avoiding her. He said, "But we're with your mother. I'm like a guest—the laws of hospitality!" Sukie said, "I hate my mother. My mother doesn't matter." She said, "Oh, God, what am I going to do! You don't want me anymore." He took her into his arms. Robin was in the next room, arranging the day's plans with Mrs. Tredwell. Marcus matched Sukie's eagerness; the wickedness of the situation so worked upon his senses that he was startled by the pleasure. Afterward, he was ashamed, and avoided looking at Sukie. Sukie said, "What's the matter?" He said, "I have a cold." He thought, Oh, God, I'm cuckoo. At lunch, he drank too much and desperately imitated the Europeans as animals—as terriers, as poodles, then as amorous cocker spaniels—for Mrs. Tredwell, who laughed. She used the baritone register of her voice and said warmly, "We've never particularly liked Jews in our family. You might call us anti-Semitic. But we're *all* terribly fond of you."

The drunken seventeen-year-old Marcus clung to the moral nicety of the point that he must not allow the mother of the girl he slept with to be fond of him, and he became surly toward Mrs. Tredwell. "That's an Irish compliment," he said. "You're more impressed with your own sentiment than with me."

I don't like her, he assured himself. He told himself that he mustn't be a whore. His thoughts were dark, astronomical. His judgments of himself and of Sukie and Robin and Mrs. Tredwell were jumbled, as if several movies were being shown at once on the same screen. On the way back to Avignon, while Robin drove the car and Mrs. Tredwell talked, Sukie in the back seat beside Marcus indulged herself in a skittish series of blandishments and displays and sidelong glances from some reservoir of erotic imagination. His nerves reacted in a strained and exaggerated way, like a child's—everything was mythological and immense; it was as if his nerves and the world were new to him: Mrs. Tredwell was fascinated by him. "You seem so old for your age." He scowled at Mrs. Tredwell. Later, he said, "Sukie, we have to straighten out." Sukie said, "You get pleasure making me hate myself." He said, "Why can't you admire me when I'm trying to do the right thing?" Mrs. Tredwell and Robin were walking ahead of them in the vineyard they were visiting above the Rhone on an afternoon when the sky was as much white as blue. Sukie went pale and said, "You're crazy. You're sick. You're really neurotic."

That evening, Robin asked Marcus why he was treating Sukie so badly. "It's a matter of honor," Marcus said. Robin blinked. "You really don't make sense, Pony." Marcus shouted at him, "You wouldn't understand! You're slimy." Robin went white. "You're self-destructive," he said, and lit a cigarette.

The hillsides above the road were green. Marcus was silent and haughty. Honor froze his face. He had always thought of love as being like the view from the windows of his father's apartment at dusk, when the taxis in great numbers flock back from upper Manhattan with the lights on their roofs—jewels on their foreheads—alight. Now he thought of it as the sprung works of a clock which moved the hands improperly. Mrs. Tredwell was growing bored with him. He observed to himself that Mrs. Tredwell did not understand Sukie, that she was not a good mother. Sukie had become hollow-eyed and captious. "You think in clichés," she said to Marcus. She said, "Everyone knows photographs can't do what painting can." She said, "You have so many opinions because you're self-conscious and can't feel anything." He lay in bed, somber in the dark.

Often at night in various towns, Robin would slip out and hunt for women. Then Marcus would lie tautly spread-eagled in bed, hating the solitude in the room, jealous of Robin, contemptuous of himself. He felt himself grow vague and sulky with concupiscence. Mrs. Tredwell was amused by him again, smiled at him again; she spoke of the noli me tangere of adolescence in her husky voice. Marcus winced, drew back, and stared at her with large eyes. She said, "You're impossible!" and ignored him. Sukie was cool.

Marcus wrote Nanna, "I think of Scantuate often. It's hard to travel with people day in and day out." He found a kind of relaxation in becoming aimless and passive. He watched Sukie and Robin giggle together in Juan-les-Pins; they walked, arms around each other, affectionate cousins. Sukie said, "He's kind to me. I feel better with him than with you." In Verona, the party went through the Castelvecchio, Mrs. Tredwell with Sukie and Robin; Marcus followed a different route through the rooms. Robin began to ridicule Marcus in public. In Venice, he said, "Tell us what you think about the view." He moved his arm in a semicircle. "What's the great man's opinion?"

Mrs. Tredwell and Sukie smiled, and Marcus said contemptuously that San Marco was like an advertising cutout: Want to feel bright? Try Brioschi.

Sukie was in love with Robin. Had always been, she said. "It was a strange—I don't know—some kind of detour or something I took with you." Robin said, "Pony, we need your help. I helped you." Sukie said, "Please, Pony, I'm not the kind of girl who can go too long without sex." She said something about being passionate. Marcus said, "Sure, I understand." He pretended to go to the movies with them, and when they sneaked up the back stairs to Robin and Marcus's room, he wandered in the *calle* behind the Piazza San Marco until he was approached by two middle-aged, dog-faced whores and their shiny-haired pimp. Then he went off with them.

The next night, he rode with Sukie and Robin and Sukie's mother in a gondola down the Grand Canal, the moonlight and the commune's floodlights playing on the façades of palaces (dozens of gondolas laden with other tourists floated by in the dark; the water breathed its sourish stench), and Mrs. Tredwell and Sukie and Robin laughed and chattered. Marcus sat quietly. It did not matter what Sukie and Robin did. He was corrupt; he looked down on them; they were children.

MARCUS SURVEYS the extras for the next shot—an old man in a straw hat, a shabby and badly dressed young man, a young girl who radiates disdain to keep at a distance the lusts of passersby, and others who are to play the bystanders, among whom, not quite touching them, the movie is to occur. Where Oskar and Liselotte are to walk has been marked on the pavement in chalk; the camera, mounted on a dolly on tracks, holds Oskar's and Liselotte's faces and the reflections in Oskar's sunglasses (of the obelisk, a spume of leaves from the underside of the trees, the old man in the straw hat). The reflected obelisks jog up and down like inverted sewing-machine needles when Oskar strolls with Liselotte, stitching the moment with the laws of optics and history. At a signal, the disdainful girl begins to walk briskly. Her reflection appears in the lower-left-hand quadrant of Oskar's sunglasses, balloons upward when Oskar's head turns to glance at her, and slides off to the right and disappears when Oskar restores his head to its former angle, parallel to his wife's.

A few weeks after the return from Europe, in the sudden quiet in Scantuate after Labor Day, Marcus went to Stedham's Moor with his camera. Sukie found him there; he looked up and saw her watching him—an ash-blond, pseudo-profound, well-bred girl standing in the gelid light, among the tall brown grasses and the rocks. "Are you going to be mean?" she asked him, a lost girl: *Who will love me? Who can I trust?* "I couldn't stand it if I thought you were going to be cold and hateful toward me."

"I'm not that kind of person," Marcus said proudly.

The scene is retaken. Between takes, Liselotte probes at her tooth with her tongue. "This is work for imbeciles, *hein?*" Marcus says to her. "No, don't look up." She tenses and petrifies with self-control. To Oskar, Marcus says, "The mouth, Oskar—emptier. You're an ordinary person, like those imbeciles"—he gestures toward the people gathered behind a barricade of sawhorses, watching them—"and your emotions are not well defined. You are bored, *mon cher,* but you do not admit it too openly. Your wife is a distinguished woman—you chose her; you respect your own judgment. Do you understand?"

Oskar's face blankens slightly. "*Ja,*" he says. "*Ich verstehe.*"

They commence the next shot. Oskar takes a step, tugging Liselotte after him; Marcus thinks, The ego and the whore. The reflection in Oskar's sunglasses is first of Liselotte's forehead, then of her breasts, then the obelisk, the street, and the leaves.

How much did Nanna see? Sukie and Robin were secretive about their affair. Marcus never discussed his sexual adventures with Nanna.

But Nanna was old, shrewd; surely she guessed. She clung tightly to his arm when they walked on the bluff. She said, "You have become an interesting-looking young man." She did not go to Florida that winter until after Christmas, but stayed in Scantuate, giving as her reason that she felt like enjoying the cold weather; but Marcus was sure it was to be near and help him. He was starting college and might get into trouble. Nanna asked him about Sukie. "She likes someone else," Marcus said evasively. "She and I are still friends." "I'm glad," Nanna said. "Gamma Foster hasn't been well. You never do your imitations anymore." He saw Sukie at college from time to time. The people he knew said of her she was a very stupid girl, a snob, shallow, affected. One of Marcus's cousins (she also told him Nanna was cold and hadn't loved her husband and children: "She was crazy about her father and nursed him, and you know that kind of thing. He was one of those citizenship-mad Jews, very anxious to win awards") mentioned that Sukie had always had a reputation in Scantuate: "Definitely loose."

Work commences on the shot that will introduce the figures of Oskar and Liselotte when the film is edited. Marcus, Alliat, and the camera are ensconced on the boom. Marcus signals, and the boom rises into the air. High above Rome, Marcus and Alliat confer in whispers. Far up the street, Oskar and Liselotte begin to walk. Oskar slightly in advance— that is, Oskar walks and Liselotte is pulled. Marcus leans forward. Liselotte teeters on the vanity of her high heels. The camera sights down through the frozen surf of leaves toward Oskar and Liselotte among the pedestrians, speckled like the street with leaf shadows and bits of light, adrift, like the leaf shadows, details of the day, and as transitory. When they come to a place where the shadow is thick and unbroken beneath the trees, Marcus shouts, *"Halt!"* and Oskar, Liselotte, and the extras pause, as still as death, while the camera whirs. Marcus shouts, "March!" and Oskar and Liselotte emerge from the shadow. Oskar points from time to time, and Liselotte nods; on the sound track, Liselotte's voice, from a distance, will say, *"Ja, ist schön."* When they pass the chalk marks of the shot before, Marcus shouts, *"Bon! Stop! Halt!"* and calls a retake for safety.

On autumn Saturday afternoons, Nanna walked with her cane in the garden. Nanna had a cyst on her leg. Marcus came down in the convertible she had bought him. On the road between college and Scantuate, he left behind the life he led at college—the moods, the self-disgust, the talk, the alcohol, the girls and women, pursued without imagination or fervor but with indignation; they ought to give in. "Everything's fine, as usual," he told Nanna. That meant he was glad to see her. When Sukie and Robin were in Scantuate at Gamma Foster's, they always came to see Nanna. Nanna had become a member of their group. Nanna, who had never been demonstrative, now kissed Marcus—not frequently: when he arrived and when he left—and she held his arm when they walked in the garden. "I may fall," she said. There is no old woman among the extras, Marcus realizes, no old Roman women, only an old man in a straw hat.

Oskar tells Marcus through Whitehart's headset telephone that Liselotte is terrible, and he asks if in the next shot he should play his part as if he is acting according to a conscious plan.

Marcus thinks and says, "No. You plan, you don't plan. It doesn't matter. You do what you do anyway. I'll tell you what it's like. Excuse me, but it's like a dog. The expression in the dog's eyes when he is going to disobey a command. Is he thinking? It is his body. He smells the woods. But plot if you like. Only remember to be innocent at the same time, a man who does not plot. You have a very fine sense of life. Play it with uncertainty." Marcus, even from the boom, can see the tension in Oskar, and he is pleased. Liselotte crosses her spindly arms stiffly over her large breasts and stands pigeon-toed while Whitehart slips a pebble into her shoe. The shot will follow the ones of Oskar and Liselotte strolling and is to be taken from the boom, from above, to suggest Oskar's aloofness, his detachment from Liselotte after the disdainful girl has passed. Marcus shouts, "All right, let's go!" and Oskar tugs Liselotte, who cannot walk very well with the pebble in her shoe. She watches Marcus tearfully, and when Marcus nods, Liselotte halts with stunning suddenness, pulls back, and passes her hand over her forehead and speaks to Oskar. On the sound track her voice will say, *"Meine Füsse"*—a child near tears. *"Gut, Lise, gut!* No, don't look at me!" Marcus shouts. He thinks, Very good and crude: an unimaginative woman. Oskar bends his head over Liselotte woodenly, to hide his confusion about the nature of the man he is playing, and to conceal his wrath with her amateurishness. In the inclination of his head and the way his hand touches her shoulder, he overacts—Oskar wants the scene done with and to be rid of having to deal with Liselotte. The concern he pretends has a vast adamancy, a coldness of spirit, and the grace Oskar cannot help displaying in his attempt to appear a gentleman. Peremptorily the man and the actor merge; he raises his arm and snaps his fingers. A taxi screeches to a halt in front of Oskar and Liselotte; Oskar helps Liselotte in, and the taxi roars in a U-turn while Marcus shouts to Alliat's assistant, *"Allez oop!"* and the boom rises and dips to suggest Oskar's sensation of freedom and release, as if he were flying above the Viale Trinità dei Monti as the taxi vanishes with Liselotte in it.

That shot will be succeeded in the movie by the close-up of Oskar standing at the railing atop the Spanish Steps, smiling at Marcus's joke about Goethe and the statue. The smile will seem to the audience to be expectant—Oskar is waiting to see what reality will emerge for him from the City of the Absolute.

As soon as the shot ends, Oskar hurries toward Marcus, who is standing beside the boom. Oskar says, "That woman! That whore! She is stupid—an amateur." His mouth assumes a bent, paranoid smile. "You put her in the movie to make me a fool. It is a plot."

Marcus says, "Oskar, I need her. I need her for the movie."

"Why?"

Marcus shrugs. "For a touch of innocence. Of soul. She is a symbol of your soul, Oskar, *mein Lieber.*" Oskar relaxes in part. "A symbol," he says. *"Ja, ich verstehe.* And I cast her off. *Ja,* I see." Marcus walks away, to end the conversation. Sweating in the sunlight, he thinks, So she's dead. How could a woman so old know so little? The minnow eyes are stilled—how strange. His heartbeat generates a haze in his chest. Whitehart, on the first landing of the Steps, a sketch in his hand, is arranging extras and instructing them in their attitudes and actions for the next shot. Marcus says to himself, "I must go down." But he knows Whitehart finds his safety in thinking he is indispensable to Marcus. Marcus tells himself, "I must give him another moment to be important."

He turns and goes down—not the Spanish Steps but the steep flight of steps that leads to the Via della Carrozze. Marcus's heart labors. He thinks it will be forty-five minutes before the sun is right for Jehane's ascent. He wants no shadows when Jehane climbs the Spanish Steps. He turns from the Via della Carrozze into the Piazza di Spagna, a middle-aged, heavyset man moving slowly. He says to himself, "It is the work; I take everything too seriously. The shots went well; if they had gone badly, I wouldn't grieve for her."

Clumsily, he bangs open the door of the costume trailer and steps inside. Jehane lies on a couch; her costume, a department-store dress, too short in the waist, too narrow in the shoulders, is bunched across her hips as she lies. Jehane sits up, her pale eyes like erasures in her face, and immediately, vivaciously cries, *"Mon amour!"* and asks him to pass on her makeup, only to break off with surprise—he has not been fervent with her for many months—when he presses his head into the hollow between her throat and shoulder, and murmurs, *"Tu es belle . . . tu es belle, belle, belle,"* and then he raises his head, ashamed. *"Ton maquillage?"* he says, and gravely studies the face she holds atilt for his inspection. It seems to him the light whispers and weeps on her skin, and it occurs to him that once, long ago, he was more forgiving of Noreen than of his father, was always more indulgent to women than to men, to the woman in him more than to the man. He does not care now. Jehane and he discuss her makeup. She is well into her part, more than half illusion.

Marcus steps outside. Whitehart is standing near Alliat by the flower stall, and as Marcus walks toward him, the reporter and the photographer from *Réalités,* who are doing a story on Marcus, intercept him. Whitehart signals that the extras are not quite ready. "I can give you a moment," Marcus says—*a gift.*

They ask him for a photograph, and while he poses expressionless in the sun, the Spanish Steps behind him, the reporter, who is a thin young man with a large nose, smiles deferentially, says, "What is the sensation when you begin the movie?"

Marcus bursts out, "It brings death closer," then he hurries on. "When I was young, it was different. *J'ai chanté.* I'd waited so long for my chance to speak. It was like when I had my first woman—one isn't careful—one feels, and then suffers when it goes wrong. The young, you know, are not *educated.* I had no technique. I felt. Though, God knows, I took the technique of feeling seriously enough. Thinking led to dishonesty. But I was wrong. The young are always wrong. They are imbeciles. They have too many lies to defend. They must go blindly or not go at all." He is embarrassed suddenly and stops, until he notices admiration in the young reporter's eyes. He goes on, "Now I plot everything. I am no longer innocent. I am corrupt with intentions. Sometimes I am rude when I work. I am rude because the idea insists on it, because I am in a state of ambition—do you understand?"

WHEN HE came back from Europe corrupt, he found that with Nanna the corrupt part of him, which she did not know about, became insignificant. But when she bought him clothes, arranged an expensive room for him at college, a large allowance, a car, he protested, "I don't need those things. I haven't earned them."

"I want you to have them," she said. He said to himself, "I am a person who has these things." His car and the money he had to spend helped make him popular, except that he was not welcome in certain places or to certain girls after they heard his name. His classmates admired him, because he was moody, and knowledgeable about vice. He attached himself to the dramatic group and persuaded them that the way to raise money was to make a movie. "A silent. A joke. A parody of a movie. People like to be swindled." The movie had as characters Buster Keaton and Charlie Chaplin, Chaplin as a petty crook, Keaton as a pickpocket; the hero was a plainclothes detective disguised as an old-clothes man; the heroine, played by a boy, was, according to the subtitles, a mistress-criminal, killer, and left-wing deviate, and at the end was revealed to be Princess Margaret, bored with palace life. The college-student audiences laughed, and the profits from the movie paid for a production of *Richard II*, Marcus as Bolingbroke. Nanna came to a performance and said jealously, "Do you intend to make acting your life?" Sweaty and covered with makeup, Marcus cried, "I don't know! Don't be a snob, Nanna." She said, "You still have some lipstick on." She said, "I've missed you the last several weeks." She touched his arm.

Marcus lost interest in being one of a troupe of actors. He met a fierce-beaked young man named Rappaport, overweeningly stoop-shouldered, a clever, militant Jew.

"Weill? Ah," Rappaport said when he was introduced to Marcus, and smiled.

"Half and half," Marcus said, smiling back, sarcastically.

"Half and half? A half Jew is a Jew who's ashamed of being Jewish." Rappaport said, "Always some of our best people get drawn away from us—Einstein, Marx, Freud. Renegades. And what did they gain? Nothing. Nothing plus nothing. They weren't treated like Jews. Did they finally feel they were the equals of the *goyim?* My God, tell me, were they equals before they started or not? Anyway, why talk about it with you—you're not a Jew. You're a half-and-half."

Marcus said, "My God, why make a fuss about it?"

"*They* make a fuss," Rappaport said. "Well, to be honest, we make a fuss, too."

"What's a Jew?" Marcus said.

"A Jew? A Jew is a kind of man who believes in God and believes that everything is a matter of religion. You can't hide or lie about it. No saints. No divine prophets. Just prophets, and they're not always right. You have the Ten Commandments. Money can't be a God. Art can't be a God. Only God is God."

Marcus shrugged. "So what?"

"Ah," said Rappaport. "So it's the truth, that's what. Listen, you think a *goy* can ever know the truth? You think Jesus is the Son of God? Mary was a virgin? Listen, you believe that when you're a child and you do something to your mind. A Christian could discover the Oedipus complex? Don't make me laugh. They want to be Jews, Christians; that's the direction: from Catholic to Protestant to Unitarian. What's a Unitarian? A Jew who can get into a country club. What's a Communist? A man trying to act like a Jew without getting mixed up with God. Listen," Rappaport said, "a Jew can suffer and a Jew can think—you don't think those are advantages?" He told Marcus the Jewish hagiology.

Marcus decided to take Rappaport to Scantuate to open Nanna's eyes. Rappaport talked about the concupiscence of art: "Anything sensual is an advertisement for sex, let's face it. Take those bronze things over there. They arouse the senses." About comparative religion: "Christianity is a debased form of Judaism; the early Christians were uneducated people and added a lot of superstition. That's why we make them nervous. There they stand with the forgery in their hands." Marcus explained to Nanna, "Rappaport likes to *épater les goyim.*" At dinner, Marcus, who thought that intellectual excitement improved Rappaport and made him almost beautiful, encouraged him to talk about the Jewish God. Nanna interrupted Rappaport. "I am not a believer." Rappaport said, "Don't you believe God's weight rests on the world?" "I strongly doubt it." "But think of God as the principles of physics." Marcus said, "Do, Nanna." "When I was a girl," Nanna said, "it was considered bad form to discuss religion. Perhaps it has become quite common nowadays, but I, for one, am unaccustomed to it."

Rappaport said, "Your grandmother doesn't like me. Nobody's as anti-Semitic as some of these old Jewish ladies."

The next weekend, when Marcus was in Scantuate, Nanna asked him, "Are you cross because I didn't get on with your friend?"

"He's odd," Marcus said. "But you have to realize he's free to think whatever he wants—he hasn't anything to lose."

"What he thinks seems to me to redound generally to his advantage," Nanna said dryly.

"That's the ego—but the superego—"

Nanna said, "I'm afraid I don't understand." She said, "I'm rather an old woman and a little behind the times."

She said he looked unwell. He said he was worried about his ideas; he didn't seem to know what was what. Nanna asked if he wanted to see a psychiatrist. Marcus said no, he wanted to meet a philosopher. He said, "A greater Jew was killed in Modigliani than in Jesus."

He said at Scantuate, at the dinner table, "The whelk is safe in its shell, and then a sea gull finds it. Sea gulls are marvelous; they have thick strong bodies like little cannons, and strong red beaks. They pick the whelk up and carry it into the air. The whelk doesn't understand the visitation, the superior force that grips it. My God, he thinks, look how wonderful I am, I'm Olympian, look how high I've come, and then the sea gull drops him, usually on concrete or stone but sometimes on wood, to crack his shell so he can be eaten."

"Marcus!" Nanna cried.

"I'm not describing Nature, Nanna. I'm describing feelings and using Nature—"

"Marcus . . ."

Marcus said, "I'm trying to learn how to think. I've got to learn how to think. Where can I practice if not with you?"

Nanna said, "Marcus, please, talk to a psychiatrist."

Marcus said, "This isn't a neurosis, Nanna. I'm just stupid."

He didn't want a psychiatrist. What good was a psychiatrist? Did a psychiatrist know how to be a genius? A psychiatrist would not understand that being Jewish was a great truth. What did a psychiatrist know about the desire and jealousy he felt for truth, or about learning how to make oneself audible, or about anything, for that matter, except psychiatry? A psychiatrist would frown on drinking and whoring and on being restless and on moodiness, and never realize they were pedagogical aids. They drove the mind into dislocation, into a broken angle where it couldn't hang on to what it had believed before and was set free to circumnavigate a thought.

He persuaded the dramatic group to make a silent movie, *Oedipus Rex*: "Changed," he said, "to Russia in the last century. With Jews." In the movie, he had Oedipus stolen as a baby and reared in Russian Orthodoxy. The climactic scene, when Oedipus learns he is Jocasta's son and a Jew, showed Oedipus standing while his nose, with the aid of stop-lens photography, becomes long and hooked. The subtitle said, "Oedipus acknowledges the spirit of God." The audiences laughed.

A rabbi wrote him a note: "Your movie is very interesting, but perhaps doesn't quite touch on the real essence of being Jewish, which is largely a joyous matter."

Rappaport said, "You're a dangerous man. You get everything wrong. That kid is a godless hoodlum. You think he'd grow up without showing a few Jewish traits?"

"He was attracted," Marcus said. "He married a Jewess. He was anti-Semitic."

"You call those Jewish traits? Your Oedipus is a snob!" Rappaport shouted. "Rex, yet!"

"What do you know about it? Who made you a chief Jew?"

"Look at you, a Jew-come-lately," Rappaport jeered, adding, "When all is said and done, you're nothing but another hard-nosed rich."

Nanna said, "I think that obsessions and theories are only useful if they add passion to a work that already has a formal structure."

Marcus said, "I'm ordinary."

Nanna said, "I do not see that anything has occurred that we cannot take philosophically. It is not as if we'd lost all our money." And she laughed. Marcus said that he wanted Nanna to read Camus and Martin Buber and discuss them with him. Nanna said she did not have time left in her life for new philosophers; she had done her reading: "I am not a lady intellectual. You must take me as I am." She said, "Sukie is such a nice girl. Why don't you see her anymore?" She said Marcus had been much more cheerful when he was seeing Sukie. She said, "Marcus, would you like a sports car?"

Marcus stayed at college for the next few weekends. He sought out Rappaport. He did not feel humiliated in Rappaport's presence. "I hate myself," Marcus said. He had trouble paying attention in class. "Mr. Weill," said the lecturer, "I will contribute one cent for your thoughts." Marcus did not say, "I was just thinking about how big the world is and about death." He said, "I was thinking how stupid I am," and drew a laugh.

Nanna telephoned and asked, "How long am I to be deprived of your company because you're so busy being unhappy?" She said she hadn't been feeling well. She said she'd heard from Gamma Foster that Sukie was coming to Scantuate for the weekend. "May I expect you on

Friday?" she asked. Her tone was mock-humble; she was an old woman, reduced to dangling the charms of a young girl to draw Marcus to Scantuate.

Marcus said, "I'm coming to see you, not Sukie." For the first time, Marcus said to her—over the telephone it was—"I love you, Nanna."

But Sukie was there. It was April, windy, and the pulleys on the flagpole banged and clanged against the metal of the pole. Marcus and Sukie went for a walk; they took shelter from the wind on the porch of Nanna's bathhouse. Sukie said, "Robin doesn't want to let the family know about him and me. Gamma isn't well. He's afraid she'll change her will. Robin's so weak." She said, "Pony, I think Robin's awful. . . ." He remembered Sukie in Paris, and he kissed her. "You're very attractive, Pony. I guess you're not going through one of your Moses periods."

He thought afterward, This is a mistake. I don't like her. Still, politeness seemed to require him to sleep with her again on Saturday afternoon.

On Sunday, he said, "Please, for God's sake, understand—I'm sorry."

Sukie's face went gray and creased; she said, frightened, "Marcus, don't you want to see me anymore?"

"My life isn't settled. God, Sukie, let's talk about something else. I'm shaking." On his way back to school, he told himself, "At least I was kind."

Four weeks later, Sukie called from New York and said, "Marcus, I've been to the doctor."

"The doctor?"

"I'm—I'm . . ." She said with a little laugh, "You may be a father."

Marcus said to her, "Where are you calling from? What's the number where you're calling from? I'll call you back in fifteen minutes." He hung up, and grabbed a coat and slammed out of the room. He couldn't think; he went to a bar and got drunk. He spent the night in a friend's room for fear Sukie would be calling him at his own, and in the morning he telephoned Robin and cautiously asked—his hand was shaking, he puffed furiously on a cigarette—if Robin had heard from Sukie lately.

Robin said, "Oh, did she ask you for money? I told her I didn't have any. Hell, she has money of her own. I can't go to my parents—she's my cousin; Gamma will raise the roof; I don't know what kind of six-different-ways mess it would be. Christ, I'm a nervous wreck. Are you going to lend her the money?"

"I don't know. I'll have to borrow it from Nanna," Marcus said. "You think it's your kid?"

"Of course," Robin said testily. "What the hell!"

Marcus hung up. He admitted to himself that he had been afraid. He said to himself, "Tough, tough, tough . . . Tough cookies," and went back to his room and showered and shaved. The phone rang. It was Nanna's companion, to say, "Your grandmother wants to be certain you're coming down this afternoon."

"Yes," he said. "I'll be d-down about f-five o'clock." His voice sounded odd to him; he hadn't stammered for a long time. He said to himself, "Keep cool." Nanna couldn't know.

Nanna was in the library. The lamps were lit. The minnow eyes would not meet his. She said, "My friend Gamma Foster spoke to me. From Boston. It would seem that her granddaughter is—is *enceinte*—by you."

Marcus, his forehead damp, stood with one foot thrust out, as if casually. Suddenly he put his hand over his eyes. "Tough," he said. "Tough."

Nanna exclaimed, "Marcus!"

"Hell, it's probably not my kid. You don't know about Sukie. She's nothing but a—"

"Marcus!" Nanna said. "Don't be ugly."

Then Marcus realized that Nanna wanted him to marry the girl.

"Nanna! She's—it's t-true!" he exclaimed. Nanna's eyes were averted. His head went forward the length of his neck to bring his mouth closer to Nanna and give his words more force. "Nanna," he said, "you don't know her. She's trying to get away with—to g-get away with— She's t-try—" He couldn't get on with the sentence.

"I did not expect you to act like this," Nanna said. She said the Weills were not light people. She said Gamma Foster knew and trusted their honor. Her voice darkened when she said, "Your appetites are not uncontrollable." She said she and Gamma Foster could give Marcus and Sukie a small allowance, "and you could spend your summers here with me."

When she was silent, Marcus, very conscious of his posture, with no intention of being cruel but trying to bring her to her senses so she could listen and he would not be so angry and so lonely, said, "Nanna, this is crazy. You're being crazy—this is all crazy."

Nanna slipped past his voice. "A gentleman would not refuse to talk

to a girl after he's— Gamma Foster said— That's not how I understand
a gentleman—"

"Like y-you and my f-father with N-Noreen!" he exclaimed. (Not
"Nanna, be fair," or "Nanna, you're unjust.") He was upset by the note
of accusation in his voice. He tried to be politely ironic, superior, to
show how good his manners were, that he was a gentleman. "One of
us is d-dreaming," he said. Nanna's face was appalled, rigid with dis-
taste, dismay, and the desire not to hear. He looked at her, to hold her
eyes while he reasoned with her. "L-Listen," he said. "Use your head.
Wh-Why did Gamma Foster go to you, anyway? Th-They h-have
enough m-money to p-pay for an a-abortion without your help. What
made her think I'd be interested in marrying Sukie? I've shown no signs
of it up until now. They're playing you for a sucker—a Jewish sucker."

Nanna said, "This is disgusting."

Marcus blinked. He let his breath out. He said, "Have it your way."
He turned on his heel and left the room.

He told Cook he would not be in for dinner, and drove back to
college. He sat in his room and drank. The telephone rang at intervals,
but he ignored it. Around midnight, he took off his clothes and lay down
and cried. Then he put on a robe. He sat by the window and thought.
The housemaster came to his door. "Your father is very worried," he
said. "I think you'd better call him." Marcus shaded his eyes with his
hands to conceal the reddened lids. "It's all right," Marcus said. "I'll call
him now. Don't worry, I'm all right."

The housemaster waited while Marcus spoke to the long-distance
operator and then when Marcus said to his father, "Hello, it's me," he
left the room.

Marcus said, "Please let's not have a long t-talk. I just called to say
I've decided to go into the army."

His father said, "Oh, Marcus."

Marcus said, "If you t-try to stop me, I'll go c-crazy—O.K.?"

His father said, "Marcus, it's time you faced the fact you have a few
responsibilities. Nanna is terribly upset."

Marcus said, "Nanna c-can cheer herself up—she can go have a
n-nice long chat with G-Gamma Foster. Look, I'm not in a m-mood
to talk."

His father said, "Do you realize how much you owe Nanna?"

"Well, why don't you p-pay it back for me," Marcus said. He
shouted, "It's not my child! You can all go to hell!"

There was a silence. His father said, "I see. All right, Marcus. Maybe the army's best right now. Let's leave it at that."

"Yes, sir," Marcus said. "G-Give my best to your family."

At first, in the army, he suffered from moments of fright, defiance, and remorse. Then he began to forget. Sometimes he felt that his skull had become a darkened, quite silent movie theater; what his mind thought and senses saw appeared in the very center of his attention, easily decipherable, distinct. Nanna sent him a Christmas card and a check—no note—and he mailed the check back to her.

The army put him in the Signal Corps, and stationed him at an air base in France. He became highly popular with the other men in his unit. They took up his habit of referring to certain officers, and to the army itself, as Grandmother: "Grandmother wants this in triplicate. . . ."

When the army released him, he migrated to Paris. His sexuality proved valuable; Paris took him in and gave him adventures. After a while, he turned against the life he was leading and became the guardian and ward of his work. He put together a small serious movie, and his career and reputation began. When, after eleven years, he saw Nanna and spent a week with her in Paris, he thought, How Euclidean—she does not know how to behave with me. He himself was helpless with irony. He thought, I can't fend off death for her. I haven't time. That's how Marcus saw the story.

H E   S A Y S to the reporter, "You see, when I was a young man I thought life was—was wet, a liquid thing, like the ocean. I didn't know I didn't mean life but only childhood. I thought a man had no leverage and had to swim all his life—currents, tides; one floated and was swept here and there. But then you come to dry land. One knows what one is doing. One makes decisions." He breaks off; it is nearly noon. He has been keeping track of the position of the sun and the quality of the light. Now the sun is striking almost directly downward on the walls of buildings. The glass of the shopwindows ripples with reflections of traffic. The palms rustle like flags overhead, and the brilliant Roman light, so different from the light in Scantuate, pours heavily upon walls, glass, birds gliding like fish in the air. Marcus says, "Dry land. I'll tell you something terrifying about life—it makes sense." He has been keeping track of the sunlight. He says, "Excuse me. It's time for the

next shot," as flatly as if he has not been on a flight of emotion, and
walks off.

He calls Whitehart and Alliat to him, says, "The sun's right. Let's get
moving, boys and girls." He is crying.

"What is it?" Alliat asks in French.

"My grandmother. She was such a stupid woman. Let's go. . . ."
Everyone is dispatched to his position.

Marcus and Alliat seat themselves on the boom, and the boom rises.
"Jehane comes from the Sistine Chapel as from her mother's womb,"
Marcus says. Alliat nods and sights the camera. The streets open to
Marcus's eye as the boom reaches its greatest height. Halfway down the
Via Condotti, Jehane starts to walk. In a white kerchief and sunglasses,
she walks in the Roman sunlight. Two boys, extras—unwashed, skull-
eyed, large-mouthed—racket on a motor scooter past her, shouting,
"*Ciao! Bella!*" then an obscenity. Jehane flinches and walks on. She
comes to the curb and makes her way out into the stream of traffic. She
breaks into a trot, nears the camera, starts up the Spanish Steps—the
stone waterfall. She climbs past the extras, who enact their assigned
motions, to the stretch that has been cleared and waits deserted in the
sunlight. She moves farther from the street, Rome, the camera; alone on
the wide Baroque sweep of the Steps, she climbs. She climbs with
indignation, in solitude. The bystanders grow quiet. They stand silent
and involved. Marcus sighs. She mounts, and it is the human spirit
mounting. He presses his hands together. A stillness accompanies her
ascent. Does Jehane enjoy silence as acclaim? She climbs—ah, the successful aerialist—and reaches the landing, where she will meet Oskar
descending.

On the Waves

In the churning wake of a motorboat from one of the luxury hotels, the gondola bobbed with graceful disequilibrium. The tall, thin, handsome man sitting in the gondola gripped the sides of the small wooden craft and said to his seven-year-old daughter, "Hold on." He thought, Gondolas are atavistic.

He wore a white polo shirt. Once he had been the sixth-ranking tennis player in the United States, and had married a rich girl; his days on the tennis circuit were five years past, and the marriage had ended in divorce twelve months before. Now he taught American history in an American school in Rome and played tennis with various members of the diplomatic set. He still kept to the course of reading he had drawn up and that he hoped would give him intelligence, or, failing that, education. Gifted with a strong body and good nerves, he had never felt so harassed by ignorance that a sense of his own worth could not come to his rescue; then in the fourth year of his marriage, his tennis game and marriage deteriorating, he had begun wanting desperately to know more about everything. He had settled down to read the philosophers, the psychologists, the historians, the poets, the critics. He had had no clear idea what he would do as an educated man, a self-made intellectual, and so he decided to teach. He had left his wife, unwilling to quarrel with her, unable to bear her restlessness at the change in him. He had gone to Europe. The divorce had depressed him. He had missed his daughter unconscionably. He wrote his former wife and asked if the child Melinda could visit him. He would pay her plane passage to Europe. His former wife agreed to permit the journey. Melinda had sent him a note in block capitals: "CAN WE SEE VENICE DADDY?"

She sat beside him in the gondola, white-skinned, thin-boned, with straight eyebrows like his and green eyes like her mother's. Her reddish-blond hair was her own. So was the dull stubbornness with which she maintained a polite and lifeless manner toward Henry. This was the fourth day of her visit, their second day in Venice.

He had a headache. He sat slouching, hands between his knees. He wondered irritably how the Venetians managed to live day after day with the illusive and watery haze, the heat, the mind-scattering profusion of reflections, of smells, of playful architectural details, with the unsettling mixture of squalor and ostentation, with the silent, silvery air, the decay, the history, and the atmosphere of vice. But he felt constrained to be honest. The truth was, he thought ashamedly, he was bored. It was dull as hell to spend so many hours in the company of a child.

They had been to the Ca' d'Oro that morning. Henry had said, "Isn't it pretty? It's supposed to be one of the prettiest houses in Europe."

"It's pretty," the child said.

She had grown restless when he'd dawdled in front of the Mantegna. "Tell me the story of that picture, Daddy," she'd said.

"The man being shot with arrows is a saint," he'd said.

So much in Venice was unsuitable for a child.

It had been perhaps a mistake, this trip: movement was half a child's charm. Children stilled—on a train, at a dinner table, in a gondola—were reduced: one was chafed by the limitations of their intellects and the hardness of their voices.

When they'd left the Ca' d'Oro, they'd hired a gondola and embarked on the Grand Canal. Noticing the child's lackluster eyes, the loose setting of her lips, Henry had asked her, "You're not seasick or anything?" He suggested, "Some people don't like gondolas. If the gondola bothers you, we can go ashore."

"Could we have lunch?"

"I forgot," Henry had said. "It's your lunchtime. Can you hold out until we get to San Marco? I know the restaurants there."

AS THE gondolier resumed his steady stroke, Melinda turned to Henry—the angle of her head upon her shoulders indicated melancholy—and asked in a weak voice, "Why did they build Venice on the water?"

Henry replied without thought, "To be safe."

"It's safe on the water?"

Henry, whose eleventh-grade history students adored him and trusted his opinions, said, "Well, children might fall in. But the people here wanted to be safe from armies."

The child waited questioningly.

Henry was thinking that a gondola was an inefficient watercraft, keelless (a bent demiquaver, a notation of the music of the water). He woke from his reverie with a start. "Armies can't fight and swim at the same time."

"They could come in little boats," the child said.

Henry dusted off the knees of his trousers. "The Venetians could swim out and overturn little boats, they could do all sorts of things to little boats. The Venetians had no trouble with armies for a thousand years." He smiled to cover any deficiencies in his explanation—he had always been extraordinarily confident of his physical charm.

"A thousand years?" the child asked.

"Yes," he said reassuringly, "a thousand years."

The child closed one eye, looked at him through the other. "Is that a long time, Daddy?"

Henry swallowed a sigh. "I'll tell you," he said. "Let's take Grandmother Beecher. You think she's old, don't you?" Henry's eyes held the child's attention. "Now imagine *her* grandmother. And keep going back for *twenty* grandmothers. Isn't that a lot of grandmothers?"

His and the child's eyes seemed hopelessly locked. Then, as he watched, the child's eyes slowly went out of focus.

Slowly, she extended her arm over the water; she observed the shadow of her hand change shape on the sun-gilt waves. She was as lifeless as a mosaic, yet she spoke: "Are the palaces so wibbly-wobbly because they're so old?"

Henry said, "Well, yes and no." He paused, then went on heartily, "The buildings are old, yes, but that's not the entire story. The islands they are built on were mudbanks—they just barely stuck out of the water, and the Venetians made them bigger by throwing stones and logs and garbage—"

"Garbage—eeugh!" The child held her nose.

"Well," her father said, "they made the islands bigger. But as the years pass, the water licks away at them. Waves are like little tongues," he said with sudden poetry. "They eat out little pieces of the islands, the islands sink, and the buildings wobble." It was sad she was too young, Henry thought, for him to tell her that suns, stars, people, intelligence, and every other bit of created matter began by law in chaos and aged into chaos.

Melinda, squinting, peered up into Henry's face. "Is Venice falling apart, Daddy?" she asked.

"Well—yes and no," Henry said. "It's *sinking,* but very slowly."

"Gee, Daddy, you know an awful lot," she said with despairing enthusiasm.

Henry felt his face heating into a blush. He said, "Any guidebook would tell you . . ." He did not finish. He gazed at the Baroque palaces along this newer stretch of the Grand Canal, palaces spotted with noon shadows, draped in cornices, pilasters, and balustrades, sad.

"It won't fall down while we're here?" the child asked. She laughed faintly.

Did she want Venice to fall? Henry said, "No. It won't fall." It was disappointment he saw in her face. He said, "You know that big tower in the Piazza—the red tower? It fell down once. . . . In Henry James's time. About sixty years ago." Melinda was watching him, he thought, expectantly. She wanted to hear more about the collapse of Venice. Good God, why did the child wish harm to this fanciful city built on mud and garbage? Was it that, betrayed, she resented the world of adults, hoped for its destruction? Henry's heart trembled: the child was a betrayed idealist. Achingly, he looked at her.

She wore the dim frown that suggested she might be grappling with a half-formulated female thought.

"What is it?" Henry asked. "Are you thinking something? What are you thinking?"

The child, startled, shook her head and drew her shoulders up.

"You can tell me," Henry said encouragingly.

"You'll get angry," she said.

"Me?" He stopped. He said slowly, "It doesn't matter if I get angry. Fathers and daughters can get mad at each other if they want. It doesn't mean a thing. We can't go through life being afraid of each other." Melinda studied her thumb. "Why, if I got angry, I might shout and wave my arms and fall into the Grand Canal—wouldn't that be funny?"

Melinda was silent.

"Go ahead," Henry said. He leaned closer. "Try to make me angry. See what happens."

"I'm too scared."

"Of me?"

"I don't know," she said tactfully. She stuck her forefinger into the water. Henry could see only the back of her head.

He felt the rush of innocence that accompanies a sense of being misunderstood. "The water's dirty!" he exclaimed.

Melinda raised her finger and held it in her other hand on her lap; drops of water darkened her pale-blue skirt.

Henry said, "I don't see that anything you can tell me would make me any angrier than I am at your *not* telling me."

Melinda whispered, "All right. . . ." The gondola rocked. A lifeboat-shaped motor vessel was chugging by, stacked with Coca-Cola cartons. "I don't really like Venice."

He had expected her to say—his hopes had grown so from the moment when he realized she wanted Venice to fall—something more illuminating, something like an admission that it saddened her, the distance that had come between her and Henry since the divorce, something like "I hate it that you and Mommy don't live together anymore," something honest like that.

He said, "You wanted to come to Venice! It was your idea!"

"It's not the way I thought it would be," she said. "Nothing here is sincere except the water."

Henry's mouth opened, then emitted laughter. He laughed rather a long time. He sobered: Would Melinda care that a city was *insincere* if Henry's leaving home had not taught her that insincerity was everywhere? He blinked at her pityingly, tenderly.

"Why did you laugh?" Her face was pink with hurt.

"Because I thought what you said was witty." He watched her. "Do you know what 'witty' means?"

"No."

"Something true—more or less—that comes as a surprise makes people laugh. That's witty."

"I did?" she said.

"Yes. You did. . . . But, Melinda, Venice is supposed to be nice, even though it's insincere," Henry said.

The child's face caved in, as if she took what he'd said for an expression of disapproval.

Henry, with that sensation of clumsiness that came to him whenever she asked him to help with one of her small buttons, tried to put things right. "But you like the water?"

"And the pigeons," the child said, anxious to please.

"Why? Are they sincere?"

"Yes," the child said, and nodded vigorously.

Why did she look so expectant? *I give up,* Henry thought, and laughed with exasperation and weariness. Melinda's face pinkened again, slowly. She smoothed her skirt. She seemed to have come into possession of a gentle incandescence. He said, "We certainly won't stay here if you don't like it. We can go to Paris."

"Paris?" The incandescence grew, then dimmed. "If you want to," she said, staring into her lap.

Henry had come to hate her pale good manners. The first days of her visit, he had thought she was still shocked that Mother-and-Daddy were no longer a single, hyphenated warm beast; he had told himself, "She will have to get used to me as an individual." He had not expected her to go on so long being mannerly and frightened with that individual. He began to rattle off words like a salesman trying to confuse a customer. "We'll go swimming—at the Lido—this afternoon. We'll take the launch over. We'll swim in the 'sincere' water, and tonight we'll eat and pack and have some ice cream, and tomorrow we'll fly to Paris. We'll fly over the Alps. You'll see the Alps—you've never seen the Alps before. We'll get to Paris in time for lunch. We'll have lunch outside on the street—"

"I know. I saw it on television."

"But you'll like it?"

The child said worriedly, "Do you have enough money?"

Oh, my God, Henry thought, *she did overhear those quarrels.* "No," he said, "I can't afford it. But we're going to do it anyway."

Melinda's eyes grew large. Her face seemed distended with pleasure. She put her hand to her mouth and laughed in the shelter of her hand.

Henry said, "What's so funny?"

"You're funny, Daddy. You're so bad." She inserted her hand inside his and gripped his fingers with an industrious and rubbery pressure— an active possession. Light dipped and danced along the swan's neck of the gondola's fantastic prow. She sighed. "Daddy," she said after a while. "You know that boy who lives across the hall?" From the apartment in the States where she lived with her mother, she meant. "Well, he likes to play dirty games."

Henry's tongue moved over his lower lip. He thought, How strangely moving it is that the child trusts me. "He does?" he said.

"Yes," she said.

"What do you mean by dirty games?" His eyes probed a corner of the Venetian sky; his voice was as calm as a psychiatrist's.

"You know."

"Give me an example."

"Oh, he wants me to go into the closet with him and take my clothes off."

The gondola slid under the Ponte dell'Accademia. Henry said, "Is that so?"

Melinda said, "Yes," nodding.

Henry switched his eyes to a different corner of the sky. "Is that all?" he asked.

"He's really silly," she said, noncommittal. ". . . He likes to push stomachs."

Henry heard the muted rumble of footsteps on the wooden bridge. "Do you like to push stomachs?"

Melinda said, "Sometimes." She drew the end of a strand of hair back from her cheek. "But I don't really like playing those games with *him.*" She looked up at her father, her brows knit. "He gets angry if I won't play those games."

"Why does that bother you? What do you care if he gets angry?"

"Well, I don't like him to get too angry. I like having him to play with when I get bored."

"Is boredom so awful?" Henry said in a louder tone.

"It depends."

Henry thought, *She wants to punish me for abandoning her. My God.* He made a mental note to do some reading about disturbed children. He said, shielding his eyes with his hand, "You stay out of that closet!"

A startled, single peal of involuntary laughter popped out of Melinda. She stared at him with pink astonishment.

"What's funny?" Henry asked.

"You are!" the child shouted. "What you're thinking! You want to kiss me!" Strands of hair bounced on her forehead in the silvery light. She spread her fingers over her mouth and cheeks, hiding them from him.

The sunlit panorama was squeezed into a rich oval in the center of which his daughter's face floated, partly veiled by her fingers. "You're right," Henry said, with amazement.

A flutter passed across the child's shoulders; a sound halfway between a choked shout and a laugh came from behind her fingers.

Along the canals, at the edge of his vision, Venice trembled on its uncertain islands, assailed by the devouring and protective and odorous wash of the sea. He kissed Melinda's hands, and as she moved them he kissed her cheek, her nose, her chin.

THE GONDOLA floated toward the seaward rim of the Piazzetta. Melinda's head lay on Henry's chest in the exhaustion following laughter. Her arm was thrown across his stomach. "We're at the Piazza," Henry said.

Melinda sat up, touched a hand to her hair. Groggily, she surveyed the approaching landfall, the stone folds of the perspective opening past the winged lion, the lozenge-patterned palace, the benign litter of Byzantine oddments, bronze horses, golden domes, pinnacles, flagpoles, and pigeons. Amiably, the child said, "*Ciao, piazza. Ciao,* lunch. *Ciao,* pigeons."

Bookkeeping

I T H I N K I am going mad, what you call loco. . . . I don't want to bother you . . . but you live so near. . . ." Annetje's voice over the telephone, fascinating, foreign, threaded on hard-breathing pauses, moved Avram Olensky unbearably. He was curly-haired, a handsome but unhappy- and nervous-looking Jew. He kept his back to his guests, Louise Kimball, now Louise von Kunnel, and her husband of eight months, the *Graf* Ulrich von Kunnel.

Avram, as usual wishing his feelings could be simple, felt embarrassed to be thinking it dreadful luck that Louise was the person he would have to abandon to help Annetje: Louise was so highly susceptible to slights. She had earlier, in her bland, quite admirable, Yankee forthrightness (she was from Ridgefield, Connecticut), warned Avram that she worried he would be anti-German with Ulrich.

Louise was a very old friend and had been briefly a mistress and had once lent Avram the money he had needed to found a small literary magazine.

Calculating the ethics of the situation rapidly, Avram said to himself, "Compassion outweighs Gratitude," and said into the telephone, "Annetje, I am *glad* you called me."

"You are a kind man!" Annetje exclaimed in her accented, exciting, telephone-flavored voice.

"No, no," Avram said truthfully. "I only wish I were. I—"

Annetje said, "I took LSD. I am having a *reaction*. I cannot eat, I cannot sleep. I am paranoid as hell."

Avram's spirits lifted; they rose a certain percentage. LSD. Ah, he thought, a little help is all that is required. "Talmudist," hissed a part of his mind.

But he had avoided Annetje for years. He had grown nervous in his middle thirties; Annetje frightened him, her prettiness was so extreme—white-blond hair, enormous seaside-gray eyes—her irrational, storm-tossed, passionate conversation so unnerving. She would say, "The story of my life is too much. I was born in a castle, a Dutch castle. My father was a banker. He was not afraid of the Nazis. Then he was. We got to Vichy, and one day my father went out to buy cigars and never came back. Never. The nuns told my mother they would save me. I was dressed as a nun and I went to Italy. I never saw my mother again. I was told after the war she died of pneumonia. But they were being kind to me, I think. I spent the war in Italy. We were often bombed. I could not go to the chapel or the cellar. I did not want to be buried alive. I used to run outside and scream at the airplanes."

As soon as the war was over, she came to America. "I didn't want to see frightened faces anymore. . . . My first husband was terribly rich—he came from Chicago. He had a tiny little airplane—he was very strange, that man—he wanted to fly everywhere. Even to horse races. He decided to fly to Rio de Janeiro. We flew from Chicago to Tennessee, from Tennessee to Florida, from Florida to the Bahamas. I wanted never to be frightened again, and here I was in this little tiny airplane with this man who wanted to be frightened all the time. It gave him *pleasure*! My God. When we flew over the jungle, I decided that was the end. In Rio, I left him. Also, he was dull."

If she was so afraid of danger—Avram had asked her—why had she married Allan? Allan was her second husband, and it was while she was married to him that Avram had met her. Allan was a professional deep-sea diver, a scuba expert, with very little money.

"He never asked me to go diving with him," Annetje said, wide-eyed. "I did not realize I would be frightened for *him*." She had left him when he gave her an ultimatum, to calm down and be reasonable or go away. He had not expected her to go away.

She had married a third time, while visiting friends in Switzerland. She told Avram what had happened, meeting him one day on Lexington Avenue, both of them shopping; they lived two blocks apart, they discovered. Avram was recently divorced—from his second wife.

"I did not want to get married again," Annetje said, brushing at the incredibly blond hair that fell across the left side of her forehead. "He *insisted*. He is very, very sophisticated. He said we would drive each other mad if we did not marry. He said, married, we would love each other less, we would have a little peace."

Her third husband, a cadaverous six-feet-five-inch semiserious novelist from Montana, as handsome as Gary Cooper, as serious a drinker as Scott Fitzgerald, wrote for the movies between novels, squandering and gambling away his enormous salary. Annetje was his fourth wife. Avram knew the man slightly—John Herbert Thompson his name was. John Herbert had what seemed to Avram a peculiarly touching quality of emotional elegance; he loved and suffered with a singleness of purpose that reminded Avram of the curved, thin legs of French antiques.

One of Avram's most intense experiences had involved John Herbert—Avram had fallen briefly, confusedly in love with an Italian poetess who was at that time loved by John Herbert. The Italian poetess had been pessimistic, very tall and bony for an Italian woman; her usual expression had been one of somber, dark-eyed, hopeless intuition. She had taken Avram as a lover and discarded John Herbert, because, she said, Avram's deadness, his endless calculations, were more needful than John Herbert's despair. "I want a man who cannot live without me," she had said. "When I love, I am a capitalist. When I love, I own." At other times, she was, of course, a Communist.

Avram had always admired John Herbert. "I am almost a C.P.A. really, in spirit, by comparison," he had said to Annetje when she told him of her marriage. "There is a spiritual grandeur about great drinkers. Me, I am prudent. Always, involuntarily, at bottom, *prudent.*"

But, he thought, Annetje had again married strangely. John Herbert was mentally and physically adventurous. He had had two nervous breakdowns, brought on by too much thinking, by exhaustion, and like many American writers afflicted with what Avram called "a virility syndrome"—he wanted to be a perfect man—he pursued farfetched sports, skydiving for one, and had once gone on a four-month expedition in the Andes and discovered a tribe that used hallucinogenic sweet potatoes as a staple of diet. Yet Avram thought there was style in the marriage of a man of such emotional elegance to a temperamental coward like Annetje. Annetje would make John Herbert want to live. She would interpose her beauty between John Herbert and his passionate carelessness.

"Where is John Herbert?" Avram asked now on the telephone.

"He has left me," Annetje said. "I told him to get out. It was the drug. He did not want to give me any sympathy. I do not deserve sympathy, but he is my husband, the bastard. Besides, I think he has a girl. I do not care. My God, my God. This is awful. They should put me on TV. The world should see me like this. No one would ever take LSD again. Ha-ha. Ha. Listen, you live so close, I want to see someone. My friends hate me. I tell you, I am paranoid. Listen, can you come over. The walls here are behaving strangely. I should throw myself out the window."

"Annetje!"

"No, I won't throw myself out the window. The windows have a very evil look. I am being persuasive. John Herbert says this is what I do. I am unfair."

Avram felt a surge of complicity with John Herbert. Annetje sounded to him like someone enjoying a minor collapse, not someone who needed immediate help. But could he take that chance?

In New York, to be without compassion was to become an outcast. Avram did not know of any circle except among lawyers, perhaps (and even then he wasn't certain), where an unwillingness to sympathize was not cause for exile. Avram had often said that intelligence was less in demand in New York than a feeling heart.

On the other hand, he was afraid of Louise. She was a rather rigid person. Within bounds, she could be flexible, but the bounds were very narrow. She was a Republican, a heavy drinker, and once slighted, she never forgot. If he left to go to Annetje, she would feel slighted; she was unyielding in points of honor. No matter how carefully he argued that he had an ethical obligation to go to Annetje, Louise would simply feel he preferred Annetje to her. If he lied and said Annetje was a very close friend, Louise would wonder, out loud—Louise never held anything back—why he had never introduced Louise to her. Louise would say, "You think I'm too dull for your interesting friends."

Avram leaped toward a compromise. "I have company," he said to Annetje, and turned his head to give Louise a warm smile. She returned a suspicious look; she sensed a slight in the air.

"Oh," Annetje said quickly, "I am terrible, I have interrupted you, I am very sorry, go, go at once, I will be all right, I am fine, I am very strong, I—"

"No, no. Listen to me. Why don't you join us? Please. Let me take you to dinner. Please?"

"I couldn't. I am going mad. I—"

"Please. I want you to join us." Avram saw that Louise was looking very angry.

Annetje said, "I can't. I am afraid. I cannot leave my apartment. I have not left for five days. I do not know what is outside my door."

"I will come and fetch you," Avram said. He put his hand over the receiver and said to Louise and Ulrich, "It's only two blocks. It will only take a moment."

Louise closed her eyes and said, with eyes closed, "Don't worry about us. Don't let us interfere."

God, Avram thought, why am I such a coward?

"I look so terrible," Annetje said.

"So do we. I'll be there in three minutes," Avram said, and hung up.

He leaned against the wall near the telephone table and smiled still more warmly at Louise. Louise's pan-shaped face was rigid. Her hair had been done by some famous man of the scissors but remained undistinguished. She was wearing pearls and a dress Avram assumed was expensive. Dear, rich Louise, Avram thought. He wondered for the fifty thousandth time since he'd met her how her mind worked—she was very family-conscious; she believed in the human personality as produced and trained by certain families. But Avram had never known her to lie, she was rarely or never devious, and she often amused him.

Avram began to talk quickly. "Look, I know this is terrible. Here we are, our first get-together since God knows when, and I want to bring in a stranger. But she's in trouble. She's married to quite a good friend of mine"—Avram hoped he would not have to explain that or name the friend; Louise would be furious he had never introduced her to someone as famous as John Herbert—"and he happens to be in California. Stupidly this girl took some LSD and she's having a bad reaction. I really don't think she should be alone. Her husband would never forgive me. And you will like her. She's a fascinating person. She was married to Langwell Eggles—you know, Chicago?" Avram tried to force a social smile from Louise by tilting his head toward her, catching her glance, and raising his eyebrows to suggest what she do with her mouth.

"Of course, of course," Ulrich said. Louise has picked a large, handsome German, Avram thought; Avram often thought in sentences. He will turn pasty later in life. He is very gracious. He doesn't like me.

Louise said, "I think we'd better go." Her mouth had the twist that Avram knew so well: she felt slighted.

"No, no," Avram said. "You must stay. I've looked forward so to seeing you." He sighed; he always did, like a stage Jew, when he felt himself forced into duplicity. *Listen to me, sounding like a Gentile*, said his sigh. He rolled his eyes slightly upward. He said, "I can't help the girl's calling. I wish she hadn't called me. But I can't leave her in the lurch. Please don't punish me by leaving. And she's quite fascinating."

Louise sat back deeper into her chair; Avram took that for an answer. He darted into the kitchen and fetched a tray, loaded it quickly with bottles of liquor and the ice bucket, talking loudly all the time. "You know how it is in New York? We're very strongly neighbors in our set. It's an emotional thing, not geographical; I mean, I don't know who lives next door to me. But Annetje is a neighbor, I feel. I—" He reentered the living room. "Please don't blame me. You mustn't let me down. We owe ourselves this evening together." He set the tray on the oiled walnut coffee table. "I'll be gone ten minutes at most, and I'll bring back this fascinating girl I do really want you to meet. Really." Avram felt a twinge of conscience; surely charity and affection were equally insulted when one tried to kill two birds with one egocentric stone: not only would Annetje be the equivalent of a floor show and make the evening special and ease this getting acquainted with Ulrich but Louise and Ulrich would protect him from Annetje.

He closed his eyes. He was keeping books, as usual.

He opened his eyes, grabbed a raincoat from the closet, paused to say, "Now please wait for me," and dashed dramatically out the door.

AVRAM DARTED down the steps of his brownstone with that quick boyishness of his which aroused the sarcasm of so many of the intellectuals who wrote for his magazine.

The street was empty of walkers, lined with parked cars, each dotted with moisture from the half fog, half drizzle that filled the air with tiny drops of light-blurring water—the air had an acrid edge of pollution.

As he loped along the sidewalk, he felt an uplift of spirits. In his life—he was between affairs, and the magazine came out only twice a year—he lately felt a dryness, a dearth of feeling and of interest. The city had lately begun to seem mere walls of brick and glass, channels for soot. But now he looked forward to the evening. He was attempting to help someone; this was an oasis.

How he pitied Annetje for being an acidhead. Avram did not approve of LSD and had never taken any. At a party given a few years before for two men who wanted to raise funds for a quasi-utopian settlement to be based on love and LSD, the men had spoken at length and incoherently of the evils of the games of ambition, of the evils of success and failure—noticeably charmless failures in a roomful of successful people well on the way to being more successful. Since then, Avram had stubbornly held that LSD was a drug for failures without good sense. He was surprised at Annetje. Yes, her marriages did not last, she was growing older, but why the hell didn't she simply make up her mind to be a better wife? Annetje had charm.

Annetje and John Herbert kept an apartment in a building just off Lexington Avenue, with doormen and elevator men. Annetje was afraid of being raped. Men on the streets did conceive enormous desire for her; Avram had observed it. Once, he had seen her walking down Lexington Avenue, quite frightened, followed by four men, four men dispersed and straggling, and when she crossed the street to greet Avram the four men had halted, like Secret Service agents, and stared while she spoke to Avram, who then walked her to Bloomingdale's, a guard.

Once, a man—it had been in the papers—had managed somehow to enter her building; he had thrown himself on her in the hallway; she had broken free and run down seven flights of stairs to the lobby. A passing police car had responded to the doorman's shout. The two policemen found the would-be rapist crouching on the roof, sobbing. He was a forty-five-year-old truckdriver with a record of sexual offenses, most of which, to Avram's surprise, were for homosexual assault of one kind or another. Annetje had said, "I am very attractive to homosexuals. I don't remind them of their mother." Annetje was thin and had that extraordinary coloring, of course, and an astonishing amount of sex appeal. She had said gloomily, "I could tell the minute he grabbed me he was homosexual. I thought, Just my luck, I am going to be raped by a homosexual."

Poor Annetje. In the end, no man is man enough for a really pretty woman, Avram thought.

He knocked on her door. She did not answer, and Avram began to worry; he was calculating what he must do if she did not answer—call the police, take her to a sanitarium, get in touch with John Herbert—when he heard footsteps. Tiny, frightened footsteps.

"Who is it?" Annetje whispered.

"Avram."

"Thank God," she said.

He heard a series of mechanical noises, of clicks and scrapes; she was unlocking the door. Seconds passed; the noises continued.

"There are so many," she said through the door. "I can't work them. I'm a prisoner."

"Take your time. Don't be upset," Avram said with patience.

Abruptly the door opened, and there was Annetje. Bedraggled, un-combed, pale inside a tattered sweater and a heavy skirt that hung lopsidedly and was sliding lower on her hips. Annetje was one of those intensely seductive women who dress stylishly for the street and then relax at home inside shapeless old clothes, clothes they've perhaps had since college, or their first marriage—mementos of lost years, vanished fashions, and the emotions that went with the fashions.

Annetje was very thin-waisted, with little cushionlike hips and thin, square shoulders, quite broad, and Avram was always aware of the small of her back; her shoulders and her hips were assertive: it was the small of her back which was private and where her vulnerability truly resided. His hands twitched, anxious to touch her there. So frail, he thought. So needful. His eyes began to film over. He caught himself; he bent semimedically to study her eyes to see if the pupils were dilated or anything like that. But that was a mistake. Avram was susceptible to Annetje; the seaside grayness of her eyes jolted his emotions. Bedraggled or not, she sent out a current of high sexual voltage. She suggested to Avram Swedish movies, summer making the Nordics carnal.

"It's you," she said, pressing fragile, long-boned arms to her breast. "I didn't think you would come." Then, with that violence Avram feared in her, she threw those frail arms around his neck.

Avram's hands fluttered, then settled helplessly on the small of her back; it felt incredibly tiny; he could feel her life coursing in her. He murmured, "I said I would come," but he was nearly mindless. He had only enough self-possession to calculate that if he tried to make her it would be shameful—taking advantage. Dull honor, he thought, gently massaging the small of her back: I will probably get an ulcer and die young. He heard himself say, "I said I would be here." It was a deeper voice than he usually used. He had started, he thought, the mating dance. He wondered if Annetje had ever seen a male unexcited by desire, a male in a more normal state.

"But I am paranoid. I told you I was paranoid. I thought you were just lying to get me off the phone. I thought you were angry that I called." She flung herself backward, away from him, turned in a half pivot, came to rest with one arm across her chest, gripping her other arm. "Do you have any cigarettes? I've been afraid to smoke. I was afraid of setting myself on fire."

He had his first impulse since her call of genuine sympathy. "Why did you do it? No one should go through such unnecessary . . ." He didn't know what word to use: agony, discomfort.

"I am a fool," Annetje said. "I thought it would help me—I wanted to understand John Herbert. There is nothing to understand. That is what I saw. He is a child, a malicious child. I am a child." She looked at Avram.

Avram thought, She is right. He himself was well into the dry plateau of growing older, that slow one-way advance into the wastes.

"I could have seen it without the drug," Annetje said with a little laugh. Suddenly she pressed her hand to her mouth. "I mustn't laugh," she said between her fingers. "My teeth will fall out."

The apartment had a stale, nervous smell. Avram commented on it and Annetje said, "I have locked all the windows. Air pollution will get in. Or I will throw myself out. No, I won't."

Avram said, "Let's go. This place isn't good for you. Get a raincoat."

"Sit with me a moment," Annetje said. "Just for a moment. Us alone." She spoke wheedlingly, almost in a child's tone. Avram was impressed by her lips—large Dutch lips, delicately flickering; their soft flutter charmed him.

"What happened with John Herbert?" he asked. He followed Annetje into the green-and-white, airless living room.

"I told him to get out, that bastard," she said. " 'Go away,' I said. He slapped me. He was furious I had taken the LSD. He said I was a pig. Oh, it was very sordid." She sat down on an innocently moss-green couch, her knees close together, her hands hovering, not quite touching her temples. "It is time to die. It is the one sordid thing I have not done," she said.

"Why don't you settle down, Annetje?" Avram said avuncularly.

"Settle down?" Annetje grimaced. "There are quicker ways to die. I cannot stand it. I have had enough of bastards," she said. "I do not need any more badness from these bastards. I am through with him. Them. Why do they eat you up? They are such babies. They want to be mothered. I am not a mother." She gave Avram a heated glance of her gray eyes as if to demonstrate in what way she was not motherly. She said, "Why can't he act like a man? Always, it is I who fail him, he says. I think it is my turn to collapse. Let him take care of me, let him worry about me. Last month he has a binge, two weeks—drinking, women, gambling. He comes home in rags, half beaten, bruises on his face. 'Help me, Annetje,' he says. I take him in my arms. I wash his face. I sit up with him all night. The next day he is refreshed, he continues with his binge. He comes home, he has nightmares, I hold his head in my lap all night. His nightmares frighten even me. Even now I am not as bad as he was then. He says he is going out of his head. I get him to the doctor. After two days, he refuses to see the doctor again. He says the doctor is stupid. Very well, let him go out of his head. Good riddance. I don't care. I am tired. I know I am unreasonable. I have had this drug. I am crazy—I know it. I am paranoid. I tell him he wants to destroy me. I tell him to get out. You know what he does? He goes. But I am glad. I want to be alone."

Avram's conscience made him say, "But he loves you, Annetje . . . and you are, I think, still in love with him."

"Of course," said Annetje. "I am always in love with bastards. It is not easy to stop loving. But if I don't see him I will be all right. I would rather die than see him."

"I don't believe you."

"Ah," Annetje said seriously, "you understand me."

Avram wriggled in his chair, blinded by her regard.

She said, "I am very tough. I am tougher than he is. He is weak!" She spoke with large-scale contempt.

Avram thought, I am afraid of her. He said, "You're not actually *tough.*"

"No. You're right," she said docilely, tensely. "That is true. I am not. But they always think I am. I need a man. I *need.* I want a man to take care of me—a strong man." She glanced at Avram. "I think you are strong."

"Not strong enough," Avram said mournfully.

Annetje said, "Why do men think women take their strength from them?"

"Well, women do, in a way," Avram said, weakly amused. "I mean, I sometimes feel very weakened by you."

Annetje's mouth turned downward with sadness. "You find me boring."

"No, no. I think you are afraid of being loved. You are tired of it." He passed his hand over his eyes. "You are not pleased when people lean

on you. You don't like it, and you are afraid, too, you won't be strong."
Annetje smiled slowly; her eyes widened. She said, "You understand
me. You are a lot like me—you are more like me than John Herbert is."
She sat on the couch, fragile and exposed. She seemed to hold his
regard to her breast, to her cheek. For comfort. If he embraced her, she
would explore her feelings of similitude to him in kisses that would be
like waves—suffocating, soft, private, dense. And then?

Avram thought with self-distaste that he was too scrupulous in his
lechery. She had taken LSD, she was out of the question. But he did not
want to fall in love with Annetje anyway; I can't afford it, he phrased
it inwardly.

"Yes," he said. "We are very much alike, like brother and sister."

"You would be good to me," Annetje said.

"No," Avram said. "I would be less patient even than John Herbert.
I am very demanding."

"Like Allan!" Annetje exclaimed with sudden comprehension. Allan
was the professional skin diver, her second husband. "Ah, God, I was
miserable with him!" Annetje said. "The sweet-tempered men are the
worst. How he nagged! And jealous! My God, he was jealous. There
I was, cooking all day, sewing, and he was jealous."

"He probably thought you liked him as a rest cure rather than for
himself," Avram said, with a touch of petulant identification.

Annetje said, "Ah. No."

"He might have thought that," Avram argued.

"But no," Annetje said. "He did not. You don't know everything, I
see. I will tell you something. You have the story all wrong. I loved him
more than he loved me. You see, when I was younger and I admired
a man, I slept with him, but sleeping was not important to me. You
understand when I say sleeping I mean the other?"

"Yes," Avram said.

"I loved the man whoever he was. But I belonged to myself. You
understand? But with Allan that changed. My God! I was crazy with
it," Annetje confided. Averting her eyes, spiritually drawing away from
him, she said, "Now it is dangerous for me to go to bed with a man.
I feel too strongly."

Avram said as if studying a cue card, "But you do love John Herbert!"
He did not like it that Annetje's retreat strengthened his desire.

"Yes," she said. "No. It makes no difference. I am through with that
bastard. Perhaps I should put my head in the oven. It is a gas oven."

"Don't be stupid, Annetje," Avram said.

"Yes, it is stupid, but I am a stupid woman. I have had no life. I have been eating tranquilizers all day—six, ten, twelve of them."

"You fool!" Avram exclaimed. "We must call a doctor."

"I did. He said I was a fool. He came. He checked my heart." Avram was glad he had not kissed her. He stood up. "Come," he said, all solid reason; even the palms of his hands were drying. "Get your raincoat. We must go. It will be good for you to get out of this apartment. My friends are very stable, middle-class people. They are just what you need at this point."

"No. Let us stay here and—" Annetje began.

"Please," Avram said firmly.

"Oh yes. I see. You don't want to be rude to them. Now, where is my coat? Let me go comb my hair."

He nodded. She left the living room. The trouble with women like Annetje, he thought, was that they did not want a man to put his life into their hands; they wanted to put their life in his. Then when he mismanaged it, they could righteously assert that they had earned their freedom. Their men's wrongdoing gave them the little freedom they had from their guilt.

"Hurry," he called. He did not want her to be in the bathroom too long. Twelve tranquilizers! "Come on."

He was standing at the doorway of the living room. Annetje came out of a bathroom down the hallway. "I should change," she said gloomily.

"No," Avram said. "You are fine. Just get a coat."

"God damn. I am afraid," she said from inside the closet. "That goddam drug. I will never take it again!" She was near tears.

"How did you get hold of it?" he asked as he helped her from the closet and into her coat.

"John Herbert. Who else? He loves drugs. Anything to die." Her disgust carried her to the door; then she halted and stared helplessly at the locks. Avram counted six. "They don't all work," Annetje said. She began to fiddle with them. "I bought some. John Herbert bought some. Whenever we were happy, we put another lock on the door." Suddenly the door opened. "There," she said with surprise. "I did it."

In the elevator, she clung to Avram's arm. They did not speak, but they glanced at each other. The doorman in the lobby held the door for them. "I am afraid of *him*," Annetje whispered to Avram. He pressed her hand reassuringly.

The air was gray, like a light flannel; the streetlamps were on. Avram said to Annetje that she had wanted to have a bad reaction to test John Herbert, but it was an unfair test. "People who love get too upset," Avram said. "No one like us"—he meant unsettled, unsuburban people—"is clever or strong or forgiving enough in love. We are impossible when we love. What we need is humor and patience, but we are too greedy to be patient. We want a perfect love. We should avoid love entirely, perhaps—good, solid, lewd friendships might be more to the point."

Annetje laughed suddenly. Her laughter rose. It was not quite normal, not quite mad. Her head was tilted back; her hair fell straight and heavy and fair, strangely alive and enticing. Her jutting, delicate face bones seemed to Avram to burn with a low light in the gray air. "My God, a lewd friendship would destroy me, I think."

Avram said crossly, "I think we could all use a bit more repression. I like repression."

He held Annetje's arm, he guided her along the sidewalk. She walked uncertainly; she leaned back as if the pavement were tilting her. Nor did she advance in a straight line—Avram kept correcting her course. "This way," he murmured as they drew near the corner. "Where emotions are concerned, I say caution! And still more caution!"

Annetje began to laugh again. "You are a clown," she said. "You are a great liar! You are not like that at all!"

"I am," Avram said.

Annetje clutched her coat and drew it tightly across her throat. She shook her head; her pale blond hair flew from side to side—an erotic cap, Avram thought. It was a flashing point of emphasis in the twilit, drizzling cityscape. He kept up his pressure on her arm, he kept her walking. He worried about Louise and Ulrich—but it was a faint concern beside his growing impatience to make Annetje walk, escape the talons of the drug, to move, to rejoin life, as it were. He tried to keep a balance between helping her and not hurrying her, between a reassuring pressure and a persecution.

"WILL THEY understand that I am mad?" Annetje was crouched against the mailbox wall in the hallway of the brownstone where Avram lived. Avram thought it a good sign that she should have social second thoughts; she was not so cut off from reality after all.

"Yes, yes," he said. "They are square but not unintelligent—not really unintelligent. The woman is an old, old friend of mine. She was always at her best with me when I was unhappy or in trouble. She likes helping people—there's some Quaker in her background."

"Quakers?" said Annetje. "Those funny rich people from Pennsylvania?"

"There are a few not quite so rich ones from Connecticut."

"Quakers in Connecticut?" Annetje put her hand over her mouth and giggled. "Yes?" she said. She nodded. "It is very interesting."

"Yes," he said. "Now let's go upstairs." He smiled at Annetje. He took her arm. "We'll have a drink, but perhaps you'd better not have a drink. Then we will eat. . . ."

He had left the door of his apartment unlocked. "We're here!" he called out, and pushed the door open. Louise and Ulrich had changed postures; they were sitting stiffly on the couch, side by side, upright, formal. Louise seemed pinker than he remembered. Avram wondered if Louise and Ulrich had been necking. Ulrich looked quite wooden. "Louise," he said brightly, "this is Annetje Thompson. Annetje, this is Louise—Louise—and . . ." He could not remember Louise's married name or Ulrich's name at all.

"My husband, Ulrich von Kunnel," Louise said coldly.

"How do you do?" Annetje said, rattling the words off with a careless, tumbled charm. She looked quite forlorn except that her face, of course, was so striking, and her hair and her shoulders and her small, pillowy hips, too. "I am in terrible shape," Annetje confided. "Avram has told you, I am strange. I am not myself. I am not always like this. No," she said pathetically. "Not like this. Avram said I should come out, but really I am not fit. I will depress you. I am very mad."

Avram took Annetje's coat from her shoulders. "Don't worry about it," he said. "We are all a little mad."

"Not from taking drugs!" Louise said, her color rising.

Incredulity made Avram giddy. He said, "Louise. You can't. Say that, I mean."

"I was merely speaking the truth."

Avram stared at her. How *did* her mind work? How could she not be interested in meeting someone who had taken LSD? How could she fail to be impressed by Annetje—unkempt, exotic, ravishingly, electrically present, and troubled? He wondered if Louise was peevish at wasting her pearls, her dress, her careful lipstick on an evening of improvised sympathy.

He thought confusedly it must be her marriage; she was stiff. He said with a nervous laugh, "Truth? Don't talk piffle, darling." It was an old routine, his speaking comic British with Louise, one he had grown tired of and not used with her in a long time, but he trotted it out eagerly; he waited for her to smile.

Her face settled into lines of battle. "I don't like drugs!" she said in a voice Avram thought unconscionably opinionated but wonderfully well bred.

He said, "Louise, as it happens, I dislike drunks, and I've seen you drunk."

Ulrich said, "What is this thing that Americans have, that they must obliterate their environment—do they find their country and their life so very ugly?" He raised his eyebrows; he smiled.

"Annetje is Dutch," Avram said. He wondered again at that German confidence which allowed them to think they were making a good impression when they were not.

Annetje turned and smiled at the sound of her name. "Yes. Dutch," she said. She glided delicately across the floor as if expecting it to trick her. "Dutch, double Dutch," she said, and collapsed into a chair in the darkest part of the room. Her hair, her pale face glimmered. "Oh, I am in terrible shape," she said obliviously. "When you take LSD," she said to Louise, "be very careful."

"I would never take a drug!" Louise exclaimed.

"Louise, you are being intolerant!" Avram cried, whining slightly in his astonishment.

Louise said, "I am sick unto death of this whole modern business—turning strong people into nursemaids."

"No one wants you to be a nurse," Avram said. He understood her now: she resented Annetje's capture of the center of attention. "But I have always thought of you as someone who could transcend her limitations."

"I am civilized," Louise said grandly. "If your friend isn't well, shouldn't she go to a hospital? They are equipped to handle this sort of thing."

Avram said, "Don't be illiterate, Louise. Nothing can be done for the aftereffects of LSD. For the moment, Annetje is confused, and needs company—that is all."

"I am very confused," Annetje said, "but I am not good company. I—"

"She's suffering from drug poisoning!" Louise said.

"It is not drug poisoning. Do you know *anything* about LSD?"

"All drugs are alike," Louise said. Avram had often thought Louise's inclination to be immoral was so strong that she had to make her private laws very stringent. And simple.

"They are not *all* alike!" he cried. "Some act on the nerves, some on the muscles, some on the—"

"You know what I mean," Louise said.

"Drugs are not alike," Annetje said, shaking her head. "I have taken many. This is the worst that has ever—"

"You see!" Louise said. She turned to Annetje. "You are a thrill-seeker, aren't you?"

Annetje said seriously, "I do not like to be bored." She put her fine-boned hands to her head. "But this is terrible. Five days now, I cannot eat, I cannot sleep, the walls look at me, I—"

"Isn't that what you ought to expect if you have recourse to drugs?" Louise asked.

"Louise!" Avram cried.

"Well, it's true," Louise said.

"Why can't we say that people who take drugs are braver than we are?" Avram demanded. "They are less afraid of aftereffects—of death."

"You are speaking nonsense," Ulrich said gravely.

"Why," said Avram, "do people think a dictum rudely expressed will pass as a convincing argument?"

"What did he say?" Ulrich asked Louise. He turned back to Avram. "My English is not perfect." He smiled politely and turned to Louise.

Avram said, "I may very well be wrong on this issue, I may very well be under the influence of fashion, my opinion may be nonsensical, but I would prefer you expressed *your* opinion at least in my own house with more respect for the notion that I don't consider my opinions nonsense."

Ulrich looked blank. Louise said, "Pooh."

"You are making a joke?" Ulrich asked Avram.

"I was not. I believe there is a spiritual bravery involved in a living death. In tampering with the mind. It is one I am incapable of, but I believe people have the *right* to ruin or expand their lives with drugs or whatever. I certainly do not think I am speaking nonsense. Nonsense requires a very special sort of talent—mathematicians have it, witness Lewis Carroll." Avram felt he was being fatuous. "I have no talent for nonsense. I mean what I say."

"You believe drugs should be *legal?*" Louise demanded.

"Yes."

"I suppose you would let drugs advertise," she said.

"Perhaps."

"You are a *visionary,*" Louise said with contempt. "You always felt you knew it all."

"He is very intelligent," Annetje said.

"Thank you, Annetje."

Annetje turned to Louise. "Don't you feel he understands women?"

"No," Louise said.

"I think he is very understanding," Annetje said imperviously.

Louise smiled ironically at Avram. Avram thought of her face as a flat, lipsticked radar screen. He said, "You mustn't confuse stodginess with pragmatism, Louise."

"Don't be rude to me," Louise said. "Just because I haven't taken a drug doesn't mean I'm stodgy." She assumed a penetrating look. "Just when did you enter the avant-garde?"

"I am not speaking as a member of the avant-garde. I am speaking as a man of compassion and intellect."

Annetje said, "Avram is Jewish."

"Ah, are you Jewish?" Ulrich asked.

"Louise didn't *tell* you?" Avram asked.

Ulrich said, "She told me you were a man of belles lettres."

"How mad," Avram said. He turned to Louise. "You charlatan," he said. "Did you try to pass me off as a Gentile gentleman?"

"I'm very interested in belles lettres," Ulrich said.

"Of course not," Louise said.

"I've never been conservative. I feel your class unjustly owns and bores this country," Avram said bitterly.

"Oh, pooh," Louise said.

"It's a hypocritical class. You are a woman who has always liked to drink and have since girlhood. How can you condemn anyone who fiddles with their senses?"

Annetje said, "I hate drunks. They are very ugly."

"Alcohol kills and maims far more people than drugs do," Avram said. "Why are you so defensive?" he went on, exalted with argument;

he pointed his finger savagely. "What are you afraid of ? Why are you jealous of Annetje's experimenting with self-illumination?"

"I am not jealous!"

"Oh, you do not want this experience," Annetje said vaguely. "It is terrible. My teeth burn like little fires."

"I am not jealous *or* defensive!" Louise said. "I am protesting this trampling on what it means to be a responsible human being."

"Except when drunk," Avram said, slyly relentless.

"Except what when drunk, please?" Ulrich asked. Annetje was staring into space.

"Responsible, darling," Louise said to him.

"Yes. I believe in that," Ulrich said.

"Even for crimes during the war?" Avram demanded, turning on *him*.

"And what of Vietnam?" Ulrich replied instantly.

"You can compare Vietnam, deplorable as it is, to the camps?"

"The camps?" said Annetje, terrified.

"I am sick of the camps," Louise said.

"Bad conscience," Avram said. "If I had any backbone, I would refuse to speak to you ever."

"You do not look Jewish," Ulrich said.

What a really inglorious evening, Avram thought. He said, "Isn't that wonderful? But you can tell I'm Jewish because I'm so brilliant."

"Oh, yes," Ulrich said agreeably.

"Please don't talk about Jews," Annetje said in a weak, frightened voice, raising her hands to her temples. With an odd flutter as of an attempt at a normal social charm, she said sweetly, "I am tired of Jews."

"Tired?" Avram demanded. "Why are you tired of them? You've never been married to one that I know of."

Ulrich smiled abruptly at Annetje.

Louise said, "Are you married?"

"Yes," said Annetje.

"Doesn't your husband care if you take LSD?"

"I do not care if he cares or not. Besides, I did it for him. A friend told me, she saved her marriage—she said, you take this drug and you have an insight, you learn to be understanding. But it was horrible. The understanding was like death. Now I cannot eat, I cannot sleep, I think I want to die."

Avram said, "There is a theory that LSD interferes with the ego—

sometimes that leads to an insight, but sometimes it leads to a view of one's self as not worth saving."

"We all have those feelings without drugs, I am sure," Louise said snappishly.

"Not you, Louise," Avram said. "Your ego is too *healthy.*"

"I don't want to be insulted anymore!" Louise said.

"Louise is very—how do you say—mature," Ulrich said.

"I've learned to live with myself," Louise said.

"But the rest of us haven't learned to live with *you,*" Avram said.

"Come, Ulrich." Louise stood. "We must go."

Annetje said, "I don't want to live with myself."

"Well, you just go on taking drugs, and Avram will be very sympathetic," Louise said.

"Oh, sit down," Avram said. "We've known each other too long to be insulted by anything."

Annetje frowned at Louise. "I think you have a very closed mind. I think it's terrible to have such a closed mind."

Avram had not thought Annetje was following the talk. He was pleased; she was coming back to the real world.

Louise said, "I don't happen to think a closed mind is a vice."

"Louise," Avram said. "Come on now."

"I don't fall for all the propaganda that comes down the pike. I don't believe in that kind of open mind. I happen to think *she* has the closed mind—a drug closed it."

"And I was hoping to help her a bit while her mind opens," Avram said.

Louise sat down. "I do not approve of drugs at all." She lifted her glass and took a straightforward, large swallow—a drinking woman's swallow. She put her glass down. "And don't tell me about alcohol!" She sat quite still while the drink moved into her bloodstream.

Ulrich said to Annetje, "Why do Americans want to change themselves?"

"Alcohol stood our ancestors in good stead," Louise remarked. "Avram, you are a very old friend. But I really don't like intellectuals."

Annetje said to Ulrich and Louise, "You are like Germans." She said it warningly. "They never listen. They thought they knew everything. Sometimes I thought they did know everything, they must be right, because they were so powerful they were winning the war. I was frightened all the time. But they did not win. But we were walking by a road, I was very little, and their planes came and shot at us. Why? It was because we didn't matter. I hate people who are so *realistic*. . . ."

"You think it realistic to hate a whole nation?" Louise exclaimed.

Avram thought, Drugs, race, *and* politics. He began to laugh. No one paid him any attention.

"Yes," Annetje said.

"If you don't forgive the Germans, why should anyone forgive you?" Louise demanded.

"Forgive her? Forgive her for *what?*" Avram demanded. "She didn't kill twenty million people."

"The Germans should have been hanged, all of them," Annetje said. "They were filthy, filthy—" She seemed close to tears.

"There is sweet reason and sympathy," Louise said to Avram, and shrugged.

"I think it is unfortunate you hate so many people," Ulrich said stiffly, "the innocent with the guilty."

"They did it first!" Annetje cried.

Avram stood up and leveled a finger at Louise. "You see! There it is! You heard her. The beauty of it, the simplicity of it—*they did it first.* Don't you see? I *lean* on people like you, Louise, I *rely* on you, but for illumination we must turn to the drug-takers, the sufferers, the penetrating souls who *see* right and wrong."

"Isn't that splendid," Louise said, and took another drink.

"It was only a very small minority who—" Ulrich's eyes were on the pale Annetje.

"Don't, please, give us that minority nonsense!" Avram cried.

"It is not nonsense. I was in Germany and I—"

"Did not know about the camps," Avram said with disgust.

"That is correct."

"I was in Holland and France and Italy and I knew," Annetje said.

Louise said, "Well, of course, we are very sorry for what you went through, but Ulrich went through a great deal, too."

Ulrich said, "You cannot believe what it was like when the Russians came—like wild beasts."

"Oh, for God's sake, why not?" Avram said. "Look what your armies had done to Russia."

"They weren't Ulrich's armies. He was a child."

"Annetje was a child, and the Germans would have killed her."

Louise said, "What is so sick about this conversation is that we don't end it."

"You don't know what it is like to be hunted," Annetje said in a deepened voice, a voice that shuddered. "They wanted to find you and kill you and there was no *reason*, there was no r—"

Ulrich said with shuttered eyes, "I think we would all be happier without memories. I try to have no memories." He opened his eyes and gazed at Annetje. That German wants her, Avram thought with a pang of jealousy. Ulrich said, "So I have come to the New World." To a rich wife, Avram thought coldly. "We must learn to live together. We—"

"When I took the drug, at first it seemed like that," Annetje said. "It seemed it was over, I did not have to remember, I could forgive the Germans. It was like a great burst of light. I could stop being afraid. But then it turned into a nightmare. There was still wickedness—wickedness goes on and on—my husband is a bastard—I cannot stand it!" She raised her hands to her temples; then, it seemed to Avram, the room went out of focus for her. She said, "Excuse me. I am crazy. I am not myself. I would not wish this on anyone!"

"Except the Germans," Louise said sotto voce.

"Yes, the Germans!" Annetje cried. "I wish they should all be put in a crazy house—"

"Ah," Ulrich said sadly. "She is talking about many innocent people."

"Yes, she is, you dolt!" Avram cried.

"There seems to be an insuperable difference of opinion," Louise said.

Avram passed his hand in front of his eyes. "Yes. I am ashamed. I am ashamed of all of us except Annetje."

"Don't be ashamed for me," Louise said, and finished her drink. "I am not the least bit ashamed of anything I've said. I'm not avant-garde. I haven't said anything sophisticated."

Avram's left hand gripped his right one. He said, "It's incredible. No one has thrown anything."

Ulrich said, "She warned me. She said with you one has to be tolerant. You make terrible arguments with everyone."

"She did, did she?" Avram passed his hand again over his eyes. "Is anyone hungry?" he said. "I thought we might eat Chinese."

"Ah, God, no," Annetje said. "I can't. I can't eat. I will go home."

Ulrich asked her, "Do you refuse to eat with a German? Are you angry?"

"I have eaten with Germans," Annetje said. "I am not angry. I am not myself. It—"

Louise said to Avram, "You didn't ask me if I was angry."

Avram said, "We have put up with so much from each other over the years! I tell myself when the time comes you'll send me CARE packages in the concentration camp."

"Oh, pooh," Louise said.

Annetje was still talking. ". . . the idea of chewing, and in a restaurant *all* the people chewing, chewing . . ."

"But you ought to eat!" Avram cried, argumentatively. "It will *help* you."

"I will make myself spaghetti at home," Annetje said in a tone of pathos. "Please don't make me go to a restaurant." She was near tears.

"Annetje, you cannot go home," Avram said. "What will you do? Stare at the walls?"

"Yes, but that is all right. It is all I can do now."

Louise said to Avram, "Perhaps it would be better if Ulrich and I left. You could stay with your friend."

"No!" said Avram.

"No, no," said Annetje. "I don't want to be that kind of person. I have asked too much of Avram already."

Avram squirmed, he calculated his own villainy, decided it was extensive but not fatal, yet he did not want to be alone with Annetje, he wanted no private responsibility for her at all.

"I'll walk you home," he said. He said to Louise and Ulrich, "I'll be right back. Please wait for me." He rose.

Annetje began to prattle, "It is better this way. I feel much better. I don't want to interfere. I am very strange just now. I cannot bear myself, really, my strangeness. I know I will get better, I must wait out my punishment—all I mind is when I think it will never end. You know, I cannot bear the feel of clothes just now? I have worn these for five days. I am afraid to touch them, these clothes."

Avram thought Louise looked resigned; he thought Ulrich listened at first with mere politeness and then with interest and even lechery. But Annetje went on and on and on, and after a while Ulrich began to utter rude little ironies: "Very interesting, I am sure. . . . You seem very interested in your own symptoms. . . ." But Annetje did not look at him.

Avram said, "Annetje, would you like to wait for me here?"

"No, no. I feel this apartment has lips." She laughed.

"You are very sensitive," Ulrich murmured.

"Yes," Annetje said. "I can hear conversations through the air, I can hear radio waves, I am quite mad."

Avram said, "You don't want to be alone."

"But it is better for me," Annetje said. She stood up. "I cannot be with people. I am too impossible." She turned to Ulrich and Louise. "I am sorry I am so crazy. Perhaps we will meet at a time when I am more myself."

Ulrich smiled politely; Louise stretched her closed lips.

Annetje slid her arms into the coat Avram held for her. He thought she appeared almost saintly in her obliviousness to the rudeness and contemptuous mood of the two on the couch. Although Louise had been angry before she could possibly have known, her anger was in part justified by how unimportant Annetje thought her—unimportant, unreal, uninteresting.

ANNETJE HESITATED twice on the stairs in the hallway. "The steps frighten me going down," she said. "It's stupid—I'm stupid, yes? The steps are all right, they won't collapse under me?"

"I don't think so," Avram said. He said, "Will you really be all right alone? Can't you call someone to be with you?"

"Everyone is tired of me," Annetje said brightly. "Everyone I liked I have called and they have been with me and they have gotten tired and left and been angry with me. Five days . . . They get so bored."

Avram minded less than he would have thought, his having been the last resort.

"I have moods all the time," Annetje was saying. "They get tired." She stepped into the lower hallway and blinked, relieved to be free of the stairs. She said, "They owe me nothing. No one owes me nothing. It is John Herbert, that bastard, who should not leave me alone. I sat up with him many times."

Outside, the air was still hung with floating drops, visible beads of moisture, faintly pewter-colored with captured light, and very beautiful, Avram thought. The sidewalk was quite wet and held the dim, damp, shapeless reflections of lights in windows and over doorways and of streetlights. Avram thought that Louise and Ulrich were very probably kinder to each other and closer to each other than Annetje and John Herbert. He said, to make it up to John Herbert that he had desired his wife, "You should not blame him. You took the LSD to hurt him."

"I wanted to help, I wanted to learn how to be good," Annetje cried, twisting her head.

"But you excluded him," Avram said. "You went off alone. You said he's been in bad shape lately. It was the same as if you abandoned him, you pushed him away. . . ."

"Yes, yes, I see that. Perhaps he isn't a bastard. I am so paranoid, I imagine so many terrible things. I—" She broke off.

At the apartment house on the corner, a doorman stood behind the glass door, staring out. Avram said, "I didn't say he wasn't a bastard. I only said you excluded him."

"Yes, yes. How clever you are," she said, and leaned more closely to him as if for comfort.

Avram's heart began to swell inside him like a piece of fruit, he thought, ripening. He guided Annetje at the corner to make the turn. Too many debits, he thought. He burst into apology. "I am *not* clever," he said. "What was I doing when I asked you to join us? How could I not have known! What was I thinking of ?"

Annetje said in a humble voice, "I am so sorry I was so terrible with your friends."

Avram halted on the pavement, in the mist. "You were terrible? No, no." Avram said, "*They* were terrible."

"They were?"

"They were unforgivably rude. They picked on you."

"They did?"

Avram peered into her face. "My God," he said. "You are confused!" He laughed, took a step onward, Annetje a weight against his arm. "You have no judgment at all, you are really quite wonderful."

Annetje said, "I thought they had closed minds, but I am so paranoid I thought it was just my imagination."

Cars trailed enormous red exclamation points along the wet macadam. Buildings ascended and disappeared behind veils of haze, which they then charged with mysterious, silvery glare. Between the buildings, the sky held patches of diluted red, of watery rouge. Avram said, "There is no ambiguity about it. They attacked you the moment you walked in the door. Annetje, I don't want to encourage you in a neurosis, but not all of a paranoid's fears are unfounded."

"Is that true? Oh," Annetje said with a little, wondering laugh. "Yes, that must be true. I see that." She stopped walking; she breathed. "I am so glad." She pressed Avram's arm. They turned and went into Annetje's apartment house. "I thought everything I felt was because I was so crazy."

"Well, you can have more faith in yourself now," Avram said firmly. He was silent in the elevator. When the elevator was gone, he said to Annetje, "There is a genuine irony for you—hostility helped make you better. The evening was not a failure." It seemed safer to him to be more emotional with her now that he knew he was the last person in her telephone book she had called. "Sometimes it horrifies me," he said, "that we dare talk about serious subjects—the camps, love, anything. We should leave the serious subjects to poets, who will tell us how to speak of them without lowering them; we should confine ourselves to the weather and the stock market like sensible people." Annetje was trying, with frightened hands, to work the locks of her door. Avram said, "Annetje, I am sorry I have to go back. I would rather stay with you."

Annetje turned and looked up, surprised, pleased, unbelieving, humble. "Would you like to stay with me?"

"Oh yes. But Louise is a very old friend. You can see she's decidedly odd—she wouldn't understand if I stayed with you. I'll tell you something about her: she never breaks a promise, she is never late for an appointment, she is utterly reliable."

"That's wonderful," Annetje said. "I would like to know people like that. Sometimes it seems to me I live in a bowl of soup; nothing is solid."

"I think you are hungry," Avram said. "Promise me you will eat, that you will make yourself a little spaghetti or something."

"Yes. Maybe."

"No maybe. Just yes."

Annetje shrugged her fine shoulders. She said, "Your friends seemed very like Germans." She was frowning.

"Ulrich *is* a German," Avram said.

"Ah," said Annetje. "So that is the story. I am sorry for you to have to spend an evening with that one."

Avram smiled shamefacedly at her. She was not clear-minded yet. "Shall I call you after they leave?" he asked.

She looked up quickly, knowingly; she saw him, he was certain. "No, no," she said. She was ashamed, he thought, of having called on him, of having fallen so low. "I think tonight I will sleep."

"You will be careful? No more tranquilizers? You won't do anything to yourself?"

"No, no," Annetje said. "I am the kind who survives."

* * *

AVRAM LISTENED to her snap the locks on her door. *Survives.* In the elevator, an elderly man and woman cast uneasy looks at him as if convinced he could not mean them well.

He hurried from the elevator; he reached the sidewalk; as he strode toward Lexington Avenue it seemed to him he startled the air. He was thinking. He did not expect simple goodness from himself or a simple anything anymore, but a minor integrity would have been nice.

He halted at the corner; he breathed in the wet, pewter-riddled dark. Louise. Annetje. For them, each living moment was muddied by rain from dead landscapes. They received spectral instructions from cemeteries. But no rain fell for him from his well-audited sky. He bent his head, thinking he ought to be depressed. It was no good—he was amused.

He thought, I am spiritually coarse. He made up his mind: I will bawl out Louise and Ulrich; I will say, "A little kindness toward people we differ from will improve the world. We mustn't shut all the doors." Louise will have all the money in the room, and I will have all the heart and niceness.

He smiled, he surrendered. He turned then and broke into an easy, boyish run up the avenue. He ran with resigned self-approval.

Hofstedt and Jean – and Others

I

This is what happened when one forty-five-year-old professor (of English) slipped into an affair with a twenty-year-old student. Whom he did not quite manage to love. I will try to make it edifying.

The narrative will be colored like a map, according to the geography of my spirit, the prickliness of my temper, my perversity, which I am told I possess to an unbearable degree, my lunges at and occasional capture of intelligence, that armored and fatal lizard, and by those other elements of my desert—sand, rock, sunbaked stone, which surround and protect the oasis, the nerve in the tooth, the exploitable ores of my spirit. Can a man indicate and not vindicate his own geography? My long-dead mother inside the glass museum case of memory is bitter with me still, as she often was when I was small: "Why are you such a fool, Leo? Why do you let people take advantage of you? Why don't you use your head?" I use my head, Momma. She saw my character as having at its center a place where I became the victim, a witless servitor, not clever, and unable to get the best of any bargain.

* * *

II

I was bicycling in Central Park with my friend Ettringhelm and his wife one Sunday in April just a few weeks after I separated from my second wife. It was too early in the year for New York to empty on weekends: is it possible a million people were in the park that day? Beneath the watery April sun, an occasional police car or jeep cruised slowly, watchfully, among the bright shoals of cyclists who floated, flushed, moist, openmouthed, above wantonly pumping legs, curiously disowned, jumping knees, and the transparent whir of wheels. While in the glens and glades and on the paths visible from the roadways a whole other crowd moved, and everywhere there was the delicate dull gleam of skin, among the bicyclists and pedestrians, in the yellow-green shrubberies, and on the black paths and roads: chests and shoulders made block forms among the slyer flickers of necks and legs. The hint of nudity enlivened this catalogue of races, life styles, hair lengths, adolescents in indescribable costumes, this example of urban swarm—cynical, carnal, mixed in degree and grade, and tautly, warily festive. Perhaps, as forty years before, as in the twenties, our national life was a party; money lit up faces and shining legs and made them Japanese lanterns for the celebration of our prosperity. God bless Technology! The clannishness, the new solicitudes, the fragile and tentative anxiety for brotherhood, reminded me of a high-school dance. So much was in abeyance, the future pivoting uncertainly in front of us, the past askew or lost, and in the present ambiguously happy disorder any emotion might emerge, any presumption occur.

"When you use a word like that—" Ett said. I had used not "presumption" but another word, some word like "quaint" or "picturesque." Ett is a molecular geneticist, the third-best in the country—"the best American-born one," he has said to me with an earnestness that softened the boast and made more patent the disappointment; we were, as I said, bicycling. "When you use a word like that," Ett asked, "is that camp?"

"You feel I can't use that word normally? That the word no longer truly refers to anything real?"

"Why?" persisted Ett. "Why do you use words like that?"

His wife, Inez, bicycling on his right, Inez who is half Spanish, half Danish (Ett is American-Swedish by descent and marvelously gloomy behind his fair, high coloring), Inez who has large breasts, is short, almost dumpy, who is unremittingly devoted to Ett, who blankets his back and sides with warmth while he stares out into the cold molecular reaches of his discipline—Inez said, "Leo feels old."

She was already puffing a bit from the unaccustomed exercise, although we had been bicycling only a short time; she had pinkened; she pedaled industriously, but she was trailing slightly behind. Ett did not slow to match his speed to hers—she was his handmaiden—and my mind, which is often somewhat out of control and never more than at a time like a divorce, watching her legs pump dutifully, thought, Rotary votary.

"Yes. Leo feels old," I said, and speeded up slightly; we were ascending a slight grade not far from the Seventy-second Street crossing, heading north, I believe. I set the pace a little faster because it is my nature to instruct, and at this headier speed they might soon see that time had made us cousins; they, too, ought to feel old.

Ett and I are friends of such very long standing. One keeps one's pike leveled when one is with him and Inez. Ett is a science-fiction, universal-rule-desiring sort, he is both New Left and New Victorian—worthy, self-approving, blind to his past, quick to use the condemnation "outmoded," anxious to substitute for any pragmatics his adored science, science being a mother whose breast teems, a father whose brain will bring us a corrected politics, tranquil psyches, and teach us useful and accurate methods for apprehending reality and fending off death: Ett's science has the attributes of Rosicrucianism. Inez is of the genus of wives who blindly uphold a husband's inanity. I say inanity with affection.

We met at Harvard, Ett and I, he a prodigy of fifteen, I a less prodigious prodigy of sixteen; we were drawn to each other with an almost audible thud, rosy-cheeked freshmen, dazzlingly new-brained and younger than everyone. But I had been adopted by half a dozen boys in my hall as a mascot, whereas by November, when Ett and I finally began to speak—I had noticed him often enough before, he was so short, so blond, so rigid-looking, so young, and so clean—he still knew no one by first name except his two roommates, both of whom he held in contempt, and a boy from Minnesota he had gone to school with and did not much care for, either. Which is to say my loneliness was transcendental—I wanted to be an effectual male, not a mascot—

and his was real. Our first conversations were at passionate cross-pur-
poses, Ett complaining in a dry, logical tone of Harvard's backwardness,
of the uselessness of most of the studies, of the aged futility of the ideas
the professors so proudly, ironically, in clumsy Massachusetts Anglophilia, offered, while I spoke of certain emptinesses that oppressed me,
a murderous atmosphere of heartless ambition. I wanted no more splen-
dors of an ambitious kind, no more heroes, but only open and active
hearts, while Ett wanted to be a superhero, the superest hero of all—he
was a Scandinavian with Persian tastes, a boy who spoke of relativity
with absolute force—and when I realized this, for I listened to him
actually once the initial nervous glare of making friends died down, it
was too late for me to disregard him. He was my friend; the train was
in motion.

I have a rather terrible drive toward teamwork, which fits into my
notion of friendship, and for a while that year I was Ett's team and
followers: he was coach, father figure, brother figure, Beau Ideal, and
perhaps even Lady of the Lake to me. I went so far as to take chemistry
to be near him, and rather self-consciously, like wearing a brother's
ruffled shirt, I took to the notion of an Elite; I, too, saw Harvard as a
reactionary bastion of daydreams, dead at the core. But not much in my
nature runs entirely through me—indeed, my life can largely be defined
as pauses and rebellions: no state endures. Ett and I, it appeared, were
ranked at the top of our class, and Ett insisted we were rivals; he
disbelieved me when I said he deserved to be top man, that I was merely
facile, and that I wanted him to be top man. He disbelieved me! He
thought me ambitious! I had been seeing a maternal and overweight
Radcliffe girl, but at that time I shifted to a thin girl from Yonkers, who
had what seemed an incurable fever blister: we kissed *around* it, as
around an externalized conscience. She egged me on against Ett, saying
with angry Freshman Percipience that I was under his influence. Under
her influence I belabored Ett with sarcastic revelations: he was malad-
justed; in any Elite I would be a more useful member than he because
I at least would be able to get along with the other members. "Here
comes Lionel Coldheart," I would say when he entered the room; it was
the usual masculine antagonism, but with that faint early-adolescent sob
in it that fills so much of our fiction, for I had been cast out of Utopia
and was bitter at my exile.

He believed my sarcasm, his sense of assurance began to crack, and
he took to reading treatises on human psychology, especially when my

grades began to inch ahead of his, which they did because I spoke to everyone, and "everyone" supplied bits of such scholastic lore as which professors liked foreign-language quotes in papers and which ones thought them precious. Also, I listened to the professors, and Ett did not. I admired his integrity, his thoughts were his own; I was intellectually corrupt, and quite thoroughly at the head of the class. Ett could no longer treat me as the first of his disciples, and he had no equipment for dealing with an equal; his solution was to look up to me briefly, then down at me, and to treat me—with averted eyes—like a mascot. It was then that I discarded any predilection I had for a notion of an Elite.

We settled into a pattern that has endured with parenthetical irruptions of simple and intense affection until the present day, a pattern in which—aha—many threads are woven. He will say, "Fiction is outmoded. I only read fact. When I read novels, I skip and read only the sexy parts."

"Ah," I reply, "I never do math at all. . . . You know, sex is to a modern-day novelist what social ethics were to Dickens. Sex is what we study, it is the area of our competence. . . ." I keep on until Ett cannot miss the point, which is my claiming a sexual experience and expertise greater than his. Inez says I am good for him, I wake him up. A blow launched by a comparative realist, of my sort, strikes him like a kick in the back of the knee; he *looks* staggered—by the new shape reality takes for him, for all realities are shaped, and a new thought, a new jog in the structure of the life of a man he knows, of the life that man might be living, shakes him.

He does the same for me with such scientific pronouncements as "It is proved that life is an electrochemical accident." He crushes and instructs me, and I require it. In me still, the peculiar adoration of Ett that began nearly thirty years ago continues with adolescent passion, in some floating park out of time, free of sequence; it is as fierce as sunlight, as self-love. Ett *is* a somebody. It is partly a joke: his father burned with ambition in the Minneapolis grain business, and said to Ett as he tossed a softball at him in the twilight, "You can be for science what Charles A. Lindbergh was for airplanes." His father managed to embody himself in Ett like a wasp laying an egg in a spider, or a sculptor working in transient bronze, or someone mailing a thought to coming time; there are ghosts in Ett, and they enlarge him somehow. He may save us all. Or a few of us. But I like the feeling I have when I part from him; some of the dust rubs off on me, that traveler's dust he has picked up while edging in his crablike—and crabbed—way through adult years toward a perhaps ill-conceived but still stirring hope (no more defective births if his experiments work out). I do not feel lessened by sharing his sensibility: he has been married only once and been faithful. When he works, he leaves behind this world's fairer aspects—fields, faces, seductions—descends into a dark where he forces his intelligence to pinch ever inward, where he is ever more and more cramped and alone as he steals toward a microthought no one has come upon before. It is not what I do at all.

I PEDALED harder; he caught up, kept up; Inez slipped a bit more behind. Ett and I are fitness-minded; Inez is, too, but chiefly in her mind. I turned and said over my shoulder, "Inez, I think your husband and I are having a race. We'll wait for you farther on."

As I turned, I briefly saw beside the road a not entirely familiar girl, her face set inside coarse-textured wavy brown-blond hair.

Ett said, "We aren't racing." His honesty has areas of clouded interference.

"I was joking," I said, for no reason that was yet clear to me, and settled back and pedaled alongside him; we were on an upward slope, and when he slowed I did not, but maintained my speed and pulled somewhat ahead, whereupon he kept up. I increased my speed modestly; he kept up. He muttered, "You've stopped doing isometrics."

I am moved by fashions in exercises as in everything, and while I was in my isometric phase my wind and stamina were far less than Ett's; however, I had in the meantime switched to aerobics, and my lungs and heart were correspondingly mightier. Ett had grown used to a noticeable superiority as a bicyclist—which is why, to cheer me during my divorce, he had suggested we go bicycling.

He is short, very muscular still; once, in a dream, he appeared to me as a general and as a dessert, a sweet Napoleon. He strengthened his leg thrust, moved faster, pulled ahead; I pulled even and passed him toward the crest of the hill, saying—untruthfully—"I'm out of breath—whew!" and sailed on downhill. He passed me halfway down; he was not coasting, he was secretly pedaling: I caught him out of the corner of my eye.

It has always been true between us that his long-term determination—one marriage!—is greater than mine, while for anything short-term my will and fruitfulness in tactics can beat him; so it was best to avoid racing openly—and he had been the one to deny we were rac-ing—until we were both tired and then to set a short sprint. I am at my best when I am in extremis, which my second wife once remarked was very tiring for everyone and gave one an entirely new attitude toward the question of whether excellence was worth bothering with or not.

I am not competently competitive; like most verbal men, who become judges, after all, or newspaper editors, or politicians of a certain type, I keep avoiding argument by pleading, "But it is obvious"—that is, past argument. I put everything past argument if I can. So a race is a bit difficult for me. My mind wanders. To help myself concentrate, I thought of myself bicycling to win the hand of Inez. It was a mental game. I increased our average speed but frequently said, "God, let's slow down! I don't want to have a coronary."

Our minds interflow, his and mine; we wear each other's thoughts.

I began to practice yoga breathing, something I had learned during the winter. Near Harlem—or rather as one turns to leave Harlem be-hind—the road becomes very steep, with a symbolic aptness. It was there that I said, "I'll race you to the boat lagoon."

The speed with which I pumped up the long hill, the way my wind lasted, the ferocity with which I kept on without looking back, attest, I think, to my jealousy that Ett was not getting a divorce. And to my wish that he love me, since he, like most of us, loves best someone he can look up to. His mind is on the stars. In beating Ett, I practically insured a weekly or even twice-weekly dinner invitation. I could hear him—his breathing is distinctive—a very short distance behind me. I saw again, somewhere on my left now, that slightly familiar girl—her face.

I BEAT Ett by a great many yards, slowing down in the end in fear that I had overdone it. I halted on the concrete bridge. The trees around me were in new leaf, shyly pointillist, but I hardly noticed. On the boating lagoon, a carefully landscaped spoon of water partly ringed with picturesque and miniature cliffs, moved an enormous regatta: a da Vinci enclosed a Guardi, multitudes of prows and figures on gray, danc-ing water, a democracy's shabby mock-festival, crowded, sordid, and beautiful.

I briefly glanced at, largely ignored the extraordinary scene.

Will someone one day soon build a model of a human personality—

soul, heart, spirit, mind, shifts, magnetic eccentricities, perverse connections? As they build models of molecules? Would such a model show
how a victory led to the adoption of certain traits possessed by the
defeated, a spiritual cannibalism? To cannibalize—can you imagine such
a word? "I'm going to cannibalize two of my essays on Rilke and do
a monograph," Malcolm Glick said to me the other day. Never mind.

Ett met Inez during an International Science Congress of some kind,
in Copenhagen, and when he returned to New York he came to my lair
(I was an assistant professor then) and said, "I have met someone."

I was newly divorced—the first divorce. It pains me now to remember suddenly how young I was. My hands, my God, my hands—I was
a great one for clasping my hands in front of me on my desk in those
days—my hands were not *thin*. How stupid I was; how cakey, sugary,
ill-nourishing, and doomed that last rim of youth is. He said, "I think
I've found the right girl, Leo," and there was a glimmer of cakey
satisfaction in his handsome, Viking's face. I had, of course, just been
parted from a *wrong* girl. Ett said pseudoscientifically of his find, "She
seems sensible." My first wife had not been sensible. I said, "You poor
ass," and began to question him, mimicking a cold-minded dean: who
were the girl's people, what was her schooling, her attitude toward
religion, was she giddy, sexually up-to-date, had he committed himself
to her?

He said, "It's half settled. She is willing to put my career first. She's
very intelligent."

"I assume she's good-looking."

"She has a fantastic body," he said with a self-satisfaction that made
me think, not for the first time, he was incapable of love.

"She does?"

"Fantastic whim-whams," he said. "Her legs are great."

Then at some point his self-satisfaction ebbed; he sat there, in my
absurdly tiny office, a squat Viking, and said with half accusation, half
envy, "I don't know if *you*'ll think she's so great-looking."

"If she's a good wife to you, I will," I said, staunchly sentimental.

He said, "You know, Leo, the wonderful thing about her is that she's
not just passionate, she's also got good sense."

I did not believe him, but I envied him his finding such a girl just in
case and his having me for a friend; I had only him.

He said, "You've always been flighty about women." I thought, Ah,
he and I are father figures for each other.

When we flew to Copenhagen—I was to be best man, of course—and I met Inez, I saw a girl, twenty-two, with a heavy coil of dark hair and blue eyes, slender legs, and a pigeony breast; she seemed a bit dowdy, quite proper. Her father was a government official concerned with teaching science or some such thing. But there was in her an astonishing sexuality. At once monomaniacal and pedestrian, she was and is a bureaucrat's Carmen.

She has some good sense, much good nature, and her attachments are profound. Ett, neuroses and all, was always quite sturdy, but he has not been able to stand up to Inez's monomaniacal assaults. Her gaieties can be as earnest and bruising as muggings. Ett has moments of sturdy jollity, but he prefers a smiling, understated gloom. Within two years Inez had reawakened in him his self-doubts. She was a fanatic mother; after their first child appeared, Ett came to see me and said in a defensive, hearty tone, "I'm jealous of my child. I'm going to see an analyst."

I was about to marry the second time, and often felt engulfed in music. I said, "Ett, look at this functionally: you have the aphrodisiac torments of Proustian jealousy without having your wife play around with another man."

But Inez *wanted* him to see an analyst. One looks on and wonders about the interplay of judgments, wishes, vengeances; youth falls away, the thumbnails grow ridged, that moral scrofula the young hate so in their elders sets in, that semipermanent, delicately power-mad and cool ambiguity. Age! Age! The body ceases to be an ally when one is twenty-eight or so; the next phase runs sourly, corruptly, on toward thirty-five, when idealism often returns, that or a nervous breakdown, and fates begin to be clearly marked. Ett became well known, his analyst became little more than a sycophant, Ett's self-approval soared eaglelike and looked down on all the kingdoms of the earth save that of the two molecular geneticists who were better m.g.'s than he. And when he was not grandiloquent Ett was querulous—his insomnia, his diets, his devious colleagues made him peevish, as if he had a vision of himself as a living statue of an eminent and gentle and useful man who was constantly being yanked into ungainly poses, who was de-pedestaled by the envy of his co-workers and the frailty of his physical being.

But he climbed back up on the pedestal again and again and did good work. It is not easy to admire him: he is absentminded and selfish, and he approves of his own selfishness, perhaps rightly; he and his analyst have decided Inez is an emotional masochist—God!—but one can observe the war in him between the analyzed monster and the gentle Ett, for he is afraid, whenever he is roused from his self-absorption, that he might be treating Inez badly. He cares for her and does not want her hurt or too badly mauled by time and himself.

She is not much wiser than he. She, too, has been analyzed; if anything, she is more monomaniacal than ever: "I must develop a sense of humor," she will say, frowning. "I am humorless on both sides, Spanish and Danish." She laughs self-deprecatingly, somewhat tragically, although whether more in the Norse or in the Iberian mode I cannot say.

Like paint on a wall, they grow cracked and yellow, those two, but they adhere. Perhaps they are weak and too frightened to change, or lazy; they are certainly not well equipped for adventures; but perhaps also they are good people, and sound in some mysterious way: they have stuck not just to the marriage but to each other. They become elegiac about the reasons they don't get along. Inez will say proudly, "We have very serious problems, Ett and I." Ett, who is practicing to be a Grand Old Man and is beginning to experiment with a folk manner, will say, "Logic doesn't suit women, and a good thing, too. If they were logical, why would they settle for being wives to a man like me?"

III

THE FACE I have glimpsed in the park, the girl I have not yet spoken to, has said to me since that day, "Your friend Ett is awful—his attitude toward his wife. He has deformed emotions." (She has also said, "You're as much married to Inez as Ett is.")

I said, "I enjoy insights. What do you mean, Ett has deformed emotions?"

"Oh, if you can't see it!" she said despairingly. "Why do you like him?"—also despairingly.

"Why shouldn't I like him?"

"He's not the sort of man a man like you should have as a friend!"

"What kind of friends do you think I should have?"

"Other men like you, sensitive and with it and sexy. . . ." She did not look at me as she spoke.

She imagines my kindness exists; she sought it in someone older—an experienced kindness, which is perhaps only the reflected safety of a bargain with someone who cannot easily afford to hurt her.

I had made it a rule never to touch a student, and when I heard of a colleague who had no such rule, I thought how fitting it would be for him to be delivered to the wrath and jealousy of the outraged parents. I don't blame the young. It is impossible for them to check their appetites and still be young; they have their youth to offer, and they will offer it. Sometimes there is love; we'll pass that by. But when a girl drifts up to a professor, looks at him with wide brown eyes, he must not respond as a man; he holds the title of professor, not of a man. But why be cruel and withhold from the girl the happiness she craves? Because she does not know what she is doing. It is not kind or sensible to imprison anyone in the consequences of a partial lust. But she will learn so much. Too much. Why cannot we be happy animals? Because that is not how happiness works—quite.

If a girl has been failed by her father and needs to find that strength in someone, or if she was so happy she wants to repeat that happiness, why be puritan?

Why, indeed?

The father of the glimpsed face, Mr. Macardling, works for Continental Electric, is an associate vice-president, is a water-worn brook pebble of a man, hard, interchangeable with others of his type, and with tints especially clear when he is in the water that shaped him. He said to me a number of times, "It's a simple matter." My affair with his daughter.

I replied, "Yes. Of course. But it *feels* complex."

"Would you say you were an indecisive man?"

"I will say almost anything, I fear."

"I don't disapprove," he said. Of the affair.

"I do."

"Ha-ha," he said, and grasped my arm. "I like you, Leo."

"I find you acceptable," I reply cautiously.

"Tell me, Leo, are you pretty much what a New York intellectual is?"

"Good God, no!"

"I didn't think so. What impresses me is your fantastic honesty."

"Well, I'm not a businessman," I say, and pat his arm. He starts to tighten up. "I am under fewer pressures," I continue. He begins to smile. I smile, too, and say, "I have different tricks up my sleeve." We both laugh. Then he looks at me with a mock—is it a mock?—scowl.

I do not know where we stand, he and I.

He is orderly, and children admire order, and he is cheerful, and children like smiling fathers; he is open and not weak and he must always be off to business. If he were my father, I would admire him—

indeed love him distractedly—I would re-create him in myself or in someone who has a good deal of time and patience or who is indebted to me, and then when I had him where I could hold his attention and devour his time I would pity him and soothe him, quarrel with him at leisure, in pain or with raw delight, I would rebel, forsake him, return to him. . . . Jeanie Macardling finds no young man so elusive, so orderly, so capable of stirring her imagination as her father. Damn her father!

I am a great lover. Of respectability. I never saw respectability as a lie or a hard bargain—harder than any other—or a trap: it can be misused, but what can't? What isn't? In return for taking heed of appearances, one is rewarded—that's what respectability means—and, of course, appearances can't quite be kept up without some reality, therefore sacrifices. When I was a child in the Midwest, there were little centers of sin every so many hundred miles, and men who could not endure respectability much longer went on business trips to Hot Springs or Cairo (Illinois) or Chicago. Respectability never omitted sin but put it in a place—and after all, why not? The worst scandals were when grownups interfered sexually with the young.

After that Sunday in the park, often in my enormous lecture course when I stood at the podium and looked out at the rows of pale, unformed faces and saw Jeanie's, I wondered if she was sturdy or neurotic, adept at affection and creating a warm atmosphere, if she was honest or giddy or hollow. It was not at first with anything more than curiosity that I searched out her face, to see if she was indeed in my course—not in simple paranoia but as reflection of something which had been vague and duplicitous in her manner that Sunday, or it could be simply that I was pleased to have had any human contact with one of that vast number of the swarming young.

There is something intoxicating in lecturing and something corrupting as well, something I spoke of in a speech to the National Conference of English Instructors, a sort of damning mythicization of the self, an overwhelming sense of one's comparative truth opposed to their comparative error, them, sitting out there, the unenlightened, Babbitts, Antichrists, blindhearts.

Sometimes it is merely a sense of one's own beauty, one's voice pouring out in almost endless profusion words of penetration, images, points, arguments. My second wife accused me of being "a vocal narcissist." I use my voice. I argued with her once, "Only three things hold people's attention: money, gaining or enjoying superiority over others, and sex." So I—oh, what a realist *I* am—build every lecture about one of those three: the money that might go with clear thought, the superiority that so delicately and firmly accompanies knowledge, and sex. I take sex where I find it; sometimes I supply it by a generic flirtation with the entire class—it is a scholarly device.

I never dwelled on her face; I merely wondered what I missed in not knowing her; I wondered if I would become as firm as Ett if I were in the care of a woman of the sort he liked. A good woman to steady me.

Now blur the faces in the lecture hall, whirl them around like a montage turning into wheels, the wheels of a plane; and there I am, in Paris, the summer after that term, delving into documents in the Bibliothèque Nationale, wandering in the Luxembourg to clear my head or to read. There had been an affair that spring, after the day in the park, with a straight-backed philosopher lady whose stinking self-assurance and righteousness had frozen my timid lust—no, not my lust, my heart. One had to cheat one's thoughts past her, bootleg notions of this or that. She was a relativist and could have easily forgiven infidelity, but never unclear thought. Infidelity is not my problem. It's belonging to people and yet wanting to think my own thoughts. As everyone knows, an affair or a marriage leaves bruises all over one's psyche and one's fantasies, and one wants to be left alone. A man of open and stupid heart, I elevated my condition into a moral style, I was chaste and I was happy, and I credited my happiness to my chastity: one must be moral or suffer. But one day, doused in French prose, pinched and stung by the French sun and by the cries of serious-eyed and somehow gently, interiorly stiffened French children at play—cries rendered haunting by the careful pessimism that seemed to be lodged in the intelligent rigidity of their bones—I plunged into another mood. It was toward three o'clock. Even though I was a tourist, and a tourist is a simpler man than a man at home, I did not at first see any further into my mood than that it was a restlessness—as if French prosody had affected me with a muscular itch. Then at three-thirty the sun clouded over; Paris became misty, became clearly the forest city it is, dominated by Druidical rites of passage (the buildings are like forest rows in stone, the air is both warm and cool with mortality and damp and with faint gradations of temperature that stir the nerve endings in the skin), and I decided I was lustful in a sense. I do not know about other men, but in me a mood is simply a climate in the skull, a quality of light, something quite real but unnamed. Sensibility is not only perceiving; it is attaching names. It was tentatively that

I put the label on my mood, saying "tourist's lust" as I walked up the long *allée* toward Montparnasse. It was with the first appearance of an argument—"Christianity seems so out of place in Paris," I began—that I realized how powerful a cramp had attacked me; other men may move more swiftly and surely among their instincts.

One's appetites nip at one's heels, distract one's senses, until one sets them on the hunt; distracted, resistant, I sat at the Coupole and drank Pernod; slowly the moral level at which I thought it necessary to live sank, until by six I had rearranged my thoughts to fit my loneliness and my body heat. It was shortly after six when in a beret sort of thing and a shiny vinyl, almost stylish raincoat, with coarse-textured hair slightly lifted by the moisture of the evening, Jeanie appeared, obviously by herself, and said with a funny, nervous, broken-breathed laugh, "You're Professor Hofstedt. You probably don't remember me. I was in your English Prose and Poetry 804B last year."

Before Paris and after the day in the park, one of the teaching fellows brought me among the sample papers from his group a paper written by Jeanie; she had written, "The goal of poetry is to excite and teach. Sometimes it teaches by being shocking." She used two quotations:

Poetry marries the mind to voluptuousness and seduces the senses to sense.

Poetry is about as much "a criticism of life" as a red-hot iron is a criticism of fire.

In Paris, when I suggested if she was not busy or did not have to rush off and meet her parents or friends or some young man, I remembered her paper and that I had thought, reading it, she was a girl of no extraordinary intelligence but of a passionate disposition.

THE AWARENESS quickens: the wallpaper in my room, and after kissing her the sudden conviction that I had ought to love this girl or not touch her because her soul was so naked, her kisses so alive, unconcealed, unself-protective, but not unskilled; then the conviction becomes a clouded French sensuousness, a preliminary regret for the loss to come of her innocence—not her virginity; innocence—and with that loss a loss of what in her held me to this line of action so contrary to my customary rules. I spoke in a sex-deepened voice as I undressed her:

"You understand, I never go to bed with my students." She sighed, she trembled, she gazed wide-eyed. "You must never take another course of mine," I said. In sensual moments even good humor blends indistinguishably into fatuity. What is wise is silence: the nerves will speak. I was immensely grateful to her for being so susceptible to me. I felt I would love her very shortly: she had only to be in essence what she was in appearance—fresh, young, simple, good—and I would love her warmly. Yes. Indeed.

The important thing soon came to be not to let her talk too much *before* lovemaking or I sometimes became unexcited; she caught on and was silent while I rambled on, winning her. Afterward was her time to talk: "I hate it in Glencoe, you really see the war between the sexes in a suburb. . . . Everyone *works* at being insensitive; I'd help Momma in the kitchen and there'd be a package of biscuit mix with some terrible picture on the front and I'd say, 'Oh, how ugly,' and Momma would say, 'Oh, Jeanie.' Or she'd say, 'I don't pay attention to those things,' but I knew it was me she didn't want to pay attention to. . . ."

Sometimes in the woods, in the sunlight, at Fontainebleau or in the Bois de Boulogne, a sweetness would seize her, a gentle lovingness that would terminate in hideous solicitude: "The future must be horrible for you to look into, isn't it? Maybe I can help you against the shadows." She meant because I was old. And she said things like "I'm good for you, I make you feel young," when I laughed at something—say, two dogs running in a circle, chasing each other, bodies, necks, legs stretched like held notes in Mozart: I am much amused by animal exuberance.

At times she would be bored; she would wait while I worked and come in suddenly to the room where I was writing and say, "I'm going out." "To do what?" "I don't know. Something." And she could not meet my gaze. *Tell me what to do, tell me something interesting to do.*

When I was young, I saw people as sheer appetites, fish leaping for flies, smooth, beautiful, and hungry. But I was perhaps appetiteful myself then. I'm older now and I see people as complex things, held in and mysterious, streaked with virtues and ridiculous with vices; I see them perched on time, each on a breaking branch the buds of which are sticky, new always, ready to unfold into green moments.

Doodling one day, I wrote, "the time and energy it takes to instruct her . . ."

I did not want to take her back to New York with me or explain her to my friends or be seen with her: Hofstedt's child, Hofstedt's embodied lust, all my secrets revealed in her reasonable sweet ordinariness.

And then there was her conversation, the words she used: "That was an icky movie." Some people are austere with silences, others not, but I feel that for us as for primitive man it is language that enables us to move in unison with others, and I did not want to totter with Jeanie.

But I liked her body.

Villon wrote:

> *Je congnois mort qui nous consomme,*
> *Je congnois tout, fors que moy mesme.*

I know death, who eats us, I know everything—but not myself. I wanted her; I wanted to set her free; I wanted to be free of her. Above all, I did not want to be guilty of any crime toward her. Gifted with intelligence, aided by thought, we advance on folly.

"Jeanie, I cannot persuade myself that what is happening is good for you or that anything is right except to separate for a while and study our feelings—"

Hofstedt at the window not long after, with his back to the girl he did not just then know if he loved or not, a girl with coarse-fibered hair, white bandages on her wrists; Hofstedt hearing echoes of the wild-voiced, unconvincing, yet wholly terrifying scene in the bathroom—a scene reflected in mirrors, in glossy white tile, in the razor blade itself she held: she had said, "You don't love me, I want to kill myself"—standing at the window after the scene had ended, Hofstedt said in reply to her (but he did not say it; he thought it), *You are a spoiled, passionate, perhaps unloving child.*

The shock echoed in him, caused concern and anger; his nerves and feelings were startled. The girl was monomaniacal—Inez-like.

"God knows," he said aloud, his back to her, his face looking out at plane trees, at what, after the scene in the bathroom, he could not help seeing as leaves spilling as if from razor-slit bolsters, "I'm a clumsy ass and a bastard and all of that, but can't we do without the melodrama?"

The girl with that childish hair and dulled eyes said simply, "No."

The wisdom of conventional rules had never seemed more unexceptionable, and the powers of my own mind more problematic. "Leo," I asked myself, "what do you want to do?"

I had no idea.

A French friend of mine, Charles N., came to Paris just then; we talked; he was killed a week later in an automobile accident. But the day we talked he said to me rather crossly—I had been saying unkind things about Sartre's prose—he said, "Leo, I don't feel your fundamental optimism proves you are a fool; it merely indicates that you occupy a private world."

I said, "But I know it for a fact. None of us is going to die."

I ᴛᴏᴏᴋ her back to New York; Ett was mad with jealousy; he said, "How do you rate such a pretty girl?" I announced Jeanie's and my engagement; the college was most indulgent; I met Jeanie's parents— they seemed normal, clumsy, child-crippling people. I began to write essays to earn money to buy furniture; my second wife had taken everything—"to teach you a lesson, Leo," she said. "You underrate what people do for you. Legally—the law thinks I did a great deal for you and that I have a right to these things."

At a party, my second wife met Jeanie and came up to me later and said, "You've shifted to plain girls, have you? Well, at least she's not a Tahitian." I have no idea what she meant.

Jean decided Jeanie was too childish an appellation, and she became Jean, giggling. "It's about time. Maybe *no one* will ever mention my light-brown hair again." She told me she was beginning a novel.

I wrote:

> It has been many years since I have had an affair of any length with an American woman who did not have a manuscript for me to read sooner or later.

One night at Inez and Ett's, Jean held forth on the magnificence and importance of movies, and I said movies were to her what sermons had been to her Presbyterian grandmother—inspiring, part of her Sunday morality, hardly ever intelligent or the source of intelligence but, rather, the source of a good deal of hypocrisy, and so on.

"Don't start a quarrel," she said.

"I didn't mean to—I was making an observation."

Ett had a special, peaceful gaze—with unwrinkled brows—with which he looked at Jeanie. I think he daydreamed about her unremorsefully always whenever he saw her.

"You're tired of me," Jeanie said.

Inez said mysteriously, "Leo is a very sophisticated man."

"My dear," I said, "if you want to quarrel, let's go home and get drunk and quarrel in peace and not upset our friends."

"We must talk about it!" Jeanie said with a sort of fine desperation. "Here?"

"You talk better than I do. When we're alone, you win the arguments. But Inez and Ett know you. They know how unreasonable you are."

"How unreasonable am I?" I asked, turning to Ett.

"God," he said, and threw up his hands.

"Very," Inez said. I smiled at her.

"You need me to bring you down to earth," Jeanie said.

I was suddenly very uncomfortable. I said peevishly, "Life will do that, don't you think? Earth or ashes. Life is instructive."

"Don't put me down," Jeanie said.

"My dear, we can't quarrel on fair terms if you make up all the rules."

"Please," Jeanie said. "You're still hostile because of last night. Tell me now why you were so mad at what I said."

I turned to Inez and Ett; I said, "Last night we were at Simmy Watts', and Alice Mary Ott said I represented the unsuccessful mating of ghetto Jew with George Bernard Shaw—no: it was George Bernard Shaw and the reform rabbinical tradition. Never mind, I can never keep her epigrams straight, but Jeanie—Jean—yelled at her, 'Don't you castrate Leo,' and—"

"She *was* trying to castrate you!" Jean exclaimed.

"Yes. Of course. But I don't need you to defend me in that fashion, I don't want the public image of a virago helpmeet."

"You know what he said to her?" Jean demanded. "He said, 'I'm afraid you've nailed me to the cross again, Alice Mary—you never miss.' I think that was wishy-washy and *awful.* "

Inez said to Jeanie, "I wish I had your courage."

J E A N I E   H A S several hundred virtues and finenesses and is not dull so much as merely young, but when I think that what I want chiefly from her is that she grow up and be like Inez, I think I must find a way to break off the affair.

I encourage her to flirt with younger men. I think she is interested in Max Rankin, who is in his late thirties and who is very celebrated; he is the one who began a novel:

Hello. My name is Max Rankin. I wish I were a poet. What is a poet? A poet is a man whose words ring—noncounterfeit.

But I am not quite sophisticated enough really to wish it or push it, not in the way I won the bicycle race that day.

IV

T HAT DAY. Let us go back to that day.
Anonymity is a tribute to virgin birth and is sought after as a quality of soul and of physical being in religious orders and by some ascetics in their marriage to sanctity and is considered a dilemma of the democracies. Hard-boned souls feel it a premature burial, as if only special voices have a special endurance, or as if to be unknown were such a grave symptom of injustice, as to be a form of Berkeleyan murder, a casting into nonexistence.

Inez has not been anonymous to me since Ett married her: I could make out her figure among the swimming cyclists some distance away. "Here comes your better half," I said to Ett, but he was not looking for her.

He said, "How long have you been doing aerobics?" She was in part anonymous to him. Isn't that odd? He was a stony-faced audience for whom Inez was no longer a star, was almost a mother to be escaped from, not to be seen as human. My mother—I have omitted her. She said to me a year or so before she died, "You get tired of people, but when they go away you miss them." I miss her. Is she necessary to explain how it is that I am cold-eyed and uncharitable? Shall I say my mother rarely reached inward toward the heart, or if she did, I managed to elude her with some Bedouin-child's play? But that on the other hand we never made each other cry?

I spoil Jeanie. I lead her into low emotional habits, I am so easily blackmailed. Is that in memory of my mother? I encourage masochism—that inept term. I do not believe that Jeanie loves *me;* I am merely the frame in which she wedges the immense Dutch landscape—all thatched villages and dancing villagers—of her great girlish lovingness; the more difficult I appear, and she will tease me into being very difficult, the sharper grows the sense that *she* is being loving, that it is her love which is occurring: and her identity glows in an ideal light.

On the other hand, although I believe in divorce, mind you—but I do think people who divorce show they are playing a different game from those who do not divorce—is this not an excellent bargain for a man like me who perhaps *needs* special lighting or a transposed love of some kind? I feel no great discomfort with Jeanie—yet. She attracts me still, if not so much that I haven't managed to stave off hungering strongly after other women. One does not want to hurt her; one will lie—lie! what a fine language English is—in the beds one makes. It is not certain we have made a bad bargain (and she claims it is no bargain at all, but love). I haven't the stringency to inscribe a finish when she is unprepared.

I am waiting to see. To see what? If Jeanie will tire soon of going on with a man who does not quite love her. If Ett or Rankin will make a move. Ett? Rankin? Rankin envies me and Ett is a friend: it is impossible to envy or admit the worth of anyone without desiring his women.

We are, in our connections, a linkage of sensibilities, like lawn mowers rigged like reapers to mow the fields of—what shall I say? American Life?

Inez: how many years have I known her? Fourteen? It does not matter if I speak to her or ignore her, if I am mannerly or forgetful, if I protect her from Ett or start mischief between them; everything I have ever done or not done, everything she has done or not done, has helped piece together an intimacy in which there are so many intertwinings of awareness, familiarities of spirit and conversation and neurosis, that it is like a garden growing rank, a wild and untouched sweetness, a tangle of leaves and stalks: it is as if we have already slept together. The smallest of incidents, and the largest of lapses of conscience, could bring us to the actuality. Inez, once a year, drunk, will complain, "I know Leo doesn't find me attractive," and she will sulk. I will reply, "But I do," and laugh. The danger comes if we permit our eyes to meet. Then the joke falters.

In Ett's feeling for her there is a masculine element of surprise; he is astonished that she is there, that he is married, that it is her voice he hears. One could easily be persuaded he was a poor husband to her, that Inez deserved consolation—but honor, so far, that tiresome notion, has made me too lazy to indulge in the wretched strain of such a strenuous insight.

The discontent is there, in her eyes, even as she bicycles, as she glides, pinkly flushed, not young, delicious, good-hearted, wicked, too, in the way of people who are not professedly wicked—that is, by accident, with eyes closed, striking blind blows. It is easy to prefigure her words; she is not clever enough—or loving enough—to be surprising. She at once serves and reassures and punishes those near her with her durable repetitiousness.

She said, first displaying the admiration she regularly hands out to Ett: "You men are so strong. You go so fast—like the wind." She said, "Oh, I'm out of breath, this must be very good for me, I don't get enough exercise, I think." She looked at Ett: "Did you win?"

It was not a hugely wicked thing for her to ask, nor was it so bad of Ett to say, without generosity, "No. He's switched his exercise routines."

But that day, at that moment, my affection for her, for Ett, passed into a sort of tantrum of a lesser order—it *felt* like weariness of spirit at the time (*Je congnois tout*), a boredom with *their* childishness; they seemed so cramped and pitiable, Inez and Ett, so petty and competitive, falling like hammers on my nerves and on each other's like parents fastening children to dead urgencies. I was tired of the dinginess of Ett's heart (actually, he has quite a good heart as hearts go: he is loyal) and of Inez's blindness (she is not so unenlightened, all in all). So that when the girl with the almost plain, nice face inside its cap of coarse-textured, unfashionable, wavy hair, with its exercise-reddened cheeks and rather dim nose and modest chin, riding by on her bicycle between two girlfriends, smiled and flicked her hand shyly at me, that girl who was most likely a student of mine, since she had that lectured look, and her smile and hand flick were so decidedly tenuous that it seemed she knew my reputation for extreme rudeness in public to students, I smiled back. I cannot abide students' pussyfooting after father surrogates, after extra attentions, their attempts at quasi or real seductions—their way of becoming instantly human. I cannot abide it, I am too easily shaken; I like formality and approaches and smiles as careful as flower arrangements. I smiled merely to express my attachment to the freshness that semi-unknown girl represented. I did not smile at *her.* I smiled to assert my separation from Inez and Ett and from the stale and intricate branchings of their still living but spindly and often graceless affection for each other. The girl's face broke. The unexpectedness of the intensity of my response pulled at her composure, gave her face a harsh twist: a collapse of preconceptions. I am not a handsome man, but I teach English prose and poetry. I stink of romance in a marginal way. Too late I wished to retract my smile.

The three girls glanced at each other, pulled over to the side of the road—I had not really looked at any of them. One of the other girls waited, I think, until my glance moved that way: she had her hand in the air—waiting. When I saw her, I smiled irritably as I usually do and continued to talk to Inez; I suggested we ride on, but Inez said, "A moment—I must catch my breath." Jeanie's friends said to her (she told me later), "He only recognizes you." Jeanie said, "He smiled at all of us." "No," said the others, "he only really smiled at you. He likes you."

Jeanie said to me later, "They teased me into talking to you."

I think Jeanie still sees me as Yeats's Vicar on earth; she was a young girl. No two souls met that day in the park: two types encountered each other.

Walking her bicycle, hands on the handlebars, her breasts pressed into a diagonal, her face naive and bold and stupid and lovely in its carnal aggression rising, a dotted square with rounded chin above the oblique lines of her twisted breast—head and breast, head and breast—she moves through the stream of cyclists on that day of easy presumption. Does she think life is safe or kind? Will she wake in my arms, naked, see me looming over her and fear me and the way I think, and cry out despairingly, inwardly, "How did this happen to me?"

That day Ett and I notice her simultaneously. It is very soon after a divorce, and what I feel chiefly is nothingness. The girl swallows bravely; a flush has overspread her nondescript face; her back is straight. Youthful inanity makes her voice gawky, touching. But I have closed my eyes to her; I am irritated, horrified by her *presumption*. She is an intruder. She says boldly, "Hello, Professor Hofstedt, do you go bicycle riding often?"

I am completely unattracted by her, but Ett is looking at her. I see him looking at her in such a way that it is as if someone is underlining a passage in a book.

"Oh," Jeanie says angrily to me from time to time, "why do you make everything so complicated?" I shrug, and have yet to reply, "I know no simple stories."

Ett's gaze drew something like a line of light around her—I thought, *He sees her as a younger Inez.* From that moment, the girl was never to be anonymous to me again.

The Shooting Range

I

Aɴɴ Kᴀᴍᴘғᴇʟ went to Millburg, Illinois, in the summer of
1934, to make a time-motion study of the manufacture of small-bore
rifles in the Axel-Lambwell Small Arms Plant. She went as a secret
member of the Communist Party. She was twenty years old, a tall, thin,
pale-faced girl with large wrists and square, nervous hands.

She believed in the Party but not as much as she believed in what she
thought Communist ideals were—the brotherhood of man and the release of men from economic pressures that distorted them and their
lives.

She was not clever. In her first year at college, a boy, shorter than she
was, and with blond hair, had seduced her and brought her into the
Party. She soon bored him, and he grew a mustache and transferred to
another college. Ann continued in the Party and grew paler and thinner
and thought often of the happiness she had lost. She had a mathematical
facility, and she was accurate and painstaking, and she entered the
Engineering Department, where she specialized in statistical studies of
mass-production techniques. The time-motion study of the manufacture
of small-bore rifles was to be her honors thesis.

It cost her five dollars a week to rent two rooms with a bath in the
downtown section of Millburg. She went by streetcar—by trolley—to

the plant every morning. The owner of the plant, on the chance her time-motion study would be useful to him, assigned his chief foreman to give her what help, information, or instruction she needed.

The foreman was in his late thirties, a neat, orderly man. He had very light brown hair. His name was Walter Campbell; he had not finished high school; he was married and had three children; he neither smoked nor drank.

He behaved toward Ann with that unremitting respect which suggests the conviction of one's inferiority to someone of a higher order, more worthy, more valuable, more delicate.

Having noticed that Ann rode the trolley, he ventured to suggest she permit him to drive her home in the evenings. He believed it must be disagreeable for a college girl, a "lady," an "efficiency expert," to ride on a crowded trolley with workingmen. Ann had tried to explain she did not mind taking the streetcar, but Walter, within his meekness and deference, proved unexpectedly stubborn.

Ann wondered if anything could be done to arouse a man who was so patently a tool of the bosses.

Driving her home one evening, Walter said worriedly, "What are your parents thinking of, letting a girl like you spend a summer living alone?" Ann meant to laugh, but smoke from her cigarette caught in her throat and she choked and coughed. Walter patted her back. He halted the car to do it. He was turned toward her and he was solicitous. Ann noticed his body smell—dry, physically healthy, warm. Ann caught her breath and said, "You shouldn't worry about me. I—I'm not a virgin." Walter said nothing. When they reached the curb in front of the building in which Ann's five-dollar-a-week apartment occupied the third floor rear, she thanked him for the ride and went inside.

She did not go to the plant the next day but stayed at home working with figures and walking up and down what her landlady called the sitting room of Ann's "suite of rooms," smoking and lecturing herself on childishness. But she was embarrassed at what she had said.

That evening Walter called to ask if she was well. She said yes. She said she'd be at the plant the next day.

When she entered the plant, she saw Walter bending over one of the workmen who was polishing a rifle barrel. He did not see her come in but he turned around as if he had felt her entrance. Ann was certain that he had begun to *have feelings* about her. It was as much to prove she felt no class distinctions as it was in the hope of winning Walter to her

Marxist ideals that she permitted herself to decide she would encourage him. She was enlightened, she thought; she could want his bodily intimacy and companionship without wanting *him*. But she would accept *him*. When she left that evening, she said, staring over his head, that she would be at home, working up the material she had already gathered. "Please stop by and see me," she said.

H E W A S shy, and Ann's boldness was a matter of principle and easier to maintain in speech than in her room. His first visit they spent talking. He said his wife and children were in Indiana for the summer, in a rented cottage on a lake. He went over on weekends. He said it was very pleasant to enjoy "a little harmless feminine companionship" in the evenings. He often grew lonely, he said. On his second visit, there were long silences. On his third, as soon as he entered her sitting room, Ann saw he had made up his mind about her. But he seemed unable to make the first move. Ann said, "I feel a little strange. I think I've been smoking too many cigarettes," and she lay down on the couch. After a while, Walter tiptoed over and began massaging her forehead. Then Ann kissed him.

She was not prepared for Walter's quickness and noisiness as a lover, or for his semitearful whisper afterward of "I love you." She thought he was joking, or that he was grateful for the sexual release. She said nothing in reply.

He had an even-featured, dull face—the eyes seemed to be in retreat, to be fleeing, then pausing to look back, then fleeing again. But his body, good-sized, strong, somewhat bony and white on the chest because he still wore a shirt when he went swimming with his family in Indiana, was handsome to her and curiously alive, jerky, overeager, highly sensitive. Her body was a feminine version of his in appearance but slow and cautious in feeling and almost always slightly cold to the touch. It drew comfort from the repeated touch of Walter's body, but Ann had never known what an older girl in the Party had described as "a woman's right" (or sometimes "*the* woman's right"), and she did not expect to find it with Walter, who had perhaps never heard of it. She did not feel like explaining it to him or requesting it.

They met usually in Casperia, the next town to the south on the railway line. There was a wooded state park and a lake behind a WPA dam. Lovemaking with Walter seemed strangely clean and innocent.

They rarely undressed completely but, with citronella smeared on their necks and foreheads and arms to discourage mosquitoes, lay on a blanket in the woods. Walter said he had never touched any woman before except his wife. He had always been shy with women, he said, "uneasy with this thing"—Ann presumed he meant sex. He said he probably wasn't as good a lover as a college man was. Ann resented it that he hadn't the courage and pride of those workingmen who felt themselves equal and even superior to everyone. She resented it that he felt her superior to him, that he felt she was experienced and worldly. She told him she had had only one lover and one experience besides the lover, that he, Walter, was as good as the college men she had known, that she felt more with him than with them. Even as she said it, she realized it was true. She felt passionately that he was as good a lover as anyone could be; she set herself and Walter on fire, and she knew, for the first time, the pleasure she hadn't known before. Now it was her turn to cry; she cried and said, "I love you," and, in a burst of melodrama, kissed both his hands.

A SUMMER on the Illinois plains has its own special quality: the nights are heavy and still with heat, the sky splits frequently with bursts of heat lightning; often after midnight, mist rises from the ground. Ann and Walter sometimes waited for the mist; they liked to sit in the mist, holding hands or embracing more closely. But usually they parted before midnight, Walter to drive back to Millburg, Ann to take the train. Walter hated Ann's taking the train but she insisted, and he understood that talk (gossip) was bad for an unmarried girl but he hoped Ann wasn't doing it for the sake of his wife. "I wouldn't hurt you for her sake," he said. But he still drove to the cottage in Indiana for Sunday visits. Ann said she understood. She never complained. She said she would leave Millburg before his family came back. "I don't ever want to be a problem or a burden to you," she said.

She daydreamed about being married to Walter and living in a small house and packing his lunch for him to take to the plant: but it was only a daydream.

When they sat on the blanket in the woody park in Casperia, Walter talked about God, about the Republican and Democratic parties, about rifles. He did not talk well. He repeated himself and he left things out. He sometimes said Ann was "beautiful, really beautiful," and that she was "the best thing that ever happened" to him. Ann realized his shyness with her and the fact that she impressed him made his tongue clumsy, because in the plant she sometimes heard him speak and he spoke sensibly and even with muted poetry: "We want the barrel to shine like a blue mirror," he instructed a youthful workman. Ann was warm and comfortable and excited too, happy, a little breathless, and both sad and anxious that the summer was going to end. But the affair would be perfect of its kind, and it would end before she bored Walter.

Meanwhile, each week, the intimacy deepened in its own way. They found out more about each other. Walter insisted she quit the Communist Party, and Ann did. She received in reply a vaguely threatening letter, but she had not been important to the Party; they had not thought highly of her; she did not hear from them again.

She described her professors at college to Walter and he would say, "He sounds like a very conceited man," and Ann would reply, "Yes, he is. That's it exactly." Walter discussed the plant with her. "It's basically a craft operation," Ann said sagely. "It would be a mistake to try for too much efficiency." Walter would nod. "Yes. I think so."

They came to know each other's clothes, even their underwear, and their physical states; Ann's headaches and Walter's nervous stomach became common property.

Finally, as the involutions of time and feeling bore them deeper and deeper into the shadows of their own inner selves, Walter said he would like to divorce his wife; he said, "I wish I could get a divorce and live with you forever, Ann."

"Oh no," Ann said. "You don't really." She laughed in an odd, twisted way. "You're not that kind of man. People would talk. You might even lose your job." He would never leave his job, she knew. He hadn't enough confidence. Nor could he support his children and then support another family. He had spoken in a helpless tone anyway. "Let's take what we are given," Ann said, flushed and earnest.

Walter continued to talk about divorce and remarriage, but not with hope or firmness. He hinted in a frightened way at her superiority, his own lack of worth, his half-guessed deficiencies and the deficiencies of the life he could offer her. Ann lost her sense of direction; she no longer remembered why divorce and remarriage were out of the question. She thought despairingly only that she would have to go away soon (if he followed her, if he was that strong, she would live with him inside or outside marriage).

II

IN THE last week of August, one morning, Walter drove his two-door Chevrolet sedan up the tree-lined street where Ann lived and parked in front of the house-turned-into-apartments Ann shared with her landlady and two other women, all widows except herself. Walter turned the wheels of his car carefully in toward the curb, put the gearshift into neutral, and pulled on the hand brake. Swallowing with difficulty, he climbed out of the car, glanced quickly and furtively up and down the street as he trotted the few feet into the hall of the building. He climbed two flights of stairs and knocked on Ann's door. "It's me—Walter," he said.

Ann opened the door.

"I couldn't go to work," Walter said pathetically. "I started to but I couldn't. I feel sick because you're going away soon. I think about shooting myself."

"Oh, Walter," Ann said, and embraced him.

Walter stroked her back. "Seeing you means a lot to me," he said, almost without inflection. He seemed to be nakedly himself—ordinary, uneducated, successful in his small fashion, a mother's boy, egocentric, lonely, hurt, shy, tender, bemused, in love, lost.

There was nothing else to do: they made love.

Ann was tense, was not satisfied, was emotional. Walter said nothing, not a word; he seemed to be too caught up in his feelings to speak. Ann lit a cigarette while Walter dressed. She thought at first his neck was flushed; when she realized those red marks were the marks of her fingers, she grew frightened. Second by second, she grew more irritable and more moved: she saw an unexpected beauty in Walter's dressing himself, and at the same time she was maddened by his silence, his self-preoccupation, his getting dressed to go off to work after all with the dull, dry conscientiousness of a man of no imagination. She loved him for having no imagination. When he was dressed, he turned toward her, and she saw he had tears in his eyes.

She cried, "I don't want to make you unhappy!"

"Ann." He swallowed. He looked stiff, wretched, stupid.

"You'd better hurry. You're already late," she said, impatient, maternal. When he was gone, she stood by her window; she saw him enter the car; she saw the car drive away. He didn't look back.

Ann sat in a chair by the window and held her bathrobe shuttered over her chest. She was drawn more and more to the idea of sacrifice, of leaving at once without saying goodbye. Walter would hate her; he would despise her for a coward. He would return to his wife. It was a great gift she would make him. If she left secretly, without seeing him again, he would not have the humiliation of having to choose between her and his wife when in truth he had no choice. It was not her own possible humiliation that she was fleeing.

She packed hurriedly, inefficiently, disturbed by a sense of disconnection as if there were two Anns, and one was throwing a tantrum; and then she went to the railroad station. She bought a ticket to Milwaukee and stumblingly lugged her suitcase to the train platform, which had a wooden roof, like a canopy, with fringes of gingerbread and spooled icicles hanging down; from the railroad tracks rose an acid metal smell, the sun beat so strongly on them. Then there was a wrought-iron fence and a view of cornfields; no one moved anywhere in her field of vision. Not even a fly buzzed anywhere near her. It seemed to her that at the heart of the universe lay a dry small-town silence. I'm not looking forward to graduate school, she thought.

AT COLLEGE, she found the boys she met to be hypocritical and tiresome, young and not acquainted with what was real, as Walter was. She wanted to say, "Why don't you all learn how to be simple and real?"

Her grief disordered her face and her temper. She said to herself, "You're turning into a gargoyle—no, into Olive Oyl," and laughed aloud. She was in the college library and saw her milky reflection in the polished top of the reading table. The other people at the table looked at her strangely.

When she thought of Walter, she thought now of his shyness as foreknowledge of passion: he had known. She saw his fine-featured (tanned) face and on it she saw his understanding of her: no one else had ever understood her at all.

She reminded herself that she was emancipated. She meant to sleep with someone. She fell into bed twice, but it was very boring.

Then she met a tall, loud, cheerful, heavyset graduate student at a party; he had some of Walter's great gaiety of spirit, Ann thought. They went to his apartment and it seemed to Ann that it could have been worse.

Her lover patted his paunch and said, "Casanova was fat, too." He said, "I've got vast appetites, like Walt Whitman."

This one is just a boy, Ann thought.

Then he said Ann should come by his room the following day after classes: "It needs a good cleaning."

He's joking, Ann thought. I must be losing my mind. "No, no, no, no, no," she said.

He stared at Ann. "You wouldn't help clean my room?" he asked in a trembling voice.

"I don't do things like that," she said nervously.

He said, "I'll tell you what you are—you're a love cheat. I thought you wanted to make me happy!"

It rained often that autumn. In her boardinghouse was a student who addressed women as "Ma'am." He was from a farm. He was younger than Ann; he was about eighteen. He always left the table immediately after dinner to get to his books, and he rose at five in the morning and walked downtown to a department store and loaded and unloaded trucks until eight and then returned to the boardinghouse for breakfast and had his first class at nine-fifteen. He was as disciplined and broad-shouldered as Walter.

She invited him to her room; she served him ragged fragments of Swiss cheese on saltines and gave him rye without ice to drink. They became lovers. Ann went and lay down on her bed, put her arm over her eyes, and said, "I'm too drunk to know what I'm doing."

It seemed to Ann that the Ann who had met Walter and the Ann who occupied the present moment were not the same: she had changed; she was not, in some essential way (it had to do with innocence), young anymore; the change was like a deformity. But she felt herself to be more intelligent, more awake, more a person—a person in agony but more a person. Half disbelieving and with a gasp of bitterness—the image in her head was of the outer skins of an onion being peeled away—she said to herself, "We're getting a lot closer to the onion now."

It made her sad that he could sleep with her and not care for her, that this was the little that should be allowed her—she had thought life was more sensibly arranged than this.

"It's all so laughable, life is, don't you think?" she asked the boy.

"I don't philosophize much," he said.

"You're young for your age," she said.

He looked at his hands—they were large and very red—and at his shoelaces, as if checking his appearance to see if he was safe from being laughed at. He said, "I guess I wouldn't know about that." He spoke with implausible politeness.

She sometimes thought she would stop sleeping with him, but then the thought of the fineness of his politeness and of his person would summon up images of rest and refreshment as if he were a movie or a vacation.

It even occurred to Ann that she liked being hurt because she felt so terrible about Walter. She never named Walter to herself anymore; she referred to him to herself as *the other one*.

She had trouble with her teeth. She went to the dentist—he said she was grinding her teeth, perhaps in her sleep. She took long walks alone through fields of crusty snow. She yearned to be moderate in her desires.

She did not care if she lived or died. She thought she might as well go home and see her parents during Easter vacation.

I t   w a s funny when her mother said, "All my children are musical except Ann—she's advanced." It amused Ann in her dark, heavy, German mood to put on one of her dresses, a loose-fitting modernistic print, and to hang a long chain around her neck and go to a dance to watch the middle-class mating ritual. It amused her that many men flirted with her, an "advanced" girl (because—she thought—the way she was dressed raised their hopes, and because they or their fathers did business with her father). And then there were the dullards who were pressed into service as her dates; they spent most of their time trying to persuade her of Roosevelt's villainy. It seemed to her for a while, that lilac-penetrated spring, that it was a terrible thing to be a woman.

She had in her face and carriage at all times something of the look of a torch singer—she looked emotional, melancholy, and proud in her lack of innocence.

At a country-club dance, a man she did not know stared at her from across the dance floor; he was a smallish, young-old man; he wore the only brown double-breasted suit—and a wrinkled one, at that—among the white dinner jackets. He approached her and tumbled out the words "Fe fi fo fum! I smell the blood of an iconoclast!" He introduced himself: "Joseph Lord Fennimore—my mother's maiden name was Lord"—nicknamed, he remarked with hopeful sullenness, Fennie, "an attorney at law and generally considered crazy as a loon because I go to a psychoanalyst that my so-called friends say I look on as God."

"Well," said Ann, with a sigh, "I guess that's not much worse than thinking Alf Landon is."

"Oh! *Touché*," Fennie cried, and looked at her with gratitude.

They went out on the terrace, each holding a cup of what Fennie called "Depression punch—mostly rum and indigestion. The orange peels are made out of Kleenex."

He said, "I'm not crazy; I'm what they call tied up inside." He was eight years older than Ann; that's why they had never met, he said; he had gone with "the older crowd." He said, "I will tell you an absolutely typical story about me."

When he was twenty, he said, he'd had a daydream about sex, "like most American boys"; his daydream was that he would meet a woman whose desires matched his, "and everything would be simple—it's a very typical daydream." He had heard about a girl who was "a genuine nymphomaniac. I met her at a college football weekend. She encouraged me, and God, when I thought there I was, included in her nymphomania, well, I just about went out of my mind. There was this party at the frat house—I took her into the den—I locked the door. . . . Now, I want you to picture this. The den is covered with animal heads—water buffalo, moose, antelope: totems. . . . This story makes my analyst go out of his head, he thinks it's so significant. I wanted this girl to think I was nonchalant—I was looped. I, ah, tossed her step-ins over the horns of the water buffalo. It was just Thorne Smith—you know—but she got on her high horse. She wouldn't have anything to do with me after that. She was a nymphomaniac, but she wanted to be treated with respect. I've never been able to handle that kind of dishonesty. I've never been a true bourgeois. I'm kind of a radical, but I guess you can tell that from the way I'm dressed. . . . Do you dream much?" Fennie asked.

"No," Ann said. A lopsided moon floated above the rolling slopes of the golf course. "*Au clair de la lune*," she said. She was a little drunk. She started down the stone steps. "I want to walk on the grass," she said.

When Fennie threw his arms about her near a grove of trees, Ann smiled gently.

The comedy did not bother her, the laboriousness of the joke. She wasn't after sex. She thought it would be nice to make Fennie's dream come true.

Fennie said, "Thank you for Paradise."

"Oh," Ann said sophisticatedly, maternally. "You've never done it outdoors?"

ANN THOUGHT that for Fennie the other night had not yet finished happening. He wanted sometimes to talk about it with her, but she refused. Fennie said, "You have such a sense of how to live!" He told her that he was known for his gloomy temper. "But that's because I'm a very dissatisfied person *au fond*," he told Ann. His father had been a judge. "I'm not an outcast," Fennie said. "I get asked to the larger parties. . . . I like people too much or too little, and show it. I'm not considered reliable." He went on at length; he disliked Milwaukee; he apologized to Ann: "I'm not romantic. Am I a great disappointment to you?"

"I'm not romantic, either," Ann said. "I loved a man once—I don't want to go through *that* again."

"Yes, me too!" Fennie said. "I've had enough *Sturm und Drang* with my mother."

They were very relaxed lovers.

Fennie said, "I've been thinking: after you go back to college, I could drive up and see you weekends—sometimes."

Ann's eyes went blank. "Fennie, there's someone else." She was slightly cross; it was all so difficult and complicated.

"Someone you love?" Fennie asked, breathing like a startled horse.

"No, no. I told you I don't love anyone."

"Does he love you?"

"No, no, no, no!"

"Ah," said Fennie. With his eyes cast down, he said, "I suppose there's an—an electricity between you."

"I don't know what there is between us," Ann said, concentrating.

Fennie was humble. "I'm jealous," he said.

Ann said casually, "You come see me if you want. Just don't make scenes."

Fennie visited her at college every other weekend. Ann admired his stubbornness; it seemed to her he was an undersized football player who knew he might be hurt but who kept on going anyway.

He thought her very knowledgeable, and he followed her lead and obeyed her hints about the best way to make love. He was in awe of her moods; he was admiring.

She was taken by a sense of poetry—the approaching summer was, she thought toughly, a time of violence; the yellow sun struck the brown, plowed farmland and left a green bruise: she was afloat on a rhetorical poetry of the senses.

It suited Fennie, who had paid thirty-five dollars for a copy of *Lady Chatterley's Lover*, to try to be a simple, uncomplicated man; he complicatedly mimicked the simplicity of such a man. Of a workman, Ann would have said. Of a gamekeeper, Fennie would have said.

Ann took Fennie one warm afternoon to a meadow outside the college town; the meadow was ringed with birches and oaks and had a dead oak in its center, and Ann and Fennie agreed the meadow looked like nature's imitation of photographs of the Place Vendôme. Ann and Fennie walked in the meadow, and the weeds and clover they crushed beneath their feet gave off a sweet, vegetable fragrance. Fennie said he was so happy that he wouldn't mind dying then and there. Then added, with surprise, "I mean it."

Ann had not stopped sleeping with the boy from the boardinghouse and in a mindless way preferred him to Fennie because she had known him longer; he had precedence. But that day in the meadow, rising from their afternoon's rest, Fennie said bitterly as he brushed off Ann's back and picked bits of grass out of her hair, "There, you look as if nothing's happened." Ann suddenly heard the truth of the terrible complaint in his voice; she had been immune to Fennie. She shivered, and broke and ran like a frightened colt toward the road.

She couldn't bear it—making a simple, uncomplicated man who admired her unhappy. . . . Fennie was pleased to see that he had that power over her. He had no other power over her at all—only this, of his unhappiness.

Fennie took Ann to a hotel one night; their room had immense red roses on the carpet. Ann lay on the bed, her shoes off, an electric fan blowing on her shoulder. Fennie, making drinks, his back to her, said jocularly, "Ann, you're the cat's pajamas, I'll tell the world." Then, with his back to her, he said he wanted to ask her a question. "The question is," he said, his back to her, "concerned with marriage."

"Oh!" Ann cried.

Fennie's confidence rose in proportion to Ann's dismay, as if any intimation of weakness in her strengthened him. He said, almost deliriously, "Why shouldn't we get married? Don't worry about my mother or my analyst!" he said, keeping his back to her the entire time. "I can take care of *them.*"

Ann began to cry. She thought, It didn't matter what I did; this was the one I was bound to end up with. This one will marry me.

III

SHE AND FENNIE went before a justice of the peace seven days later. Ann had been determined to have a civil ceremony, with no family present; indeed, neither family knew of the marriage yet. "I don't want *their* emotions," Ann said. "This is private, Fennie. It's embarrassing enough as it is."

After the ceremony, she and Fennie sat in the used 1932 Plymouth he had bought to have his own car to come up and see her on weekends. Her hands were shaking and so were his. The early-morning heat and sun and the Sunday stillness enclosed the car in a fragile envelope. The heat, the stillness held an unfocused and shaming memory; Ann stared palely out the window—perhaps she was listening for an approaching train. Suddenly Fennie leaned forward and put his head in her lap. "You make me so happy," he said, as if apologizing for having married her.

Ann kissed the back of his head with straightforward tenderness: "I'll be a good wife to you, Fennie." She thought, June 16, 1935, and I'm married.

Ann walked into her family's house in Milwaukee while Fennie waited in the car. Ann's mother exclaimed, "I said to your brother at Easter—'That girl's ready to get married'!"

Then Ann called Fennie inside. She thought he would be put off by her mother's air of triumph, but later, when they were driving toward his house, he told Ann he liked her mother very much. Ann said, "Maybe you just like mothers—period."

At Fennie's house, a maid let them in; Fennie's mother was sitting in the upstairs parlor. Fennie said from the doorway of the room, "Mother, this is Ann Kampfel Fennimore. I married her this morning. You may have lost the battle but you've won a wonderful daughter."

Fennie's mother, a large, plain woman, said, "Oh, Fennie! Can't we talk this over?"

Ann covered her face with her hands.

She meant to protect Fennie from his mother, take care of him, but he did not let her; he was very busy over the next few weeks; he was in a very trance of warfare, fighting with his mother, with his analyst—"I've outgrown analysis, Ann. You've given me maturity"—and baby-talking with Ann, calling her "wifey-ifey" and getting hurt when she forgot her name was Mrs. Fennimore. Fennie would say, "My mother is a hysterical old *bitch*! I have a headache." His mother would telephone late at night—hoping, Fennie claimed, to interrupt his and Ann's love-making—to say she heard prowlers and wished she had a loyal watch-dog; to say she had forgotten to ask Fennie about her rental property in Waukegan; or simply to say good night. She was polite. She said, "Perhaps I shouldn't phone so late, but I don't sleep much." Ann thought Fennie was neurotic about his mother. Ann and Fennie would quarrel; Fennie would shout, "All I'm asking is that you stroke my forehead!" Ann would shout, "You stroke my forehead! I have a head-ache, too." Ann's mother compounded the strain by telling Ann, "That dreadful woman has been saying dreadful things about you all over town." Ann, who did not mean to be upset, burst into tears when she told Fennie. (And Ann's brother's wife was difficult; and Fennie's cous-ins and the young women who gave teas were envious: now that he was married, Fennie was a catch; and inquisitive: how had Ann caught him; and pushy, pushy, pushy.) Fennie said, "That woman will stop at noth-ing to get her own way." "Which woman?" Ann asked tearfully. "Fen-nie, which woman?"

Fennie had dragged her into this world; Ann sometimes woke up from strangely anonymous daydreams, in which a man had a rendez-vous with her in a woods, in the country, to find that Fennie was staring at her. "Ann," he said, "I think the sex you and I have is very interesting. Do you think it's good?"

One evening, when the windows in her apartment were open and electric fans whirred, blurring the wine-colored twilight outside, Ann contemplated suicide or divorce. She struggled with her mood. Finally, she said, "Fennie, I think we should leave Milwaukee."

Fennie, wet, wrapped partially in a towel, appeared in the door of the room. "What did you say?" She repeated it. Fennie caught his breath. The difficulties were immense, he pointed out; there were any number of things to be afraid of, such as being disinherited. He paused. "I've always wanted to leave Milwaukee," he said. "I never had the nerve." He said, "I'll be grateful to you for this, I think, for the rest of my life."

Fennie found a job through a college classmate. He would work for the government in Washington.

It took Ann and Fennie a week to pack; Fennie had a special system for packing their books in alphabetical order so they could easily be arranged on shelves in Washington. Ann said, "I feel a great burden has been lifted from me. I think I've been afraid the whole time we've been here. Well, I won't be frightened anymore. What we must remember, Fennie, is that the past is dead."

She thought it strange that there were so many beginnings in the beginnings of a marriage.

A N N   S A I D of Washington, "It feels like a Southern town."

She worked as a statistician and earned eleven hundred and fifty-five dollars a year. Fennie, at the Department of Commerce, as a junior member of its panel of legal advisers, earned three thousand. Fennie had nine hundred and fifty dollars a year from a trust fund. His mother had said she would send him fifty dollars a month, but she sometimes forgot. Ann's share of her family's business was eleven hundred dollars a year. Ann and Fennie knew themselves to be prosperous.

They took a three-room apartment near Dupont Circle. Ann thought the apartment beautiful; she dreamed about it in her sleep and woke to find herself there. Fennie sometimes said to her in the morning, "You're my s-wheatie, my breakfast of champions."

Ann believed that Fennie should share in the work of running the apartment. "Men and women are equals," Ann said; Fennie agreed. "There's a lot of dead lumber to be cleared away in these matters," he said.

In those early months, they would meet after work and drive home together and shop together. At the grocery, Fennie was excited and unreliable. He would hurry to Ann's side while she studied two cans of green peas and did the complicated weight-price figuring necessary to determine which was the best buy—Ann felt American industry should be policed by intelligent consumers—and he would whisper, "Honey" (he had started to pick up bits of a Southern speech), "the butcher says he has Virginia smoked ham, the real McCoy."

"How much is it?" Ann would ask.

Fennie was inclined to take Ann's frugality as a criticism of his masculinity.

Sometimes Ann and Fennie would be stiff and silent in each other's company after the difficulties of shopping together, depressed at the differences there were between them. Ann would be the one to break the silence: "Why are all the lights in the windows so yellow, Fennie? Is it because of the dust in the atmosphere?" He had once explained to her that dust in the air caused the brilliance of sunsets. It was her way of making peace.

Relieved, Fennie would say something silly like "Because chickens cross the road." Ann thought Fennie's humor was surrealist; the silliest of his remarks could plunge her into hilarity. She would laugh. Fennie would laugh at the sight of her laughing. Giggling, laughing, and sighing, they would continue home, their laughter following them like tame birds.

Fennie did not go on very long helping her shop. He did not help her with the apartment, either. Exhausted in the evenings, after a long day of being a new man in the office, he would collapse and ask Ann to make him a drink. "You like to baby me," Fennie said. "You like to do it because you love me," he said to her.

She did not contradict him.

Ann found it hard to get used to—that people thought of her as fortunate, young, and happy. And interesting. She wanted to be left alone and not have men make suggestive remarks to her or put ideas into her head, and she did her hair in a bun and wore loose-fitting clothes to hide her figure, which was considered in Washington to be very good-looking—long-limbed and slender.

Fennie pressed on her volumes of Havelock Ellis to read, and *Ulysses*, and *Women in Love*, and popular accounts of Freudian theories; Ann grew angry and said he was silly and she would not read them. She knew more about sex than any book, she said.

On those occasions when Fennie would say that he knew she did not love him as much as he loved her, Ann would say angrily, "That's stupid, Fennie. Stupid, stupid, stupid."

In some ways—so it seemed to Ann—Fennie was simply an overeducated, overtalkative, middle-class male who overcomplicated things. She was menaced by what she felt in him to be a destructive male element: "Don't think too much," she would say to him. She did love him, but she did not want her feelings examined. She sometimes thought of Walter. She would be pale and worn out and sprawled in a chair. "You're tired," Fennie would say.

"No, I'm not," Ann would cry, and jump up and start cleaning out ashtrays. He did not know everything.

Sometimes it brought her close to terror when he spoke of her moods, as if he had lunged out at her in a dark hallway and said, "Boo!" in a ringing voice. Her heart would take several minutes to settle down.

Ann's and Fennie's new friends, men and women alike, condemned dishonesty—dishonesty of emotion, of fact, in sex, and in government. They disliked snobbery but could not help thinking that people who were unlike them were unfortunate, foolish, or greedy. The couples spent what money they had on war relief for Spain, Ethiopia, or China, on books, whiskey, superior dentists, and cleaning women; they paid three dollars a week for their cleaning women. They agreed that the world was not fit for people to bring children into and that the men should not be distracted by more responsibilities. Yet an alarming number of Ann's friends became pregnant as the months went by, especially when the stock market went up. Ann read the stock-market news and did not admit that she wanted to be pregnant. Fennie did not want children just now. Ann said, with a little laugh, "You want to be the only baby in the family." Fennie said, "Be reasonable," and Ann bit her lip and tried to be reasonable.

It became a point of honor not to think of Walter anymore, and his honesty and his dignity. She was not disloyal to Fennie.

She thought it almost comic how soon after marriage Fennie stopped respecting her mind. Sometimes he asked her what she was thinking of when they made love; lately he complained. He would say, "Concentrate on me more." He did not have so much interest in making Ann happy. It was as if love were a long board and he could not carry it from his end and wanted to lay it down, although he loved her sadness—only he could ease it. Suddenly he was interested in his own life again, that part of him that was not attached to Ann.

"There's an intelligent man at the office," Fennie said. He said Clerkenwall Franklyn came from a distinguished Quaker family, was brilliant, was a genuine Philadelphia lawyer. "Franklyn," Fennie announced, "says we have to come to terms with the bourgeoisie. We can use them and steal the country back from them at the same time! We can do it just the way they stole it from us—*legally!*"

"Oh," said Ann, her lips disapproving, "how can you think you can compromise with the *bourgeoisie!*"

"We have to!" Fennie said enthusiastically. "Who else can run local enterprises?"

"The brighter workingmen," Ann said, breathing irregularly.

"My dear wifey-ifey, the brighter workingmen *are* bourgeois, only without the broader commercial imagination," Fennie said.

"No, no, no, no, no," Ann said.

"Well, let's talk about it some other time," Fennie said.

When Ann was certain she was pregnant, she went to Fennie and told him that if he thought it was a bad time to have a child she would, of course, as three of her friends had, get an abortion. Fennie reminded her of their dream of working for the good of the country. "First things first," he said. "Am I right?" he asked, omitting to ask if she wanted the child.

Ann took an afternoon off from work and went to Baltimore by train to have her abortion. Very weak, she took a train back to Washington. Fennie was frightened, when he came home, to see her so pale; she was on her feet, her mouth set in an unreal smile; Fennie had the impression that Ann hated him.

She refused for a long time to speak of what had happened; sometimes her hand would creep to her stomach and rest there as if to warm it.

She and Fennie quarreled. Fennie suddenly complained that Ann had a piercing, Wisconsin accent.

"You never complained before!" Ann said in just that piercing voice.

"I never noticed it before."

Ann said, "I'll tell you what, Fennie. I'll kill myself. Will that make you happy?"

Fennie said, "Oh, shut up." Then he looked amazed. He said emotionally, "You can't let things fester. . . . I think you're still upset about the—er—abortion incident. But what's happened to our ideals, Annie-annie? You know we're not after the ordinary things in life. We're after big game."

There was something sexual and slatternly about Ann as she stood there in her despair; Fennie felt himself fascinated by her anew.

Two months later, she miscarried. The doctor said her system had been weakened by the abortion. Ann said, "I didn't tell you I was pregnant, Fennie, because I knew it would be all right." She talked as if she were proud of herself, but she would drop suddenly into soliloquies of self-accusation: "I'm a terrible fool—stupid, stupid. . . ." She was often apologetic: "I don't know if I'm coming or going. I'd lose my head if it wasn't fastened to my shoulders." When she drank, she would turn on Fennie: she twisted up her face and said, "You're a rat, Fennie. You're a genuine rat."

Fennie, quite pale and patient, said, "I know you're not yourself."

Ann replied, "No, I'm not myself. I'm your mother, Fennie, you rat."

Fennie said, "You haven't been your real self since the babies."

"Don't talk to me that way, you crypto-Fascist!" Ann cried. "Well, the honeymoon is over," she would say by way of apology. "I'm sorry. I said a lot of true things I shouldn't have said."

She would be silent and devoted for days. "Marriage is not easy," she would say to friends. "Fennie and I have made a good adjustment." She thought of Fennie as Men. "You know what men are like," she would say. She had been married four years. To have given a specific description of Fennie would have made her weep: *He is a smallish man who had a bad mother. He drinks too much because he's self-centered. He gets overexcited. He isn't always easy with me. He's tempted to bite his nails but he wants to believe analysis cured him and so when he starts to bite a nail he stops. But every couple of months he gives in and bites a nail or two. He is not very good with people. The skin over his chest is almost blue and there is a reddish-blue mark on his paunch where his belt rubs. His collarbones stick out.* If she had been asked to list his defects, she would have cried, "We have values! We don't look at people that way!"

If asked to describe herself, she would have said, "I'm something of an intellectual. My mind is very erratic, but I'm not ashamed of being a woman." If pressed, she might have added, "I'm a good wife to my husband. I don't bother him with my moods. I know when to say goodbye." She would have said that she and Fennie labored to "bring to birth" better "conditions" for the country. Her life and Fennie's were not at all meaningless.

Fennie's mother fell ill. Fennie went out to Milwaukee. When he returned to Washington, he said to Ann that his mother would like to see a grandchild. "Why don't we have a child?" Fennie said as if it had been Ann who had not wanted one.

"Fennie, a child?" Ann ran her finger across an invisible veil in front of her eyes. She smiled haltingly, one hand covering the corner of her mouth. "Is it fair to bring a child into the world just now, Fennie?" Her hands dropped into her lap. "I wouldn't mind having a child," she said.

She carried to term and gave birth to a daughter, named Louise, after Fennie's mother.

ANN CALLED the child Baby. She felt inside herself the baby's moods, her rages, appetite, sleepiness, and comfort; these feelings in Ann were like a model of an unusual solar system: blank and primitive, very unreasonable and private, an enormous space and a sun and a moon. Light leaped from the sun to the moon. She played—she did not fully know what she meant by the phrase—the sun-moon game with the baby, each taking turns being the sun, being the moon.

She was with the baby all the time; she never said goodbye to the baby. During the day, a colored maid came in; the maid was affectionate in a false and distant way, was proud, thought people were plotting against her. Ann hardly knew the maid was there.

Fennie was rarely home; he worked late at the office; he did not get in Ann's way. He said war was coming; he had lately begun to admire Harold Ickes and he modeled his speech on that of the secretary of the Department of the Interior. He said, "War is coming just as sure as God made little green apples."

The baby was colicky, and cried at night; Fennie would wake—he was not as tired as Ann and did not sleep with her desperate unconsciousness—and he would nudge Ann awake; at the thin edge where her mind met the night world was the baby's cry. Ann would leap out of bed—sometimes Fennie would laugh—and bound across the room, rebounding from chairs, even from the wall, to the baby's crib, her senses dulled, her pride dissolved in a preoccupation with digestion and infantile excrement.

It frightened and pleased her that motherhood was difficult. She looked into the mirror at her harassed face, her undone hair: she was doing all she could.

Fennie and Ann could not talk together as they had. They did not make love for three and a half months. Fennie was pale, his stomach was acting up. His best tenderness had an undertone of sarcasm. In a burst of concern, Ann, half asleep one evening, struggling to stay awake, gave herself to him. Since the baby came, she often thought Fennie was difficult—if not childish; he did not bother his head to understand how important it was for her to concentrate on being a good mother.

She wondered if Fennie would ever give up talking about the "male" and the "female" and D. H. Lawrence. He said, "It isn't good to fight the life of the instincts. . . . I don't think you read enough anymore, Ann." He thought she was not being a good sport. Ann no longer listened to Fennie when he spoke. He would say, "I heard about a book called *A New Look at Female Happiness*. Should I get hold of a copy? Will you read it?"

She replied, "I think I'll get some ivy for the window box."

She seemed mysterious and elusive to Fennie. She became pregnant again and announced the news to Fennie, and added, with her eyes large and in a calm voice, "We have to get a house."

Fennie said, "Ann, it's too soon for you. You know the doctor said it was too soon."

"I'm not going to do anything to this baby!"

Fennie said, "The baby, the baby. Women don't care about their husbands. Only their toys, their dolls . . . that's what Lawrence says a baby is to a woman."

"There's always suffering in a marriage," Ann said in a strangely light tone. "Everyone has it, Fennie," she said. "We have to buy a house."

She chose one across the river in Alexandria. It cost thirteen thousand dollars and was made of peach-colored brick; it had white stone windowsills. An old woman had lived her last years in it and it was shabby. Ann cleaned it room by room. The house possessed, Ann thought, an undeniable goodness.

Ann tried to be a better companion to Fennie. She read the newspapers: "Hitler is insane," she said; "you can tell by his face"; and she sat down when Fennie came home and had a drink with him and tried to get him to talk about the office. He could not get over how much having children had changed Ann. He did not trust her. "Don't bother your little head about the office," he said.

"The Germans bomb civilians, you know," Ann said vaguely, glancing around at her backyard. "People's houses . . ."

She bought almost no furniture; many of the rooms in her house remained empty, filled with sunlight during the day but empty. "This is not a time to become attached to material possessions," Ann said. Her house and her babies, the one born, the one not yet born, had to be taken care of and appreciated, but they could lead her astray. "People lose their moral judgment and turn into appeasers because of possessions," she said with a kind of grief.

The doctor said she was doing too much housework, going up and down stairs too often.

She said, "I look like a dope fiend. I'm letting everything slide."

France was falling. Ann was in her seventh month. Fennie came home early one afternoon and told her the Germans had entered Paris. "The French didn't stop them at the Marne this time?" Ann asked. She said, "We'll have to fight now, won't we, Fennie? Are they bombing refugees?"

She did not like to complain or be self-indulgent during a time of crisis. It was a difficult and premature birth. The baby, a girl, was healthy but very small. Ann did not recover properly, and the doctor said she would have to have an operation. "You won't be able to have any more children."

Ann refused to permit the operation. "I'm strong as a horse," she said to Fennie. "I'll be all right. Don't be a worrywart."

Fennie told her their elder daughter kept asking for Ann. He had tears in his eyes, and he was angry, too. "Why are you so stubborn? You're the stubbornest person I ever knew." He said, "Children aren't everything."

The doctor said to her, "You are a very high-strung, unreasonable woman."

"Doctor, look at your peasant woman," Ann said. "She—"

The doctor said, "Do you know anything about the death rate among peasant women?"

"Is it high," asked Ann, the statistician, "if the women aren't overworked?"

"All women are overworked," the doctor said dryly. "If they're not, they become hypochondriac. I can't let you go home," the doctor said. "You can hemorrhage at any time."

Ann said to the doctor, "My husband always wanted a son."

The doctor shrugged.

Ann thought of her house and the two waiting children. She said, "I guess he will just have to do without."

The doctor said, "You just keep your sense of humor, Ann, and everything will be all right."

Five days after the operation, Ann went home.

IT SEEMED to Ann that Fennie was as stirred and uplifted by the excitement of the war as he had once been by her. He was distended with excitement: "People don't realize that *this* is *Götterdämmerung*," he said. He drank at the office to keep himself going. It tired her that Fennie felt important because he was involved behind the scenes. She wanted to tell Fennie to watch the way he spoke; she needed to draw from him—she put no name to it—a sense of being worthwhile, because she could no longer draw it from herself.

She often did not make sense when she talked. She said tactfully, "You know, the children see you when you talk as if you *like* the war. . . ." She halted. He's a good husband, she thought. It seemed to her silly suddenly to blame him, just as it was silly to blame children—everyone knew what children were like. Goodness was not something people talked about, and anyway, she had lost her sense of moral direction. Nothing in marriage was ever settled. Marriage was not a completed state.

Fennie broke the silence. He said, "Dearest, what are you trying to tell me?" She turned away; he was being patient with her. He was a more successful human being than she was; he was a good bureaucrat. She was not certain if she liked him anymore. She stuck out her lips. Fennie said again, "Dearest, what are you trying to tell me?"

"I've forgotten," Ann said, and gave a small, placating laugh.

She rarely mentioned her feelings, but when she did—"I'm sad," or "Fennie, I don't know why I go on living"—she spoke almost lightly so that it would not cause a quarrel. Fennie would say, "You should get out more. You think about yourself too much."

It was as if there had been a long, long struggle between them and Fennie had won it and she didn't care much.

She followed her Negro maid from room to room. She said, "Last night I had the oddest dream. I was in China. I was a little, tiny, doll-like, *perfect* Chinese woman—" She meant one who had never undergone an operation, who was pretty and hopeful and high-spirited. "I think you missed a dust kitty under that chair, Mary Lou," Ann said.

Mary Lou turned a sad, furtive, half-psychotic gaze toward Ann, toward a spot to the right and above Ann's ear, so that Ann remained an unseen, bleached presence. "Nobody ever said I wasn' a good cleanin' woman. I don' lie, I don' steal, I don' owe a dollar to no man alive—"

"I'll do it. Hand me the broom. Let me tell you about my dream," Ann said as she swept. "I had a terrible husband. I was a slave. I was black and blue from head to toe, all my children died of impetigo or beriberi except one, so I ran away. I took my baby with me. I left it in a railroad station, just for a moment. Then a bomb fell—I saw it like a tear falling. It exploded; the air rang and rang like a crystal glass when you tap it. A man was on top of me, but it wasn't a man, it was a piece of wood—you know how dreams are. And my baby was crying in the

ruins of the railroad station—have you seen that famous photograph—"
Mary Lou denied having stolen any photograph. "No, no," Ann
said, "I'm talking about a photograph that was in all the newspapers
years ago."

"I wouldn' want one of your photographs noway," Mary Lou said,
smiling richly. "I got photographs of my own."

"Mary Lou," Ann said. "Don't you understand? I would never accuse
you." Ann trembled with sympathy for Mary Lou, whose sorrows had
cramped her mind. "But listen to my dream: The railroad station was
burning, but the *Panay* was coming to rescue us, and Wallace Beery was
the captain, only it wasn't Wallace Beery, it was Mussolini. . . . Mary
Lou," Ann said, "you never tell me your dreams."

"I has only religious dreams," Mary Lou replied.

Mary Lou's skin was rough, black, exotic; she had a foreign, sweet
odor, like soap. Ann followed Mary Lou with her eyes. One day Ann
stubbed her toe; she cried out, lifted the hurt foot, stood, her eyes closed,
her leg lifted, balanced like a heron on one foot. Mary Lou said, "Did
you hurt you'self ?" She uttered a low, crooning noise, "Ooo-lee-doo,
oo-lee-doo, did you hurt you'self," and put her arms around Ann. Ann
leaned against her, but then she said, "I'm not going to be one of those
women who turn into parasites on their maid. You have a life of your
own, Mary Lou." She pulled away from Mary Lou. "Oh, we in America
owe the Negro so much!" she said.

Mary Lou grew more careless after that; in one day, she broke a dish,
a glass, a rung off the back of a dining-room chair. She was rude and
shouted at the children; she pilfered Ann's sheets. Ann told Fennie, and
Fennie fired the maid. He said, "We're doing this for *your* self-respect,
Mary Lou."

S O M E T I M E S , on the street in Washington, Ann saw the new Selec-
tive Service inductees, freckled farm boys among them, a few with
reddish-yellow hair; she could imagine what the smell of such a boy's
body would be like, the naiveté of his conversation.

Ann and Fennie went to parties, informal parties, usually held outdoors, in someone's backyard. Often, at these affairs, the men in the
earlier, soberer portion of the evening would congregate at one end of
the yard to discuss the war and the government. The women chattered
about servants and prices.

Ann drank a lot because she wanted to be drunk. Then, when it grew late and the moon had risen and the men rejoined the women and boozy versions of friendliness, nostalgia, innocence, and seduction appeared, she hinted at her despair to whoever approached her. She often sat alone, bleak-eyed and erect.

A man, his face a lopsided plate swimming in the broken dark, put his hand on Ann's knee. Ann saw it was Fennie, and he was drunk, too. He said in his Harold Ickes voice, "How's life treating you, sweetie pie?"

To Ann's right, a voice said, "For my money, far and away your best right-handed pitcher in the major leagues today is Bucky *Walters.* . . ." Ann said, "Life is black. The Fascists are coming. I wish I was dead."

"Oh, you're in a bad mood," Fennie mumbled, and made his way off into the seesawing flurry, the feathery, flapping geese wings of voices at the party.

AFTER Pearl Harbor, Fennie worked so late at his office that he had a bed moved in and sometimes slept there. Ann never contemplated infidelity; it would make Fennie unhappy. On a cold Thursday night, he telephoned her and said he was in love with his secretary.

IV

ANN THOUGHT it was bureaucratic of Fennie to break the news to her over the telephone, and she meant to be rude. She said— Fennie shared his secretary stenographically with a man named Aswell—"Doesn't Aswell mind?"

Fennie said, "You don't care. You never cared."

"Me?" Ann said, but he had already hung up.

He telephoned back to shout that he was nearly forty years old and had high blood pressure and deserved a little happiness before he died.

He telephoned a third time: He wanted to bring the girl to the house; there was no reason why he, Ann, and the girl should not discuss the situation like civilized human beings, he said. Ann said, "All right, Fennie. Anything to give you a little happiness before you die."

Ann had not realized to what extent despair had wrapped itself around her spirit until the girl came to the house that evening with Fennie. She was Southern, young, and timid, and Ann minded terribly that the girl was brainless and had soft, plump legs—"But her legs are neither here nor there," Ann said to herself—and she minded the girl's compliments on the house and furniture. "What a truly lovely old house this is," the girl said tensely. "This is the girl I love," Fennie said. Ann said she was perfectly willing to divorce Fennie. He said—in front of the girl—that Ann was in no fit condition to make a decision. Ann said, "Then why are we talking? Why did you bring the girl here?" Fennie said Ann was making a scene, and the recriminations began.

THE PSYCHOANALYST'S office was not far from the Mall. Ann said, her hand partly shielding her eyes, "My life's in pieces. I'm married to a bastard. I don't know why things have turned out so badly for me. I was happy once. There was a man—he was a golden-haired working-man in Illinois. . . . It was the only love I ever knew." She went on about Walter.

The analyst said, "I think we can say you have problems that need, that *deserve* treatment." He was an affluent-looking man, not very tall, with a full body, not very fat, with gray hair, not very thick. He suggested, somehow, childhood; he shed an aroma of it—the darkened room, the leather couch, the privacy suggested those secret places, under beds, in garages, inside a closet, where children met. He spoke slowly and warmly: "I think we can say that no one should be as alone as you are."

The second time she saw him, she was uncomfortable, and he said, "Analysis is not easy; it is not for everyone."

Ann began to cry. "Neither is love," she said.

Session after session, for the first dozen weeks, she cried. She apologized for crying so much.

"It is all right if you cry here," the doctor said over and over, with the same little smile.

One day, Ann cried, "But I was happy *once!*"

The doctor said, "You were happy—the happiness you refer to, was it more in your body or in your mind?"

"Why—it wasn't in my mind!" Ann cried. "I knew in my mind it couldn't last!"

The next day, she said to the doctor, "You're very, very sensitive."

The doctor said, "There is a sympathy between us. We are congenial."

He dressed like a social climber, but Ann liked him, and told him so.

The doctor told her he hoped she was making a transference. "Your feelings about me are a major part of your analysis—because *they* are not in the past."

She said her feelings toward the doctor were warm. He said yes, that was a step toward transference, and smiled.

Ann did not talk about Walter anymore. She did not sleep with Fennie. When the doctor asked her if she ever thought about taking a lover, she said, "Where would I get the time?"

The doctor asked if there was no one she was attracted to, and Ann said there was a man who ran a filling station in Alexandria—"But I don't want to make a habit of the working class." She said, "I'm attracted to you—mildly. As a matter of fact," she added, "no one ever seduces *me.*" She broke off. "I'm not the sort of woman who gets crushes on her doctor." She said, "Why aren't you a famous psychoanalyst? Is there something wrong with you?" she whispered.

The doctor said proudly, "I do not belong to any organized camp. I walk my own path. There is no publicity *apparat* to inflate my reputation. You think I do not get enough recognition? You would like to be prouder of me?"

"Yes," Ann whispered.

Long after she had left the office each day, she went on speaking to him—until two or three o'clock in the morning, hardly pausing even when she heard Fennie let himself into the house and get ready for bed on the second floor; Ann slept on the third floor, or rather lay awake on the third, too interested in what she had to say to the doctor to sleep.

She said to the doctor, "Last night I dreamed you and I lived alone in a pretty house on a hill. It was in the country. We were very good friends. It was a happy dream." She giggled. "Can you imagine?" She burst into tears: "I'm overintense."

He spoke to her of the collective unconscious, of introversion, of the libido, of the superego. They discussed her dreams. They discussed her transference. They discussed her passionate nature.

At first, she could not believe it when she began to lust after the doctor. She felt—he gave her the symbol in a discussion of a dream—the heavy roots of wings enter her back. She talked about Walter, and the farm boy, and Fennie, and it seemed to her the wings beat restlessly, clubbed her about the head. She suffered an erotic concussion.

The doctor said to her she did not understand transference, that she was transposing to the doctor feelings meant for her father: "The incest taboo confuses you." He said it was all right for her to lustafterhim—lust was not unhealthy. The doctor said, "You are living out an archetypal pattern in your life."

When she slept, she slept badly. She dreamed. Even when she did not recognize the doctor in her dreams, he pointed out that he was present: the windows in her dream that she threw herself out of, that she tried to open, were him; his first name, as she knew, was Winthrop.

"It would be nice," Ann said, staring at the ceiling, "to have a sexual thing with a really perceptive man, a man I could talk to."

"You are experimenting with one of the modes used by patients to interfere with transference."

Ann asked, "Am I ugly?"

The doctor said she had a distinctive charm.

Ann took a deep breath. "How ugly am I?"

"You are not ugly."

"How far am I from being beautiful?"

The doctor said she was asking a meaningless question.

Ann began to cry. "I think I'm too old for decency," she said. "No man wants a woman as she really is. Men want women to be imaginary."

The doctor said, "You are under severe tension. The middle years are difficult. Marriages last too long. Well, our time is up. Dry your eyes. I will see you on Thursday."

She said, "There is a lie in this analysis. You take my money. You make me feel terrible things. It's like a terrible love affair."

The doctor said, "Your analogy is not a true one. You do not want to go to bed with me. You want to go to bed with your *father.*" Ann made a hissing noise. "We analysts know that transference is not love."

Ann said, "You should never have interfered with me. You never intended to be sincere."

Another day, she said, "If there's a Hell, there's a place in it for women like me."

"Now, now," the doctor said. "Let's not exaggerate."

Ann said, "No one else's face is real to me. If you loved me, I would never make a scene. I wouldn't bother you. I wouldn't get in your way. . . ."

The doctor said, "Let us examine what you said. *You promise to be good.* Here we have the psychological heart of Christianity: the libido in a state of longing will promise anything. Christianity represents a great psychological advance over paganism. It reproduces the *family*. It invented romantic love. Is this not why?"

"I suppose so," Ann said dully.

"Paganism allows to the woman only the god's *animal* presence. A woman deserves more than that."

Ann said, with tears in her eyes, "I was happy with Walter."

The doctor said, "But what does it mean when a woman wants *only* the animal presence? *It means she hates herself and desires to be superior to the analyst.*"

Ann laughed; then she cried. She said, "I'm not sure I understand about Christianity. Tell me more about Christianity. You're such a moral man. You're a *good* man."

The doctor closed his eyes and said, "I am so glad you wish at last to meet me halfway." The next day, he said, "Yesterday we made a breakthrough—we came to an end of childish egoism."

THE DOCTOR told her she had always been inhibited because it had been dangerous for her as a female child to have feelings. "But now you have been freed. You are ready to be more giving. You have overcome much of your self-involvement. You can be your womanly self—warm and sympathetic. . . . Tell me," the doctor said sternly, "you are feeling well? You are feeling happy?"

Ann could not bring herself ever to disappoint him. She said, "Yes. I'm *much* better. You *are* a wonderful doctor."

Fennie came home two evenings a week to see the children. Ann noticed his exhaustion and said in a voice very like the doctor's, "Fennie, is something troubling you at this time?"

Fennie said that the Department was falling apart, two of his memos had been sidetracked that week; that the Russians and the English, the left and right wings, and the State Department had factions in the Department. "It's a mess," Fennie said dejectedly.

"Fennie," Ann said, "that's not very different from what you've always said about the Department. We have to go deeper. Let's try and find out what you're trying to hide."

"The Department won't recover from this mess," Fennie said. "The end of the war is coming, and no one's loyal to the Department anymore. Franklyn's diddled everyone. He's a disappointed man. He didn't make under secretary; he has a grudge. There's no one to turn to. He's got everyone lined up. They're playing footsie with the right wing. The future is being undermined, and there's nothing anyone can do."

Ann sat quite still. Slowly, she raised her eyes to Fennie's face. She was possessed by, if not the spirit, then the style, of the doctor. "There must be a lot of men who don't like Franklyn," she said. "Tell me, Fennie, why don't you form your own conspiracy?"

S H E   S A I D to the doctor, "It's better if Fennie and I are friendly. It's much better for the children." She wondered if the analyst was listening. If he was preoccupied, she did not want to intrude. She became tongue-tied. She said, "I don't know what to talk about."

The doctor said, "How is your novel coming?"

"My novel?"

"I'm speaking metaphorically," the doctor said.

"A metaphor? What metaphor?"

"I am being too abstruse," the doctor said—patronizingly, Ann thought.

"Perhaps you've mixed me up with another patient," Ann said.

"We must not overreact," the doctor said gently.

"You have such a healthy ego," Ann said, and turned her head to the wall.

That evening, Fennie telephoned to say he wanted to stop by the house, to talk to her. "Two days in a row?" she said ironically.

She was sitting on the second floor, in the living room, when Fennie came in, with his briefcase, and sat down and said the suggestion she'd given him had led to complications: "There's a lot of interest, but we've got to have a safe place to talk. You know what the office is like. . . ." Yes, she did, Ann said; the secretaries eavesdrop, she said maliciously. Fennie wanted to have the men to the house.

Ann said, "Why not?"

Fennie said he was worried that news of what he was up to would leak out and the fat would be in the fire.

"So what?" Ann said. "This is an *honest* conspiracy." She said, "Publicity might help—the fence-sitters will rally around if they know there's a lesser evil. People are always on the lookout for a really lesser evil."

"Analysis seems to have sharpened your wits," Fennie said.

Ann looked at Fennie. A husband was on the whole a lesser evil than a psychoanalyst; she had no real hope of finding a happy love anywhere.

When she saw the doctor, her feelings for him struck her anew, they were so strong, so unyielding still. She said, "You have to play with people's minds, it's all propaganda, love is in the imagination." She said, "That's the way it is. Fennie has no mystery."

She said, "It doesn't do much good to hold a man's feet of clay against him. A woman who loves can't go looking for a lesser evil—she wouldn't know a lesser evil if she found one. . . . I'm always trying to grow an apple orchard in a flowerpot." Her love for the doctor was colored now by hopelessness, devotion, resignation.

She lay still while the doctor said she was worried about acting as a hostess for Fennie. "The incest taboo in your case has become a flirtation taboo. Therefore, social life is impossible for you."

At five that afternoon, she was at home and heard a car drive up: it was Fennie with a colleague. Ann shook hands dreamily with him when he entered the living room; she let her glance linger; her eyelids drooped with sexuality. It had been a year and a half since she had slept with anyone. Fennie's colleague smiled, pleased by the welcome he'd received.

Ann said to the doctor the next day, "Last night there were five men at the house. I flirted with all of them. I thought I was exaggerating about their liking me, but two of them followed me to the kitchen and made propositions. Not at the same time. Fennie noticed. He didn't say anything. He was drunk. After I went to bed, I was thinking of you, I was thinking about analysis. I wanted—I wished I was about to have a— I—" She wanted to say that lust was not the word to describe her desire; she said, "I wasn't—I wasn't— I was in a *mood.*" She cried, "I wish you would explain it to me! Women's desire is so much worse than men's!"

"What do you mean by that?" the doctor asked.

"I don't know. I thought you might explain it to me."

The doctor said, "Freud remarked toward the end of his life that he had never been able to discover what it was that women really wanted."

Ann laughed dutifully because it would please the doctor. She said, "I slept with Fennie."

"Did you do it to punish me?" the doctor asked.

She said, "I don't know. Maybe. All the doors in the house were open, to catch the breeze. I heard the children; I heard Fennie tossing—he was making noises in his sleep. He called my name. At least, I think it was my name. It could have been a kind of snore—'Ann' or—" She imitated a sound, stertorous n's, drawn out. "I know the body and mind are one," she said loyally, "but it wasn't like that. It was a—a bodily thing."

She climbed out of bed and stood. She tiptoed to the second floor; she whispered, "Fennie, what is it?" She said to the doctor, "He didn't answer. He really was asleep." She said, "I felt like giggling but I analyzed my emotions and decided I was nervous and didn't really want to giggle—I made myself stop and think about my motives. They seemed all right. I thought, Everybody else does what they want. He didn't misunderstand. He was asleep at first, and then he was only half awake, and when he really woke up he didn't talk. I don't know if he ever was really awake. Yes. He was. Afterward he said, 'What do—' No. He was grammatical. He said, 'To what do I owe this—' " She thought, she strove to recall his speech. " '—this token of affection?' And then I did giggle a little bit." She laughed, coaxingly. She said quickly, "I'm sure I did it a little to get even with you. And besides, I was starved for—for $that$. " She said, "I don't know why I use euphemisms with you. I never used to use them."

The doctor said, "You are not rebellious anymore."

She said, "I don't want to sleep with strangers—there's no room in my life for strangers."

The next day she said, "You know what I feel like? I feel like a sea gull. I've had to fly for years and years in a storm, but now I can rest. I've found help. I've found you. The steep waves won't drown me."

The doctor said, "What a lovely image for the stage in analysis you have reached! It projects so beautifully your wish to spread your newly strong wings and fly into maturity."

Ann was silent. There was no end to what that son of a bitch expected of her; now that son of a bitch wanted her to be cured.

One night Fennie said, "Are you ever coming to visit me again after I'm asleep?" Ann said, "Why don't we talk things over, Fennie?" But Fennie said she should save her words for her analyst. He was abrupt in a not very bitter way. He and Ann went to bed together. Ann said, "My own, my very own Fennie." He stiffened; he seemed put out. Ann said in a comradely voice, "My pal Fennie," and he relaxed.

She said to the doctor, "What I have is, I have a lot of nothing!"

The doctor did not comment. She could not see him. He was only a presence.

She cried on the streetcar going home.

She played with her children for a little while and then sent them upstairs with the maid, a Norwegian refugee girl. Fennie was bringing more men home. He was in one of his most bastardly moods. He came down to the kitchen to get ice. Ann was making sandwiches. She said, "Don't get overexcited. Nobody wants to deal with an overexcited conspirator."

"Get off my back," Fennie said.

He went upstairs. Ann sliced tomatoes for the sandwiches; the tomatoes looked like fat, malformed hearts. It was going to rain. Outside, the wind puffed and rustled, fell silent, started up again. Ann rushed out into the backyard; she uttered a muted, gooselike honking, an *onh, onh, onh,* a sound that harmonized with the wind, half humor, half breathlessness. She gathered up two dolls, some tin teacups and saucers—dime-store toys her daughters played with. The light was strange and pure; Ann thought of it as a mystic butter spread on the earth's bread. From the house came the sound of Fennie shouting. Ann hurried inside, dropped the toys into a box; she hurried in the kitchen; she gathered the sandwiches already made and piled them on a plate. She hurried down the dark hallway and climbed the stairs to the living room. Fennie was still shouting. To control her fright, she pretended the living room was full of psychoanalysts.

She said, "I have sandwiches. Two kinds. Swiss cheese," she said, "and lettuce and tomato." She felt the tension in the room focus on her—then the tension broke.

"The idea of food is relaxing to worried men," Ann said to the doctor. "I'm a help to Fennie now in a way that he understands."

The doctor said, "It is a beautiful moment when a patient achieves objectivity in her self-evaluations."

Ann said, "Fennie still sees that girl occasionally." She decided on Fennie's motives: "He doesn't want to give in too easily. . . . He wants to punish his mother for needing her. . . ." She spoke with triumph, like a successful detective in a murder mystery, and in psychoanalytic terms, like the doctor: "Fennie's highly Oedipal—"

"An excellent insight," the doctor said.

Ann said with good-natured malice, "I see through Fennie, but I don't mind." She said to the doctor, "I owe my new maturity to you." Her warmth was tempered by open irony now, life being what it was.

Early in November, she told the doctor, "He doesn't see the girl anymore, but he hasn't confessed it. He spends two nights a week out. He wants me to think he's still seeing her."

"How do you know he's not?"

"I can tell in bed," Ann said triumphantly.

Ann said, "Fennie and I might place our libidos more firmly if we had a grand get-it-off-our-chests reconciliation scene, but I'm afraid Fennie's telling me how he felt about the girl might cause me to have a violent ego reaction."

She was enthusiastic about psychoanalysis, evangelical. But she did not like to think back over her analysis; she did not want to remember the agony. "You woke me from a living death." She said, "My chief pleasure comes from my home life. My children mean more to me than anything." She said, "Fennie is the keystone of the family hearth." She said, "I can live in and cope with real-life situations."

Ann said to the doctor, "Analysis is the first relationship I have ever carried through." She said, "The way I threw myself at you—I completely misunderstood transference." She laughed. She said, "This is a little like it was after Walter, except that all the neurotic patterns have been broken." She said, "You were always as much a Walter figure to me as a father figure. Of course I realize Walter was a father figure." She said, "Life is war, I guess. Affection makes it bearable." She said affection itself was one of the cruelties, like death—one of the perils, along with the egos of other people. She said, "I ought to write a novel about men."

The doctor said, "Patients never forget what they think are their doctor's blunders."

"Reality is reality," Ann said.

The doctor sighed. "You are handling yourself very well," he said.

Ann said, "Perspective is what matters. . . . I try to be objective and amused. . . . I am very fond of my husband. After all, that's the point of analysis, isn't it—if you can be fond of your analyst, you can be fond of anyone?"

The doctor said, "Talking to you, seeing you so *womanly*, makes me wonder how some people can think Freud was mistaken."

He said in a voice that imparted parental reassurance while at the same time establishing a lack of faith in her, "You can always come back and see me when you get into trouble." He said, "I want to make you a little present: there will be no charge for this hour."

"You'll make me cry," Ann said—she wasn't afraid of ambiguity.

Later, she found that she missed the doctor and Walter both.

V

F o r a long time after analysis, Ann thought of honesty as being the ability to admit the paramount importance of toilet training in the formation of character. She thought of herself as having a "relationship" with Fennie and "relationships"—necessarily "ambivalent"—with her daughters. She said to herself, "I think things through." Ann did not find that analysis had prepared her for life—it had been a tunnel out of the shadows into the here. She was forceful. She imitated a woman from Philadelphia who served with her on three charitable committees and had a way of imposing her will. "Hoo-de-hoo hooey to that!" the woman would say forcefully. Ann took it up: "Hoo-de-hoo hooey!" she would cry.

She avoided mental intimacy with anyone. She became bored and restless and then angry if Fennie talked about ideas or her mind too much. She did not like to talk about ideas; she and Fennie were bohemians and liberals. She who had rarely gossiped when she was young gossiped now. She liked only to talk about people. She was delighted by anecdotes. She wanted her daughters "free to develop themselves," she said—"healthy." She tried not to invest too much emotion in them.

Fennie gardened and played bridge twice a week with men from the Department. Ann joined a bird-watching group. "Ann's a whizbang at warblers," Fennie said; he talked like an Ivy Leaguer more and more the older he grew, and it was never clear how much or how little irony he intended. "Fennie has the touch when it comes to delphiniums," Ann said; she retained her Middle Western accent; it took people a while to realize she, too, was ironic.

Fennie never talked about love. Ann said, "We're not like people who have been psychoanalyzed and talk of nothing else." She said, "Fennie and I fulfill each other's needs."

She was ambitious for Fennie's sake. She angled to advance his interests and the interests of her family. She used her plainness; people trusted her. She spoke dryly of "life's combats—blood on the teeth." She was a dry woman—that was her own opinion of herself. She had no daydreams.

Something they did constantly, she and Fennie, was to measure themselves and the way they lived against other couples' methods; a large part of living consisted of convincing themselves that they deserved to be the better part of any comparison. She said, "I'm as happy as any woman has a right to be."

When Ann was forty-five years old, she began to feel unwell, angry, and oppressed. "I've been a servant all my life," she said. She argued, "Women are the true lower classes." She consulted a gynecologist. Ann had expected to enter old age without difficulty because of the operation she'd had before the war, but the gynecologist told her she had been mistaken. "You mean I have to go through the whole song and dance?" Ann said angrily.

Fennie told their daughters to be careful of Ann—"Your mother isn't herself."

One morning when an autumn light filled the kitchen, and the maid, an Austrian immigrant (a telephone lineman had broken her heart, or, as Ann believed, her ego), was scurrying tragically between the stove and the back porch—the back porch had been, Ann put it, "fixed up as our eating area: it's not just a dining area," she would explain; "we breakfast and lunch there, too"; her wit was of that sort that year—and her daughters were quarreling, Ann thought she could not bear to be in despair again.

Ann said to the maid, to her daughters, to Fennie, "Be big! Be big! Be big!"

She walked out of the kitchen, out the front door of the house and down the street. Fennie told the maid and the girls to stay where they were, and he hurried after Ann. He caught up to her before she reached the corner. He said, "Do you feel nervous today?"

"It's not all just in my mind, Fennie!" Ann cried.

Fennie mixed a touch of complaint with solicitude: "You don't feel well?"

Scornfully, Ann said, "Nothing's ever just in the body, either, Fennie!"

Fennie murmured, "The neighbors."

Ann said, "I mean it, Fennie. I'm tired of being small. I don't care about the neighbors."

Fennie chewed on his lip. "No one's had any breakfast," he said.

"Be big," Ann said. "Fast. Fasting's good for you."

Fennie smiled. "Come back to the house. We'll all be big."

He was joking, but to placate Ann he tried being bolder and larger;

so did the girls. Nobility became a family style; Ann worried that her family seemed foolish and doomed. "Why can't you be realistic?" she would cry. If it was not the younger girl's refusing to mention the pains in her stomach that turned out to be appendicitis, it was the elder's confessing the following year that she was not a virgin: "Mother, he was so sad." That was when Ann cried, "Why can't you be realistic?" The children continued to quarrel: "Mummie," said the younger, "Louise is being small and won't lend me her blouse." The nobility of soul Ann longed for appeared, came into focus, grew frail, transparent—was it there or not? She did not know. She thought, Once I was a woman; now I am objective and amused. But at moments the souls of her daughters and of her husband did seem to blossom into largeness of feeling.

Ann would burst out laughing, seemingly for no reason.

"What's funny?" Fennie would ask.

"We are," Ann said. "I am. Everything is." At first, she laughed alone, but after a while Fennie laughed with her.

They drank, the two of them, together, heavily. Ann had two martinis before dinner, and then a succession of highballs until bedtime. She would become benevolent or quarrelsome—Fennie could not predict her mood.

Ann went to see an endocrinologist. She said, "Actually, my condition is mild, but lately I've developed an upsetting symptom. I have—ah—desires for men in public life." She spoke quickly: "It used to be particularly Anthony Eden but now it's Nehru." She said, "I don't like upsetting my husband." The doctor gave her an injection. Ann said, "It's so silly." After the injection she felt faint. "Being a woman isn't easy," she told the doctor. He was not a bad-looking man.

At the time when the furor over Communists in Washington was very great, Ann said, "Fennie, will they dig up my old membership in the Party? Will they hurt you?"

Fennie said, "It was a long time ago and you changed your name—when you married; it isn't likely anyone would remember such a marginal member as you were—"

Ann said, "I'm glad I was a Communist! I didn't just talk. I tried to do something for mankind!"

Fennie said crossly, "You were an idiot then, you're an idiot now, you'll always be an idiot, and you can't hold your liquor worth a good goddam."

When they were tired of quarreling and of being defiant—safely, with each other—they went up to bed and, frightened, fell asleep holding hands.

After the Army-McCarthy hearings, Ann's youthful dereliction not having been discovered, Fennie took Ann to New York City for a four-day vacation. They stayed at the Biltmore and went to the theater and to a few museums. Fennie laughed at himself; he said, "We're on a real spree."

He said she was a pretty good wife for him.

They always walked to the theater. Ann fussed that Fennie would catch cold. She was an unpretentious, odd-looking, ugly-handsome woman. She admired New York; it seemed to her to be a city where people did things for amusement.

When she and Fennie returned to Alexandria, to the empty house—the girls away at college—and Ann was alone and began to think, she felt a mild carelessness; she was not young anymore, not cautious. Her thoughts more and more dwelt on Fennie. At first, Fennie was taken aback by the new warmth—not quite indiscreet but not discreet, either—of her interest in him. He said she surprised him.

Ann said, making a joke of herself, "I'll tell you my thinking on the subject, Fennie. At our age, we're obscene anyway. We may as well enjoy ourselves."

In bed, Ann was sometimes shaken by alternate fits of laughter and weeping.

One evening she and Fennie went to a dinner party. Afterward, Fennie accused her of drinking too much and sitting with her skirt above her knees. "A woman your age with her skirt rucked up," he said.

Ann said nothing. She wore a vacuous look and would not speak. Fennie came home from the office early the next day; he was fascinated by her mood. He kept touching her, not in a gentle but in a restless, edgy way; Ann responded with taut, difficult glances. It was the maid's day off. Ann was washing up. Fennie said, "Let me help with the dishes." He and Ann worked with a silent efficiency and familiarity with each other that slowly revealed itself to be erotic.

Ann felt that she cultivated her days and the nights with Fennie, a little Netherlands.

She wished she had a good memory for jokes. She wanted to make Fennie laugh. She thought, He really is a very masculine man.

She did not want to be honest; she wanted to be sympathetic. She wanted him to enjoy himself; she admired him. He was good-looking in a heavyset way; his opinions were important in the affairs of the Department.

Fennie said, "Ann, what are you up to? A little middle-aged romance?"

Charlotte, the younger daughter, home for Thanksgiving—Louise was visiting her roommate's family in Vermont—said of Ann and Fennie to her friends, "They're very close. They're very unclinging as parents."

When Ann or Fennie forgot and was selfish or too casual, Fennie, susceptible to doubts now, and Ann, sensitive again, hated each other. But then the atmosphere between them would shift into a familiar comfort, somewhat apologetic in tone—as if they were humbled by a sense of the compromises each knew the other was making.

If Fennie was worn out or restless, Ann might be sulky or she might be patient. Fennie became exasperated if Ann paid him too much attention, or if when he was home she gave too much attention to her reading and not enough to him. It was roulette.

At moments when the responsiveness of herself to Fennie and his, reluctantly, to her became intense, Ann would experience an indefinably numbing, even shameful happiness; she would think, My God, it's still going on.

She did not really expect it to happen, the excitement, the somewhat dry, angular passion of argument, of companionship, and of sensuality. When it did happen, its recurrence struck her like the rattle of a drum. The passions of the middle-aged were strong, she thought, because the middle-aged had an empty space inside themselves; inside, she was as empty as a parade ground across which the shattering rattle could resound without obstruction.

Fennie began, only a little at first, to show traces of a Middle Western accent again in his speech. He took to calling the house from the office, once or twice a day, never at the same times; he would ask Ann what she was doing and she would tell him. In the evening again he would ask her what she had done during the day, checking up on her.

She made scenes when he was late to dinner: "If you know you're going to be late, call me. Don't make me worry!"

She did not want him to be able to read her emotions. If he was certain of her feelings, he might become bored; he might wish her to be different; it was best to be elusive, hypocritical, to seem to have as many moods as possible, to practice sleight of hand.

It startled her, she thought it funny, that the emotional side of a love affair should so quickly come to outweigh the physical, to take precedence, to guide it, to make it, if not minor, then lesser.

She was often tired and took an hour's rest in the afternoon. Sometimes when she was resting, she thought. It seemed to her that just as when a person talked to himself he let himself exaggerate and dream in a way that was a little insane, so what went on between a wife and husband was like that solitary lunacy: a wife and husband talked to themselves, alone together, the world outside.

She had come to an age where she did not value herself or her time so highly that she wanted anything better or other than what she had. She thought it wasn't marriage so much as a love affair complicated by marriage that she was living.

Fennie wanted to go away with Ann, on a trip, to get away from everything and everyone, to be alone with Ann. He thought of her as a subtle and clever companion, and not at all a disappointment to him.

They went to England first. Standing in front of the stony grace of the Elgin Marbles, she said, "Oh, Fennie, you're so good to me." That night, she said, "Fennie, don't take too long in the shower."

"Don't nag," he said.

(The cleverer she was, the happier they were, the more he expected of her.)

In Brussels, it seemed to Ann that there were so many states to be passed through in the course of a day spent with Fennie—appetite and surprise, curiosity, peevishness (glossed over), middle-aged passion, and unexpected sorrow—that there was no place and no peace wide enough to hold her and Fennie.

Ann knew now—away from home, grateful to Fennie—that she loved him. In Paris, she memorized the shape of his hands. In Rome, she filed away the look of his eyes squinting in the sun on the Palatine. "A Man in Sunlight," she labeled the sight of him waving to her from one of the upper tiers of the Colosseum. The adventures of traveling and the patterns of her and Fennie's feelings involved Ann in a tension and watchfulness that seemed to her now the outward symptoms of love.

In the Greek Islands, she and Fennie rode on donkeys up a winding track to a hilltop temple, honey-colored and in ruins. Ann watched the sunlight move like melting porcelain across Fennie's white shirt. Far away, on the Aegean, a large white ship with a single funnel shouldered

Innocence

I *Orra at Harvard*

ORRA PERKINS was a senior. Her looks were like a force that struck you. Truly, people on first meeting her often involuntarily lifted their arms as if about to fend off the brightness of the apparition. She was a somewhat scrawny, tuliplike girl of middling height. To see her in sunlight was to see Marxism die. I'm not the only one who said that. It was because seeing someone in actuality who had such a high immediate worth meant you had to decide whether such personal distinction had a right to exist or if she belonged to the state and ought to be shadowed in, reduced in scale, made lesser, laughed at.

Also, it was the case that you had to be rich and famous to set your hands on her; she could not fail to be a trophy, and the question was whether the trophy had to be awarded on economic and political grounds or whether chance could enter in.

I was a senior, too, and ironic. I had no money. I was without lineage. It seemed to me Orra was proof that life was a terrifying phenomenon of surface immediacy. She made any idea I had of psychological normalcy or of justice absurd since normalcy was not as admirable or as desirable as Orra; or rather she was normalcy and everything else was a falling off, a falling below; and justice was inconceivable if she, or someone equivalent to her if there was an equivalent once you had seen her, would not sleep with you. I used to create general hilarity in my room by shouting her name at my friends and then breaking up into laughter, gasping out, "God, we're so small-time." It was grim that she existed and I had not had her. One could still prefer a more ordinary girl but not for simple reasons.

A great many people avoided her, ran away from her. She was, in part, more knowing than the rest of us because the experiences offered her had been so extreme, and she had been so extreme in response— scenes in Harvard Square with an English marquess, slapping a son of a billionaire so hard he fell over backwards at a party in Lowell House, her saying then and subsequently, "I never sleep with anyone who has a fat ass." Extreme in the humiliations endured and meted out, in the crassness of the publicity, of her life defined as those adventures, extreme in the dangers survived or not entirely survived, the cheapness undergone so that she was on a kind of frightening eminence, an eminence of her experiences and of her being different from everyone else. She'd dealt in intrigues, major and minor, in the dramas of political families, in passions, deceptions, folly on a large, expensive scale, promises, violence, the genuine pain of defeat when defeat is to some extent the result of your qualities and not of your defects, and she knew the rottenness of victories that hadn't been final. She was crass and impaired by beauty. She was like a giant bird, she was as odd as an ostrich walking around the Yard, in her absurd gorgeousness, she was so different from us in kind, so capable of a different sort of progress through the yielding medium of the air, through the strange rooms of our minutes on this earth, through the gloomy circumstances of our lives in those years.

People said it was worth it to do this or that just in order to see her—seeing her offered some kind of encouragement, was some kind of testimony that life was interesting. But not many people cared as much about knowing her. Most people preferred to keep their distance. I don't know what her having made herself into what she was had done for her. She could have been ordinary if she'd wished.

She had unnoticeable hair, a far from arresting forehead, and extraordinary eyes, deep-set, longing, hopeful, angrily bored behind smooth, heavy lids that fluttered when she was interested and when she was not interested at all. She had a great desire not to trouble or be troubled by supernumeraries and strangers. She has a proud, too large nose that gives her a noble, stubborn dog's look. Her mouth has a disconcertingly lovely set to it—it is more immediately expressive than her eyes and it shows her implacability: it is the implacability of her knowledge of life in her. People always stared at her. Some giggled nervously. *Do you like me, Orra? Do you like me at all?* They stared at the great hands of the Aztec priest opening them to feelings and to awe, exposing their hearts, the dread cautiousness of their lives. They stared at the incredible symmetries of her sometimes anguishedly passionate face, the erratic pain for her in being beautiful that showed on it, the occasional plunging gaiety she felt because she was beautiful. I like beautiful people. The symmetries of her face were often thwarted by her attempts at expressiveness—beauty was a stone she struggled free of. A ludicrous beauty. A cruel clown of a girl. Sometimes her face was absolutely impassive as if masked in dullness and she was trying to move among us incognito. I was aware that each of her downfalls made her more possible for me. I never doubted that she was privately a pedestrian shitting-peeing person. Whenever I had a chance to observe her for any length of time, in a classroom for instance, I would think, *I understand her.* Whenever I approached her, she responded up to a point and then even as I stood talking to her I would fade as a personage, as a sexual presence, as someone present and important to her, into greater and greater invisibility. That was when she was a freshman, a sophomore, and a junior. When we were seniors, by then I'd learned how to avoid being invisible even to Orra. Orra was, I realized, hardly more than a terrific college girl, much vaunted, no more than that yet. But my God, my God, in one's eyes, in one's thoughts, she strode like a *Nike*, she entered like a blast of light, the thought of her was as vast as a desert. Sometimes in an early winter twilight in the Yard, I would see her in her coat, unbuttoned even in cold weather as if she burned slightly always, see her move clumsily along a walk looking like a scrawny field-hockey player, a great athlete of a girl half-stumbling, uncoordinated off the playing field, yet with reserves of strength, do you know? and her face, as she walked along, might twitch like a dog's when the dog is asleep, twitching with whatever dialogue or adventure or daydream she was having in her head. Or she might in the early darkness stride along, cold-faced, haughty, angry, all the worst refusals one would ever receive bound up in one ridiculously beautiful girl. One always said, "I wonder what will become of her." Her ignoring me marked me as a sexual nonentity. She was proof of a level of sexual adventure I had not yet with my best efforts reached: that level existed because Orra existed.

What is it worth to be in love in this way?

II   *Orra with Me*

I DISTRUST summaries, any kind of gliding through time, any too great a claim that one is in control of what one recounts; I think someone who claims to understand but who is obviously calm, someone who claims to write with emotion recollected in tranquillity, is a fool and a liar. To understand is to tremble. To recollect is to reenter and be riven. An acrobat after spinning through the air in a mockery of flight stands erect on his perch and mockingly takes his bow as if what he is being applauded for was easy for him and cost him nothing, although meanwhile he is covered with sweat and his smile is edged with a relief chilling to think about; he is indulging in a show-business style; he is pretending to be superhuman. I am bored with that and with where it has brought us. I admire the authority of being on one's knees in front of the event.

In the last spring of our being undergraduates, I finally got her. We had agreed to meet in my room, to get a little drunk cheaply before going out to dinner. I left the door unlatched; and I lay naked on my bed under a sheet. When she knocked on the door, I said, "Come in," and she did. She began to chatter right away, to complain that I was still in bed; she seemed to think I'd been taking a nap and had forgotten to wake up in time to get ready for her arrival. I said, "I'm naked, Orra, under this sheet. I've been waiting for you. I haven't been asleep."

Her face went empty. She said, "Damn you—why couldn't you wait?" But even while she was saying that, she was taking off her blouse.

I was amazed that she was so docile; and then I saw that it was maybe partly that she didn't want to risk saying no to me—she didn't want me to be hurt and difficult, she didn't want me to explode; she had a kind of hope of making me happy so that I'd then appreciate her and be happy with her and let her know me: I'm putting it badly. But her not being able to say no protected me from having so great a fear of sexual failure that I would not have been able to be worried about her pleasure, or to be concerned about her in bed. She was very amateurish and uninformed in bed, which touched me. It was really sort of poor sex; she didn't come or even feel much that I could see. Afterward, lying beside her, I thought of her eight or ten or fifteen lovers being afraid of her, afraid to tell her anything about sex in case they might be wrong. I had an image of them protecting their own egos, holding their arms around their egos and not letting her near them. It seemed a kindness embedded in the event that she was, in quite an obvious way, with a little critical interpretation, a virgin. And impaired, or crippled by having been beautiful, just as I'd thought. I said to myself that it was a matter of course that I might be deluding myself. But what I did for the rest of that night—we stayed up all night; we talked, we quarreled for a while, we confessed various things, we argued about sex, we fucked again (the second one was a little better)—I treated her with the justice with which I'd treat a boy my age, a young man, and with a rather exact or measured patience and tolerance, as if she were a paraplegic and had spent her life in a wheelchair and was tired of sentiment. I showed her no sentiment at all. I figured she'd been asphyxiated by the sentiments and sentimentality of people impressed by her looks. She was beautiful and frightened and empty and shy and alone and wounded and invulnerable (like a cripple: what more can you do to a cripple?). She was Caesar and ruler of the known world and not Caesar and no one as well.

It was a fairly complicated, partly witty thing to do. It meant I could not respond to her beauty but had to ignore it. She was a curious sort of girl; she had a great deal of isolation in her, isolation as a woman. It meant that when she said something on the order of "You're very defensive," I had to be a debater, her equal, take her seriously, and say, "How do you mean that?" and then talk about it, and alternately deliver a blow ("You can't judge defensiveness, you have the silly irresponsibility of women, the silly disconnectedness: I *have* to be defensive") and defer to her: "You have a point: you think very clearly. All right, I'll adopt that as a premise." Of course, much of what we said was incoherent and nonsensical on examination, but we worked out in conversation what we meant or thought we meant. I didn't react to her in an emotional way. She wasn't really a girl, not really quite human: how could she be? She was a position, a specific glory, a trophy, our local upper-middle-class pseudo-Cleopatra. Or not pseudo. I couldn't revel in my luck or be unselfconsciously vain. I could not strut horizontally or loll as if on clouds, a demigod with a goddess, although it was clear we were deeply fortunate, in spite of everything: the poor sex, the differences in attitude which were all we seemed to share, the tensions and the blundering. If I enjoyed her more than she enjoyed me, if I lost consciousness of her even for a moment, she would be closed into her isolation

again. I couldn't love her and have her, too. I could love her and have
her if I didn't show love or the symptoms of having had her. It was like
lying in a very lordly way, opening her to the possibility of feeling by
making her comfortable inside the calm lies of my behavior, my inscrib-
ing the minutes with false messages. It was like meeting a requirement
in Greek myth, like not looking back at Eurydice. The night crept on,
swept on, late minutes, powdered with darkness, in the middle of a
sleeping city, spring crawling like a plague of green snakes, bits of
warmth in the air, at 4 a.m. smells of leaves when the stink of automobiles died down. Dawn came, so pink, so pastel, so silly: We were talking
about the possibility of innate grammatical structures; I said it was an
unlikely notion, that Jews really were God-haunted (the idea had been
broached by a Jew), and the great difficulty was to invent a just God,
that if God appeared at a moment of time or relied on prophets, there
had to be degrees in the possibility of knowing Him so that He was by
definition unjust; the only just God would be one who consisted of what
had always been known by everyone; and that you could always identify
a basically Messianic, a hugely religious, fraudulent thinker by how
much he tried to anchor his doctrine to having always been true, to
being innate even in savage man, whereas an honest thinker, a nonliar,
was caught in the grip of the truth of process and change and the
profound absence of justice except as an invention, an attempt by the
will to live with someone, or with many others without consuming
them. At that moment Orra said, "I think we're falling in love."

I figured I had kept her from being too depressed after fucking—it's
hard for a girl with any force in her and any brains to accept the whole
thing of fucking, of being fucked without trying to turn it on its end,
so that she does some fucking, or some fucking up; I mean, the mere
power of arousing the man so he wants to fuck isn't enough: she wants
him to be willing to die in order to fuck. There's a kind of strain or
intensity women are bred for, as beasts, for childbearing when childbearing might kill them, and child rearing when the child might die at
any moment: it's in women to live under that danger, with that risk, that
close to tragedy, with that constant taut or casual courage. They need
death and nobility near. To be fucked when there's no drama inherent
in it, when you're not going to rise to a level of nobility and courage
forever denied the male, is to be cut off from what is inherently female,
bestially speaking. I wanted to be halfway decent company for her. I
don't know that it was natural to me. I am psychologically, profoundly,

a transient. A form of trash. I am incapable of any continuing loyalty and silence; I am an informer. But I did all right with her. It was dawn, as I said. We stood naked by the window, silently watching the light change. Finally, she said, "Are you hungry? Do you want breakfast?"

"Sure. Let's get dressed and go—"

She cut me off; she said with a funny kind of firmness, "No! Let me go and get us something to eat."

"Orra, don't wait on me. Why are you doing this? Don't be like this."

But she was in a terrible hurry to be in love. After those few hours, after that short a time.

She said, "I'm not as smart as you, Wiley. Let me wait on you. Then things will be even."

"Things are even, Orra."

"No. I'm boring and stale. You just think I'm not because you're in love with me. Let me go."

I blinked. After a while, I said, "All right."

She dressed and went out and came back. While we ate, she was silent; I said things, but she had no comment to make; she ate very little; she folded her hands and smiled mildly like some nineteenth-century portrait of a handsome young mother. Every time I looked at her, when she saw I was looking at her, she changed the expression on her face to one of absolute and undeviating welcome to me and to anything I might say.

So, it had begun.

III *Orra*

S HE HADN'T COME. She said she had never come with anyone at any time. She said it didn't matter.

After our first time, she complained, "You went twitch, twitch, twitch—just like a grasshopper." So she had wanted to have more pleasure than she'd had. But after the second fuck and after the dawn, she never complained again—unless I tried to make her come, and then she complained of that. She showed during sex no dislike for any of my sexual mannerisms or for the rhythms and postures I fell into when I fucked. But I was not pleased or satisfied; it bothered me that she didn't come. I was not pleased or satisfied on my own account, either. I thought the reason for that was she attracted me more than she could satisfy me, maybe more than fucking could ever satisfy me, that the more you cared, the more undertow there was, so that the sexual thing drowned—I mean, the sharpest sensations, and yet the dullest, are when you masturbate—but when you're vilely attached to somebody, there are noises, distractions that drown out the sensations of fucking. For a long time, her wanting to fuck, her getting undressed, and the soft horizontal bobble of her breasts as she lay there, and the soft wavering, the kind of sinewlessness of her legs and lower body, with which she more or less showed me she was ready—that was more moving, was more immensely important to me than any mere ejaculation later, any putt-putt-putt in her darkness, any hurling of future generations into the clenched universe, the strict mitten inside her: I clung to her and grunted and anchored myself to the most temporary imaginable relief of the desire I felt for her; I would be hungry again and anxious to fuck again in another twenty minutes; it was pitiable, this sexual disarray. It seemed to me that in the vast spaces of the excitement of being wel-comed by each other, we could only sightlessly and at best half organize our bodies. But so what? We would probably die in these underground caverns; a part of our lives would die; a certain innocence and hope would never survive this: we were too open, too clumsy, and we were the wrong people: so what did a fuck matter? I didn't mind if the sex was always a little rasping, something of a failure, if it was just prepara-tion for more sex in half an hour, if coming was just more foreplay. If this was all that was in store for us, fine. But I thought she was getting gypped in that she felt so much about me, she was dependent, and she was generous, and she didn't come when we fucked.

She said she had never come, not once in her life, and that she didn't need to. And that I mustn't think about whether she came or not. "I'm a sexual tigress," she explained, "and I like to screw but I'm too sexual to come: I haven't that kind of daintiness. I'm not selfish *that* way."

I could see that she had prowled around in a sense and searched out men and asked them to be lovers as she had me rather than wait for them or plot to capture their attention in some subtle way; and in bed she was sexually eager and a bit more forward and less afraid than most girls; but only in an upper-middle-class frame of reference was she *a sexual tigress.*

It seemed to me—my whole self was focused on this—that her not coming said something about what we had, that her not coming was an undeniable fact, a measure of the limits of what we had. I did not think we should think we were great lovers when we weren't.

Orra said we were, that I had no idea how lousy the sex was other people had. I told her that hadn't been my experience. We were, it seemed to me, two twenty-one-year-olds, overeducated, irrevocably shy beneath our glaze of sexual determination and of sexual appetite, and psychologically somewhat slashed up and only capable of being partly useful to each other. We weren't the king and queen of Cockandcunt-dom yet.

Orra said coming was a minor part of sex for a woman and was a demeaning measure of sexuality. She said it was imposed as a measure by people who knew nothing about sex and judged women childishly.

It seemed to me she was turning a factual thing, coming, into a public-relations thing. But girls were under fearful public pressures in these matters.

When she spoke about them, these matters, she had a little, superior inpuckered look, a don't-make-me-make-mincemeat-of-you-in-argument look—I thought of it as her Orra-as-Orra look, Orra alone, Orra-without-Wiley, without me, Orra isolated and depressed, a terrific girl, an Orra who hated cowing men.

She referred to novels, to novels by women writers, to specific scenes and remarks about sex and coming for women, but I'd read some of those books, out of curiosity, and none of them were literature, and the heroines in them invariably were innocent in every relation; but very strong and very knowing and with terrifically good judgment; and the men they loved were described in such a way that they appeared to be examples of the woman's sexual reach, or of her intellectual value, rather than sexual companions or sexual objects; the women had sex generously with men who apparently bored them physically; I had thought the books and their writers and characters sexually naive.

Very few women, it seemed to me, had much grasp of physical reality. Still, very strange things were often true, and a man's notion of orgasm was necessarily specialized.

When I did anything in bed to excite her, with an eye to making her come, she asked me not to, and that irritated the hell out of me. But no matter what she said, it must have been bad for her after six years of fucking around not to get to a climax. It had to be that it was a run on her neural patience. How strong could she be?

I thought about how women coming were at such a pitch of uncontrol they might prefer a dumb, careless lover, someone very unlike me: I had often played at being a strong, silent dunce. Some girls became fawning and doglike after they came, even toward dunces. Others jumped up and became immediately tough, proud of themselves as if the coming was *all* to their credit, and I ought to be flattered. God, it was a peculiar world. Brainy girls tended to control their comes, doling out one to a fuck, just like a man; and often they would try to keep that one under control, they would limit it to a single nozzle-contracted squirt of excitement. Even that sometimes racked and emptied them and made them curiously weak and brittle and embarrassed and delicate and lazy. Or they would act bold and say, "God, I needed that."

I wondered how Orra would look, in what way she would do it, a girl like that going off, how she'd hold herself, her eyes, how she'd act toward me when it was over.

To get her to talk about sex at all, I argued that analyzing something destroyed it, of course, but leaves rotted on the ground and prepared the way for what would grow next. So she talked.

She said I was wrong in what I told her I saw and that there was no difference in her between mental and physical excitement, that it wasn't true her mind was excited quickly and her body slowly, if at all. I couldn't be certain I was right, but when I referred to a moment when there had seemed to be deep physical feeling in her, she sometimes agreed that had been a good moment in her terms; but sometimes she said, no, it had only been a little irritating then, like a peculiarly unpleasant tickle. In spite of her liking my mind, she gave me no authority for what I knew—I mean, when it turned out I was right. She kept the authority for her reactions in her own hands. Her self-abnegation was her own doing. I liked that: some people just give you themselves, and it is too much to keep in your hands: your abilities aren't good enough. I decided to stick with what I observed and to think her somewhat mistaken and not to talk to her about sex anymore.

I watched her in bed; her body was doubting, grudging, tardy, intolerant—and intolerably hungry—I thought. In her pride and self-consciousness and ignorance she hated all that in herself. She preferred to think of herself as quick, to have pleasure as she willed rather than as she actually had it, to have it on her own volition, to her own prescription, and almost out of politeness, so it seemed to me, to give herself to me, to give me pleasure, to ignore herself, to be a nice girl because she was in love. She insisted on that but that was too sentimental, and she also insisted on, she persuaded herself, she passed herself off as dashing.

In a way, sexually, she was a compulsive liar.

I set myself to remove every iota of misconception I had about Orra in bed, any romanticism, any pleasurable hope. It seemed to me what had happened to her with other boys was that she was distrustful to start with and they had overrated her, and they'd been overwrought and off balance and uneasy about her judgment of them, and they'd taken their pleasure and run.

And then she had in her determination to have sex become more and more of a sexual fool. (I was all kinds of fool: I didn't mind her being a sexual fool.) The first time I'd gone to bed with her, she'd screamed and thrown herself around, a good two or three feet to one side or another, as she thought a sexual tigress would, I supposed. I'd argued with her afterward that no one was that excited, especially without coming; she said she had come, sort of. She said she was too sexual for most men. She said her reactions weren't fake but represented a real sexuality, a real truth. That proud, stubborn, stupid girl.

But I told her that if she and a man were in sexual congress, and she heaved herself around and threw herself a large number of inches to either the left or the right or even straight up, the man was going to be startled; and if there was no regular pattern or predictability, it was easy to lose an erection; that if she threw herself to the side, there was a good chance she would interrupt the congress entirely unless the man was very quick and scrambled after her, and scrambling after her was not likely to be sexual for him: it would be more like playing tag. The man would have to fuck while in a state of siege; not knowing what she'd do next, he'd fuck and hurry to get it over and to get out.

Orra had said on that first occasion, "That sounds reasonable. No one ever explained that to me before, no one ever made it clear. I'll try it your way for a while."

After that, she had been mostly shy and honest, and honestly lecherous in bed but helpless to excite herself or to do more to me than she did just by being there and welcoming me. As if her hands were webbed and her mind was glued, as if I didn't deserve more, or as if she was such a novice and so shy she could not begin to do anything *sexual*. I did not understand: I'd always found that anyone who *wanted* to give pleasure could: it didn't take skill, just the desire to please and a kind of, I don't know, a sightless ability to feel one's way to some extent in the lightless maze of pleasure. But upper-middle-class girls might be more fearful of tying men to them by bands of excessive pleasure; such girls were careful and shy.

I set myself for her being rude and difficult although she hadn't been rude and difficult to me for a long time, but those traits were in her like a shadow, giving her the dimensionality that made her valuable to me, that gave point to her kindness toward me. She had the sloppiest and most uncertain and silliest and yet bravest and most generous ego of anyone I'd ever known; and her manners were the most stupid imaginable alternation between the distinguished, the sensitive, the intelligent, with a rueful, firm, almost snotty delicacy and kindness and protectiveness toward you, and the really selfish and bruising. The important thing was to prevent her from responding falsely, as if in a movie, or in some imitation of the movies she'd seen and the books she'd read—she had a curious faith in movies and in books; she admired anything that made her feel and that did not require responsibility from her, because then she produced happiness like silk for herself and others. She liked really obscure philosophers, like Hegel, where she could admire the thought but where the thought didn't demand anything from her. Still, she was a realist, and she would probably learn what I knew and would surpass me. She had great possibilities. But she was also merely a good-looking, pseudorich girl, a paranoid, a Perkins. On the other hand, she was a fairly marvelous girl a lot of the time, brave, eye-shattering, who could split my heart open with one slightly shaky approving-of-me brainy romantic heroine's smile. The romantic splendor of her face. So far in her life she had disappointed everyone. I had to keep all this in mind, I figured. She was fantastically alive and eerily dead at the same time. I wanted for my various reasons to raise her from the dead.

IV   *Orra: The Same World,*
a Different Time Scale

ONE AFTERNOON, things went well for us. We went for a walk, the air was plangent, there was the amazed and polite pleasure we had sometimes merely at being together. Orra adjusted her pace now and then to mine; and I kept mine adjusted to her most of the time. When we looked at each other, there would be small, soft puffs of feeling as of toy explosions or sparrows bathing in the dust. Her willed softness, her inner seriousness or earnestness, her strength, her beauty, muted and careful now in her anxiety not to lose me yet, made the pleasure of being with her noble, contrapuntal, and difficult in that one had to live up to it and understand it and protect it, against my clumsiness and Orra's falsity, kind as that falsity was; or the day would become simply an exploitation of a strong girl who would see through that sooner or later and avenge it. But things went well; and inside that careless and careful goodness, we went home; we screwed; I came—to get my excitement out of the way; she didn't know I was doing that; she was stupendously polite; taut; and very admiring. "How pretty you are," she said. Her eyes were blurred with half-tears. I'd screwed without any fripperies, coolly, in order to leave in us a large residue of sexual restlessness but with the burr of immediate physical restlessness in me removed: I still wanted her; I always wanted Orra; and the coming had been dull; but my body was not very assertive, was more like a glove for my mind, for my will, for my love for her, for my wanting to make her feel more.

She was slightly tearful, as I said, and gentle, and she held me in her arms after I came, and I said something like "Don't relax. I want to come again," and she partly laughed, partly sighed, and was flattered, and said, "Again? That's nice." We had a terrific closeness, almost like a man and a secretary—I was free and powerful, and she was devoted: there was little chance Orra would ever be a secretary—she'd been offered executive jobs already for when she finished college—but to play at being a secretary who had no life of her own was a romantic thing for Orra. I felt some apprehension, as before a game of tennis that I wanted to win, or as before stealing something off a counter in a store: there was a dragging enervation, a fear and silence, and there was a lifting, a preparation, a willed and then unwilled, self-contained fixity of purpose; it was a settled thing; it would happen.

After about ten minutes or so, perhaps it was twenty, I moved in her: I should say that while I'd rested, I'd stayed in her (and she'd held on to me). As I'd expected—and with satisfaction and pride that everything was working, my endowments were cooperating—I felt my prick come up; it came up at once with comic promptness, but it was sore—Jesus, was it sore. It, its head, ached like hell, with a dry, burning, reddish pain.

The pain made me chary and prevented me from being excited except in an abstract way; my mind was clear; I was idly smiling as I began, moving very slowly, just barely moving, sore of pressing on her inside her, moving around, lollygagging around, feeling out the reaches in there, arranging the space inside her, as if to put the inner soft-oiled shadows in her in order; or like stretching out your hand in the dark and pressing a curve of a blanket into familiarity or to locate yourself when you're half asleep, when your eyes are closed. In fact, I did close my eyes and listened carefully to her breathing, concentrating on her but trying not to let her see I was doing that because it would make her self-conscious.

Her reaction was so minimal that I lost faith in fucking for getting her started, and I thought I'd better go down on her; I pulled out of her, which wasn't too smart, but I wasn't thinking all that consequentially; she'd told me on other occasions she didn't like "all that foreign la-di-da," that it didn't excite her, but I'd always thought it was only that she was ashamed of not coming and that made being gone down on hard for her. I started in on it; she protested; and I pooh-poohed her objections and did it anyway; I was raw with nerves, with stifled amusement because of the lying and the tension, so much of it. I remarked to her that I was going down on her for my own pleasure; I was jolted by touching her with my tongue there when I was so raw-nerved, but I hid that. It seemed to me physical unhappiness and readiness were apparent in her skin—my lips and tongue carried the currents of a jagged unhappiness and readiness in her into me; echoes of her stiffness and dissatisfaction sounded in my mouth, my head, my feet; my entire tired body was a stethoscope. I was entirely a stethoscope; I listened to her with my *bones;* the glimmers of excitement in her traveled to my *spine;* I felt her grinding sexual haltedness, like a car's broken starter motor grinding away in her, in my *stomach,* in my *knees.* Every part of me listened to her; every goddamned twinge of muscular contraction she had that I noticed or that she should have had because I was licking her clitoris and she didn't have, every testimony of excitement or of no-excitement in her, I listened for so hard it was amazing it didn't drive her out of bed with self-consciousness; but she probably couldn't tell what I was doing, since I was out of her line of sight, was down in the shadows, in the basement of her field of vision, in the basement with her sexual feelings where they lay, strewn about.

When she said, "No . . . No, Wiley . . . Please don't. No . . ." and wiggled, although it wasn't the usual pointless protest that some girls might make—it was real, she wanted me to stop—I didn't listen because

I could feel she responded to my tongue more than she had to the fucking a moment before. I could feel beads sliding and whispering and being strung together rustlingly in her; the disorder, the scattered or strewn sexual bits, to a very small extent were being put in order. She shuddered. With discomfort. She produced, was subjected to, her erratic responses. And she made odd, small cries, protests mostly, uttered little exclamations that mysteriously were protests although they were not protests, too, cries that somehow suggested the ground of protest kept changing for her.

I tried to string a number of those cries together, to cause them to occur in a mounting sequence. It was a peculiar attempt: it seemed we moved, I moved with her, on dark water, between two lines of buoys, dark on one side, there was nothingness there, and on the other, lights, red and green, the lights of the body advancing on sexual heat, the signs of it anyway, nipples like scored pebbles, legs lightly thrashing, little *ob*s; nothing important, a body thing; you go on: you proceed.

When we strayed too far, there was nothingness, or only a distant flicker, only the faintest guidance. Sometimes we were surrounded by the lights of her responses, widely spaced, bobbing unevenly, on some darkness, some ignorance we both had, Orra and I, of what were the responses of her body. To the physical things I did and to the atmosphere of the way I did them, to the authority, the argument I made that this was sexual for her, that the way I touched her and concentrated on her, on that partly dream-laden dark water or underwater thing, she responded; she rested on that, rolled heavily on that. Everything I did was speech, was hieroglyphics, pictures on her nerves; it was what masculine authority was for, was what bravery and a firm manner and musculature were supposed to indicate that a man could bring to bed. Or skill at dancing; or musicianliness; or a sad knowingness. Licking her, holding her belly, stroking her belly pretty much with unthought-out movements—sometimes just moving my fingers closer together and spreading them again to show my pleasure, to show how rewarded I felt, not touching her breasts or doing anything so intensely that it would make her suspect me of being out to make her come—I did those things but it seemed like I left her alone and was private with my own pleasures. She felt unobserved with her sensations, she had them without responsibility, she clutched at them as something round and slippery in the water, and she would fall off them, occasionally gasping at the loss of her balance, the loss of her self-possession, too.

I'd flick, idly almost, at her little spaghetti-ending with my tongue, then twice more idly, then three or four or five times in sequence, then settle down to rub it or bounce it between lip and tongue in a steadily more earnest way until my head, my consciousness, my lips and tongue were buried in the dark of an ascending and concentrated rhythm, in the way a stoned dancer lets a movement catch him and wrap him around and become all of him, become his voyage and not a collection of repetitions at all.

Then some boring stringy thing, a sinew at the base of my tongue, would begin to ache, and I'd break off that movement, and sleepily lick her, or if the tongue was too uncomfortable, I'd worry her clit, I'd nuzzle it with my pursed lips until the muscles that held my lips pursed grew tired in their turn; and I'd go back and flick at her tiny clitoris with my tongue, and go on as before, until the darkness came; she sensed the darkness, the privacy for her, and she seemed like someone in a hallway, unobserved, moving her arms, letting her mind stroke itself, taking a step in that dark.

But whatever she felt was brief and halting; and when she seemed to halt or to be dead or jagged, I authoritatively, gesturally accepted that as part of what was pleasurable to me and did not let it stand as hint or foretaste of failure; I produced sighs of pleasure, even gasps, not all of them false, warm nuzzlings, and caresses that indicated I was re-warded—I produced rewarded strokings; I made elements of sexual pleasure out of moments that were unsexual and that could be taken as the collapse of sexuality.

And she couldn't contradict me because she thought I was working on my own coming, and she loved me and meant to be cooperative.

What I did took nerve because it gave her a tremendous ultimate power to laugh at me, although what the courtship up until now had been for was to show that she was not an enemy, that she could control the hysteria of fear or jealousy in her or the cold judgments in her of me that would lead her to say or do things that would make me hate or fear her; what was at stake included the risk that I would look foolish in my own eyes—and might then attack her for failing to come—and then she would be unable to resist the inward conviction that I was a fool. Any attempted act confers vulnerability on you, but an act devoted to her pleasure represented doubled vulnerability since only she could judge it; and I was safe only if I was immune or insensitive to her; but if I was immune or insensitive I could not hope to help her come; by making myself vulnerable to her, I was in a way being a sissy or a creep because Orra wasn't organized or trained or prepared to accept responsibility for how I felt about myself: she was a woman who wanted to be left alone; she was paranoid about the inroads on her life men in their egos tried to make: there was dangerous masochism, dangerous hubris, dangerous hopefulness, and a form of love in my doing what I did: I nuzzled nakedly at the crotch of the sexual tigress; any weakness in her ego or her judgment and she would lash out at *me;* and the line was very frail between what I was doing as love and as intrusion, exploitation, and stupid boastfulness. There was no way for me even to begin to imagine the mental pain—or the physical pain—for her if I should fail and, to add to that, if I should withdraw from her emotionally, too, because of my failure and hers and our pain. Or merely because the failure might make me so uncomfortable I couldn't go on unless she nursed my ego, and she couldn't nurse my ego, she didn't know how to do it, and probably was inhibited about doing it.

Sometimes my hands, my fingers, not just the tops, but all of their inside surface and the palms, held her thighs, or cupped her little belly, or my fingers moved around the lips, the labia or whatever, or even poked a little into her, or with the nails or tips lightly nudged her clitoris, always within a fictional frame of my absolute sexual pleasure, of my admiration for this sex, of there being no danger in it for us. No tongues or brains handy to speak unkindly, I meant. My God, I felt exposed and noble. This was a great effort to make for her.

Perhaps that only indicates the extent of my selfishness. I didn't mind being feminized except for the feeling that Orra would not ever understand what I was doing but would ascribe it to the power of my or our sexuality. I minded being this self-conscious and so conscious of her; I was separated from my own sexuality, from any real sexuality; a poor sexual experience, even one based on love, would diminish the ease of my virility with her at least for a while; and she wouldn't understand. Maybe she would become much subtler and shrewder sexually and know how to handle me, but that wasn't likely. And if I apologized or complained or explained in that problematic future why I was sexually a little slow or reluctant with her, she would then blame my having tried to give her orgasm, she would insist I must not be bored again, so I would in that problematic future, if I wanted her to come, have to lie and say I was having more excitement than I felt, and that, too, might diminish my pleasure. I would be deprived even of the chance for honesty: I would be further feminized in that regard. I thought all this while I went down on her. I didn't put it in words but thought in great misty blocks of something known or sensed. I felt an inner weariness I kept working in spite of. This ignoring myself gave me an odd, starved feeling, a mixture of agony and helplessness. I didn't want to feel like that. I suddenly wondered why in the theory of relativity the speed of light is given as a constant: was that more Jewish absolutism? Surely in a universe as changeable and as odd as this one, the speed of light, considering the variety of experiences, must vary; there must be a place where one could see a beam of light struggle to move. I felt silly and selfish; it couldn't be avoided that I felt like that—I mean, it couldn't be avoided by *me*.

Whatever she did when I licked her, if she moved at all, if a muscle twitched in her thigh, a muscle twitched in mine, my body imitated hers as if to measure what she felt or perhaps for no reason but only because the sympathy was so intense. The same things happened to each of us but in amazingly different contexts, as if we stood at opposite ends of the room and reached out to touch each other and to receive identical messages which then diverged as they entered two such widely separated sensibilities and two such divergent and incomplete ecstasies. The movie we watched was of her discovering how her sexual responses worked: we were seated far apart. My tongue pushed at her erasure, her wronged and heretofore hardly existent sexual powers. I stirred her with varieties of kisses far from her face. A strange river moved slowly, bearing us along, reeds hid the banks, willows braided and unbraided themselves, moaned and whispered, raveled and faintly clicked. Orra groaned, sighed, shuddered, shuddered harshly or liquidly; sometimes she jumped when I changed the pressure or posture of my hands on her or when I rested for a second and then resumed. Her body jumped and contracted interestingly but not at any length or in any pattern that I could understand. My mind grew tired. There is a limit to invention, to mine anyway: I saw myself (stupidly) as a Roman trireme, my tongue as the prow, *bronze,* pushing at her; she was the Mediterranean. Tiers of slaves—my God, the helplessness of them—pulled oars, long stalks that metaphorically and rhythmically bloomed with flowing clusters of short-lived lilies at the water's surface. The pompous and out-of-proportion boat, all of me hunched over Orra's small sea—not actually hunched: what I was was lying flat; the foot of the bed was at my waist or near there, my legs were out, my feet were propped distantly on the floor, all of me was concentrated on the soft, shivery, furry delicacies of Orra's twat—the pompous boat advanced lickingly, leaving a trickling, gurgling wake of half-response, the ebbing of my will and activity into that fluster subsiding into the dark water of this girl's passivity, taut storminess, and self-ignorance.

The whitish bubbling, the splash of her discontinuous physical response: those waves, ah, that wake rose, curled outward, bubbled, and fell. Rose, curled outward, bubbled, and fell. The white fell of a naiad. In the vast spreading darkness and silence of the sea. There was nothing but that wake. The darkness of my senses when the rhythm absorbed me (so that I vanished from my awareness, so that I was blotted up and was a stain, a squid hidden, stroking Orra) made it twilight or night for me; and my listening for her pleasure, for our track on that markless ocean, gave me the sense that where we were was in a lit-up, great, ill-defined oval of night air and sea and opalescent fog, rainbowed where the lights from the portholes of an immense ship were altered prismatically by droplets of mist—as in some 1930s movie, as in some dream. Often I was out of breath; I saw spots, colors, ocean depths. And her protests, her doubts! My God, her doubts! Her *No, don't, Wiley*s and her *I don't want to do this*es and her *Wiley, don't*s and *Wiley, I can't come—don't do this—I don't like this*es. Mostly I ignored her. Sometimes I silenced her by leaning my cheek on her belly and watching my hand stroke her belly and saying to her in a sex-thickened voice, "Orra, I like this—this is for me."

Then I went down on her again with unexpectedly vivid, real pleasure, as if merely thinking about my own pleasure excited and refreshed me, and there was yet more pleasure, when she—reassured or strengthened by my putative selfishness, by the conviction that this was all for me, that nothing was expected of her—cried out. Then a second later she *grunted*. Her whole body rippled. Jesus, I loved it when she reacted to me. It was like causing an entire continent to convulse, Asia, South America. I felt huge and tireless.

In her excitement, she threw herself into the air, but my hands happened to be on her belly; and I fastened her down, I held that part of her comparatively still, with her twat fastened to my mouth, and I licked her while she was in midheave; and she yelled; I kept my mouth there as if I were drinking from her; I stayed like that until her upper body fell back on the bed and bounced, she made the whole bed bounce; then my head bounced away from her; but I still held her down with my hands; and I fastened myself, my mouth, on her twat again; and she yelled in a deep voice, *"Wiley, what are you doing!"*

Her voice was deep, as if her impulses at that moment were masculine, not out of neurosis but in generosity, in an attempt to improve on the sickliness she accused women of; she wanted to meet me halfway, to share; to share my masculinity: she thought men were beautiful. She cried out, *"I don't want you to do things to me! I want you to have a good fuck!"*

Her voice was deep and despairing, maybe with the despair that goes with surges of sexuality, but then maybe she thought I would make her pay for this. I said, "Orra, I like this stuff, this stuff is what gets me excited." She resisted, just barely, for some infinitesimal fragment of a second, and then her body began to vibrate; it twittered as if in it were the strings of a musical instrument set jangling; she said foolishly—but sweetly—"Wiley, I'm embarrassed, Wiley, this embarrasses *me*. . . . Please stop. . . . No . . . No . . . No . . . Oh . . . Oh . . . Oh . . . I'm very sexual, I'm too sexual to have orgasms, Wiley, stop, please. . . . Oh . . . Oh . . . Oh . . ." And then a deeper shudder ran through her; she gasped; then there was a silence; then she gasped again; she cried out in an extraordinary voice, "I FEEL SOMETHING!" The hair stood up on the back of my neck; I couldn't stop; I hurried on; I heard a dim moaning come from her. What had she felt before? I licked hurriedly. How unpleasant for her, how unreal and twitchy had the feelings been that I'd given her? In what way was this different? I wondered if there was in her a sudden swarming along her nerves, a warm conviction of the reality of sexual pleasure. She heaved like a whale—no: not so much as that. But it was as if half an ocean rolled off her young flanks; some element of darkness vanished from the room; some slight color of physical happiness tinctured her body and its thin coating of sweat; I felt it all through me; she rolled on the surface of a pale blue, a pink and blue sea; she was dark and gleaming, and immense and wet. And warm.

She cried, *"Wiley, I feel a lot!"*

God, she was happy.

I said, "Why not?" I wanted to lower the drama quotient; I thought the excess of drama was a mistake, would overburden her. But also I wanted her to defer to me, I wanted authority over her body now, I wanted to make her come.

But she didn't get any more excited than that: she was rigid, almost boardlike after a few seconds. I licked at her thing as best I could but the sea was dry; the board collapsed. I faked it that I was very excited; actually I was so caught up in being sure of myself, I didn't know what I really felt. I thought, as if I were much younger than I was, Boy, if this doesn't work, is my name mud. Then to build up the risk, out of sheer hellish braggadocio, instead of just acting out that I was confident—and in sex, everything unsaid that is portrayed in gestures instead is twice as powerful—when she said, because the feeling was less for her now, the feeling she liked having gone away, "Wiley, I can't—this is silly—" I said, "Shut up, Orra, I know what I'm doing. . . ." But I didn't know.

And I didn't like that tone for sexual interplay either, except as a joke, or as role playing, because pure authority involves pure submission, and people don't survive pure submission except by being slavishly, possessively, vindictively in love; when they are in love like that, they can *give* you nothing but rebellion and submission, bitchiness and submission; it's a general rottenness: you get no part of them out of bed that has any value; and in bed, you get a grudging submission, because what the slave requires is your total attention, or she starts paying you back; I suppose the model is childhood, that slavery. Anyway, I don't like it. But I played at it then, with Orra, as a gamble.

Everything was a gamble. I didn't know what I was doing; I figured it out as I went along; and how much time did I have for figuring things out just then? I felt strained as at poker or roulette, sweaty and a little stupid, placing bets—with my tongue—and waiting to see what the wheel did, risking my money when no one forced me to, hoping things would go my way, and I wouldn't turn out to have been stupid when this was over.

Also, there were sudden fugitive convulsions of lust now, in sympathy with her larger but scattered responses, a sort of immediate and automatic sexuality—I was at the disposal, inwardly, of the sexuality in her and could not help myself, could not hold it back and avoid the disappointments, and physical impatience, the impatience in my skin and prick, of the huge desire that unmistakably accompanies love, of a primitive longing for what seemed her happiness, for closeness to her as to something I had studied and was studying and had found more and more of value in—what was of value was the way she valued me, a deep and no doubt limited (but in the sexual moment it seemed illimitable) permissiveness toward me, a risk she took, an allowance she made as if she'd let me damage her and use her badly.

Partly what kept me going was stubbornness because I'd made up my mind before we started that I wouldn't give up; and partly what it was was the feeling she aroused in me, a feeling that was, to be honest, made up of tenderness and concern and a kind of mere affection, a brotherliness, as if she were my brother, not different from me at all.

Actually this was brought on by an increasing failure, as the sex went on, of one kind of sophistication—of worldly sophistication—and by the increase in me of another kind, of a childish sophistication, a growth of innocence: Orra said, or exclaimed, in a half-harried, half-amazed voice, in a hugely admiring, gratuitous way, as she clutched at me in approval, "Wiley, I never had feelings like these before!"

And to be the first to have caused them, you know? It's like being a collector, finding something of great value, where it had been unsuspected and disguised, or like earning any honor; this partial success, this encouragement gave rise to this pride, this inward innocence.

Of course that lessened the risk for this occasion; I could fail now and still say, *It was worth it,* and she would agree; but it lengthened the slightly longer-term risk; because I might feel trebly a fool someday. Also, it meant we might spend months making love in this fashion—I'd get impotent, maybe not in terms of erection, but I wouldn't look forward to sex—still, that was beautiful to me in a way, too, and exciting. I really didn't know what I was thinking: whatever I thought was part of the sex.

I went on; I wanted to hit the jackpot now. Then Orra shouted, "It's *there!* It's THERE!" I halted, thinking she meant it was in some specific locale, in some specific motion I'd just made with my tired tongue and jaw; I lifted my head—but couldn't speak: in a way, the sexuality pressed on me too hard for me to speak; anyway, I didn't have to; she had lifted her head with a kind of overt twinship and she was looking at me down the length of her body; her face was askew and boyish—every feature was wrinkled; she looked angry and yet naive and swindleable; she said angrily, naively, *"Wiley, it's there!"*

But even before she spoke that time, I knew she'd meant it was in her; the fox had been startled from its covert again; she had seen it, had felt it run in her again. She had been persuaded that it was in her for good.

I started manipulating her delicately with my hand; and in my own excitement, and thinking she was ready, I sort of scrambled up and, covering her with myself, and playing with her with one hand, guided my other self, my lower consciousness, into her. My God, she was warm and restless inside; it was heated in there and smooth, insanely smooth, and oiled, and full of movements. But I knew at once I'd made a mistake: I should have gone on licking her; there were no regular contractions; she was anxious for the prick, she rose around it, closed around it, but in a rigid, dumb, faraway way; and her twitchings played on it, ran through it, through the walls of it and into me; and they were uncontrolled and not exciting, but empty: she didn't know what to do, how to be fucked and come. I couldn't pull out of her, I didn't want to, I couldn't pull out; but if there were no contractions for me to respond to, how in hell would I find the rhythm for her? I started slowly, with what seemed infinite suggestiveness to me, with great dirtiness, a really grown-up sort of fucking—just in case she was far along—and she let out a huge, shuddering, hour-long sigh and cried out my name and then, in a sobbing, exhausted voice, said, "I lost it. . . . Oh, Wiley, I lost it. . . . Let's stop. . . ." My face was above hers; her face was wet with tears; why was she crying like that? She had changed her mind; now she wanted to come; she turned her head back and forth; she said, "I'm no good. . . . I'm no good. . . . Don't worry about me. . . . You come. . . ."

No matter what I mumbled, "Hush," and "Don't be silly," and in a whisper, "Orra, I love you," she kept on saying those things, until I slapped her lightly and said, *"Shut up, Orra."*

Then she was silent again.

The thing was, apparently, that she was arrhythmic: at least that's what I thought; and that meant there weren't going to be regular contractions; any rhythm for me to follow; and any rhythm I set up as I fucked, she broke with her movements: so that it was that when she moved, she made her excitement go away. It would be best if she moved very smally: but I was afraid to tell her that, or even to try to hold her hips firmly, and guide them, to instruct her in that way for fear she'd get self-conscious and lose what momentum she'd won. And also I was ashamed that I'd stopped going down on her. I experimented— doggedly, sweatily, to make up for what I'd done—with fucking in different ways, and I fantasized about us being in Mexico, someplace warm and lushly colored where we made love easily and filthily and graphically. The fantasy kept me going. That is, it kept me hard. I kept acting out an atmosphere of sexual pleasure—I mean of my sexual pleasure—for her to rest on, so she could count on that. I discovered that a not very slow sort of one-one-one stroke, or fuck-fuck-fuck-Orra-now-now-now, really got to her; her feelings would grow heated; and she could shift up from that with me into a one-two, one-two, one-two, her excitement rising; but if she or I then tried to shift up farther to one-two-three, one-two-three, she'd lose it all. That was too complicated for her: my own true love, my white American. But her feelings when they were present were very strong, they came in gusts, huge squalls of heat as if from a furnace with a carelessly banging door, and they excited and allured both of us. That excitement and the dit-dit-ditting got to her; she began to be generally, continuingly sexual. It's almost standard to compare sexual excitement to holiness; well, after a while, holiness seized her; she spoke in tongues, she testified. She was shaking all over; she was saved temporarily and sporadically: that is, she kept lapsing out of that excitement, too. But it would recur. Her hands would flutter; her face would be pale and then red, then very, very red; her eyes would stare at nothing; she'd call my name. I'd plug on one-one-one, then one-two, one-two, then I'd go back to one-one-one: I could see as before—in the deep pleasure I felt even in the midst of the labor—why a woman was proud of what she felt, why a man might kill her in order to stimulate in her (although he might not know this was why he did it) these signs of pleasure. The familiar Orra had vanished; she said, "GodohGodohGod"; it was sin and redemption and holiness and visions time. Her throbs were very direct, easily comprehensible, but without any pattern; they weren't in any regular sequence; still, they were exciting to me, maybe all the more exciting because of the piteousness of her not being able to regulate them, of their being like blows delivered inside her by an enemy whom she couldn't even half domesticate or make friendly to herself or speak to. She was the most out-of-control girl I ever screwed. She would at times start to thrust like a woman who had her sexuality readied and well understood at last, and I'd start to distend with anticipation and a pride and relief as large as a house; but after two thrusts—or four, or six—she'd have gotten too excited, she'd be shaking, she'd thrust crookedly and out of tempo, the movement would collapse; or she'd suddenly jerk in midmovement without warning and crash around with so great and so meaningless a violence that she'd lose her thing; and she'd start to cry. She'd whisper wetly, "I lost it"; so I'd say, "No, you didn't," and I'd go on or start over, one-one-one; and of course, the excitement would come back; sometimes it came back at once; but she was increasingly afraid of herself, afraid to move her lower body; she would try to hold still and just *receive* the excitement; she would let it pool up in her; but then, too, she'd begin to shake more and more; she'd leak over into spasmodic and oddly sad, too large movements; and she'd whimper, knowing, I suppose, that those movements were breaking the tempo in herself; again and again, tears streamed down her cheeks; she said in a not quite hoarse, in a sweet, almost hoarse whisper, "I don't want to come, Wiley, you go ahead and come."

My mind had pretty much shut off; it had become exhausted; and I didn't see how we were going to make this work; she said, "Wiley, it's all right—please, it's all right—I don't want to come."

I wondered if I should say something and try to trigger some fantasy in her; but I didn't want to risk saying something she'd find unpleasant or think was a reproach or a hint for her to be sexier. I thought if I just kept on dit-dit-ditting, sooner or later she'd find it in herself, the trick of riding on her feelings, and getting them to rear up, crest, and topple. I held her tightly, in sympathy and pity, and maybe fear, and admiration: she was so unhysterical; she hadn't yelled at me or broken anything; she hadn't ordered me around: she was simply alone and shaking in the middle of a neural storm in her that she seemed to have no gift for handling. I said, "Orra, it's O.K.: I really prefer long fucks," and I went on, dit-dit-dit-dit, then I'd shift up to dit-dot, dit-dot, dit-dot, dit-dot. . . . My back hurt, my legs were going; if sweat was sperm, we would have looked like liquefied snowfields.

Orra made noises, more and more quickly, and louder and louder; then the noises she made slackened off. Then, step by step, with shorter and shorter strokes, then out of control and clumsy, simply reestablishing myself inside the new approach, I settled down, fucked slowly. The prick was embedded far in her; I barely stirred; the drama of sexual movement died away, the curtains were stilled; there was only sensation on the stage.

I bumped against the stone blocks and hidden hooks that nipped and bruised me into the soft rottenness, the strange, glowing, breakable hardness of coming, of the sensations at the approaches to coming.

I panted and half rolled and pushed and edged it in, and slid it back, sweatily—I was semiexpert, aimed, intent. Sex can be like a wilderness that imprisons you: the daimons of the locality claim you. I was achingly nagged by sensations; my prick had been somewhat softened before, and now it swelled with a sore-headed but fine distension; Orra shuddered and held me cooperatively; I began to forget her.

I thought she was making herself come on the slow fucking, on the prick which, when it was seated in her like this, when I hardly moved it, seemed to belong to her as much as to me; the prick seemed to *enter* me, too: we both seemed to be sliding on it; the sensation was like that; but there was the moment when I became suddenly aware of her again, of the flesh and blood and bone in my arms, beneath me. I had a feeling of grating on her, and of her grating on me. I didn't recognize the unpleasantness at first. I don't know how long it went on before I felt it as a withdrawal in her, a withdrawal that she had made, a patient and restrained horror in her, and impatience in me: our arrival at sexual shambles.

My heart filled suddenly—filled; and then all feeling ran out of it—it emptied itself.

I continued to move in her slowly, numbly, in a shabby hubbub of faceless shudderings and shufflings of the midsection and half-thrusts, half-twitches; we went on holding each other, in silence, without slackening the intensity with which we held each other; our movements, that flopping in place, that grinding against each other, went on; neither of us protested in any way. Bad sex can be sometimes stronger and more moving than good sex. She made sobbing noises—and held on to me. After a while sex seemed very ordinary and familiar and unromantic. I started going dit-dit-dit again.

Her hips jerked up half a dozen times before it occurred to me again that she liked to thrust like a boy, that she wanted to thrust; and then it occurred to me that she wanted me to thrust.

I maneuvered my ass slightly and tentatively delivered a shove, or rather, delivered an authoritative shove, but not one of great length, one that was exploratory; Orra sighed, with relief it seemed to me; and jerked, encouragingly, too late, as I was pulling back. When I delivered a second thrust, a somewhat more obvious one, more amused, almost boyish, I was like a boy whipping a fairly fast ball, in a game, at a first baseman—she jerked almost wolfishly, gobbling up the extravagant power of the gesture, of the thrust; with an odd shudder of pleasure, of irresponsibility, of boyishness, I suddenly realized how physically strong Orra was, how well knit, how well put together her body was, how great the power in it, the power of endurance in it; and a phrase—absurd and demeaning but exciting just then—came into my head: *to throw a fuck;* and I settled myself atop her, braced my toes and knees and elbows and hands on the bed and half-scramblingly worked *it—it* was clearly mine; but I was Orra's—worked *it* into a passionate shove, a curving stroke about a third as long as a full stroke; but amateur and gentle: that is, tentative still; and Orra screamed then; how she screamed: she made known her readiness; then the next time, she grunted: "Uhnn-nnahhhhhh . . ." a sound thick at the beginning but that trailed into refinement, into sweetness, a lingering sweetness.

It seemed to me I really wanted to fuck like this, that *I* had been waiting for this all my life. But it wasn't really my taste, that kind of fuck: I liked to throw a fuck with less force and more gradations and implications of force rather than with the actual thing; and with more immediate contact between the two sets of pleasures and with more admissions of defeat and triumph; my pleasure was a thing of me reflecting her, her spirit entering me; or perhaps it was merely a mistake, my thinking that; but it seemed shameful and automatic, naive and animal, to throw the prick into her like that.

She took the thrust: she convulsed a little; she fluttered all over; her skin fluttered; things twitched in her, in the disorder surrounding the phallic blow in her. After two thrusts, she collapsed, went flaccid, then toughened and readied herself again, rose a bit from the bed, aimed the flattened, mysteriously funnel-like container of her lower end at me, too high, so that I had to pull her down with my hands on her butt or on her hips; and her face, when I glanced at her beneath my lids, was fantastically pleasing, set, concentrated, busy, harassed; her body was strong, was stone, smooth stone and wet-satin paper bags and snaky webs, thin and alive, made of woven snakes that lived, thrown over the stone; she held the great, writhing-skinned stone construction toward me, the bony marvel, the half-dish of bone with its secretive, gluey-smooth entrance, *the place where I was*—it was undefined, except for that: *the place where I was;* she took and met each thrust—and shuddered and collapsed and rose again: she seemed to rise to the act of taking it; I thought she was partly mistaken, childish, to think that the center of sex was to meet and take the prick thrown into her as hard as it could be thrown, now that she was excited; but there was a weird wildness, a wild freedom, like children cavorting, uncontrolled, set free, but not hysterical, merely without restraint; the odd, thickened, knobbed pole springing back and forth as if mounted on a web of wide rubber bands: it was a naive and a complete release. I whomped it in and she went, "UHNNN!" and a half-iota of a second later, I was seated all the way in her, I jerked a minim of an inch deeper in her, and went, "UHNNN!"

too. Her whole body shook. She would go, "UHN!" And I would go,
"UHN!"

Then when it seemed from her strengthening noises and her more
rapid and jerkier movements that she was near the edge of coming, I'd
start to place the whomps, in neater and firmer arrangements, more
obviously in a rhythm, more businesslike, more teasing, with pauses at
each end of a thrust; and that would excite her up to a point; but then
her excitement would level off, and not go over the brink. So I would
speed up: I'd thrust harder, then harder yet, then harder and faster; she
made her noises and half-thrust back. She bit her lower lip; she set her
teeth in her lower lip; blood appeared. I fucked still faster, but on a
shorter stroke, almost thrumming on her, and angling my abdomen
hopefully to drum on her clitoris; sometimes her body would go limp;
but her cries would speed up, bird after bird flew out of her mouth while
she lay limp as if I were a boxer and had destroyed her ability to move;
then when the cries did not go past a certain point, when she didn't
come, I'd slow and start again. I wished I'd been a great athlete, a master
of movement, a woman, a lesbian, a man with a gigantic prick that
would explode her into coming. I moved my hands to the corners of
the mattress; and spread my legs; I braced myself with my hands and
feet; and braced like that, free-handed in a way, drove into her; and the
new posture, the feeling she must have had of being covered, and
perhaps the difference in the thrust got to her; but Orra's body began
to set up a babble, a babble of response, then—I think the posture played
on her mind.

But she did not come.

I moved my hands and held the dish of her hips so that she couldn't
wiggle or deflect the thrust or pull away: she began to "Uhn" again but
interspersed with small screams: we were like kids playing catch (her
poor brutalized clitoris), playing hard hand: this was what she thought
sex was; it was sexual, as throwing a ball hard is sexual; in a way, too,
we were like acrobats hurling ourselves at each other, to meet in midair
and fall entangled to the net. It was like that.

Her mouth came open, her eyes had rolled to one side and stayed
there—it felt like twilight to me—I knew where she was sexually, or
thought I did. She pushed, she egged us on. She wasn't breakable this
way. Orra. I wondered if she knew, it made me like her, how naive this
was, this American fuck, this kids-playing-at-twilight-on-the-neighbor-
hood-street fuck. After I seated it and wriggled a bit in her and moozed

on her clitoris with my abdomen, I would draw it out not in a straight line but at some curve so that it would press against the walls of her cunt and she could keep track of where it was; and I would pause fractionally just before starting to thrust, so she could brace herself and expect it; I whomped it in and understood her with an absurd and probably unfounded sense of my sexual virtuosity; and she became silent suddenly, then she began to breathe loudly, then something in her toppled; or broke, then all at once she shuddered in a different way. It really was as if she lay on a bed of wings, as if she had a half-dozen wings folded under her, six huge wings, large, veined, throbbing, alive wings, real ones, with fleshy edges from which glittering feathers sprang backward; and they all stirred under her.

She half-rose; and I'd hold her so she didn't fling herself around and lose her footing, or her airborneness, on the uneasy glass mountain she'd begun to ascend, the frail transparency beneath her, that was forming and growing beneath her, that seemed to me to foam with light and darkness, as if we were rising above a landscape of hedges and moonlight and shadows: a mountain, a sea that formed and grew; it grew and grew; and she said "oн!" and "oннннн!" almost with vertigo, as if she were airborne but unsteady on the vans of her wings, and as if I were there without wings but by some magic dispensation and by some grace of familiarity; I thunked on and on, and she looked down and was frightened; the tension in her body grew vast; and suddenly a great, a really massive violence ran through her, but now it was as if, in fear at her height, or out of some automatism, the first of her three pairs of wings began to beat, great fans winnowingly, great wings of flesh out of which feathers grew, catching at the air, stabilizing and yet lifting her: she whistled and rustled so; she was at once so still and so violent; the great wings engendered, their movement engendered in her, patterns of flexed and crossed muscles: her arms and legs and breasts echoed or carried out the strain, or strained to move the weight of those winnowing, moving wings. Her breaths were wild but not loud and slanted every which way, irregular and new to this particular dream, and very much as if she looked down on great spaces of air; she grabbed at me, at my shoulders, but she had forgotten how to work her hands; her hands just made the gestures of grabbing, the gestures of a well-meaning, dark but beginning to be luminous, mad, amnesiac angel. She called out, "Wiley, Wiley!" but she called it out in a *whisper*, the whisper of someone floating across a night sky, of someone crazily ascending, someone who was going crazy, who was taking on the mad purity and temper of angels, someone who was tormented unendurably by this, who was unendurably frightened, whose pleasure was enormous, half human, mad. Then she screamed in rebuke, "Wiley!" She screamed my name: *"Wiley!"*—she did it hoarsely and insanely, asking for help, but blaming me, and merely as exclamation; it was a gutter sound in part, and ugly; the ugliness destroyed nothing, or maybe it had an impetus of its own, but it whisked away another covering, a membrane of ordinariness—I don't know—and her second pair of wings began to beat; her whole body was aflutter on the bed. I was as wet as—as some fish, thonking away, sweatily. Grinding away. I said, "It's O.K., Orra. It's O.K." And poked on. In midair. She shouted, *"What is this!"* She shouted it in the way a tremendously large person who can defend herself might shout at someone who was unwisely beating her up. She shouted—angrily, as an announcement of anger, it seemed—*"Oh my God!"* Like: *Who broke this cup?* I plugged on. She raised her torso, her head, she looked me clearly in the eye, her eyes were enormous, were bulging, and she said, *"Wiley, it's happening!"* Then she lay down again and screamed for a couple of seconds. I said a little dully, grinding on, "It's O.K., Orra. It's *O.K.*" I didn't want to say *Let go* or to say anything lucid because I didn't know a damn thing about female orgasm after all, and I didn't want to give her any advice and wreck things; and also I didn't want to commit myself in case this turned out to be a false alarm; and we had to go on. I pushed in, lingered, pulled back, went in, only half on beat, one-thonk-one-thonk, then one-one-one, saying, "This is sexy, this is good for me, Orra, this is very good for me," and then, "Good Orra," and she trembled in a new way at that, *"Good* Orra," I said, *"Good . . . Orra,"* and then all at once, it happened. Something pulled her over; and something gave in; and all three pairs of wings began to beat: she was the center and the source and the victim of a storm of wing beats; we were at the top of the world; the huge bird of God's body in us hovered; the great miracle pounded on her back, pounded around us; she was straining and agonized and distraught, estranged within this corporeal-incorporeal thing, this angelic other avatar, this other substance of herself: the wings were outspread; they thundered and gaspily galloped with her; they half-broke her; and she screamed, *"Wiley!"* and *"Mygodmygod"* and "IT'S NOT STOPPING, WILEY, IT'S NOT STOPPING!" She was

pale *and* red; her hair was everywhere; her body was wet, and thrashing. It was as if something unbelievably strange and fierce—like the
holy temper—lifted her to where she could not breathe or walk: she
choked in the ether, a scrambling seraph, tumbling and aflame and
alien, powerful beyond belief, hideous and frightening and beautiful
beyond the reach of the human. A screaming child, an angel howling
in the Godly sphere: she churned without delicacy, as wild as an angel
bearing threats; her body lifted from the sheets, fell back, lifted again;
her hands beat on the bed; she made very loud hoarse tearing noises—
I was frightened for her: this was her first time after six years of playing around with her body. It hurt her; her face looked like something
made of stone, a monstrous carving; only her body was alive; her arms
and legs were outspread and tensed and they beat or they were weak
and fluttering. She was an angel as brilliant as a beautiful insect infinitely enlarged and irrevocably foreign: she was unlike me: she was a
girl making rattling, astonished, uncontrolled, unhappy noises, a girl
looking shocked and intent and harassed by the variety and vicious-
ness of the sensations, including relief, that attacked her. I sat up on
my knees and moved a little in her and stroked her breasts, with
smooth sideways winglike strokes. And she screamed, *"Wiley, I'm
coming!"* and with a certain idiocy entered on her second orgasm or
perhaps her third since she'd started to come a few minutes before;
and we would have gone on for hours but she said, "It hurts, Wiley,
I hurt, make it stop. . . ." So I didn't move; I just held her thighs with
my hands; and her things began to trail off, to trickle down, into little
shiverings; the stoniness left her face; she calmed into moderated
shudders, and then she said, she started to speak with wonder but
then it became an exclamation and ended on a kind of a hollow
note, the prelude to a small scream: she said, "I *came*. . . ." Or
"I ca-a-a-ammmmmmmme. . . ." What happened was that she had
another orgasm at the thought that she'd had her first.

That one was more like three little ones, diminishing in strength.
When she was quieter, she was gasping, she said, "Oh, you *love*
me. . . ."

That, too, excited her. When that died down, she said—angrily—"I
always knew they were doing it wrong, I always knew there was
nothing wrong with me. . . ." And that triggered a little set of ripples.
Sometime earlier, without knowing it, I'd begun to cry. My tears fell
on her thighs, her belly, her breasts, as I moved up, along her body,

above her, to lie atop her. I wanted to hold her, my face next to hers; I wanted to hold her. I slid my arms in and under her, and she said, "Oh, Wiley," and she tried to lift her arms, but she started to shake again; then, trembling anyway, she lifted her arms and hugged me with a shuddering sternness that was unmistakable; then she began to cry, too.

Play

S OMETIMES WHEN I wake, I am eleven years old; and the underside of the bedsprings, the rows of coils that face me, sag, squeak, clatter against the wooden bed frame, flabbily press air—a slow sound—when I grip the curved enameled wires of the coils with my hands and bare feet, and move horizontally, hand over hand, foot over foot. No part of me touches the floor. I can climb sideways or toward the foot or head of the bed, my head in any direction. I am in my underpants and otherwise naked. And sweaty. That child's bare feet are crudely large, intrusions from next year's body. The weighty endowments to come shove and push unimaginably at a mind that refuses to name or predict them, shove and push at the childish bones and skin, too; his wrists have a grossness no other part of his arms yet has. Some time-ridden force hives and swarms in him, with no due proportion, swelling out here and there, enlarging his lips: his mouth is dull and harsh, the lips flattened planes, unchildish in his high-colored face; his eyes are cold, abstract, and hurt and vengeful eleven-year-old eyes; whatever hives in him secretes a honey and he has pale, summer skin, but also secretes a venom and he is sullen; his disposition is rough, unhoneyed, cynical, bloated with impatience. He is, with desperate weariness and unamusement, sly. He is not under the bed alone; he is with another child, one considerably smaller, seven years old, perhaps. The other child is in his underpants, and barefooted, and lies atop him as he climbs, suspended, on the underside of the bedsprings. The other child clings with his arms around my neck, his legs slide from side to side within the guardrails of my skimpy thighs; I shift my abdomen often to change the plane on which he slides, to block or interrupt a slide, to contradict the loose bony slippage of his uncoordinated frame on me: he bounces and bumps and slips on my abdomen and chest. I scuttle within the confines of a game of Tarzan. If his mother or grandmother comes in, they may or may not object; I don't care. The bedsprings are a matted tangle of jungle growth; sweatily, intensely, I disturb the dust of habitation in the half-grave beneath the bed.

Any memory of private play that year would be of play in barely lit garages or thin-windowed basements, in the most distant and the weediest parts of fields, in the corners or on the hidden side of roofs of half-built houses, or in the hidden tunnels in clumps of shrubbery, among the prickle-edge leaves and nagging spines of evergreens, or on tree branches leafed in, or in windowless shanty-clubhouses, by candlelight at noon, anywhere out of sight—perhaps I speak only of myself. I wanted to be unobserved. Boys and girls already adolescent mysteriously shamed me by their notice or even their mere presence, grownups wore me out and humiliated me—younger children spied and bore tales, were stings administered by another world: all faces held the threat or actuality of humiliation closing in; to be eleven was humiliating, the powerlessness, the lie of looking like a child still; we had been more lovable a few years before; now we got on everybody's nerves. In our view, we were the only true humans, the only complete, rational beings, clearer-headed than angels—no adult understood this. They thought we stammered with unease; it was with contempt. We did not believe we were temporary; we were too rational for miracles, for puberty; there was no hair on me below that of my eyelashes except childish fuzz—we waited. I had almost the cold heart and the will and austere obsessiveness of a man. Not quite. The moment before puberty is perhaps the clearestminded of any but it is full of errors: still, we were all brain, eyes, logic, will, and a working coldness. I did not believe in time and change, in anyone's honesty or promises—my cynicism was absolute. What passionate, relentless scoffers we were. We were like actors in a movie who know they will be murdered shortly, and everything about them, arms, legs, soul, will be carted away, will vanish from the plot, and not our parents, not our friends, not even memory would find *us* again. We were as cold and sly and temporary, as full of basking and venom, and with a peculiar suitable treacherous cold irking beauty, as snakes.

It was dark under the bed, a gray-lit—not a green-tinged—jungle, and the smell of dust took the place of the smell of leaves. Randolph was pretty and he was dull. We had no language of useful abuse; it was all done in inflection: *Him?* As I understood it, nothing could come before a game, not one's mother's fears, not one's own. There could be no safety, no prearranged rules, no set order to appeal to: everything was re-created every day; yesterday's everything died in one's sleep, in the furnace of one's dreams; what dreams allowed to stand, luck burned: your friends were busy or had allied themselves to someone else or had entered some other sphere of influence, or you had. To appeal to logic or any law outside immediate precedent, to any law outside childhood and a range of two days, was to be past our ability to describe in language the sort of person you were and why it was no good to play with you. The only acceptable mental set was that of a profoundly irreconcilable anarchist. I don't know how much we lied, how attached we were to logic and safety after all—I don't think much. To a sickening extent, the real world was curtained off from us: we tried to make our world real; we were grubby, we were little militarists, soldiers in a garrison town. Would we be six feet tall? Would we be creepy? What would luck do to us? While we waited, we thought it shameful to be organized in any way. To be a Little Leaguer was a terrible thing. We liked to explore sewer outlets and the sewers themselves; we liked to hunt rats; we put rat corpses on streetcar tracks and studied the parts of the exploded cadavers—"Lookit the thing like a bean." We liked to sit around in grubby, abandoned places, derelict corners of the park, and say crude things about our teachers. We had moments of fastidiousness and delicacy, of concentration, and of limpness. We doted on violence; we were sexually inadequate; the rage spilled out: we liked banditry, thievishness, treachery. We liked to spit on the floor of the garages of Catholic families. We vandalized sporadically. You could be crazy and ugly, but as long as you realized other people were alive and as long as you had no rules, you were eligible for companionship. But no rules—none of that leverage. We were sick to death of innocence.

Randolph was a lousy playmate; he didn't realize the bedsprings didn't squeak, it was the monkeys chattering. When I told him, he said, "Monkeys?" Then he said, "Tell me again." What he liked was being told. His mother was close to my mother, and Randolph had a little-child's crush on me, so I had to play with him. But I was ashamed of it and was playing this naked game in order to get something not too

boring out of it and also maybe to shock his mother and get that over
with. You could snort and refuse to play and say sharply to someone,
"Aw, you don't do it right," and stalk off, but then the mother of who
you stalked off from might strike back through the school psychologist,
who was erratic as hell and might accuse you of being unstable: then
it was war between the families and between teachers at school, some
of whom thought you were crazy and some of whom liked you: to the
towers, to the towers. The phrase was *It's hopeless.* Randolph is uplifted
by the rapture of hearing an untrue statement made with passionate faith
in its usefulness inside a frame of pleasure and for no other purpose
except selfishness; the delight for him is not in the logic that opens out
of any game and one's adherence to the game; his delight was in the
willfulness of speaking the blasphemies of private imagination as truths.
He will be a lawyer, an advertising man, a drunken grammatical loveless
poet, a wit who does not amuse. The idea of willed pleasure will always
exalt him because of the trick of it, which he will never have but will
claim to have. He will at intimate moments make the wrong confession.
The unhappiness he experiences bores me—not all unhappiness is
worth respect. He will maybe never realize he is boring and plays games
badly. He expected to be liked, to be a toy; his mother and grandmother
had reared him as a toy for themselves; he was pruned and undone, a
harem male. He was startled into a dependent, tense, always brief, and
soon doubting pleasure, by whatever I said. He keeps his arms around
my neck, his body lies on mine, and he waits to be amazed some more.
Meanwhile I maneuver in the scrofulous hot jungle dust beneath the
bed, acting out my notions of adventure and of physical splendor, and
I largely ignore him.

MY FATHER has been ill; he's had a series of heart attacks; sometimes he asks me to sit near him; he holds my hand and tells me bitter
things; sometimes almost with dim amusement, as if from a great distance, as if he floated out away from everyone on an inner sea, he refuses
to be interested in something I ask him; he will say, "You don't need
me to tell you what to do—you know how to be a fool all by yourself."
He says it often with affection, a kind of affection; he makes jokes of that
kind; I don't understand why he doesn't worry about me.

My mother is a very pretty, overweight, tense woman, who has had
a large-scale social life which is done for, for the moment. She says of

my father, "He pities no one but himself." She nagged him to try harder to live; he told her to be gentler, to smile, to be nice; she said, "I can't be a fool just to make you happy—be reasonable." My father had decided he hated her, and his hatred was slow and far and unrelenting; he called her Madame The Great Horned Toad and Your Highness Our Own Killer Bitch and Mrs. Hellmouth. She did not think much of the masculine sensibility; she thought my father and I ought to be inspired by our feelings for her and do great things for her; but my father did not want just to be a father, breadwinner, husband, man uplifted by love, and she didn't want to deal with him as a person. She was willing to play her roles for him for a while—she did not expect him or want him, maybe, to see her as a person, but to love her instead. She was casual that way. My mother made me play with Randolph. She liked to make me do things. She would say, "Take off my shoes for me—I'm all worn out." But I didn't want to; if I refused, there might be no dinner. She minds it that I am young, that she is supposed to take care of me, that I am a boy and will never be stuck as she has been as a nurse for someone. In an idle, terrible way she hates being a nurse and lets herself be cruel. She tells my father it makes her sick to take care of him—there is more to her than a maid and a cook. She often tries to wheedle me or crazily orders me to run the house—"Fix your father's dinner—if it isn't cooked right, he won't kill you—you're the one he likes." She said, "I suppose you expect me to give you a happy childhood?" They were all crazy.

She was fond of me in a way, but now that my father was ill people were concerned about me and not about her: they expected her to sacrifice herself. She gets even for that, she endangers me, in a casual way; in a casual way, she indulges her moods, her impulses. She is good-looking and dangerous and aging. Other people say that of her, that she is dangerous and aging. I know she feels animosity toward me, and she lets herself feel it, and I am sickened and afraid, but what should I do? My father tells me to have nothing to do with her. When I avoid her, she cries and says, "You, too, you're going to turn on me?" It is part of my wildness, those tears of hers, the animosity and then those tears.

I tried to avoid going to play with Randolph. That is, I made myself invisible, I forgot invitations, but my mother outwaited me. She said, "Don't be so full of yourself. Be more willing to do someone a favor. Maybe he'll help you someday. You never know what will happen—

you might have a good time. You should be flattered he likes you. Believe me, you haven't an easy personality to like."

She began to yell, "Go play with him! Don't make a fool of me in front of his mother! I owe her a favor! Be kind to someone for a change! It won't hurt you!"

IN THAT SUBURB, among boys my age, games of acquisition and of gambling, marbles, trading baseball cards, playing mumblety-peg for stakes, or tossing pennies, and games of real or of mock violence, pea-shooter wars, cops and robbers (with mock brawls, mock agony, often elaborate plots), Robin Hood, Tarzan, Space Search, and Torture, were more common than sports. We played scratch baseball, stoop ball, stickball, catch, touch football, wall ball, and various two-man games of imaginary baseball; it was hard when you were young to get up a real baseball game; we did not have easy access to a field, and if we got the field, older boys or grownups could easily dislodge us and take over; and where could we get eighteen kids anyway? Our parents sometimes lobbied for or paid for or set up sports to keep us from the happy nastiness of children, from our other games, but my parents did not have any interest in sports, and I had perhaps a larger acquaintance with the nastiness—and liked it more—than other children did. I don't know that that was so. Our powerlessness, the reality of that physical fact, was dinned into us over and over: you might get asked to fill in on a baseball team of older boys, but your reach, your power at the plate were so limited that any older boy who showed up was welcomed and you were kicked off.

Of the games we could control, Torture was, from the time we were six until we were about ten and began to have the coordination and freedom for large-scale activities and actual bullying, the most common game. It was most often played by three children, but the third was really more a referee, a magical companion, a safety factor. It was popular in spurts and not everyone played it all the time but everyone played it some, everyone who was a *player*—there were children we did not play with, who were what their parents wanted them to be, and who we thought were disgusting (and maybe the future belonged to them: we didn't know). Not all children have free will; and among those who have it, some have it more than others. Inflexible children, those who could not explore a moment's exotic possibilities and perversities, were excluded. Torture was straightforward: one of you was a captive and was helpless; the game hardly ever involved escape. Usually the central drama was that of interrogation; you could rise up and try to hit or actually did hit your interrogator, but then he or she would bring down an imaginary whip and you had to howl in agony. Girls played, too, but they were very strange, not easily controlled. In most cases, no real pain was essential; there were other games where the pain had to be real, but then it was shared or mutually inflicted. The basic plot of Torture was helplessness, and the reality of ruthlessness, and the survival of the will or its breaking. When you were very young, you played with every-thing imaginary—chains, whips, branding irons—but you might use an old shoelace or a piece of string as a lash: you know what children are like. Among the children I played with, the girls were the first to become realistic: cuticle scissors for stabbing (not deeply) or clipping off bits of the padded finger end. It was odd, and funny, that at that point Torture often turned into her giving you a manicure: the game's voltage was too full of intimations, had too much resonance, was too nasty, and we would, as it were, forget what we were doing and slide into some-thing else.

Girls insisted you be tied up. We played Torture perhaps for an hour on three days running and then maybe only four times more that whole year; I should not have said it was the most popular but that it was the most universal. If you went to another neighborhood, that was the game you were most likely to wind up in. Anyway, to be tied up we would use bent clothes hangers or bits of clothesline. Often the preparations would be the only part of the game we would play full-heartedly. Few girls or boys could say, "I'm going to put your eye out if you don't talk," except without conviction. I mean to say that the horror tended to evaporate: the expectation was frightening.

Sometimes the horror didn't evaporate. In a neighborhood of richer children, I found myself tied up one time, tied to a chair in a basement. There were two other boys, and a girl was supposed to join us but she never showed up. One of the boys was named Lewis: his mother was a widow, Lewis was very handsome, very shy and silent in class, and well behaved; and I had not expected this side of him. He did not talk much, and most of most Torture games was talk, so I thought this would be dull. He and the other boy heated up a soldering iron and over my protests singed my hair; then they wanted to singe my eyelashes—Lewis was very proud of his steady hand. I told him to go fuck himself (I did not know what fuck meant but I knew it was a serious term). He said I was tied up and he was going to do what he wanted: my blood ran cold and I began to twist, so he was afraid to come too near me; but he brought the iron close to my *chin*, threatening to burn me if I didn't stop twisting around. It was considered shameful ever to appeal to a grownup or to tell one anything, but I told him to get the hell away from me or I would scream and I would tell. He backed away. Complainingly, the other boy untied me, and then I hit Lewis—on the cheek, but not all that hard, hard enough only to show displeasure, not rage. Lewis said he didn't understand me; he and the other boy showed me how they played; the other boy put his finger in a vise (we were in a basement workroom); and Lewis swung the nipple-ended underbar of the vise and worked it tighter on the boy's finger. The boy began to sweat and undulate faintly, and stared at Lewis with protruding eyes. Lewis tightened the vise still more.

There were stories of fairly severe injuries—but mostly among quite rich children (we lived on streets that ran parallel along the slope of a very long rise; on the top were mansions; street by street the houses grew smaller until you came to the valley, where they were quite small).

We were sexually latent—I knew no one my age who knew about sex; we talked toward it often, but were strangely blank. We had intense bursts of sympathy toward each other, periods when we were drawn to some other child's company: I had been drawn to Lewis's. Lewis and I went to visit a girl named Myrna, who had a white bedroom: Lewis and Myrna were Episcopalians, but it was an insanely fluffy, vulgar, princess-in-the-movies sort of bedroom; and afterward, Lewis and I played Torture, my way, in a nearby woods (near the school), using our imaginations and a skinny branch or two to lash lightly at each other's legs. I thought Lewis would be wowed by my version of the game and I was stunned—and hurt—when he said he preferred the soldering-iron, finger-in-the-vise version he played.

Games were *real* when money was involved—or marbles—when loss was possible or pain. Not otherwise. A girl who was not agonized when we played catch with her doll got her doll back rapidly. Another game, played in boredom but sometimes played in high spirits, was jumping with both feet together or hopping on one foot or simply stamping on each other's feet while trying to dodge and using one's elbows or hands as fenders or to straight-arm the opponent. The oddest version of a hurt-the-feet game was one a Tom Sawyerish–looking boy I liked a lot thought up: we stood facing each other and first he dropped a brick on my toes from about knee height, then I dropped one on his toes; we both were wearing shoes; then he dropped his brick from higher on my feet; and I yowled, and dropped the brick from as high on his feet as he had on mine. Meanwhile there was a lot of quibbling about whether the brick was dropped from the right height. The first person to writhe and not to be able to stop writhing lost. I remember covering our shoes were rags and pieces of cardboard cartons so they wouldn't be too badly scratched by the bricks, so our parents couldn't figure out what we did.

Everything we did hinged on pleasure and on some kind of gamble or contest involving a fall into humiliation or an escape, or an escape from humiliation with great honor. Once, where a new house was being built, my Tom Sawyer friend suggested a game of leaping from a second-story window onto a pile of sand. And I was afraid. There were five of us, two girls; the other four sailed off, arms spread; I could not make myself do it. No. I did it once and could not make myself do it the second time.

I started a fight, a wrestling match with my Tom Sawyer friend in front of everyone then and there; the others pulled me off him; I was stronger than Tom Sawyer and so the bout wasn't fair; but also perhaps I ran things with too hard a hand too much of the time; and it was not my turn to be on top for a while; and my friends liked having me at a real disadvantage. I suffered.

In everything we did there were moments when we measured cowardice or skill or strength: a Catholic church with a high steeple was being built, and we climbed the scaffolding, not the ramps but the scaffolding, and the children who dropped out were treated with a perfect friendliness indicating their unimportance until they reestablished their importance in playing marbles or by riding a bicycle free-handed down the street with legs and arms outspread.

This measuring was sometimes joint—all of us were tested—and sometimes relative, each of us against the other; and the moments of triumph or of humiliation were so heady, and so heavy with throbs of nerves or beatings of the heart, that it seemed there were entire neurological festivals our systems waged, as rampant with noise and ceremonial—with blushes or silence or modesty or sudden acts of cruelty or of tenderness—as when the Doge married Venice to the sea: sometimes the implication of physical pleasure, the whiff of life, that rank smell, that force, that outward pressure in us nearly inundated the identity—

the body would seem to be on the verge of leaking or melting. The scaffolding we climbed left marks on my hands, deep reddened gouges, small callused ridges, a blister; into the sensation of having hands half my spirit flowed after I climbed down from the scaffolding having gone the highest of anyone, having gone to the top. I did not have to smile. I did not have to mention what I had done. I merely found it hard to focus my eyes; my eyes stared off into the distance; and some odd feeling—I would call it contentment but it writhed and rose and changed shape and taste (sometimes it was dry, sometimes moist and half sweet)—filled me to the brim, filled me, oddly, with admiration and love for my companions that they did not necessarily feel back toward me, the winner on that occasion.

Winning was like standing at the edge of a really nice view of reeds and water and pretty light in the sky. A handsome world. More dangerous was winning in a certain way, ruthlessly, too willfully: everyone objected if you won that way; they did not necessarily avoid you; you were considered, though, a wolf among children. Character and perseverance were O.K.; but this other was shocking, as was trickery; but nearly everyone used trickery. Not me. I was too Olympian for trickery except when others asked me to invent a trick for them. But the focused will, the naked appetite, as opposed to the hidden will, the indirect appetite, was shocking, shocking even to experience when it was one's own focused will, the panting, odd-eyed (as if one's eyes were on stalks and not in one's skull) concentration and brutal power of forcing someone to do something: to squeeze them until they begged for release; or to twist an arm or use a headlock or box them into submission, into having them do what you wanted them to do.

Sometimes they jumped up, or you jumped up, or I did, when I'd been forced to the ground and forced to admit I was a pig's ass, say, and you took it back and ran. Or you struck back in another way. Girls were particularly vengeful; grown-up ones, too; sometimes it seemed to me that girls never moved except in vengeance or love; otherwise they just sat on their asses, but they always had to get up to get even with some boy or some girl or their parents or who knew what. Small boys were like that, too. My Tom Sawyer friend, if his mother was nice to me, invariably suggested we play paper-stone-scissors: he had strong fingers and could make my wrist sting more than I could make his sting. Power, bits of power, lay everywhere; sometimes it was as if some Red Indian daimon possessed us, oversaw our play, made us peculiarly American.

Or we were frontier children, half Indians, half religious fanatics. But so hungry for life. The suburb sat baldly on wild ground; beneath our feet, beneath the lawns, the real ground was close, tall grass, sunlight, silence. One thing more than any other guided us, boy and girl alike, in our play, and that was an affinity for our fathers and a funny enmity toward our mothers, an enmity that had nothing to do with our furious loyalty: the one truly certain way to provoke a fight was to insult someone's mother; but still we were guided in our play not only by the Indian daimon but by another, paler Spirit, an intellectual spirit of deduction: we were fascinated by and wanted to play whatever we knew would upset our mothers most if they knew we were doing it; we had to do, *had* to, whatever they forbade or disliked; it was as if there was a law that said whatever there was that was pleasurable, we could be guided toward it by thinking of what would trigger our mothers' embarrassment and disapproval.

My mother said often it was no joy to be a mother, children enjoyed tormenting you. And in a complicated way that was true. We enjoyed what tormented them.

Sometimes older boys went on rampages—four or five tougher boys, not necessarily poorer, would go tramping through the streets, making trouble; sometimes a squadron of older boys came in on bicycles from other suburbs, sometimes from a richer one, sometimes from a poorer one, like Vikings, and they tormented who they could: they were miserably unhappy; they seemed starved—and violent—somewhat incomprehensible. *If* they caught you, you might be fastened by your belt to the back of a bicycle and forced to run behind it while the boy, bicycling with a shamed closed face, turned to watch you from time to time. They had seen this in the movies. Or they'd take your pants off, or they'd toss you in their arms until you screamed. Sometimes they twisted your arm and made you kneel and say their suburb was better than yours. Or they might make you say your mother was dirty. Or a whore. Sometimes the invaders were accused of sexual molestation, of exposing themselves in driveways, or to women afraid to get out of their cars, or of making some small boy do something faintly obscene. But it was a polite suburb and such things were hushed up.

As relatively small boys we admired the magnetic fields of the emotional power and projection of women—a woman could stand on her porch and look stern or nice, or come to school and look sure of herself and awe you. We admired women's tempers—not their hysteria. I am not certain, but with a lot of girls and women everything but their temper seemed sappy or calculated to us. And precarious and out of reach. Their temper was familiar. And permitted a sort of reality. And so it was warming.

In men we admired chiefly muscles and large hands. A really generously muscled man awed us even if he was bad-tempered. I didn't know anybody (although such existed) who failed to admire the shirtless heroes of comic strips and the narrow-hipped, masked do-gooders in certain kinds of movie romances. Casually we expected physical perfection, but our eyes were generous and perhaps saw more perfection than there was. An older boy named Stanley, who had an acne-pitted face and who was known as a troublemaker and sullen at that, was discovered one day when he was exercising in his backyard to have a remarkable body, with squared off, three-quarters-of-an-inch-thick muscles on his chest and other muscles everywhere. It was a body much grander (although small on the whole) than that of any other boy in the neighborhood that year, and often when he exercised in his backyard, some kid would scout around and gather a gang, and we would go and watch Stanley and observe his muscles while he did things to encourage them to get bigger yet.

My friends put me up to asking him how he got his chest muscles and Stanley said push-ups had done it. About nine of us, like some new species of panting crickets, promptly began doing push-ups in imitation of him. A herd of crickets.

We would pretend to stumble and we would then fall on the ground near an older girl and roll and try to look up her skirt—then we would report to each other: "Did you see anything?" We never did; we did not know what to look for; but it was exciting anyway. And necessary. When I did it I thought I'd recognize it when I saw it, whatever was remarkable under a girl's skirt, but all that ever impressed me was the sullen silent splendor of the shadows and the hint of slightly stale, close air. And secrecy. We often spied on girls who were being visited by boys. We would run to stand outside the house of an older girl we'd heard was going to a dance: we loved to see girls all rigged out. It is hard to believe how moved we were by rich regalia on a woman: furs, jewelry, expensive clothes, special shoes. But everything was suggestive: leaves blowing, a thunderhead roiling up, the smell of a cellar. To coast downhill on a bicycle was to go slightly berserk with pleasure (no hill was long enough). Things touched the palms of one's hand—concrete, the wood of a porch floor, the roughness of brick, the rust-scarred handles of a bicycle. We streamed here and there on errands that mostly had to do with the obscene. Anger in men frightened us half to death; we tried to elicit it in women; only the most frightened children never teased a woman. We might stalk a girl, an older girl, throw pebbles at her, run wildly and laugh when she chased us through a weedy lot, laugh in a strange, weak, trailing, maybe overexcited fashion. We were often good children, passive and stern, but never for long. The obscene beckoned us. Boys and a few girls often got together to discuss the meanings of the dirty words that our sexual latency prevented us from understanding: fuck was explained to me at least fifty times by older boys, but I hadn't the faintest idea what it meant. I drowned it all out. I agreed with another boy when I was six (and then, oddly, had no definition for fuck at all, and did not see the oddity) that fuck must mean something like—because it upset mothers so—going peepee on your mother. We lived in a sensual and passionate immediacy, as if the suburb were a walled and gated garden; I was quite old before I guessed the suburb had not been beautiful. Our world was shadowy and violent and unclean. But decent because of our powerlessness. We knew even parental love to be a physical attachment: weren't we loved and stroked, touched and bathed, and bidden to embrace our parents? We knew our parents lied to themselves about us; sometimes we tried to be as good as they thought we were; but it wasn't so important usually—it was only terrible sometimes. We were used to hurting people. Not always, though. Some of us had an added element of self-consciousness—that's all that virtue was then. Or that it came from. In some ways we couldn't wash off in the flow of childhood some of the things we did. In some ways we could live our lives only at moments; in front of grownups I felt it necessary to have no life but to be an observer, a referee—of dreams, of expectations. Meanwhile I was a child. The children I knew hugged and seduced thousands. After a game in the snow, or in the heat, we might lie on the ground or the snow and roll over and over and then on top of each other, until our cheeks touched, until our eyes looked into each other's eyes; we bartered our hugs or had them bartered for us; we spun and dropped and climbed into and out of perches and pockets, into and out of secrets, our secrets. We understood nothing yet. Only a few stubborn, maybe unreliable children were spared the primacy of the physical and lived in the realm of deprivation and loneliness and waiting to come into their intellectual and spiritual kingdoms. The rest of us inhabited a garden, and we knew that no one was sympathetic unless you charmed them physically first. We were children, little whores—the whole suburb was a bordello—how could it have been otherwise, how can it ever be otherwise? Blood moved in us: the light came through the shattered jasper of the trees. Heat rose from the macadam of the streets. The snow triggered briskness, forced us to dance as if it were music, to frisk, to skip. Among the trees and the living, heated people, it has to be the same no matter how much they lie or how much they forget. It is a sensual wonder to be young. We are alive from a very early age.

THE BLUE JEANS lie on the floor, the slightly smelly, stained sneakers, socks, the flimsy, discarded shirts, twisted, outspread, frail, their buttons like the eyes of fish. Other boys and I often undressed as part of playing Tarzan, or as part of playing Torture (but we did not always undress). Randolph's mother is not home; what I am doing in part is baby-sitting. Randolph's grandmother, a stern, half-crazy woman, is on patrol downstairs; I dislike her interrupting whatever I do with Randolph—she likes to open the door, come in, and check; and I have told her not to do that ever. Sometimes she peers from the doorway. Not now: Randolph has protested volubly to her (he does not like it when I am upset or bored) that she should not come in when his door is closed. On this occasion she has once or twice called out through the closed door, "What are you two doing? Is everything all right?" "We're playing: go away, Grandma." The old woman thinks ill of me, of anyone Randolph likes, and it is partly in careless defiance of her that I have taken off nearly all my clothes. There are toys near the door, and if the old woman tries to open the door, it will make a noise. I really don't give a damn about her.

I thought that what I was doing was exercising, doing something like push-ups as Stanley suggested, so I would be muscular maybe someday. A good deal of everything we did as children we did as anger—or as escape—anger with adults, escape from them. They cannot play Tarzan. The great weighted, dangling, waiting sensuality of the suburb is not obviously present. I was maybe like a foal nuzzling with its mouth, its whole bare body, at the belly of the world. The child lay atop my stomach, and as I climbed along the underside of the springs, Randolph bounced a little on me; his smooth hide rubbed on mine. Whenever I reached out with one arm or shifted my weight, it altered the plane on which he lay; he was uncoordinated; and he slid; he was almost always about to fall; I held him, as part of the effort of climbing, with the inside of my upper arms, as I moved my arms, and with my thighs, as I moved my thighs. I kept wiggling, adjusting my abdomen, adjusting the angle of the plane on which he lay to keep him balanced as best I could while I climbed.

The peculiar stagnation of the air beneath the bed, the dim dustiness, the faint sweatiness of the game were acceptable, the whole thing was something that wasn't a hole in life (as sitting still at a dinner table might be, or playing checkers often was) but it was just barely not a totally useless game; and then a very brief, faint sensation I'd never had before happened to me, and I was, after a brief passage of time, a half second or so of that childish gaping at something strange, considerably interested. It had been fairly faint; and it was as if maybe if I could find enough of it, I might be addicted to it someday—as I was to bicycle riding.

I did not have any idea what had caused the sensation, and I continued to do what Randolph and I had been doing, but I was much more inwardly alert, and the sensation recurred, faintly the second time. It more or less struck me (as logical) that this feeling was maybe a simple concomitant of *exercise,* of building up your muscles, and it was why older boys could exercise for so long and with such concentration and so without complaint; and also maybe this was why muscular boys had that look of comfort about them, of having been comforted. But when I climbed along the underside of the bed more energetically, when I exercised harder, so to speak, so that Randolph bounced on my stomach and drove the breath out of me, the sensation did not come back until, tired by that effort, I lowered my behind to the floor and caught my breath, and shifted my abdomen to support Randolph's weight, and Randolph, cooperatively, gathered himself to balance more adroitly along the central axis of my body. As he stirred and reangled his arms around my neck, in that comparative stillness, the sensation returned. So it could not be part of exercise.

At the time it seemed perfectly sensible and like the rest of life that such an interesting sensation should be mysterious and not straightforwardly available. And it was O.K. that I should set out on the hunt for the sensation. All that was typical, not strange at all. It was an almost triangular sensation, mostly blue and white, and very small but sort of hot, almost like a flame, and around it the mind darkened. That is, the sensation appeared, blue-and-white, triangular, sail-like, pennon-like (like a pennon on its end), and very interesting and seemingly worthwhile in the darkness. Part of the good thing about the sensation was the heaviness and soft drama and novel sweetness of that darkness, which was just there, so to speak, but which was maybe part of what happened, and a large part of what was felt. The little triangle was more like a guess that an inward eye made about the shape of something that had no shape. Which had only duration and amazement. An amazement of the nerves, of the body, of the semiastonished mind, this surprising part of playing Tarzan.

If I lay still, it did not come back, although it would seem to be there but would not quite form, like a ghost refusing to materialize. If I moved very, very slowly the sensation would form but sometimes so dimly that it made me irritable. If I threw myself around violently from side to side, the sensation appeared, but it was *crowded*, crowded in among other sensations, those of bumping around and of breathlessness, and was not so satisfactory. I did not know Randolph was necessary, or suspect it. In a way the hunt was a curtain between him and me, but in a way it joined us since as the moments passed there began to be a glory in the game and in the now greatly warmed up, sweaty *anguish* of the plot of the child's version of Tarzan that we were playing, that I was still to some extent playing, thinking that the game held the pleasure as a cup did tea. The actions of Tarzan and of the African chief that he carried on his stomach gave birth to the glory; it sprang from the adhesion, more and more exaggerated, satisfying, and continuous, of our chests and bellies. We were sewn together by the game, although we played it in different ways, and experienced it in widely differing ways, and by an increasing impatience in me, an abrupt liking for playing with him. And an increasing, odd, and oddly agreeable languor in him: he grew sleepy, quieter, heavy, floppy. Passive.

I climbed up and down the underside of the bed.

The more of those sensations I had, the more likable Randolph seemed. But those sensations were likable, too, except that they were so unnamed and so elusive that my liking them was like my being drawn to a boy whose house was miles away from mine and who I could not see much of or count on seeing at all: I partly held back; I felt a sort of trickery-ridden *calm* interest in what I was doing in order that I would not feel the wounded, the victimized, bitter liking and shy, half-determined, half-careless obsession that sometimes drove friends away. And that sometimes attached them to you with hoops of steel, with sudden passionate connivance. When the sensation did appear, I couldn't always remember what I had just done. And even when I did remember and repeated a movement, the sensation did not always recur. I was really struck, in a half-minded way—I seemed to have only half a mind—by the discovery that if a sensation came soon after another one, it was doubled or even quadrupled in interest to me. Sometimes then the sensation was startling, it was so strong, and it made me shiver and set up what seemed like a clatter in me.

It was unbearably strange . . . but it was bearable. It was as excruciating as if one had found a new woods and was exploring them and might be killed or be run off by a frightening man with a shotgun or might find who knew what. One moved in places—it seemed like places—shadowy, then sunlit, where one had never been before. There had been nothing so new in my life since I'd learned to read. It was a little like making one's way in the dark to spy on a lit-up large house, a mansion, to see what very rich people did. Or like landing on an island. It was like being in a strange place, too, in that all your physical stances were strange and you couldn't move in a familiar way; you didn't know if eyes spied on you, or what the footing was like, or what the odds were on stumbling; your balance, your crouch were necessarily unlike what they were at any other time; or it was like building a treehouse: you perched on a branch, gripped it with your legs, gripped another with one hand, and hammered without getting a full swing with your remaining hand. It was like that.

The strangeness was very great, but almost everything in life then was strange to me, and strangeness was more or less a familiar thing, and that was why I was so calm in a way, and why I acted as I did and went ahead.

I began to sweat in a peculiar way, or rather the sweat on me and on Randolph seemed strangely heavy and oily; it seemed to register with a really unlikely sensitivity the pressure and direction of Randolph's torso when it was sliding on mine. Or when his elbows dug into me: it was very strange and echoing.

After a while my ignorant attention was fixed so firmly on what was going on inside me that the outside world became nearly dark. I kept track of my arms and legs and I moved sensibly enough in the now silent mimicry and oddly tempoed game; but Randolph was no longer real to me; my own movements in the game were not entirely real—part of each movement splintered into a kind of shattered edge of brief trembling or twisting (like a thin piece of wood warping and then being struck, and vibrating, and then breaking into thin slivers), into movement unreal to me, indecipherable, that I could not keep track of, and that I ignored. What was real was this search by some feeling self in me for something increasingly required but unknown and increasingly anguishing but increasingly, almost infinitely desirable. In one sense, I fainted to the world, as a Christian does in an access of faith. My consciousness moved in catacombs, in tunnels.

I did not in any way caress Randolph—it did not even occur to me. I did not associate the sensation with any part of my body. It was simply a sensation in *me*. My mind moved in tunnels that were dark and sometimes cool and sometimes hot, and that would, as I continued to move my body, suddenly open into large, airy chambers that would lose their air abruptly and resound with sensations: chapels almost, they were such special places, places of such special feeling. Sometimes they were filled with a spattering of gleams accompanied by a thunder or succeeded by an aftereffect having a throbbing or pulsing quality as of echoes and of reechoes, on and on. Sometimes there was only a whisper, or such a minor pulse of feeling that the sensation was the merest imaginable dot of something found in a place which seemed to have as its chief distinction that it was a place where one was lost, and disappointed, but even the faintest sensation seemed to leave a trace, a thin bit of something, a residue that had weight in a strange way; and a number of these whisperings would pile up until their weight seemed immense: there would be a sudden rush, a long, heavy, peculiarly white-veined spill of something, of *feeling*, very strange and infinitely welcome. Even as I realized while it was happening that it was a desirable sensation, it would already be passing; and inwardly and outwardly—inwardly and outwardly childish—I would tighten myself, like a fist, make myself into a fist, a knot of will and muscle to hold it; but it was not of the order of things that could be held; it was not breath or willpower. It was strange how ignorant the body could be. The sensation was in its essence independent of me and yet it was mine; it was maddening in its paradox but O.K. in spite of being maddening. It was like a mother-feeling, it aroused feelings as one's mother did, similar feelings. And yet not quite. It was almost a matter of tears when one of the heavy throbs occurred and faded away, and it was almost a matter of tears when after I'd failed to find the sensation for several seconds it returned.

Sometimes the sensation seemed cruel and clumsy, like some event in a comic movie where what was funny was absentmindedness, stupidity, and constantly defeated haste.

I could not for a long time get a sensation to appear with any regularity right after another sensation. When I did succeed at last, the successive sensations would develop attributes, as of wind (perhaps my expelled breath), of sound, of coolness and heat both, of tactility as if I moved on a slide in a children's park, a slide made of fur, of closegrained feathers, of silk; and there were attributes of light, silver light mostly, often like a flash of silver foil, or like a series of interrupted flashes beaming at me a mystic or lunatic code, a message I could not read but enjoyed immensely although in no way that I had ever known enjoyment to form itself before. Enjoyment had never been so mixed with pain, so sad, so physical before. Or rather it had, in games of teasing and in other things, but never like this. My body had not been like this before.

Sleepily, Randolph complained; he stirred; he said he wanted to change the game. It was inconceivable, his complaining. At first, it seemed imaginary, part of the game, his drowsy whining that made me stiffen, with loss, with irritation, with the irritation of authority quibbled with; it made me lose and then sometimes more strongly regain the sensation. But I was wrong: it wasn't part of the Tarzan game. He said, "Nothing is happening. You're not talking to me. You're not paying attention to me—you're supposed to play with me."

He really was not necessary to the hunt except in a peculiar way.

I did talk to him. My lips were a little thick and hard to move, but I could talk, and outside of a disinclination to speak I saw no reason not to speak. I told him Tarzan and the chief were having a fight to the death. I could not talk and climb; but when I slowed down, Randolph started to climb off. I dropped my legs to the floor and lowered the upper part of us more gently. Mimicking a death fight, I rolled over and over with him to the middle of the floor of his room. I was gloved in sweat; my consciousness was lined with soft grayness, like moleskin. I told him, "I can't release you—you'd kill me if I let you go."

He said, "I don't want to be the chief."

"O.K. You're Tarzan. I'm the chief. I can't let you go. If I do, you'll kill me." I tightened my legs around Randolph in a scissors lock. "Try to escape," I told him; he tried; I told him to try harder, to try to wiggle loose mostly in the center. He complained I was holding him too tightly. "Well, then try harder to escape," I said, innocent of what I was doing and yet not innocent in the sense that I knew I was playing a different game from the one he was playing and that I was using him, sort of; but then he was using me—but he also tried to do what I told him. The sensation seemed to use the inside of the usual senses so that with my eyes closed I *saw* a light that would not have been visible to my real eyes, and my ears heard a noise that did not come from the outside. I had no idea that this pursuit of a sensation might come to an end other than that Randolph and I would grow tired and I would go home. I knew that when I released Randolph—as I did twice—I felt suddenly bored and hurt and almost nervous; so I seized him between my legs again; and he struggled. It upset me that when the sensation decomposed it left behind no hint how it was to be reconstituted. I had to learn everything. *"Try harder,"* I said suddenly, with disgust, to Randolph; things had become so tangled in me that it was unendurable; and at the same time, it was more interesting than it ever had been; but it was oppressive. I squeezed Randolph with my legs so that he really did struggle, he wiggled very hard. Suddenly I was entirely interested: I stared but not with my real eyes; I listened; behind a curtain a world began to roll across the wooden floor. Five closely attached ascending sensations disconnected me; the curtains flew apart: I was on the edge of a vast black emptiness; the round thing rolled out, flashing thunder and lightning, but not so noisily as before, not so glaringly, almost nicely. But I was frightened. But the fright was not so bad. And I went over a—a thing, tumbled over the round globe, and off into the darkness, scattering warm, strangely liquescent sparks, uncolored but scorching; something scorched me; I felt something like a wire whip through me; it was drawn through me and then from me, eviscerating me; I was thrown into grief, into astonishment, into a strange nothingness, a blankness of feeling unlike anything I'd ever known. In the posture of a dead man listening to the floor, I rolled over. There was another, fainter brief whistling in me, a feeling of softened light rising and filling something, like a thunderhead, and then a hand, a hand broke through the ceiling of the room, took hold of me, and shook me, and squeezed me, so that I thought I would die. I could not breathe or keep from exuding breath and, I didn't know what, whatever was in me. It squeezed me until I was dead, and then I was boneless and limp, and without comprehension. I curled up on my side, my hand beneath my cheek, the side of my finger to my lips, while Randolph, as Tarzan, pretended to be choking me. I hardly noticed what he was doing. I was terrified and thought I had broken something in me—I was waiting to see if like my father I would have a heart attack, and die or come close to dying. The terror was there and yet I did not feel it. I did not feel anything. There were veils of anesthesia. There was a small spot on my underpants. I saw it, it was about the size of a dime, I did not know what it was, I thought I'd think about it later. I could not easily think. When my mind did begin to stir at all—Randolph was saying I was dead, he had won, what should Tarzan do next?—Ah, ah, I thought first in a strange dull way: What was that? It was without a name. I did not even make a guess at what it was. I thought, I wonder what it was. The world, my time on it, seemed different; I felt that in a moment I could place the difference. I lay on the floor curled up and Randolph sat on my shoulder, a child I hardly knew and who liked me and who had access to me whether I liked him or not. After a while, with a certain amount of sturdy self-evaluation, I decided I'd liked it whatever it was, and I wasn't dead. I said to Randolph, "I like to play Tarzan—we'll have to play Tarzan again."

After I left him, on my way home, to my parents, to that house, I found I was not as sad and as frightened as I usually was going home (I never knew if my father was worse or even dead or how my mother would be acting); and on a suburban street, empty except for me, beneath trees whose leaves lightly clashed in a pale spring breeze, I began to suspect that I had found something very special.

An unfailing hot mitigation.

A Story in an Almost Classical Mode

MY PROTAGONISTS are my mother's voice and the mind I had when I was thirteen.

I was supposed to have a good mind—that supposition was a somewhat mysterious and even unlikely thing. I was physically tough, and active, troublesome to others, in mischief or near delinquency at times and conceit and one thing and another (often I was no trouble at all, however); and I composed no symphonies, did not write poetry or perform feats of mathematical wizardry. No one in particular trusted my memory since each person remembered differently, or not at all, events I remembered in a way that even in its listing of facts, of actions, was an interpretation; someone would say, "That's impossible—it couldn't have happened like that—I don't do those things—you must be wrong."

But I did well in school and seemed to be peculiarly able to learn what the teacher said—I never mastered a subject, though—and there was the idiotic testimony of those peculiar witnesses, IQ tests: those scores invented me.

Those scores were a decisive piece of destiny in that they affected the way people treated you and regarded you; they determined your authority; and if you spoke oddly, they argued in favor of your sanity. But it was as easy to say and there was much evidence that I was stupid, in every way or in some ways or, as my mother said in exasperation, "in the ways that count."

I am only equivocally Harold Brodkey. I was adopted when I was two in the month following my real mother's death, and Harold was a name casually chosen by Joseph Brodkey because it sounded like Aaron, the name I'd had with my real mother. I was told in various ways over a number of years, and I suppose it's true, that my real father blamed me because I became ill at my mother's death and cried and didn't trust him: I had been my mother's favorite; he kept my brother, who was older than me, and more or less sold me to the Brodkeys for three hundred and fifty dollars and the promise of a job in another town. I saw my brother once a year, and he told me I was lucky to be adopted. I never told him or anyone else what went on at the Brodkeys'.

The Brodkeys never called me Harold—Buddy was the name they used for me. Brodkey itself is equivocal, being a corruption of a Russian name, Bezborodko. To what extent Harold Brodkey is a real name is something I have never been able to decide. No decision on the matter makes me comfortable. It's the name I ended with.

In 1943, in the middle of the Second World War, I was thirteen. Thirteen is an age that gives rise to dramas: it is a prison cell of an age, closed off from childhood by the onset of sexual capacity and set apart from the life one is yet to have by a remainder of innocence. Of course, that remainder does not last long. Responsibility and Conscience, mistaken or not, come to announce that we are to be identified from then on by what we do to other people: they free us from limitations—and from innocence—and bind us into a new condition.

I do not think you should be required to give sympathy. In rhetoric and in the beauty of extreme feeling, we confer sympathy always, but in most of life we do quite otherwise, and I want to keep that perspective. The Brodkeys were a family that disasters had pretty completely broken. My father was in his early forties and had blood pressure so high the doctors said it was a miracle he was alive. He listened to himself all the time, to the physiological tides in him; at any moment he could have a stroke, suffer a blood clot, and pass into a coma: this had happened to him six times so far; people said, "Joe Brodkey has the constitution of a horse." He was not happy with a miracle that was so temporary. And my mother had been operated on for cancer, breast cancer: that is, there'd been one operation and some careful optimism, and then a second operation, and there was nothing left to remove and no optimism at all. She was forty-five or so. My mother and father were both dying. There was almost no end to the grossness of our circumstances. There had been money but there was no money now. We lived on handouts from relatives who could not bring themselves to visit us. I used to make jokes with my parents about what was happening, to show them I wasn't horrified, and for a while my parents were grateful for that, but then they found my jokes irritating in the light of what they were suffering, and I felt, belatedly, the cheapness of my attitude. My mother was at home, not bedridden but housebound; she said to my father such things as, "Whether you're sick or not, I have to have money, Joe; I'm not getting the best medical treatment; Joe, you're my husband: you're supposed to see to it that I have money." Joe signed himself into a Veterans Hospital, where the treatment was free, so she could have what money there was and so he could get away from her. I was in ninth grade and went to Ward Junior High School.

We lived in University City, U. City, or Jew City—the population then was perhaps thirty-five percent Jewish; the percentage is higher now. St. Louis swells out like a gall on the Mississippi River. On the western edge of St. Louis, along with Clayton, Kirkwood, Normandy, Webster Groves, is U. City. The Atlantic Ocean is maybe a thousand miles away, the Pacific a greater distance. The Gulf of Mexico is perhaps seven hundred miles away, the Arctic Ocean farther. St. Louis is an island of metropolis in a sea of land. As Moscow is. But a sea of Protestant farmers. Republican small towns. A sea then of mortgaged farms.

It used to give me a crawling feeling of something profound and hidden that neither Joe nor Doris Brodkey had been born in the twentieth century. They had been born in years numerically far away from me and historically unfamiliar. We'd never gotten as far as 1898 in a history course. Joe had been born in Texas, Doris in Illinois, both in small towns. Joe spoke once or twice of unpaved streets and his mother's bitter concern about dust and her furniture, her curtains; I had the impression his mother never opened the windows in her house: there were Jewish houses sealed like that. Doris said in front of company (before she was ill), "I remember when there weren't telephones. I can remember when everybody still had horses; they made a nice sound walking in the street."

Both Joe and Doris had immigrant parents who'd made money but hadn't become rich. Both Joe and Doris had quit college, Joe his first week or first day, Doris in her second year; both their mothers were famous for being formidable, as battle-axes; both Joe and Doris believed in being more American than anyone; both despised most Protestants (as naively religious, murderously competitive, and unable to have a good time) and all Catholics (as superstitious, literally crazy, and lower-class). They were good-looking, small-town people, provincially glamorous, vaudeville-and-movie instructed, to some extent stunned, culturally stunned, liberated ghetto Jews loose and unprotected in the various American decades and milieus in which they lived at one time or another—I don't know that I know enough to say these things about them.

I loved my mother. But that is an evasion. I loved my mother: how much did I love Doris Marie Rubenstein? Doris Brodkey, to give her her married name. I don't think I loved her much—but I mean the *I* that was a thirteen-year-old boy and not consciously her son. All the boys I knew had two selves like that. For us there were two orders of knowledge—of things known and unknown—and two orders of persecution.

Joe and Doris had not been kind in the essential ways to me—they were perhaps too egocentric to be kind enough to anyone, even to each other. At times I did not think they were so bad. At times, I did. My mind was largely formed by U. City; my manners derived from the six or seven mansions on a high ridge, the three or four walled and gated neighborhoods of somewhat sternly genteel houses, the neighborhoods of almost all kinds of trim, well-taken-care-of small houses, of even very small houses with sharp gables and fanciful stonework, houses a door and two windows wide, with small, neat lawns; and from districts of two-family houses, streets of apartment houses—we lived in an apartment house—from rows of trees, the branches of which met over the streets, from the scattered vacant lots, the unbuilt-on fields, the woods, and the enormous and architecturally grandiose schools.

Every afternoon without stopping to talk to anyone I left school at a lope, sometimes even sprinting up Kingsland Avenue. The suspense, the depression were worst on rainy days. I kept trying to have the right feelings. What I usually managed to feel was a premature grief, a willed concern, and an amateur's desire to be of help any way I could.

It was surprising to my parents and other people that I hadn't had a nervous breakdown.

I spent hours sitting home alone with my mother. At that time no one telephoned her or came to see her. The women she had considered friends had been kind for a while, but it was wartime and my mother's situation did not command the pity it perhaps would have in peacetime.

Perhaps my mother had never actually been a friend to the women who did not come to see her: my mother had been in the habit of revising her visiting list upward. But she said she'd been "close" to those other women and that they ought to show respect for her as the ex-treasurer of the Jewish Consumptive Relief Society. She wanted those women to telephone and come and be present at her tragedy. From time to time she'd make trouble: she'd call one of them and remind her how she had voted for her in this or that club election or had given her a lift downtown when she had a car and the other woman hadn't. She told the women she knew they were hardhearted and selfish and would know someday what it was to be sick and to discover what their friends were like. She said still angrier things to her sister and her own daughter (her daughter by birth was ten years older than I was) and her brothers. She had been the good-looking one and in some respects the center of her family, and her physical conceit was unaltered; she had no use for compromised admiration. She preferred nothing. She had been a passionate gameswoman, a gambler: seating herself at a game table, she had always said, "Let's play for enough to make it interesting."

People said of her that she was a screamer, but actually she didn't scream very loudly; she hadn't that much physical force. What she did was get your attention; she would ask you questions in a slightly high-pitched pushy voice that almost made you laugh, but if you were drawn to listen to her, once you were attentive and showed you were, her voice would lose every attribute of sociability, it would become strained and naked of any attempt to please or be acceptable; it would be utterly appalling; and what she said would lodge in the center of your attention and be the truth you had to live with until you could persuade yourself she was crazy: that is, irresponsible and perhaps criminal in her way.

To go see my father in the hospital meant you rode buses and streetcars for three hours to get there; you rode two streetcar lines from end to end; and then at the end of the second line you took a city bus to the end of *its* line and then a gray army bus that went through a woods to the hospital, which stood beside the Mississippi. My father thought it was absurd for me to do that. He said, "I don't need anything—sickness doesn't deserve your notice—go have a good time." To force me to stop being polite, he practiced a kind of strike and would not let me make conversation; he would only say, "You ought to be outdoors." My mother said of my father, "We can't just let him die." Sometimes I thought we could. And sometimes I thought we couldn't. If it had mattered to my father more and not been so much a matter of what I thought I ought to do, it would have been different. He was generous in being willing to die alone and not make any fuss, but I would have preferred him to make a great fuss. When he wouldn't talk, I would go outside; I would stand and gaze at the racing Mississippi, at the eddies, boilings, and racings, at the currents that sometimes curled one above the other and stayed separate although they were water, and I would feel an utter contentment that anything should be that tremendous, that strong, that fierce. I liked loud music, too. I often felt I had already begun to die. I felt I could swim across the Mississippi—that was sheer megalomania: no one even fished in the shallows because of the logs in the river, the entire uprooted whirling trees that could clobber you, carry you under; you would drown. But I thought I could make it across. I wanted my father to recognize the force in me and give it his approval. But he had come to the state where he thought people and what they did and what they wanted were stupid and evil and the sooner we all died the better—in that, he was not unlike Schopenhauer or the Christian Apologists. I am arguing that there was an element of grace in his defeatism. He said that we were all fools, tricked and cheated by everything; whatever we cared about was in the end a cheat, he said. I couldn't wish him dead as he told me I should, but when I wished he'd live it seemed childish and selfish.

Sometimes my father came home for weekends—the hospital made him, I think (letting him lie in bed was letting him commit suicide), but sometimes he did it to see me, to save me from Doris. Neither Joe nor Doris liked the lights to be on; they moved around the apartment in the shadows and accused each other of being old and sick and selfish, of being irresponsible, of being ugly.

It seemed to me to be wrong to argue that I should have had a happier home and parents who weren't dying: I didn't have a happier home and parents who weren't dying; and it would have been limitlessly cruel to Joe and Doris, I thought, and emotionally unendurable for me to begin to regret my luck, or theirs. The disparity between what people said life was and what I knew it to be unnerved me at times, but I swore that nothing would ever make me say life should be anything. . . . Yet it seemed to me that I was being done in in that household, by those circumstances.

* * *

WHO WAS I? I came from—by blood, I mean—a long line of magic-working rabbis, men supposedly able to impose and lift curses, rabbis known for their great height and temperament: they were easily infuriated, often rhapsodic men.

On the other side I was descended from supposedly a thousand years or more of Talmudic scholars—men who never worked but only studied. Their families, their children, too, had to tend and support them. They were known for their inflexible contempt for humanity and their conceit; they pursued an accumulation of knowledge of the Unspeakable—that is to say, of God.

I didn't like the way they sounded, either. In both lines, the children were often rebellious and ran away and nothing more was heard of them: my real father had refused to learn to read and write; he had been a semiprofessional gambler, a brawler, a drunk, a prizefighter before settling down to be a junkman. He shouted when he spoke; he wasn't very clean. Only one or two in each generation had ever been Godly and carried on the rabbinical or scholarly line, the line of superiority and worth. Supposedly I was in that line. This was more important to Doris than it was to me; she was aware of it; it had meaning to her. Doris said, "If we're good and don't lie, if you pray for me, maybe God will make Joe and me well—it can't hurt to try."

We really didn't know what to do or how to act. Some people, more ardently Jewish than we were, said God was punishing Joe and Doris for not being better Jews. My real relatives said Joe and Doris were being punished for not bringing me up as a rabbi, or a Jewish scholar, a pillar of Judaism. "I don't think the Jews are the chosen people," Joe would say, "and if they are, it doesn't look as if they were chosen for anything good." He said, "What the world doesn't need is another rabbi." At school, the resident psychologist asked my classmates and me to write a short paper about our home life, and I wrote, *It is our wont to have intelligent discussions after dinner about serious issues of the day.* The psychologist congratulated Doris on running a wonderful home from her sickbed, and Doris said to me, "Thank you for what you did for me—thank you for lying." Maybe I didn't do it for her but to see what I could get away with, what I could pass as. But in a way I was sincere. Life at home was concerned with serious questions. But in a way I wasn't ever sincere. I was willing to practice any number of impostures. I never referred to Doris as my *adopted* mother, only as my mother. I had a face that leaked information. I tried to be carefully inexpressive except to show concern toward Doris and Joe. I forgave everyone everything they did. I understood that everyone had the right to do and think as they did even if it harmed me or made me hate them. I was good at games sporadically—then mediocre, then good again, depending on how I regarded myself or on the amount of strain at home. Between moments of drama, I lived inside my new adolescence, surprised that my feet were so far from my head; I rested inside a logy narcissism; I would feel, tug at, and stroke the single, quite long blond hair that grew at the point of my chin. I would look at the new muscle of my right forearm and the vein that meandered across it. It seemed to me that sights did not come to my eyes but that I hurled my sight out like a braided rope and grappled things visually to me; my sight traveled unimaginable distances, up into the universe or into some friend's motives and desires, only to collapse, with boredom, with a failure of will to see to the end, with shyness; it collapsed back inside me: I would go from the sky to inside my own chest. I had friends, good friends, but none understood me or wanted to; if I spoke about the way things were at home, or about my real father, they disbelieved me and then didn't trust me; or if I made them believe, they felt sick, and often they would treat me as someone luckless, an object of charity, and I knew myself to be better than that. So I pitied them first. And got higher grades than they did, and I condescended to them. Doris said to me a number of times, "Don't ever tell anybody what goes on in this house: they won't give you any sympathy; they don't know how—all *they* know is how to run away. . . . Take my advice and lie, say we're all happy, lie a lot if you want to have any kind of life." I did not see how it was possible for such things as curses to exist, but it seemed strange I was not ill or half crazy and my parents were: it didn't seem reasonable that anything except the collapse of their own lives had made Joe and Doris act as they did or that my adoption had been the means of introducing a curse into the Brodkeys' existences; but it seemed snotty to be certain. I didn't blame myself exactly; but there was all that pain and misery to be lived with, and it was related to me, to my life; and I couldn't help taking some responsibility for it. I don't think I was neurotic about it.

It seemed to me there were only two social states, tact and madness; and madness was selfish. I fell from a cliff face once, rode my bicycle into a truck on two occasions, was knocked out in a boxing match because I became bored and felt sorry for everyone and lowered my guard and stood there. I wanted to be brave and decent—it seemed braver to be cowardly and more decent not to add to the Brodkeys' list of disasters by having any of my own or even by making an issue of grief or discomfort, but perhaps I was not a very loving person. Perhaps I was self-concerned and a hypocrite, and the sort of person you ought to stay away from, someone like the bastard villains in Shakespeare. Perhaps I just wanted to get out with a whole skin. I thought I kept on going for Doris and Joe's sake but possibly that was a mealymouthed excuse. I didn't know. I tended to rely on whatever audience there was; I figured if they gaped and said, "He's a really good son," I was close to human decency. I was clear in everything I did to make sure the audience understood and could make a good decision about it and me. I was safe in my own life only when there was no one to show off to.

Doris insisted I give her what money I earned. And usually I did, so that I would not have to listen to her self-righteous begging and angry persuasiveness. The sums involved were small—five dollars, ten; once it was eighty-nine cents. She had, as a good-looking woman, always tested herself by seeing what she could get from people; hysteria had inflected her old habits and made them grotesque, made her grotesque. No other man was left. No one else at all was left. Not her mother, not her own daughter by blood, not her sister: they ran away from her, moved out of town, hung up if she called. Her isolation was entire except for me. When a nephew of Joe's sent me ten dollars for my birthday, Doris said, "I need it, I'm sick, I have terrible expenses. Don't you want to give me the money? Don't you want me to have a little pleasure? I could use a subscription to a good magazine." I used to hide money from her, rolled up in socks, tucked behind photographs in picture frames, but it would always disappear. While I was at school, she would hunt it out: she was ill and housebound, as I said, and there wasn't much for her to do.

Doris never said she was my mother; she never insisted that I had to love her; she asked things of me on the grounds that I was selfish by nature and cold and cut off from human feeling and despised people too much, and she said, "Be manly—that's all I ask." She said, "I don't ask you things that aren't good for you—it's for your own good for you to be kind to me." She would yell at me, "It won't hurt you to help me! You have time for another chance!" Doris yelled, "What do you think it does to me to see you exercising in your room—when I have to die?"

I said, "I don't know. Does it bother you a lot?"

"You're a fool!" she screamed. "Don't make me wish you'd get cancer so you'd know what I'm going through!"

If I ignored her or argued with her, she became violent, and then temper and fright—even the breaths she drew—spoiled the balance of pain and morphine in her; sometimes then she would howl. If I went to her, she would scream, "Go away, don't touch me—you'll hurt me!" It was like having to stand somewhere and watch someone being eaten by wild dogs. I couldn't believe I was seeing such pain. I would stop seeing: I would stand there and be without sight; the bottom of my stomach would drop away; there is a frightening cold shock that comes when you accept the reality of someone else's pain. Twice I was sick, I threw up. But Doris used my regret at her pain as if it were love.

She would start to yell at me at times, and I would lift my arm, my hand, hold them rigidly toward her and say, "Momma, don't . . . don't . . ." She would say, "Then don't make me yell at you. Don't cause me that pain."

It seemed the meagerest imaginable human decency not to be a party to further pain for her. But the list of things that she said caused her pain grew and grew: It upset her to see high spirits in me or a long face; and a neutral look made her think I'd forgotten her predicament; she hated any reference to sports, but she also hated it if I wasn't athletic—it reflected on her if I was a momma's boy. She hated to talk to me—I was a child—but she had no one else to talk to; that was a humiliation for her. She hated the sight of any pleasure near her, even daydreaming; she suspected that I had some notion of happiness in mind. And she hated it when anyone called me—that was evidence someone had a crush on me. She thought it would help her if I loved no one, was loved by no one, if I accepted help from no one. "How do you think it makes me feel? They don't want to help me, and I'm the one who's dying." She could not bear any mention of the future, any reference especially to my future. *"Don't you understand! I won't be here!"*

Sometimes she would apologize; she would say, "It's not me who says those things; it's the pain. It's not fair for me to have this pain: you don't know what it's like. I can't stand it, Buddy. I'm a fighter."

She said, "Why don't you know how to act so I don't lose my temper? You aggravate me and then I scream at you and it's not good for me. Why don't you understand? What's wrong with you? You're supposed

to be so smart but I swear to God you don't understand anything—
you're no help to me. Why don't you put yourself in my place? Why
don't you cooperate with me?"

She had scorned whatever comfort—or blame—her family had offered her; she said it was incompetent; and she scorned the comfort
tendered by the rabbi, who was, she said, "not a *man*—he's silly"; and
she suspected the doctors of lying to her, and the treatments they gave
her she thought were vile and careless and given with contempt for her.
"They burned me," Doris whimpered, "they burned *me.*" Her chest
was coated with radium burns, with an unpliable, discolored shell. She
was held within an enforced, enraged, fearful stiffness. She couldn't take
a deep breath. She could only whisper. Her wingspan was so great I
could not get near her. I would come home from school and she would
be lying on the couch in the living room, whimpering and abject, crying
with great carefulness, but angry: She would berate me in whispers: "I
hate to tell you this, but what you are is selfish, and it's a problem you're
going to have all your life, believe me. You don't care if anyone lives
or dies. No one is important to you—but you. I would rather go through
what I'm going through than be like you." At two in the morning, she
came into my room, turned on the ceiling light, and said, "Wake up!
Help me. Buddy, wake up." I opened my eyes. I was spread-eagled
mentally, like someone half on one side of a high fence, half on the other,
but between waking and sleeping. We sometimes had to go to the
hospital in the middle of the night. The jumble of words in my head
was: *emerging, urgent, murderer, emergency.* I did not call out.

She said, "Look what they've done to me. My God, look what they've
done to me." She lowered her nightgown to her waist. The eerie colors
of her carapace and the jumble of scars moved into my consciousness
like something in a movie advancing toward the camera, filling and
overspreading the screen. That gargoylish torso. She spoke first pite-
ously, then ragingly. Her eyes were averted, then she fixed them on me.
She was on a flight of emotion, a drug passage, but I did not think of
that: I felt her emotion like bat wings, leathery and foreign, filling the
room; and I felt her animosity. It was directed at me, but at moments
it was not and I was merely the only consciousness available to her to
trespass upon. She said, "I scratched myself while I slept—look, there's
blood."

She had not made me cry since I was a child; I had not let her; nothing
had ever made me scream except dreams I'd had that my first mother

was not dead but was returning. Certain figures of speech are worn smooth but accurate: I was racked; everything was breaking; I was about to break.

I shouted, "Stop it."

She said, enraged, "Am I bothering you? Are you complaining about me? Do you know what I'm suffering?"

I said, "No." Then I said—I couldn't think of anything sensible—"It doesn't look so bad, Momma."

She said, "What's wrong with you? Why do you talk stupidly?" Locks of hair trailed over her face. She said, "No one wants to touch me."

I raised my eyebrows and stuck my head forward and jerked it in a single nod, a gesture boys used then for O.K. when they weren't too pleased, and I climbed out of bed. My mother told me at breakfast the next day not to mind what she had done, it had been the drug in her that made her do what she did; the bat wings of her drug flight seemed when I stood up to fold back, to retreat inside her: she was not so terrifying. Merely unlikable. And sickening. I put my arms around her and said, "See. I can hug you."

She let out a small scream. "You're hurting me."

"O.K., but now go back to bed, Momma. You need your sleep."

"I can't sleep. Why don't you want to kill the doctor for what he's done to me . . . ?"

She said for weeks, whenever she was drugged, "If I was a man, I'd be willing to be hanged for killing a man who did this to a woman I loved."

She'd had five years of various illnesses and now cancer and she still wasn't dead.

I would come home from school to the shadowy house, the curtains drawn and no lights on, or perhaps one, and she would be roaming barefooted with wisps of her hair sticking out and her robe lopsided and coming open; when I stood there, flushed with hurrying, and asked, "Momma, is it worse?" or whatever, she would look at me with pinched-face insanity and it would chill me. She would shout, "What do you mean, is it worse? Don't you know yet what's happened to me? What else can it be but worse! What's wrong with you? You're more of my punishment, you're helping to kill me, do you think I'm made of iron? You come in here and want me to act like your valentine! I don't need any more of your I-don't-know-what! You're driving me crazy, do you hear me? On top of everything else, you're driving me out of my mind."

Feelings as they occur are experienced as if they were episodes in Kafka, overloaded with hints of meaning that reek of eternity and the inexplicable and that suggest your dying—always your dying—at the hands of a murderousness in events if you are not immediately soothed, if everything is not explained at once. It is your own selfishness or shamefulness, or someone else's or perhaps something in fate itself, that is the murderer; or what kills is the proof that your pain is minor and is the responsibility of someone who does not care. I didn't know why I couldn't shrug off what she did and said; I didn't blame her; I even admired her when I didn't have to face her; but I did not see why these things had to happen, why she had to say these things. I think it mattered to her what I felt. That is, if I came in and said, "Hello, Momma," she would demand, "Is that all you can say? I'm in *pain*. Don't you care? My God, my God, what kind of selfish person are you? I can't stand it."

If I said, "Hello, Momma, how is your pain?" she would shriek, "You fool, I don't want to think about it! It was all right for a moment! Look what you've done—you've brought it back. . . . *I don't want to be reminded of my pain all the time!*"

She would yell, "What's wrong with you? Why don't you know how to talk to me! My God, do you think it's easy to die? Oh my God, I don't like this. I don't like what's happening to me! My luck can't be this bad." And then she would start in on me: "Why do you just stand there? Why do you just listen to me! It doesn't do me any good to have you there listening! You don't do anything to help me—what's wrong with you? You think I'm like an animal? Like a worm? You're supposed to be smart, but you don't understand anything, you're no good to me, you were never any good to me. I'd laugh at you, you're so useless to me, but it hurts me to laugh: what good are you to me? Do something for me! Put yourself in my place! Help me! Why don't you help me?"

Sometimes she would say in a horrible voice, "I'll tell you what you are—I'll tell you what everyone is! They're trash! They're all trash! My God, my God, how can my life be like this? I didn't know it would be like this. . . ."

I really did not ever speak to anyone about what went on at home, but one of the teachers at school suggested that I apply for a scholarship to Exeter, so that I could get away from the "tragedy in your home." And get a good education as well. I was secretly hopeful about going

to boarding school a thousand miles away. I did not at all mind the
thought that I would be poorer and less literate than the boys there. I
figured I would be able to be rude and rebellious and could be hateful
without upsetting my mother and I could try to get away with things.

I remember the two of us, Doris and me, in the shadowy living room:
I'm holding some books, some textbooks. She's wearing a short wrap-
around housecoat, with a very large print of vile yellow and red flowers
with green leaves on a black background. I've just told her casually I can
go away to school; I put it that I would not be a burden on her anymore
or get on her nerves; I told her I did not want to be a burden—I said
something like that; that was my attempt at tact. She said, "All right—
leave me too—you're just like all the rest. You don't love anyone, you
never loved anyone. You didn't even mourn when your real mother
died, you don't ever think about her. I'll tell you what you are: you're
filth. Go. Get out of here. Move out of here tonight. Pack up and go.
I don't need you. No one will ever need you. You're a book, a stick,
you're all book learning, you don't know anything about people—if I
didn't teach you about people, people would laugh at you all the time,
do you hear me?"

I went into another room and I think I was sitting there or maybe
I was gathering together the ten or fifteen books I owned—having with
a kind of boy's dishonesty, I suppose, taken Doris's harangue as permis-
sion to leave her, as her saying yes in her way to my going away, my
saving myself—when she came in. She'd put on lipstick and a hair
ribbon; and her face, which had been twisted up, was half all right: the
lines were pretty much up and down and not crooked; and my heart
began to beat sadly for myself—she was going to try to be nice for a little
while; she was going to ask me to stay.

AFTER THAT she seemed to feel I'd proved that I belonged to her;
or it had been proved I was a man she could hold near her still. Every
day, I came home from school, and Doris fluttered down from her filthy
aerie of monstrous solitude and pain: in a flurry of dust and to the
beating of leathery wings, she asked me a riddle. Sometimes she threat-
ened me: she'd say, "You'll die in misery, too—help me now and maybe
God will be good to you." Or she'd say, "You'll end like me if you don't
help me!" She'd say it with her face screwed up in fury. She'd say,
"Why don't you put yourself in my place and understand what I'm

going through." It occurred to me that she really didn't know what she was saying—she was uttering words that sounded to her close to something she really wanted to say; but what she said wasn't what she meant. Maybe what she meant couldn't be said. Or she was being sly because she was greedy and using bluff or a shortcut and partly it was her own mental limitation and ineptness: that is, she couldn't say what she hadn't thought out.

It wasn't enough that I stayed with her and did not go to Exeter. She railed at me, "You're not doing me any good—why don't you go live in the Orphans' Home: that's where heartless people who don't deserve to have a family belong." We both knew that I didn't have to go to the Orphans' Home, but maybe neither of us knew what she meant when she demanded I help her. It was queer, the daily confrontations, Doris and me not knowing what she wanted from me or even what the riddle really was that she was asking. She crouched there or seemed to at those moments, in the narrow neck of time between afternoon and evening, between the metaphorical afternoon of her being consigned to death and the evening of her actual dying, and she asked me some Theban riddle while she was blurred with drugs, with rage, and I looked at her and did not know what to do.

But after a while I knew sort of what she was asking: I knew sort of what the riddle was; but I couldn't be sure. I knew it was partly she wanted me to show I loved her in some way that mattered to her, that would be useful; and it was wrong of her to ask, I knew because she was ashamed or afraid when she spoke to me and she averted her eyes, or they would be sightless, unfocused from the morphine. In a way, pity could not make me do anything, or love. The final reasons are always dry ones, or rational and petty: I wanted to do something absolutely straightforward and finally loyal to her, something that would define my life with her in such a way that it would calm her and enable me to be confident and less ashamed in the future and more like other people. And also if I was going to live with her for a while, things had to change; I wanted to know that life for me did not have to be like *this*. Things had to be made bearable for both of us.

It doesn't sound sensible—to make her dying and my being with her bearable. But it is language and habit that make the sense odd. It was clear to me that after a process of fantastic subtraction I was all that was left to her. And for me, what with one odd subtraction and another, she was the only parent I had left to me; she was my mother.

* * *

I COULD half see, in the chuffing, truncated kind of thought available to my thirteen-year-old intelligence, that the only firm ground for starting was to be literal: she had asked me to put myself in her place. O.K. But what did that mean? How could I be a dying, middle-aged woman walking around in a housedress?

I knew I didn't know how to think; I guessed that I had the capacity—just the *capacity*—to think: that capacity was an enormous mystery to me, perhaps as a womb is to a woman. When I tried to think, I wandered in my head but not just in my head; I couldn't sit down physically and be still and think: I had to be in movement and doing something else; and my attention flittered, lit, veered, returned. Almost everyone I knew could *think* better than I could. Whenever I thought anything through, I always became a little angry because I felt I'd had to think it out to reach a point that someone better parented would have known to start with. That is, whenever I thought hard, I felt stupid and underprivileged. I greatly preferred to feel. Thinking for me was always accompanied by resentment, and was in part a defensive, a rude and challenged staring at whatever I was trying to think about; and it was done obstinately and blunderingly—and it humiliated me.

Death, death, I said to myself. I remembered Doris saying, "I don't want to be shut up in a coffin." That was fear and drama: it didn't explain anything. But it did if she wasn't dead yet: I mean I thought that maybe the question was *dying. Dying.* Going toward a coffin. Once when I was little I'd found a horizontal door in the grass next to a house; I had been so small the door had been very hard to lift and to lay down again because my arms were so short; when the door was open, you saw stairs, unexpected in the grass, and there was a smell of damp and it was dark below, and you went down into an orderly place, things on shelves, and the light, the noises, the day itself, the heat of the sun were far away; you were coolly melted; your skin, your name dissolved; you were turned into an openness, into being a mere listening and feeling; the stillness, the damp, the aloneness, the walls of earth, of moist, white-washed plaster, soaked you up, blurred you; you did not have to answer when anyone called you.

And when you fell from your bike, while you were falling, the way everything stopped except the knowledge that pain was coming. The blotting out of voices, the sudden distance of everything, the hope, the conviction almost that this was a dream, the way time drew out, was airy, and nothing was going to happen, and then everything turned to stone again; it was going to happen; the clatter of your bike crashing, your own fall; and then finally you sat up with disbelief and yet with knowledge: you saw your torn pants; you poked at the bleeding abrasions on your elbow that you had to twist your arm to see. You felt terrible but you didn't know yet, you couldn't know everything that had happened to you.

I remembered in pictures, some quite still, some full of motion, none of them rectangular; and what I meant, while it was clear enough to me at first, became liquid and foggy when I tried to establish in words what it was I meant, what it was I now knew; it slid away into a feeling of childishness, of being wrong, of knowing nothing after all.

Doris wouldn't have those feelings about dying. And my feelings were beside the point and probably wrong even for me. Then my head was blank and I was angry and despairing; but all at once my scalp and neck wrinkled with gooseflesh. I had my first thought about Doris. She wouldn't think in those pictures, and they didn't apply to her because she wouldn't ever think in pictures that way, especially about dying: dying was a fact. She was factual and pictureless.

Then after that I made what I called an equation: Doris-was-Doris. I meant that Doris was not me and she was really alive.

That made me feel sad and tired and cheated—I resented it that she was real and not me or part of me, that her death wasn't sort of a version of mine. It was going to be too much goddamned work this way.

I went off into "thinking," into an untrained exercise of intellect. I started with x's and y's and Latin phrases. I asked myself what was a person, and after a while, I came up with: A person is a mind, a body, and an I. The I was not in the brain, at least not in the way the mind was. The I is what in you most hurts other people—it makes them lonely. But the mind and body make it up to people for your I. The I was the part that was equal in all men are created equal and have the same rights to life, liberty, and the pursuit of happiness. The emotions of the I were very different from the emotions of the body and the mind. When all three parts of you overlapped, it was what people meant by "the heart."

Doris's heart. Doris's mind, Doris's body, Doris's I.

Inside a family, people have mythologically simple characters—there's the angry one, the bookish one, and so on, as if everyone was getting ready to be elevated and turned into a constellation at any moment. Notions of character were much less mythical once you got outside a family, usually. Doris in her family was famous for her anger, but she had also said of herself a number of times that she had more life in her than her husband or her mother and sister and brothers and daughter. It had always made me curious. What did it mean to have more life in you? She'd never said I had much life in me, or a little. It seemed to me on reflection that Doris had meant her temper. A lot of her temper came from restlessness and from seeing people and things the way she did. She'd meant she couldn't sit quietly at home or believe in things that weren't real. Or be a hypocrite. She'd meant she was a fighter; active—but she never played any sport, not any; she was the most unexercised woman I knew of: she never did housework, never went dancing anymore (I meant before she'd been sick), never swam or played tennis, never gardened or walked, never carried groceries—if she shopped she paid a delivery boy to bring the groceries home for her. She never failed to sleep at night although she complained of sleeping badly—she didn't have so much life she couldn't sleep. She dreamed a lot; she liked to have things happen, a lot every day. She liked to go places, to get dressed up, to get undressed and be slatternly: she was always acting, always busy being someone, performing in a way. Was that the life in her? She insisted on people controlling their minds and not thinking too much and she didn't approve of bodies being too active—she really was mostly interested in the *I: I like to live, I want a good life, you don't know how to live, I know what life is, I know how to live, there's a lot of life in me, I have a lot of life in me.*

I thought these things at various times; they occurred to me over a number of days. My mind wandered into and out of the subject. Preoccupied with it at times, I dropped and broke things or got off the bus at the wrong stop or stumbled on the curbstone, holding my textbooks in one hand, their spines turned upward leaning against my thigh, in the style of a sharp high-school boy. Girls at school told me I was looking "a lot more mature."

Every once in a while, I would remember something: Doris saying angrily, "I pushed my brothers, I put every idea they had into their heads, I was somebody in that little town"—in Illinois—"people thought I was something, it was me that gave my brothers a name; that's all it takes to win an election, a name. J.J. was mayor, Mose was police commissioner— You don't think it did them some good? And I put them over. They looked *Jewish*—it was *my* looks, me and Joe; Joe was in the American Legion: believe me, that helped. And it was all my idea. Momma never wanted us to do nothing, Momma thought the Gentiles would kill us if we got to be too outstanding. She was always in Russia in her mind. I was the smartest one—Momma and my brothers weren't as smart as I was. I could always get people to do what I wanted. Who do you think told J.J. what to wear? I taught him how to look like a businessman so he could go into St. Louis and people wouldn't laugh at him. I found him his wife, he owes me a lot. But I have to give him credit, he's the only one who had brains, he's the only one who did anything with what I told him. If you ask me, Mose can't count to fifteen without getting a headache, and Joe was not smart, either. Joe was vain: when he went bald I had to fight with him to take off his hat in the house. He did have pretty hair; he was too blond to be a Jew. But everything was a pose with him, he never did anything because it was smart, it was always Joe putting his hand in his pocket and being a big shot—believe me, a lot of women thought he was attractive. But you couldn't talk to Joe, no one could ever talk to Joe, he wouldn't listen, he had his own ideas—ideas! I'm the one to say it, I married him, I made my bed—he was dumb: I had to have the brains for both of us. But good-looking, my God. The first time I saw him I couldn't believe it, he was so good-looking: I didn't think he was Jewish. He was in an officer's uniform. You can imagine. I was never photogenic but I was something to look at, myself. Joe took one look at me and he didn't know if he was coming or going. He cut in on me at a dance and asked me to marry him just like that and he meant it. He meant well. I really wasn't bad-looking: people always told me everything. I was too pretty when I was young to make it in St. Louis—older women ran things in St. Louis—you think I didn't catch on? St. Louis is a good town for a woman when you get older: I know what I'm talking about. I knew the right time to move here. If Joe had been a businessman, we could have caught up with J.J.—we had good chances, people liked me, but Joe didn't go over, he didn't make friends with smart people, he wouldn't take my advice. I should have been the type who could get divorced but I never believed in divorce: it would just be the frying pan into the fire: marriage is never easy. Listen, I'm smart: I'd've liked to try my luck in Chicago, I've always been outstanding, I've always impressed people. . . ."

It seemed to me from what little I could remember about her when

I was little, and before Joe became ill, that she had interested the people around her. Everyone had looked at her wherever she went and people waited for her to arrive for the excitement to start. And they had been afraid of her too. When she was all dressed up—and even when she wasn't—she often looked glamorous and interesting: she'd worn things like a black suit with wide lapels, very high-heeled black shoes, longish black gloves, a diamond bracelet on the outside of one glove, a fur neckpiece, fox heads biting their tails, a tight-fitting hat with a long feather fastened to it by a red jewel, and a veil drawn over her face; and behind the veil a very red lipsticked mouth.

I hadn't as a child clearly understood what we were to each other. She'd been so different in her moods, she hadn't ever seemed to be one person, to be the same person for long, to be the same person at all. When I was little, I'd been allowed to sit on her bed and watch her get dressed—this had been a privilege awarded me and a kind of joke and thing of affection. She'd been a slightly dumpy, slack-skinned, nervous woman with a wried mouth and eyes muddy with temper. She would arrange a towel around her shoulders and bosom while she sat at a vanity table, and then she would brush her hair; she would beat at her hair with the brush; she would stick out her chin and brace against the force of her brushing. What was wonderful was that as she brushed, a faint life, like a sunrise, would creep into her face—a smoothness; she'd be less wrinkled, less skewed in anger or impatience, in bitterness or exhaustion; a pinkness, very faint, would spread around the line of her hair; her face would not look so ashen then. Part of it was that her hair would begin to shine, part was that her face would reveal an increasing, magical symmetry, part was the life in her eyes, but she became pretty. I would stare at her reflection in the mirror. I had to keep looking at her because if I closed my eyes or ran out of the room, the prettiness would disappear from my head, and then I'd have to run back and look at her. Seated at the vanity table, she'd say things that were strange to me and grown-up (I thought) and private. "I had good coloring when I was young but you know what they say: you don't stay young forever." Or "I look like a ghost." On the spur of the moment she would change the curve of her eyebrows and the shape of her lips or use another shade of powder and of lipstick: it would be very strained while she did it, she would be intent and bold and willful, like a gambler. God, the hushed niceness of the looks, the romantic, whispery, gentle niceness she would often end with. Sometimes she tried for startlingly dramatic looks and got them or partly got them; sometimes she failed and had to wipe her face clean and redo her hair and start over. She would get, at this point, if things seemed to be working, a blunt, broad, female, and sarcastic excitement, a knowing gaiety, a tough-fibered, angry pleasure and a despair that moved me. If I said, "You're pretty, Momma," she would say in the new voice of her new mood, "Do you think I'm the cat's miaow?" Sometimes she would keep repeating that but in changing, softening voices until she came to a gentle, teasing voice, one as sweet as a lullaby with agreeable and patient inner themes. She was a complete strategist. Sometimes she would sing "Yes, Sir, That's My Baby." As if she was a man and was admiring herself. Sometimes her voice would be quavering and full of half-suffocated, real pleasure, readily amorous or flirtatious. I think she was always the first to be affected by her looks.

Three times that I can think of, when I was alone at home, I sneaked a look into my mother's bureau, at her underwear . . . but also at her jewelry and handkerchiefs and sweaters: I wanted to see what was hidden. Other motives I pass over. Once, and maybe twice, I tried on a nightgown of hers and danced on the bed and saw myself in the bureau mirror. I don't remember feeling that I was like a woman in any way. I can remember moments of wanting to be one, when I was fairly young—to wear a turban and be opinionated and run everything in the house and not ever have to prove myself—but the wish wasn't sexual, so far as I know, or profound or long-lived. It was envy of women having power without having to serve apprenticeships for it. And also it was a daydream about safety and being taken care of and undoing some of the mistakes of having grown to be seven or eight years old: a woman, like a little boy, was a specialist in being loved.

My ignorance about women was considerable—why were women so secretive? I knew my mother and my sister faked just about absolutely everything they did with men, but why? Their temper, their good nature, their unhappiness, their happiness were almost always fake—but why? I didn't understand what the need was for all the fraud.

No man or boy was ever permitted to be outspoken near a woman. In U. City, there weren't too many docile, crushed women or girls; I didn't know any. In U. City, women sought to regulate everyone in everything; they more or less tried to supersede governmental law, instinct, tradition, to correct them and lay down new rules they insisted were the best ones. Nearly everything they wanted from us—to be polite, to sit still, to be considerate, to be protective—was like a dumb drumming of their wanting us to be like women. The rarest thing in a woman was any understanding of the male. And that wasn't asked of them. Women were highly regarded, and in U. City it was considered profoundly wicked to be rude to any of them. One simply fled from them, avoided them. Their unjust claims. I mean we respected women as women, whatever they were as people.

I thought about my mother's name, Doris Marie Rubenstein Brodkey, as mine. It seemed intensely silly to be called Doris. Then one day I thought about being a woman called Doris who was all dressed up and then was being pushed headfirst into a keg of oil. It was unbearable. And disgusting. I thought I had imagined what it was like to be Doris dying, to be a dying woman. I woke the next day from a night's sleep having realized in my sleep I had not imagined my mother's dying at all.

She was in her forties and she had cancer and she had some twist to her character so that she drove people away. People said she had "a bad mouth"—she was cutting and shrill, demanding, she said true things in full malice. The more I thought about being her, the more masculinely I held myself: even my thoughts were baritone.

She had an odd trait of never blaming herself, and nothing anyone ever said about her affected her in a way that led her to change. She never listened to my father at all, or to her mother, or her daughter, or her friends. That simmered in my head a few days before it took another shape. I was at football practice. We were running up and down the football field lifting our knees high as we were told. I was afraid of the coach. Suddenly it occurred to me my mother was undisciplinable, ineducable and independent: she refused to be controlled by sexual pleasure, so far as I could see, or by conventional notions of what was maternal or by what people thought or by their emotional requirements. But it was a queer independence and one of the mind or of the pride: she felt it in her mind: but it wasn't what I'd call independence: she was tied to her family; she couldn't conceive of moving far away; she couldn't bear to be alone; she needed to have someone in love with her: she was independent of the claims of the person in love with her, but she needed the feelings directed at her for her to be independent of something. Time after time, after quarrels with certain friends or with her family, she would say, "I don't care, I don't need them," but she was peculiarly defenseless and *always* let people come back, even if they were just wastes of time and drains on her energy. She couldn't bear to lose anyone. She was like a creature without a shell and without claws and so on—she was rather a soft person—and she sort of with her mind or mother wit made a shell and claws, and needed, and wanted, and pursued people, men and women, who would be part of her—of her equipment—who would care about her and outfit her and help her. She fawned on such people to get them to like her until she felt, correctly or paranoiacally, that they didn't care about her, that they had failed her; then she would assail them behind their back for practice and when the scurrility was polished she'd deliver it to their faces.

It seemed hot and airless even to begin to work on imagining what it was like to be my mother.

One thing I did not know then but half know now was that I was not independent of her. I thought then I did not love her exactly; she struck me as having no aptitude for happiness, and so there was no point in being attached to her or having a lot of feeling about her—she'd only use it against me. I knew she was no mother in any conventional sense; she herself often said as much; but the fact that she was such a terrible mother made me feel aristocratic and amused as well as tired me: I saw other mothers charging around half destroying their kids, crippling them, blinding them, and I felt protective toward my mother—this was a dry, adolescently sarcastic, helpless feeling, almost part of my sense of humor, my sense of aristocracy, if I can call it that, this being protective toward her. Also, I figured that when I was an infant someone had been kind to me: I was comparatively strong physically, and surprisingly unfrightened of things, and I gave credit for this to Doris.

But I know now I was frightened of a lot of things; I just didn't pay much attention to the fright. My ignorance, my character scared me. I could hide behind taking care of her. I leaned on the fact of having her near me; her presence, having to take care of her, supplied an answer to a lot of questions, supplied a shape. I didn't have to know who I was. Girls pushed me around a lot: there was a dim shadowy hysteria in me about that. I didn't often feel it, but I needed and resented Doris. I thought I was objective and emotionless and so on, but I wasn't: she was important to me.

I had noticed that she never blamed herself, but then I saw that she never blamed any woman much, even women she was angry with; she'd say such and such a woman was selfish and a lousy friend and that she never wanted to see her again, but my mother really only launched diatribes against men. She had a brother who'd become rich, and she said he was ruled by his wife, that his wife kept this brother from being nice to Doris, but what Momma did was stop speaking to her brother and she went on being friends with her sister-in-law.

I couldn't see how Momma managed this presumption of sinlessness in women. Finally, I worked it out that she felt women were in an unfair situation, and had to do what they did. She never thought women were bound by honor or by any of the things men were bound by. At one point, enraptured with my daring, I wondered if my mother was basically a lesbian. But then it seemed to me she was much more afraid of women than she was of men, so maybe she was merely trying to get along with other women who were the real danger and so on.

She never forgave, never forgot anything I said to her in anger—she remembered rudenesses I'd committed when I was four years old. But she said that what *she* said didn't matter and didn't mean anything. The same with complaints; she went on and on about how grim life was and how terrible most people were, but if I even so much as said that school was dull, she said, "Be a man—don't complain."

I couldn't figure out that one-sidedness: how did she expect not to irritate me, not to bore me? Then suddenly I had an inspiration, which maybe had nothing to do with the truth, but I could imagine she might want to be independent of absolutely everything, even of having to be fair in the most minor way. . . .

My poor mother's freedom. She was utterly wretched, and at this point in her life she screamed most of the time rather than spoke. "I have no life. . . . Why did this happen to me. . . ." And: "My brothers are filth. . . ." And so on.

One day she was ranting about one of her brothers, "He used to be in love with me but now he won't come near me because I'm ugly and sick," and it occurred to me that she was enraged—and amazed—to discover selfishness in anyone except her. No one had the right to be selfish except Doris.

She remembered everything she had ever done as having been a favor for someone. And this wasn't just madness, although I thought so at first; it was her cold judgment of how life operated: it was her estimate of what she was worth. Or a bluff. She thought or hoped she was smarter and prettier and more realistic than anyone.

To watch somebody and think about them is in a way to begin to have the possibility of becoming them.

It seemed to me I could see certain ways we were already alike and that I had never noticed before. I had never noticed that I had almost no pity for what men suffered—in a war, say; I didn't care if men got hurt, or if I hurt boys in a fight, so I was always more comfortable with men than with women. And I caught sight of something in me I hadn't admitted to consciousness but it was that I judged all the time how well I was being taken care of, even while thinking I did not ask to be taken care of at all. And she was like that. She thought pain belonged to women; she did not like men who suffered; she thought suffering in men was effeminate. She didn't think men deserved help: she was a woman and too exposed; she had to be taken care of first. I tried to imagine a conscious mind in which all this would seem sensible and obvious.

I heard a woman say, "It's easy for me to be nice—I have a husband who is good to me. . . ."

It was terrifying to contemplate the predicament hinted at in such a speech.

I could believe a lot of what my mother was was what had been done to her.

She said to me once, "I would have been happy married to a gangster." I knew people did not always say what they meant: they uttered words that seemed to make the idea in their heads audible but often the sentence said nothing or said the opposite to anyone outside their heads who did not know all the connections. Partly because the idea was defective, but more often because in simple egoism and folly one could say, especially if one was a woman, "Why don't you understand me?" and never think about the problem of having to make oneself clear. Men had to make themselves clear in order to run businesses and to act as judges, but in order to be clear they said less and less: they standardized their speeches. Or were tricky or— But anyway, when my mother said something it seemed easiest to take her literally because the literal meaning would cover more of her intention than any interpretive reading would. She often became very angry with me for taking her literally, but since no one else understood her at all, ever, I thought my system was the best possible, and also, by taking her literally I could control her a little.

When she said she would have been happy with a gangster, it was hard to know what she meant: did she need violence, did she want a man who could be violent because of how he would act toward her or because of the way he'd act toward other people? I guessed she wanted someone to be tough toward the world, who would be her fists, who would be no fool, and who, busy with his own life, would give her a certain freedom. My mother did not like needing anyone—"If you don't need anybody, you don't get hurt"—but she needed people all the time. She said of my real mother, "She was brave—she went where she wanted to go, she would go alone, she didn't need anyone, I don't know where she got the strength, but she could stand alone. I envied her, I wanted to be like her. I wanted to adopt you because I thought you would be like her."

I thought, without much confidence, that women were held under the constraint of social custom more than men were: almost all of *civilization* had to do with the protection and restraint of women; but *that* seemed to be true of men too. My mother lived a half fantasy of being tough, she was verbally tough: a failed adventurer. She wanted to have her own soul and to stand outside the law: she thought she could be independent if only she had a little help. My mother was willing, up to a point, to blaspheme, to try to defraud God.

Then, more and more, it seemed to me my mother hated all connections; even her bones did not seem to be fastened to each other, I noticed; my mother was soft, fluid, sea-y, a sea-y creature. What harrowed her most was the failure of her maneuvers, of her adaptations, her lack of success. It seemed to *me* that her illness was an experience, an act of destiny outside the whole set of things that made up that part of life where you were a success or a failure. Will and charm and tactics could manage just so much—then you had to believe in God or luck or both, which led you into theological corruption of a very sickening kind (I could not believe God would help you make money). They were two different orders of experience, but my mother thought they were one. She thought your luck as far as having looks was part of the other, even though she said, "Anyone can be good-looking—you have to try, you have to carry yourself right; sometimes ugly people are the best-looking of all. . . ." She was generous enough to admit of some women, "I was much prettier than her once but she's outdistanced me: she knows how to dress, she's taken care of herself. . . ."

Riding on the bus I tried to imagine myself—briefly—a loose-fleshed, loose-boned soft-looking woman like my mother with her coarse ambitiousness and soulful public manner (when she wasn't being shrill) and the exigent fear of defeat that went with what she was. . . . I did it sort of absently, almost half drowsing, I thought it was so, well, dull, or unilluminating. But suddenly I experienced an extraordinary vertigo, and a feeling of nausea, and I stopped quickly.

I didn't know if I'd felt sick because I was doing something I shouldn't do—I mean I started with that notion, and it was only a day or so later I thought maybe the nausea had gone with imagining defeat. So far as I knew, I did not mind defeat—defeat hurt but it offered an excuse for being indulgent and sexual and so on.

I didn't even conceive of total defeat. Being a hobo would be a fate, getting meningitis and dying, being a homosexual, a drunk, a lifelong shoe salesman would be a fate, maybe even amusing. None of that really frightened me. I wondered if it was the war that had done this to me or if I'd been cheated out of a certain middle-classness. Maybe it was that in never having been given much by Doris I'd come not to expect much in general, or maybe I just didn't fear failure properly, or it had to do with being masculine.

So I had to *imagine* what it would be like to really hate failure. I worked out a stupid idea that Doris needed family, social position, charm, looks, clothes, or she couldn't begin to have adventures; something that didn't require those things was not a real adventure. She maybe needed those things as someone might need a hearing aid or glasses or a tractor or a car: a woman deprived of them was deaf, blind, reduced to trudging hopelessly along.

I was not obsessed with understanding my mother; I worked on this when I had the time.

I sometimes imagined myself in combat conditions, I tried to imagine myself undergoing humiliations, deprivations. It was a matter of pride not to run away from painful thoughts.

I knew my mother had never made an imaginative leap into my life or into any man's life; she'd said so: "I know nothing about being a boy...." She'd said to my father, "I know nothing about being a man...." She did not like movies that were about men. She never asked me to tell her about myself. Perhaps she was defiant because Jewish women were supposed to be respectful toward men—I couldn't handle that thought—but it seemed to me *very* clear she was interested only in her own fate as a woman. She thought everyone dealt in ruses, in subterfuge, but that she did it best. Her world bewildered me. I assumed she did not love me. I did not know to what extent I loved her. I saw that my insensitivity to her, as long as she behaved the way she did, was the only thing that made it possible for me to be halfway decent to her. If I reacted to her directly, I would become a major figure in the drama, and it would become clear she was a terrible pain in the neck, a child, and a fool. She thought if I became sensitive to her I would be struck with admiration for her in what she was going through, as once men had fallen in love with her at first sight. But I knew that would not happen. The depth of pain she suffered did not make her beautiful, could not make her beautiful: what she did, how she acted, was the only thing that could make her beautiful. Maybe once sheer physical glory had made her redoubtable but I figured she'd had to work on her looks. There was nothing you could be without effort except catatonic. If I became sensitive to her and she was careless of me, I would not care if she died.

Obviously, between her and me there were two different minds and sensibilities and kinds of judgment operating: she wanted to control my mind—but without taking responsibility for it. She wanted to ascribe not a general value but a specifically masculine value to my being sympathetic toward her pain. It seemed to me she did not have that right because she had not carried out any specifically feminine side to our relationship, to any bargain. I mean she was working a swindle. She was also trying to help me. She wanted her condition considered a heroic, serious event, but I had nearly died twice in my childhood, and both times she had said, "Be brave." She had experienced no discomfort, only "aggravation" when I'd been ill—"I'm not good at illness," she'd said. You couldn't hold the past against people, but on the other hand, what other contract did you have with anyone except that past?

My mother did not expect gentleness from people, on the whole, but when she was desperate she wept because there was no gentleness in anyone near her. She preferred to go to Catholic hospitals when she was ill, because of the nuns: they forgave her over and over. She lied to them and told them she would convert, and then she took it back and said God would punish her if she stopped being Jewish. She screamed and railed at people but the nuns always forgave her. "They're good—they understand women," she said. She whispered, "I'm a terrible person but they don't mind."

She said she could not bear it when people came near her and thought of themselves.

I did not do anything merely in order to be good to her. I decided to fiddle around with being—with being a little taken advantage of. I did it as a profanation, as a gesture of contempt for the suburb and toward people who pitied Doris; I did it as an exercise in doing something illicit and foul, as an exercise in risk-taking and general perversity. I figured, well, what the hell, why not do it, what did I have to lose?

I was probably already wrecked and I'd probably be killed in the war besides.

I trained myself to listen to her talk about how she felt; I didn't wince or lose my appetite when she went on and on about what she was going through. Actually I was losing weight and having nightmares, but I'd get up in the middle of the night and do push-ups so I'd sleep and look healthy the next day. I wanted her to know I accepted what she went through as "normal."

She could of course describe only with limited skill, thank God, her pain.

"I have a burning—it begins here"—her eyes would fill with tears—"and then it goes to *here!*" And she would start to tremble. "I want to kill everybody," she would whisper, "I've become a terrible person—" (She'd been terrible before, though.) "I don't know what to do. Why is this happening to me?"

She said, "If I believed in Heaven, if I thought I could go there and see my father and my sister Sarah—they were always good to me—I wouldn't be so afraid." She said, "It always seemed to me the good died young but I wasn't good and I'm dying young."

I was much too shy to imagine myself a woman physically, in exact detail, cleft and breasted.

My mother's room had a wallpaper of roses, large roses, six or seven inches across, set quite close together. One day, sitting with her in a chair by her bed, it occurred to me that she could not bear any situation in which she could not cheat. What she said was, "I don't know what good morphine is! It doesn't help enough—I can't get away with anything." She may have meant *from* anything but I took her meaning as the other thing. She also said, "If I pray it doesn't help, the pain doesn't stop."

"Do you believe in God, Momma?"

"I don't know—why doesn't He help me?"

"You're supposed to praise Him whether you're in pain or not."

"That's unfair."

"Well, we're not supposed to judge *Him.*"

"I don't want a God like that," she said.

"If you believed what the Catholics believed, you could pray to the Virgin Mary."

"No woman made this world. I couldn't pray to a woman."

Much of her restlessness and agony came from comparing what the movies said life was and death was and what pain was for women with what she actually had to confront in her life. She didn't think movies lied—like many liars, she saw truth everywhere.

One day I was listening to her and I grew sad. She said angrily, "Why are you looking sad?"

I said, "Out of sympathy."

She said, "I don't want that kind of sympathy—I want to be cheered up." It was much worse, much more hysterical and shrill, than I'm showing.

"How do you want to be cheered up?"

"I don't know—you're so smart: you figure it out." But if I tried to cheer her up she'd say, "You're talking like a fool."

The Golden Rule seemed to me inadequate; she wanted something given to her that had nothing to do with what I wished for myself.

I finally caught on; she yearned for a certain kind of high-flown, movie dialogue: "Mother, is the pain *any* better today?" "No. . . . No! I can't bear it." "Didn't the nurse come today and give you the morphine shots?" I would say, sounding like a doctor, calm, fatherly. "Don't mention the morphine! I don't want to think about the morphine!" she would say like a rebellious girl or flirtatious woman.

She liked it if I pretended to be floored by her bravery whether she was being brave or not. Often she made herself up for these scenes. Doris could not bear to be just another patient for her doctors and nurses and could not bear her relative unimportance to them. My father had minded that too. But Doris plotted; she kept my report card face up on her bed when the doctor came; one day she told me to stay home from school and to cry when I let the doctor in. I said I couldn't cry. She became enraged.

It was her notion that people were good for their own pleasure or out of stupidity and were then used by people who were capable of extorting love: love was based on physical beauty, accident, and hardness of soul: that is to say, hardness of soul aroused love in other people.

It was a perfectly good set of notions, I suppose, but I have never noticed that women thought more clearly than men.

One day I decided just to do it, finally, to sit down and actually imagine myself being her, middle-aged, disfigured, and so on.

I bicycled to some woods at the edge of town—a woods cut down since—walked and carried my bicycle through the trees, until I came to a glade I knew about where there was a tiny stream between mudbanks that were in spots mossy. Enough kids used the glade that the undergrowth had been worn away in the center and the ground was mud, moist, smooth, quivering, lightly streaked with colors. As woods went, that one was threadbare, but I thought it very fine.

I'd cut my classes.

I leaned my bicycle against a tree and I sat on the moss. I'd asked Doris's sister things about what Doris was going through, and the nearly senseless answers I'd gotten had unnerved me; the casual way people expressed things so that they did not tell you anything or care or ever in words admit to what they knew really bothered me. Perhaps they didn't admit it to themselves. Doris had a niece who was very intelligent and talkative but she didn't like me: it wasn't anything personal, but in the family there were assignments, and she'd been assigned to my sister; and my sister hated me, and out of politeness to my sister this cousin did not show any liking for me. She was rigorous in this (until one day she had a quarrel with my sister, and after that she was medium friendly to me). This particular cousin was outspoken and talked about things like menstruation and desiring boys, but she would not talk to me, although she was polite about not talking to me. So I didn't know if Doris was going through menopause while she was dying of cancer or not. I didn't know if one canceled the other out or not.

I don't think I made it clear to myself what I was doing. I did and I didn't know, I was definite and yet I crept up on it. Sitting in the glade, I thought it was all right and not upsetting to imagine oneself a young pretty girl especially if you didn't do it in detail but it seemed really foul to imagine oneself a middle-aged *woman*. It would be easiest to imagine being a very old woman, a witch, or a rude dowager—that was even sort of funny. But to think of myself as a middle-aged woman seemed to me filthy.

I wondered if I thought middle-aged women sacrosanct, or monstrous, or disgusting, or too pathetic or what. It seemed a great transgression, a trespass to think so ill of them, although a lot of boys that I knew laughed at and scorned middle-aged women, married women and teachers both. Simply contemplating the fact, the phenomenon of middle-aged women, I seemed to myself to have entered on obscenity.

Well, then, I ought just to take them for granted and avert my eyes. But then I could not imagine what it was to be Doris or what she was going through.

All at once I did imagine myself a girl, a girl my own age; it was a flicker, a very peculiar feat—clearly I was scared to death of doing any of this. But I did it a couple of times without really pausing to experience what it was I was as a girl: I just performed the feat, I flickered into it and out again. Then, carried away by confidence, I did pause and was a girl for a second but it was so obliterating, so shocking that I couldn't stand it. I was sickened. The feeling of obliteration or castration or whatever it was was unsettling as hell.

I had more than once imagined having breasts. Other boys and I had discussed what it must be like to have breasts: we'd imitated the way girls walked; we'd put books inside our shirts to simulate the weight of breasts. But I had not imagined breasts as part of a whole physical reality. Now suddenly, almost with a kind of excitement—well, with a dry excitement as in writing out an answer to an essay question on a test, working out an outline, a structure, seeing a thing take shape—I suddenly saw how shy I'd been about the physical thing, and with what seemed to me incredible daring (and feeling unclean, coated with un-cleanliness), I imagined my hips as being my shoulders: I hardly used my hips for anything; and my shoulders, which were sort of the weighty center of most of my movements and of my strength, as being my hips. I began to feel very hot; I was flushed—and humiliated. Then after a moment's thought, going almost blind with embarrassment—and sweat—I put my behind on my chest. Then I whacked my thing off quickly and I moved my hole to my crotch. I felt it would be hard to stand up, to walk, to bestir myself; I felt sheathed in embarrassment, impropriety, in transgressions that did not stay still but floated out like veils; every part of me was sexual and jutted out one way or another. I really was infinitely ashamed—there was no part of me that wasn't dirty, that wouldn't interfere with someone else's thoughts and suggest things. I seemed bound up, packaged, tied in this, and in extra flesh. To live required infinite shamelessness if I was like this. I was suddenly very bad-tempered. . . . (Possibly I was remembering dreams I'd had, ideas I'd had in dreams.)

I felt terrible. I tried to giggle and make it all a joke, giggle inwardly—or snort with laughter. But I felt a kind of connected hysteria, a long chain of mild hysteria, of feeling myself to be explosive, hugely impor-tant, and yet motionless, inclined to be motionless. I suddenly thought that to say no was what my pride rested on; saying yes was sloppy and killing. All this came in a rush. I was filled with impatience and incred-ible defiance and a kind of self-admiration I couldn't even begin to grasp.

The life in me, in her, seemed a form of madness (part of me was still masculine, obviously, part of my consciousness) and maddened and mad with pleasure and also unpleasantly ashamed or stubborn. I really did feel beyond the rules, borne over the channels laid down by rules: I floated over *everything*. And there was a terrible fear-excitement thing; I was afraid-and-not-afraid; vulnerable and yet emboldened by being *dirty* and not earthbound—it was like a joke, a peculiar kind of exalted joke, a tremendous, breathless joke, one hysterical and sickening but too good for me to let go of.

I began to shake.

I had only the vaguest idea of female physical weakness—women controlled so much of the world I was familiar with, so much of University City; but all at once, almost dizzyingly, almost like a monkey, I saw—I saw *connections* everywhere, routes, methods (also things to disapprove of, and things to be enthusiastic about): I was filled with a kind of animal politics. But I was afraid of having my arms and legs broken. When I was a man, I saw only a few logical positions and routes and resting places, but as a woman I saw routes everywhere, emotional ways to get things, lies, displays of myself: it was dazzling. I saw a thousand emotional strings attached to a thousand party favors. I felt a dreadful disgust for logic: logic seemed crippling and useless, unreal; and I had the most extraordinary sense of danger: it almost made me laugh; and I had a sort of immodest pride and a kind of anguished ambition and a weird determination not to be put in danger. . . . I was filled and fascinated by a sense of myself. Physical reality was a sieve which I passed through as I willed, when my luck was good. (I had read a number of books about women: *Gone With the Wind, Pride and Prejudice, Madame Bovary*.)

Then I saw why, maybe, Doris was a terrible person—it was her attempt at freedom. Her willfulness was all toward being free; now she was ill and caught. Briefly, I felt I understood Doris a little, only a little, for the first time. I felt I understood part of the stormy thing in her, and the thing where her pains blocked out the world and her obstinate selfishness and the feeling of having a face. I did not have entire confidence in my penetration, but still I admired my sympathy for her, but dully, almost boredly—with an open mouth, half wondering what to think about next—when suddenly, without warning, I really imagined myself her, Doris, middle-aged, disfigured, with loose skin, my voice different from what it had been: my voice was not that of a young woman. My mouth hurt with the pressure of my bitterness: my mouth was scalded. (In my own life, when I was unhappy, it was my *eyes* that hurt; my vision would hurt me: people would look like monsters to me and would seem to have evil glances, as if black cats inhabited their eyes.) It was almost as if there was steam somewhere in my throat; really, I burned with the pressure of angry words, with a truth I wasn't willing to modify, a truth meant to be wholly destructive to the errors and selfishness of others. To their complacency. I imagined all of it—not being liked by my family anymore, my husband hating me, being forsaken by my mother and sister. By my friends. As myself, as someone young, I could bear a good deal; but it takes energy to feel depressed, and when I imagined myself to be Doris, when I was Doris, I hadn't the energy anymore to die; too many things had gone wrong; I was too angry to die; I felt too much; there was no end to what I felt—I could do nothing but scream.

I DIDN'T know if I was faking all or any of this. What does imagination consist of ? I was thirteen and perhaps a superficial person. There was no guarantee I felt deeply or that I possessed any human grace at all. The trees around me, the tiny creek (like an endless parade of silvery snakes of varying thinnesses rustling over pebbles), the solitude suggested to me a gravity, a decency, a balance in life that was perhaps only the reflection of my Middle Western ignorance, or idealism. It is hard to know. But as long as I held on to the power to pity her, even while I imagined myself to be her, I did not, in my deepest self, suffer what I imagined her suffering. With what I would consider the equivalent confidence and folly of a boy playing at chemistry in the basement, I held up a mental snapshot of what I had in the second before half experienced in imagining myself to be Doris: it was a condition of mind, of terror and bitterness and hate, and a trying to win out still, all churning in me, and it was evil in that it was without bounds, without any fixity or finality, and suggested an infinite nausea—I was deeply afraid of nausea. It was a condition of mind, a sickening, lightless turmoil, unbearably foul, staled; and even to imagine it without going crazy myself or bursting into tears or yelling with horror, not to live it but just to conceive of it without going through those things was somehow unclean. But with nearly infinite coldness, a coldness that was a form of love in me, I held the thought. The mind's power to penetrate these realities is not distinguishable from the mind's power merely to imagine it is penetrating reality. My father had twice contemptuously called me the Boy Scout. Did Doris live much of the time in that foulness? I thought there was no end to her wretchedness, no end—I was thirteen—to the uselessness of her misery.

The thing about being a bad person, the thing about being free and a little cheap and not letting yourself be owned by other people at all, by their emotions, was that then you had to succeed, at everything you did, all the time: failure became an agony. And there was no alternative to that agony when it began except to become a good person. Not a saint, nothing extreme. It was just that if I imagined myself a middle-aged woman like Doris with both my breasts cut off and my husband dying, hating me while he died, turning his back on me and saying all the years he'd spent with me were foul, and with myself as selfish and hungry for triumph still, I was deprived of all justice, of all success, and my pain and terror were then so great that I would of course be insane.

Which magnified the agony.

Clearly—it seemed obvious to me as I sat there and reasoned about these things—unselfishness lessened such pain if only in the way it moved you outside your own nervous system. Generosity emptied you of any feeling of poverty anyway. I knew that from my own experience. Extended generosity predisposed you to die; death didn't seem so foul; you were already without a lot of eagerness about yourself; you were quieted.

I BICYCLED home, to bear the news to Momma, to tell her what I'd found out.

I was adolescent: that is, I was half formed, a sketch of a man. I told Doris unselfishness and generosity and concern for others would ease most pain, even her pain; it would make her feel better.

God, how she screamed.

She said that I came from filthy people and what I was was more filth, that I came from the scum of the earth and was more scum. Each thing she said struck her with its aptness and truth and inspired her and goaded her to greater anger. She threw an ashtray at me. She ordered me out of the house: "Sleep in the streets, sleep in the *gutter*, where you belong!" Her temper astounded me. Where did she get the strength for such temper when she was so ill? I did not fight back. My forbearance or patience or politeness or whatever it was upset her still more. I didn't catch on to this until in the middle of calling me names ("—you little bastard, you hate everybody, you're disgusting, I can't stand you, you little son of a bitch—" "Momma . . . Come on, now, Momma . . .") she screamed, "Why do you do things and make me ashamed?"

It was a revelation. It meant my *selfishness* would calm her. At first I said, "Do you really want me to go? You'll be alone here." I was partly sarcastic, laughing at her in that way, and then I began muttering, or saying with stubborn authority that I would not leave, I wanted my comfort considered, I wanted her to worry about my life. She said, huffing and gasping but less yellow and pinched and extreme, "You're a spoiled brat." I mean she was calmed to some extent; she was reduced to being incensed from being insane. But she screamed still. And I kept on too: I did not care what grounds she used—it could be on the grounds of my selfishness—but I was really stubborn: I was determined that she try being a good woman. I remember being so tense at my presumption that I kept thinking something physical in me would fail, would burst through my skin—my nerves, or my blood, my heart, everything was pounding, or my brain, but anyway that particular fight ended sort of in a draw, with Doris insulted and exhausted, appalled at what I'd said. At the stupidity. But with me adamant. I couldn't have stopped myself, actually.

After that, with my shoulders hunched and my eyes on the ground or occasionally wide open and innocent for inspection and fixed on her, I referred to her always as brave and generous. I dealt with her as if she was the most generous woman imaginable, as if she had been only good to me all my life. I referred to her kindness, her bravery, her selflessness. She said I was crazy. I suppose certain accusations, certain demands, were the natural habitat of her mind. At one point she even telephoned the junior-high-school principal to complain I was crazy. He wouldn't listen to her. I went right on behaving as if I remembered sacrifice after sacrifice she had made for me. She was enraged, then irritated, then desperate, then bored, then nonplussed, and the nonsense of it depressed her: she felt alone and misunderstood; she did not want me to be idealistic about her; she wanted me to be a companion to her, for her. But she stopped screaming at me.

I don't know if she saw through me or not. I don't think I consciously remembered over the weeks that this went on what had started all this or its history; continued acts develop their own atmosphere; that I

sincerely wanted a home of a certain kind for us was all that it seemed
to be about after a while. That I had to protect myself. When she gave
in, it was at first that she indulged the male of the family, the fool, the
boy who was less realistic than she was. Then to conceal her defeat, she
made it seem she couldn't bear to disillusion me. Also, while she more
or less said that she hadn't the energy to do what I expected of her, she
must have realized it took energy to fight me. She may have said to
herself—as I said to myself before I imagined myself to be her—Why
not? I think, too, my faith seduced her, my authority: I was so sure of
myself. And besides, the other didn't work anymore.

Of course, it was a swindle all the way: she could no longer ask things
of me so freely, so without thought of what it would do to me. She
became resigned, and then after a while she became less sad—she even
showed a wried amusement. She almost became good-tempered. She
was generous to some extent with everyone or I was hurt. She recon-
ciled with her mother and her daughter, with her brothers and her sister,
with the neighbors sometimes at my insistence—even with my advice—
but after a while she did it on her own in her own way. It seemed to
me it was obvious that considering all the factors, she was much kinder
to us than any of us were, or could be, to her, so that no matter what
bargain she thought she was negotiating, she really was unselfish now.
The bargain was not in her favor. She practiced a polite death or
whatever, a sheltering politeness, which wasn't always phony, and a
forgiveness of circumstances that was partly calculated to win friends:
she comforted everyone who came near her, sometimes cornily; but still
it was comfort. I was a little awed by her; she was maybe awed and
instructed by herself; she took over the—the *role*, and my opinions were
something she asked but she had her own life. Her own predicament.
She still denounced people behind their backs but briefly, and she
gloated now and then: when her rich brother died suddenly, she said
with a gently melancholy satisfaction, "Who would have thought I
could outlast J.J.?" She showed a shakily calm and remarkable daily
courage; she made herself, although she was a dying woman, into a
woman who was good company. She put together a whole new set of
friends. Those friends loved her actually, they looked up to her, they
admired her. She often boasted, "I have many, many very good friends
who have stuck by me." But they were all new friends—none of her old
friends came back. Young people always liked her now and envied me.
What was so moving was her dying woman's gaiety—it was so unex-

pected and so unforced, a kind of amusement with things. Sometimes when no one was around she would yell at me that she was in pain all the time and that I was a fool to believe the act she put on. But after a certain point, that stopped, too. She said, "I want to be an encouragement—I want you to remember me as someone who was a help to you." Do you see? After a certain time she was never again hysterical when I was there. Never. She was setting me an example. She was good to me in a way possible to her, the way she thought she, Doris, ought to be to me. But she was always Doris, no matter how kind she was. If at any time restlessness showed in me or if I was unhappy even about something very minor at school she would be upset; I had to have no feelings at all or stay within a narrow range for her comfort; she said often, "I know I'm unfair but wait until I die—can't you bear with me?" When I stayed out sometimes because I had to, because I was going crazy, when I came home she would say pleadingly, "Don't ask too much of me, Buddy." She would sit there, on the couch in the living room, having waited fully dressed for me to come home, and she would say that.

All right, her happiness rested on me. Her sister and one brother and her daughter told me I couldn't go to college, I couldn't leave Doris, it would be a crime. Her cancer was in remission; she had never gotten on so well with her own family (she was patient with them now), I owed it to her to stay. I am trying to establish what she gained and what she lost. Her family often said to me bullyingly, without affection or admiration, "Her life is in your hands." I hadn't intended this. Doris said they were jealous of me. I wanted to go to college; I wanted to use my mind and all that: I was willing for Doris's life to be in her mother's and sister's hands. I was modest about what I meant to Doris—does that mean I didn't love her?

The high school, when I refused to apply to Harvard, asked me why and then someone went to see Doris, and Doris went into her bedroom and locked the door and refused to eat until I agreed to go away to college. To leave her. And she made her family and her doctor ask me to go (they pounded on her door but she wouldn't eat until they did what she told them). Doris's sister Ida came and shouted through the bedroom door at her and then said to me in a cutting, angry voice, blaming me, that Doris was killing herself. This was when I was sixteen.

I said I wasn't that important. My modesty stymied Ida.

That sacrifice, if it was that, was either the first or second thing Doris had ever done for me. But perhaps she did it for herself, to strengthen her hand for some Last Judgment. Perhaps she was glad to be rid of me. I only lost my nerve once in accepting it from her, this gift. I was lying on my bed—it was evening in early spring and I should have been doing physics—and I was thinking about college, Harvard, about a place, the Yard, that I'd never seen, grass and paths and a wall around it, and buildings and trees, an enclosed park for young people. The thought took me to a pitch of anticipation and longing and readiness unlike anything I'd felt in years; all at once it was unendurable that I had that and Doris had nothing—had what she had. It was terrible to think how Doris was cheated in terms of what she could see ahead of her. I felt I'd tricked her in some way. Not that that was wrong but she was too nice, now that she was cheated, for me to—I don't know what. I suppose I was out of control. Clumsy, even lumbering, I blundered into her room and without warning or explanation began to say I was sorry and that I'd better back out of going to Harvard. She breathed in the loud, nervous way of a woman concerned about herself, but then she got herself in hand and said in the detached, slightly ironic voice, gentle, convivial, and conspiratorial, that she used at that time, a Middle Western voice, "Sorry for what? What is it? Buddy, you have nothing to be sorry for."

I'd never brought up in conversation with her matters that had to do with feelings of mine that were unclear or difficult: what good would it have done? She would not have made the effort to understand; she did not know how; she would only have felt lousy and been upset. I was silenced by a long tradition of lying to her and being lucid. I could at this time only say over and over that I was sorry—I couldn't try to explain any of it to her.

She said, "You're being silly. I think you're too close to me, Buddy. I don't want you to grow up to be a mother's boy."

I said, "What will you do when I go away?"

"You think I can't manage? You don't know much about me. Don't be so conceited where you're concerned." (But I'd put that idea into the air.) She said, "I can manage very well, believe me." I expressed disbelief by the way I stared at her. She said, "Go into my top bureau drawer. Look under the handkerchiefs."

There was a bottle there. I held it up. "What is it?"

"My morphine."

"You hide it?"

"I know how boys like to try things. . . ."

"You hide it from *me?*"

"I don't want you to be tempted—I know you're often under a strain."

"Momma, I wouldn't take your *morphine.*"

"But I don't use it much anymore. Haven't you noticed I'm clearer lately? I don't let myself use it, Buddy—look at the date on the bottle: it's lasted over a year. The doctor can't believe I'm so reformed; he'll ask me to marry him yet. Just sometimes I take it on a rainy day. Or at night. I thought you knew I wasn't using morphine anymore."

I hadn't noticed. I hadn't been keeping track. I didn't like to be too aware of her.

She could have had another bottle hidden; there was a nurse who came twice a week and who could, and I think did, give Doris injections of morphine. I didn't want to investigate. Or know. I just wanted to go on experiencing the release of having her care about me. Worry about me. She said, "You've been a help to me. You've done more than your share. You know what they say—out of the mouths of babes. I'll be honest with you: I'd like to be young again, I'd like to have my health back. But I'm not unhappy. I even think I'm happy now. Believe me, Buddy, the pain is less for me than it was."

AT HARVARD, I began to forget her. But at times I felt arrogant because of what she and I had done; I'd managed to do more than many of my professors could. I'd done more than many of them would try. I knew more than they did about some things.

Often I felt I was guilty of possessing an overspecialized maturity. At times I felt called upon to defend Doris by believing the great world to which Harvard was a kind of crooked door was worthless in its cruelty and its misuse of its inhabitants, and Doris was more important than any of it. Than what I had come to Harvard for. But I didn't go home.

And Doris wanted me to enter that great world: the only parts of my letters she really enjoyed were about things like my meeting a girl whose mother was a billionairess. By the standards of this new world I was sentimental and easily gulled and Doris was shrill. I did not want to see beyond a present folly or escape from one or be corrected or remember anything. Otherwise the shadow of Doris lay everywhere. I began to forget her even while she was alive.

The daughter of the billionairess was, in addition to everything else, a really admirable and intelligent girl. But I didn't trust her. One night she confessed various approaches she followed for winning the affection of boys. If you don't want to be silly and overly frail, you have to be immune and heartless to the fine-drawn, drawn-out, infinitely ludicrous, workable plots that women engage in. The delicacy and density of those plots. But I wasn't confident and I ran away from that girl. It seemed to me my whole life was sad. It was very hard to bear to see that in the worldly frame of Harvard Doris was, even in her relative nobility, unimportant. I had never been conscious before of the limitations of her intelligence. She had asked me to send her money and I did, my freshman year. I had a scholarship and I worked. It wasn't any longer that she was jealous of my life but she wanted me to show I cared about her still. She had changed her manner just before I left her; she had become like a German-Jewish matron of the sort who has a son at Harvard. And her letters were foolish, almost illiterate. It was too much for me, the costliness of loyalty, the pursuit of meanings, and everything savage from the past, half forgotten or summarized (and unreal) or lost in memory already. How beautiful I thought the ordinary was. I did not go home to live with her and she did not ask me to, when, after three years of remission, and three months after my leaving her, her cancer recurred.

H o w   c a n I even guess at what she gained, what she lost?

I spent the summer with her. I had a job and stayed home with her in the evenings. My manner unnerved her a bit. I was as agreeable as I knew how to be; I tried to be as Middle Western as before. When company came, Doris would ask me to stay only for a little while and then to excuse myself and leave: "People pay too much attention to you, and I like a little attention for myself."

The Christmas after that, I traveled out to be with her, fell ill, and was in a delirium for most of two weeks. Doris was curiously patient, not reproachful that I'd been ill, not worried, and when we spoke it was with a curious peace, and caution, too, as if we were the only two adults in the world. She said for the first time, "I love you, Buddy."

I n   M a y I was called to her bedside because she was about to die. Her family had gathered and they stood aside, or else Doris had told them to leave us alone; perhaps they recognized my prior right to her;

they had never been able to get along with her, they had only loved her. Doris said, "I was waiting for you. It's awful. Mose comes in here and complains about his health and carries on about me and doesn't hear me ask for water, and Ida cries and says it's terrible for her—Ida was never any good at a deathbed—and your sister comes in here and says, 'Have a little nap,' and when I close my eyes she runs to the dresser and looks at things: she's afraid I left it all to you; she already took my compact and she uses it in front of me. I wasn't a good mother but she doesn't have to rub it in. She thinks I'm dead already. Her feelings are hurt. How is college? What I'd like to hear about is the rich people you've met. . . ."

When I started to speak, she cut in: "I was afraid you wouldn't get here in time. I didn't want to interrupt your studies and I was afraid I waited too long. I didn't let them give me a morphine shot today. I want to talk to you with a clear head. The pain is not good, Buddy, but I don't want to be drugged when we talk. I've been thinking what I would say to you. I've been thinking about it all week. I like talking to you. Listen, I want to say this first: I appreciate what you did for me, Buddy."

"I didn't do anything special for you." I did not remember clearly—I had put it out of my mind. . . . I did not want any responsibility for Doris.

"Buddy, you were good to me," she said.

"Well, Momma, you were good to *me.*" I was too shy, too collegiate, too anxious to praise her, too rattled by the emergency, by the thought she was dying, to say anything else. I thought it would be best for us to go on to the end as we had gone on for so long. For so many years I'd calmed and guided her this way: it was an old device. I assumed I couldn't be honest with her now. I had no notion that dying had educated her. I was eighteen, a young man who had a number of voices, who was subject to his own angers, to a sense of isolation that made him unwilling to use his gifts. In Cambridge, people I knew applied adjectives to me in the melodramatic way of college sophomores: interesting, immature, bad-tempered. There were people who were in love with me. I was intensely unhappy and knew that a great deal of it I owed to Doris.

Doris said, "I've been waiting for you. I missed you, Buddy. Listen, I'm not as strong as I was. I can't put on too good a show—if I make faces or noises, don't get upset and run for the nurse: let me talk: you make things too easy for me. Now listen, don't get mad at me but you have to promise me you'll finish college—you tend to run away from things. You're lazy, Buddy. Promise me; I have to make you promise: I want to be a good mother—will wonders never cease?"

"You always were a good mother."

"Oh, Buddy, I was terrible."

"No, Momma. No, you weren't." But I think she wanted companionship, not consolation; I guessed wrong on that last occasion. She said, "We don't have to be polite to each other now—Buddy, will you say you forgive me?"

She thought I was happy and strong, that I'd survived my childhood. I wanted her to think that. So far as I knew I didn't blame her, not for anything; but not blaming someone is very unlike forgiving them: if I was to forgive her it meant I had first to remember. I would have collapsed sobbing on her bed and cried out, God, it was so awful, so awful, why did those things have to happen, oh God, it was so awful. . . .

I don't know if I was cruel or not. I told her I wasn't being polite, that I had nothing to forgive her for: "You were a good mother."

She said, "Buddy, you helped me—I can bear the pain."

"Momma!" I refused to understand. "You did it all yourself. You were always better than you thought."

Each breath she took was like a seesaw noisily grinding aloft, descending. Her life was held in a saucer on that seesaw. I have no gift for bearing human pain. I kept thinking, I can accept this, I can do this without getting hysterical.

"It was always easier for me than you thought, Mother; you never hurt me much; you always thought you were worse than you were. A lot of what you blame yourself for was always imaginary: you were better to me than anyone else was—at least you lived."

"Buddy, I can face the truth, I know what I did."

"I don't know what you did."

And she even forgave me that. She said, "I understand. You don't want to face things now. Maybe it's better not to bring it up."

"Do what you like, Momma. I'll understand sooner or later."

She said, "Kiss me, Buddy. Am I very ugly?"

"No, Momma."

"You always thought I was pretty. Listen: at the end, Buddy, I tried. I loved you. I'm ready to die; I'm only alive because I wanted to talk to you, I wanted that to be the last thing—do you understand, I want you to know now how much I think of you."

"Momma—"

"I'm going to die soon, I'm very bad, Buddy. Listen: I don't want you to grieve for me. You've done your share already. I want you to have a good time. I want you to enjoy yourself." Then she said, "I can't be what you want; I don't want to upset you; just say you forgive me."

"I will if you give me your forgiveness, Momma."

"My forgiveness? Oh, Buddy. I bet you're good with girls. What a liar you are. And I always thought I was a liar. I forgive you, Buddy. Don't you know what you did for me? You made it so the pain was less."

"Momma, I didn't do anything."

"Isn't it funny what people are ashamed of?" She was silent for a small second; then she said, "Do you forgive me?"

"I forgive you, Momma, but there's nothing to forgive you for. If it wasn't for you I'd be dead."

"That was a long time ago; you were still a baby then. Oh. Run now and get the nurse. I don't think I can stand the pain now. Tell her I want my shot."

After the nurse had gone, Doris said, "Buddy, I went in a wheelchair to the ward where people had cancer and were frightened, and I tried to help them—I thought you would be proud of me."

For a moment, I remembered something. *"Momma, I was a stupid boy."*

"Hold my hand while I fall asleep, Buddy. I don't know if I think Harvard is such a good place—you don't face things as well as you used to. Buddy, I'm tired of it all. I don't like my family much. Is it terrible to say I don't think they're nice people? In the end you and my father were the only ones. I wish you could have known him. I loved you best. Don't let it go to your head. You never thought you were conceited but you were—that's always the part of the story you leave out—and how you like to domineer over people. It's a miracle no one's killed you yet. It's terrible to be sorry for things. Buddy, do you know why that is—why is it terrible to be sorry? I don't know why things happened the way they did. I kept thinking as I lay here it would be interesting if I understood things now and I could tell you—I know how you like to know things. Buddy, I promised your mother you would remember her—promise me you'll think well of her. She was your real mother and she loved you, too. Buddy?"

"Yes."

"Find someone to love. Find someone to be good to you." Then she said, "I love you, Buddy. . . . I'm sorry."

She seemed to sleep. Then her breathing grew rough. I thought I ought to go get the doctor but then I sat down again and stared at the ceiling. I was afraid my feeling for her or some flow of regret in me or anything in me she might as a woman feel as a thread requiring her attention would interfere with her death. So I said to myself, You can die, Momma; it's all right; I don't want you to live anymore. From time to time, in her sleep, in her dying, she shouted, "Haven't I suffered enough?" and "Buddy, are you still there? Don't have anything to do with those terrible people!" Then she came to and said, "Am I shouting things? . . . I thought so. I don't want you to go away, but when you're this close I don't feel right."

"Do you want me to go into the hall?"

"No. Don't leave me. But don't sit too close to me, don't look at me. Just stay near. . . . I want you here."

"All right, Momma."

I listened to her breathing grow irregular. I said to myself, Die, Momma. On this breath. I don't want you to live anymore. Her breath changed again. It began to be very loud, rackety. I began to count her breaths. I counted fifteen and then neither her breath nor her actual voice was ever heard again.

A F T E R   S H E   D I E D , I had a nervous breakdown. I couldn't believe I missed her that much. I'd loved her at the end, loved her again, loved and admired her, loved her greatly; of course, by that time, she did not ask that the love I felt express itself in sacrificing myself for her. I loved her while I enjoyed an increasing freedom from her but still I needed her; and, as I said, I had a nervous breakdown when she died. After a while, I got over it.

I don't know all that I gained or lost, either. I know I was never to be certain I was masculine to the proper degree again. I always thought I knew what women felt.

Make what use of this you like.

His Son, in His Arms,
in Light, Aloft

M Y FATHER is chasing me. My God, I feel it up and down my spine, the thumping on the turf, the approach of his hands, his giant hands, the huge ramming increment of his breath as he draws near: a widening effort. I feel it up and down my spine and in my mouth and belly—Daddy is so swift: who ever heard of such swiftness? Just as in stories . . .

I can't escape him, can't fend him off, his arms, his rapidity, his will. His interest in me.

I am being lifted into the air—and even as I pant and stare blurredly, limply, mindlessly, a map appears, of the dark ground where I ran: as I hang limply and rise anyway on the fattened bar of my father's arm, I see that there's the grass, there's the path, there's a bed of flowers.

I straighten up. There are the lighted windows of our house, some distance away. My father's face, full of noises, is near: it looms: his hidden face: is that you, old money-maker? My butt is folded on the trapeze of his arm. My father is as big as an automobile.

In the oddly shrewd-hearted torpor of being carried home in the dark, a tourist, in my father's arms, I feel myself attached by my heated-by-running dampness to him: we are attached, there are binding oval stains of warmth.

IN MOST social talk, most politeness, most literature, most religion, it is as if violence didn't exist—except as sin, something far away. This is flattering to women. It is also conducive to grace—because the heaviness of fear, the shadowy henchmen selves that fear attaches to us, that fear sees in others, is banished.

Where am I in the web of jealousy that trembles at every human movement?

What detectives we have to be.

WHAT IF I am wrong? What if I remember incorrectly? It does not matter. This is fiction—a game—of pleasures, of truth and error, as at the sensual beginning of a sensual life.

MY FATHER, Charley, as I knew him, is invisible in any photograph I have of him. The man I hugged or ran toward or ran from is not in any photograph: a photograph shows someone of whom I think, Oh, was he like that?

But in certain memories, *he* appears, a figure, a presence, and I think, I know him.

It is embarrassing to me that I am part of what is unsayable in any account of his life.

WHEN MOMMA'S or my sister's excesses, of mood, or of shopping, angered or sickened Daddy, you can smell him then from two feet away: he has a dry, achy little stink of a rapidly fading interest in his life with us. At these times, the women in a spasm of wit turn to me; they comb my hair, clean my face, pat my bottom or my shoulder, and send me off; they bid me to go cheer up Daddy.

Sometimes it takes no more than a tug at his newspaper: the sight of me is enough; or I climb on his lap, mimic his depression; or I stand on his lap, press his head against my chest. . . . His face is immense, porous, complex with stubble, bits of talcum on it, unlikely colors, unlikely features, a bald brow with a curved square of lamplight in it. About his head there is a nimbus of sturdy wickedness, of unlikelihood. If his mood does not change, something tumbles and goes dead in me.

Perhaps it is more a nervous breakdown than heartbreak: I have failed him: his love for me is very limited: I must die now. I go somewhere and shudder and collapse—a corner of the dining room, the back stoop or deck: I lie there, empty, grief-stricken, literally unable to move—I have forgotten my limbs. If a memory of them comes to me, the memory is meaningless. . . .

Momma will then stalk into wherever Daddy is and say to him, "Charley, you can be mad at me, I'm used to it, but just go take a look and see what you've done to the child. . . ."

My uselessness toward him sickens me. Anyone who fails toward him might as well be struck down, abandoned, eaten.

Perhaps it is an animal state: I-have-nothing-left, I-have-no-place-in-this-world.

Well, this is his house. Momma tells me in various ways to love him. Also, he is entrancing—he is so big, so thunderish, so smelly, and has the most extraordinary habits, reading newspapers, for instance, and wiggling his shoe: his shoe is gross: kick someone with that and they'd fall into next week.

SOME MEMORIES huddle in a grainy light. What it is is a number of similar events bunching themselves, superimposing themselves, to make a false memory, a collage, a mental artifact. Within the boundaries of one such memory one plunges from year to year, is small and helpless, is a little older: one remembers it all but it is nothing that happened, that clutch of happenings, of associations, those gifts and ghosts of a meaning.

I can, if I concentrate, whiten the light—or yellow-whiten it, actually—and when the graininess goes, it is suddenly one afternoon.

I COULD NOT live without the pride and belonging-to-himness of being that man's consolation. He had the disposal of the rights to the out-of-doors—he was the other, the other-not-a-woman: he was my strength, literally, my strength if I should cry out.

Flies and swarms of the danger of being unfathered beset me when I bored my father: it was as if I were covered with flies on the animal plain where some ravening wild dog would leap up, bite and grip my muzzle, and begin to bring about my death.

I had no protection: I was subject now to the appetite of whatever inhabited the dark.

A child collapses in a sudden burst of there-is-nothing-here, and that is added onto nothingness, the nothing of being only a child concentrating on there being nothing there, no hope, no ambition: there is a despair but one without magnificence except in the face of its completeness: *I am a child and am without strength of my own.*

I HAVE—in my grief—somehow managed to get to the back deck: I am sitting in the early-evening light; I am oblivious to the light. I did and didn't hear his footsteps, the rumble, the house thunder dimly (behind and beneath me), the thunder of his-coming-to-rescue-me. . . . I did and didn't hear him call my name.

I spoke only the gaping emptiness of grief—that tongue—I understood I had no right to the speech of fathers and sons.

My father came out on the porch. I remember how stirred he was, how beside himself that I was so unhappy, that a child, a child he liked, should suffer so. He laid aside his own mood—his disgust with life, with money, with the excesses of the women—and he took on a broad-winged, malely flustering, broad-winged optimism—he was at the center of a great beating (of the heart, a man's heart, of a man's gestures, will, concern), dust clouds rising, a beating determination to persuade me that the nature of life, of *my* life, was other than I'd thought, other than whatever had defeated me—he was about to tell me there was no need to feel defeated, he was about to tell me that I was a good, or even a wonderful, child.

HE KNEELED—a mountain of shirtfront and trousers; a mountain that poured, clambered down, folded itself, re-formed itself: a disorderly massiveness, near to me, fabric-hung-and-draped: Sinai. He said, "Here, here, what is this—what is a child like you doing being so sad?" And: "Look at me. . . . It's all right. . . . Everything is all right. . . ." The misstatements of consolation are lies about the absolute that require faith—and no memory: the truth of consolation can be investigated if one is a proper child—that is to say, affectionate—only in a nonskeptical way.

"It's not all right!"

"It is—it is." It was and wasn't a lie: it had to do with power—and limitations: my limitations and his power: he could make it all right for me, everything, provided my everything was small enough and within his comprehension.

Sometimes he would say, "Son"—he would say it heavily—"don't be sad—I don't want you to be sad—I don't like it when you're sad—"

I can't look into his near and, to me, factually incredible face—incredible because so large (as at the beginning of a love affair): I mean as a *face:* it is the focus of so many emotions and wonderments: he could have been a fool or was—it was possibly the face of a fool, someone self-centered, smug, an operator, semicriminal, an intelligent psychoanalyst; it was certainly a mortal face—but what did the idea or word mean to me then—*mortal?*

There was a face; it was as large as my chest; there were eyes, inhumanly big, humid—what could they mean? How could I read them? How do you read eyes? I did not know about comparisons: how much more affectionate he was than other men, or less, how much better than common experience or how much worse in this area of being fathered my experience was with him: I cannot say even now; it is a statistical matter, after all, a matter of averages: but who at the present date can phrase the proper questions for the poll? And who will understand the hesitations, the blank looks, the odd expressions on the faces of the answerers?

The odds are he was a—median—father. He himself had usually a conviction he did pretty well; sometimes he despaired—of himself—but blamed me: my love: or something: or himself as a father: he wasn't good at managing stages between strong, clear states of feeling. Perhaps no one is.

Anyway, I knew no such terms as *median* then: I did not understand much about those parts of his emotions that extended past the rather clear area where my emotions were so often amazed. I chose, in some ways, to regard him seriously: in other ways, I had no choice—he was what was given to me.

I cannot look at him, as I said: I cannot see anything: if I look at him without seeing him, my blindness insults him: I don't want to hurt him at all: I want nothing: I am lost and have surrendered and am really dead and am waiting without hope.

H E K N O W S how to rescue people. Whatever he doesn't know, one of the things he knows in the haste and jumble of his heart, among the blither of tastes in his mouth and opinions and sympathies in his mind and so on, is the making yourself into someone who will help someone who is wounded. The dispersed and unlikely parts of him come together for a while in a clucking and focused arch of abiding concern. Oh how he plows ahead; oh how he believes in rescue! He puts—he *shoves*—he works an arm behind my shoulders, another under my legs: his arms, his powers shove at me, twist, lift, and jerk me until I am cradled in the air, in his arms: "You don't have to be unhappy—you haven't hurt anyone—don't be sad—you're a *nice* boy. . . ."

I can't quite hear him, I can't quite believe him. I can't be *good*—the confidence game is to believe him, is to be a good child who trusts him—we will both smile then, he and I. But if I hear him, I have to believe him still. I am set up that way. He is so big; he is the possessor of so many grandeurs. If I believe him, hope and pleasure will start up again—suddenly—the blankness in me will be relieved, broken by these—meanings—that it seems he and I share in some big, attaching way.

In his pride he does not allow me to suffer: I belong to him.

H E   I S   R I S I N G , jerkily, to his feet and holding me at the same time. I do not have to stir to save myself—I only have to believe him. He rocks me into a sad-edged relief and an achingly melancholy delight with the peculiar lurch as he stands erect of establishing his balance and rectifying the way he holds me, so he can go on holding me, holding me aloft, against his chest: I am airborne: I liked to have that man hold me—in the air: I knew it was worth a great deal, the embrace, the gift of altitude. I am not exposed on the animal plain. I am not helpless.

The heat his body gives off! It is the heat of a man sweating with regret. His heartbeat, his burning, his physical force: ah, there is a large rent in the nothingness: the mournful apparition of his regret, the proof of his loyalty wake me: I have a twin, a massive twin, mighty company: Daddy's grief is at my grief: my nothingness is echoed in him (if he is going to have to live without me): the rescue was not quite a secular thing. The evening forms itself, a classroom, a brigade of shadows, of phenomena—the tinted air slides: there are shadowy skaters every- where; shadowy cloaked people step out from behind things that are then hidden behind their cloaks. An alteration in the air proceeds from openings in the ground, from leaks in the sunlight, which is being disengaged, like a stubborn hand, or is being stroked shut like my eyelids when I refuse to sleep: the dark rubs and bubbles noiselessly—and seeps—into the landscape. In the rubbed distortion of my inner air, twilight soothes: there are two of us breathing in close proximity here (he is telling me that grownups sometimes have things on their minds, he is saying mysterious things that I don't comprehend); I don't want to look at him: it takes two of my eyes to see one of his—and then I mostly see myself in his eye: he is even more unseeable from here, this holder: my head falls against his neck. "I know what you like—you'd like to go stand on the wall—would you like to see the sunset?" Did I nod? I think I did: I nodded gravely: but perhaps he did not need an answer since he thought he knew me well.

We are moving, this elephant and I, we are lumbering, down some steps, across grassy, uneven ground—the spoiled child in his father's arms—behind our house was a little park—we moved across the grass of the little park. There are sun's rays on the dome of the Moorish bandstand. The evening is moist, fugitive, momentarily sneaking, half welcomed in this hour of crime. My father's neck. The stubble. The skin where the stubble stops. Exhaustion has me: I am a creature of failure, a locus of childishness, an empty skull: I am this being-young. We overrun the world, he and I, with his legs, with our eyes, with our alliance. We move on in a ghostly torrent of our being like this.

My father has the smell and feel of wanting to be my father. Guilt and innocence stream and restream in him. His face, I see now in memory, held an untiring surprise: as if some grammar of deed and purpose—of comparatively easy tenderness—startled him again and again, startled him continuously for a while. He said, "I guess we'll just have to cheer you up—we'll have to show you life isn't so bad—I guess we weren't any too careful of a little boy's feelings, were we?" I wonder if all comfort is alike.

A man's love is, after all, a fairly spectacular thing.

He said—his voice came from above me—he spoke out into the air, the twilight—"We'll make it all right—just you wait and see. . . ."

He said, "This is what you like," and he placed me on the wall that ran along the edge of the park, the edge of a bluff, a wall too high for me to see over, and which I was forbidden to climb: he placed me on the stubbed stone mountains and grouting of the walltop. He put his arm around my middle: I leaned against him: and faced outward into the salt of the danger of the height, of the view (we were at least one hundred and fifty feet; we were, therefore, hundreds of feet in the air);

I was flicked at by narrow, abrasive bands of wind, evening wind, veined with sunset's sun-crispness, strongly touched with coolness.

The wind would push at my eyelids, my nose, my lips. I heard a buzzing in my ears that signaled how high, how alone we were: this view of a river valley at night and of parts of four counties was audible. I looked into the hollow in front of me, a grand hole, an immense, bellying deep sheet or vast sock. There were numinous fragments in it—birds in what sunlight was left, bits of smoke faintly lit by distant light or mist, hovering inexplicably here and there: rays of yellow light, high up, touching a few high clouds.

It had a floor on which were creeks (and the big river), a little dim, a little glary at this hour, rail lines, roads, highways, houses, silos, bridges, trees, fields, everything more than half hidden in the enlarging dark: there was the shrinking glitter of far-off noises, bearded and stippled with huge and spreading shadows of my ignorance: it was panorama as a personal privilege. The sun at the end of the large, sunset-swollen sky was a glowing and urgent orange; around it were the spreading petals of pink and stratospheric gold; on the ground were occasional magenta flarings: oh, it makes you stare and gasp; a fine, astral (not a crayon) red rode in a broad, magnificent band across the Middle Western sky: below us, for miles, shadowiness tightened as we watched (it seemed); above us, tinted clouds spread across the vast shadowing sky: there were funereal lights and sinkings everywhere. I stand on the wall and lean against Daddy, only somewhat awed and abstracted: the view does not own me as it usually does: I am partly in the hands of the jolting—amusement—the conceit—of having been resurrected—by my father.

I understood that he was proffering me oblivion plus pleasure, the end of a sorrow to be henceforth remembered as Happiness. This was to be my privilege. This amazing man is going to rescue me from any anomaly or barb or sting in my existence: he is going to confer happiness on me: as a matter of fact, he has already begun.

"Just you trust me—you keep right on being cheered up—look at that sunset—that's some sunset, wouldn't you say? Everything is going to be just fine and dandy—you trust me—you'll see—just you wait and see. . . ."

D I D   H E mean to be a swindler? He wasn't clear-minded—he often said, "I mean well." He did not think other people meant well.

I don't feel it would be right to adopt an Oedipal theory to explain what happened between him and me: only a sense of what he was like as a man, what certain moments were like, and what was said.

It is hard in language to get the full, irregular, heavy sound of a man.

He liked to have us "all dressed and nice when I come home from work," have us wait for him in attitudes of serene all-is-well contentment. As elegant as a Spanish prince, I sat on the couch toying with an oversized model truck—what a confusion of social pretensions, technologies, class disorder there was in that. My sister would sit in a chair, knees together, hair brushed: she'd doze off if Daddy was late. Aren't we happy! Actually, we often are.

One day he came in plungingly, excited to be home and to have us as an audience rather than outsiders who didn't know their lines and who often laughed at him as part of their struggle to improve their parts in his scenes. We were waiting to have him approve of our tableau—he usually said something about what a nice family we looked like or how well we looked or what a pretty group or some such thing—and we didn't realize he was the tableau tonight. We held our positions, but we stared at him in a kind of mindless what-should-we-do-besides-sit-here-and-be-happy-and-nice? Impatiently he said, "I have a surprise for you, Charlotte—Abe Last has a heart after all." My father said something on that order: or "a conscience after all"; and then he walked across the carpet, a man somewhat jerky with success—a man redolent of vaudeville, of grotesque and sentimental movies (he liked grotesquerie, prettiness, sentiment). As he walked, he pulled banded packs of currency out of his pockets, two or three in each hand. "There," he said, dropping one, then three, in Momma's dressed-up lap. "There," he said, dropping another two: he uttered a "there" for each subsequent pack. "Oh, let me!" my sister cried, and ran over to look—and then she grabbed two packs and said, "Oh, Daddy, how much *is* this?"

It was eight or ten thousand dollars, he said. Momma said, "Charley, what if someone sees—we could be robbed—why do you take chances like this?"

Daddy harrumphed and said, "You have no sense of fun—if you ask me, you're afraid to be happy. I'll put it in the bank tomorrow—if I can find an honest banker. Here, young lady, put that money down: you don't want to prove your mother right, do you?"

Then he said, "I know one person around here who knows how to enjoy himself—" and he lifted me up, held me in his arms.

He said, "We're going outside, this young man and I."

"What should I do with this money!"

"Put it under your mattress—make a salad out of it: you're always the one who worries about money," he said in a voice solid with authority and masculinity, totally pieced out with various self-satisfactions—as if he had gained a kingdom and the assurance of appearing as glorious in the histories of his time; I put my head back and smiled at the superb animal, at the rosy—and cowardly—panther leaping; and then I glanced over his shoulder and tilted my head and looked sympathetically at Momma.

My sister shouted, "I know how to enjoy myself—I'll come, too! . . ."

"Yes, yes," said Daddy, who was *never* averse to enlarging spheres of happiness and areas of sentiment. He held her hand and held me on his arm.

"Let him walk," my sister said. And: "He's getting bigger—you'll make a sissy out of him, Daddy. . . ."

Daddy said, "Shut up and enjoy the light—it's as beautiful as Paris, and in our own backyard."

Out of folly, or a wish to steal his attention, or greed, my sister kept on: she asked if she could get something with some of the money; he dodged her question; and she kept on; and he grew peevish, so peevish he returned to the house and accused Momma of having never taught her daughter not to be greedy—he sprawled, impetuous, displeased, semifrantic in a chair: "I can't enjoy myself—there is no way a man can live in this house with all of you—I swear to God this will kill me soon. . . ."

Momma said to him, "I can't believe in the things you believe in—I'm not a girl anymore: when I play the fool, it isn't convincing—you get angry with me when I try. You shouldn't get angry with her—you've spoiled her more than I have—and how do you expect her to act when you show her all that money—how do you think money affects people?"

I looked at him to see what the answer was, to see what he would answer. He said, "Charlotte, try being a rose and not a thorn."

AT ALL TIMES, and in all places, there is always the possibility that I will start to speak or will be looking at something and I will feel his face covering mine, as in a kiss and as a mask, turned both ways like that: and I am inside him, his presence, his thoughts, his language: *I* am

languageless then for a moment, an automaton of repetition, a bagged
piece of an imaginary river of descent.

I can't invent everything for myself: some always has to be what I
already know: some of me always has to be him.

When he picked me up, my consciousness fitted itself to that position:
I remember it—clearly. He could punish me—and did—by refusing to
lift me, by denying me that union with him. Of course, the union was
not one-sided: I was his innocence—as long as I was not an accusation,
that is. I censored him—in that when he felt himself being, consciously,
a father, he held back part of his other life, of his whole self: his shadows,
his impressions, his adventures would not readily fit into me—what a
gross and absurd rape that would have been.

So he was *careful*—he *walked on eggs*—there was an odd courtesy of
his withdrawal behind his secrets, his secret sorrows and horrors, behind
the curtain of what-is-suitable-for-a-child.

Sometimes he becomes simply a set of limits, of walls, inside which
there is the caroming and echoing of my astounding sensibility ampli-
fied by being his son and in his arms and aloft; and he lays his sensibility
aside or models his on mine, on my joy, takes his emotional coloring
from me, like a mirror or a twin: his incomprehensible life, with its
strengths, ordeals, triumphs, crimes, horrors, his sadness and disgust, is
enveloped and momentarily assuaged by my direct and indirect childish
consolation. My gaze, my enjoying him, my willingness to be him, my
joy at it, supported the baroque tower of his necessary but limited and
maybe dishonest optimism.

O N E T I M E, he and Momma fought over money and he left: he
packed a bag and went. Oh, it was sad and heavy at home. I started to
be upset, but then I retreated into an impenetrable stupidity: not knowing was better than being despairing. I was put to bed and I did fall
asleep; I woke in the middle of the night: he had returned and was sitting
on my bed—in the dark—a huge shadow in the shadows. He was
stroking my forehead. When he saw my eyes open, he said in a sentimental, heavy voice, "I could never leave *you*—"

He didn't really mean it: I was an excuse; but he did mean it—the
meaning and not-meaning were like the rise and fall of a wave in me,
in the dark outside of me, between the two of us, between him and me
(at other moments he would think of other truths, other than the one

of he-couldn't-leave-me). He bent over sentimentally, painedly, not nicely, and he began to hug me; he put his head down, on my chest; my small heartbeat vanished into the near, sizable, anguished, angular, emotion-swollen one that was his. I kept advancing swiftly into wakefulness, my consciousness came rushing and widening blurredly, embracing the dark, his presence, his embrace. It's Daddy, it's Daddy—it's dark still—wakefulness rushed into the dark grave or grove of his hugely extended presence. His affection. My arms stumbled: there was no adequate embrace in me—I couldn't lift *him*. I had no adequacy yet except that of my charm or what-have-you, except things the grownups gave me—not things: traits, qualities. I mean, my hugging his head was nothing until he said, "Oh, you love me. . . . You're all right. . . ."

M o m m a   s a i d : "They are as close as two peas in a pod—they are just alike—that child and Charley. That child is God to Charley. . . ."

H e   d i d n ' t always love me.

In the middle of the night that time, he picked me up after a while, he wrapped me in a blanket, held me close, took me downstairs in the dark; we went outside, into the night; it was dark and chilly but there was a moon—I thought he would take me to the wall but he just stood on our back deck. He grew tired of loving me; he grew abstracted and forgot me: the love that had just a moment before been so intently and tightly clasping and nestling went away, and I found myself released, into the cool night air, the floating damp, the silence, with the darkened houses around us.

I saw the silver moon, heard my father's breath, felt the itchiness of the woolen blanket on my hands, noticed its wool smell. I did this alone and I waited. Then, when he didn't come back, I grew sleepy and put my head down against his neck: he was nowhere near me. Alone in his arms, I slept.

O v e r   a n d   o v e r a moment seems to recur, something seems to return in its entirety, a name seems to be accurate: and we say it always happens like this. But we are wrong, of course.

I was a weird choice as someone for him to love.

So different from him in the way I was surprised by things.
I am a child with this mind. I am a child he has often rescued.
Our attachment to each other manifests itself in sudden swoops and
grabs and rubs of attention, of being entertained, by each other, at the
present moment.
I ask you, how is it possible it's going to last?

S O M E T I M E S   W H E N   we are entertained by each other, we are
bold about it, but just as frequently it seems embarrassing, and we turn
our faces aside.

H I S   R E C O L L E C T I O N S   of horror are more certain than mine. His
suspicions are more terrible. There are darknesses in me I'm afraid of,
but the ones in him don't frighten me but are like the dark in the yard,
a dark a child like me might sneak into (and has)—a dark full of unseen
shadowy almost glowing presences: the fear, the danger, are desirable—
difficult—with the call-to-be-brave: the childish bravura of *I must endure
this* (knowing I can run away if I choose).

The child touches with his pursed, jutting, ignorant lips the large,
handsome, odd, humid face of his father, who can run away too. More
dangerously.

He gave away a car of his that he was about to trade in on a new one:
he gave it to a man in financial trouble; he did it after seeing a movie
about crazy people being loving and gentle with each other and everyone else: Momma said to Daddy, "You can't do anything you want—
you can't listen to your feelings—you have a family. . . ."

After seeing a movie in which a child cheered up an old man, he took
me to visit an old man who probably was a distant relative, and who
hated me at sight, my high coloring, the noise I might make, my father's
affection for me: "Will he sit still? I can't stand noise. Charley, listen,
I'm in bad shape—I think I have cancer and they won't tell me—"

"Nothing can kill a tough old bird like you, Ike. . . ."

The old man wanted all of Charley's attention—and strength—while
he talked about how the small threads and thicker ropes that tied him
to life were being cruelly tampered with.

Daddy patted me afterward, but oddly he was bored and disappointed
in me, as if I'd failed at something.

He could not seem to keep it straight about my value to him or to the world in general; he lived at the center of his own intellectual shortcomings and his moral pride: he needed it to be true, as an essential fact, that goodness—or innocence—was in him or was protected by him, and that, therefore, he was a good *man* and superior to other men, and did not deserve certain common masculine fates—horrors—tests of his courage—certain pains. It was necessary to him to have it be true that he knew what real goodness was and had it in his life.

Perhaps that was because he didn't believe in God, and because he felt (with a certain self-love) that people, out in the world, didn't appreciate him and were needlessly difficult—"unloving": he said it often—and because it was true he was shocked and guilty and even enraged when he was "forced" into being unloving himself, or when he caught sight in himself of such a thing as cruelty, or cruel nosiness, or physical cowardice—God, how he hated being a coward—or hatred, physical hatred, even for me, if I was coy or evasive or disinterested or tired of him: it tore him apart literally—bits of madness, in varying degrees, would grip him as in a Greek play: I see his mouth, his salmon-colored mouth, showing various degrees of sarcasm—sarcasm mounting into bitterness and even a ferocity without tears that always suggested to me, as a child, that he was near tears but had forgotten in his ferocity that he was about to cry.

Or he would catch sight of some evidence, momentarily inescapable—in contradictory or foolish statements of his or in unkept promises that it was clear he had never meant to keep, had never made any effort to keep—that he was a fraud; and sometimes he would laugh because he was a fraud—a good-hearted fraud, he believed—or he would be sullen or angry, a fraud caught either by the tricks of language, so that in expressing affection absentmindedly he had expressed too much; or caught by greed and self-concern: he hated the evidence that he was mutable as hell: that he loved sporadically and egoistically, and often with rage and vengeance, and that madness I mentioned earlier: he couldn't stand those things; he usually forgot them, but sometimes when he was being tender, or noble, or self-sacrificing, he would sigh and be very sad—maybe because the good stuff was temporary. I don't know. Or sad that he did it only when he had the time and was in the mood. Sometimes he forgot such things and was superbly confident—or was that a bluff?

I don't know. I really can't speak for him.

* * *

I LOOK at my hand and then at his; it is not really conceivable to me that both are hands: mine is a sort of hand. He tells me over and over that I must not upset him—he tells me of my power over him—I don't know how to take such a fact—is it a fact? I stare at him. I gasp with the ache of life stirring in me—again: again: *again*—I ache with tentative and complete and then again tentative belief.

For a long time piety was anything at all sitting still or moving slowly and not rushing at me or away from me but letting me look at it or be near it without there being any issue of safety-about-to-be-lost.

This world is evasive.

But someone who lets you observe him is not evasive, is not hurtful, at that moment: it is like in sleep where *the other* waits—the Master of Dreams—and there are doors, doorways opening into farther rooms where there is an altered light, and which I enter to find—what? That someone is gone? That the room is empty? Or perhaps I find a vista, of rooms, of archways, and a window, and a peach tree in flower—a tree with peach-colored flowers in the solitude of night.

I AM DYING of grief, Daddy. I am waiting here, limp with abandonment, with exhaustion: perhaps I'd better believe in God. . . .

MY FATHER'S virtues, those I dreamed about, those I saw when I was awake, those I understood and misunderstood, were, as I felt them, in dreams or wakefulness, when I was a child, like a broad highway opening into a small dusty town that was myself; and down that road came bishops and slogans, Chinese processions, Hasidim in a dance, the nation's honor and glory *in its young people*, baseball players, singers who sang "with their whole hearts," automobiles and automobile grilles, and grave or comic bits of instruction. This man is attached to me and makes me light up with festal affluence and oddity; he says, "I think you love me."

He was right.

HE WOULD move his head—his giant face—and you could observe in his eyes the small town that was me in its temporary sophistication, a small town giving proof on every side of its arrogance and its prosperity and its puzzled contentment.

He also instructed me in hatred: he didn't mean to, not openly: but I saw and picked up the curious buzzing of his puckered distastes, a nastiness of dismissal that he had: a fetor of let-them-all-kill-each-other. He hated lots of people, whole races: he hated ugly women.

He conferred an odd inverted splendor on awfulness—because *he* knew about it: he went into it every day. He told me not to want that, not to want to know about that: he told me to go on being just the way I was—"a nice boy."

When he said something was unbearable, he meant it; he meant he could not bear it.

In my memories of this time of my life, it seems to be summer all the time, even when the ground is white: I suppose it seems like summer because I was never cold.

A H : I wanted to see. . . .

My father, when he was low (in spirit), would make rounds, inside his head, checking on his consciousness, to see if it was safe from inroads by *the unbearable:* he found an all-is-well in a quiet emptiness. . . .

In an uninvadedness, he found the weary complacency and self-importance of All is Well.

(The women liked invasions—up to a point.)

O N E D A Y he came home, mysterious, exalted, hatted and suited, roseate, handsome, a little sweaty—it really was summer that day. He was exalted—as I said—but nervous toward me, anxious with promises.

And he was, oh, somewhat angry, justified, toward the world, toward me, not exactly as a threat (in case I didn't respond) but as a jumble.

He woke me from a nap, an uneasy nap, lifted me out of bed, me, a child who had not expected to see him that afternoon—I was not particularly happy that day, not particularly pleased with him, not pleased with him at all, really.

He dressed me himself. At first he kept his hat on. After a while, he took it off. When I was dressed, he said, "You're pretty sour today," and he put his hat back on.

He hustled me down the stairs; he held my wrist in his enormous palm—immediate and gigantic to me and blankly suggestive of a meaning I could do nothing about except stare at blankly from time to time in my childish life.

We went outside into the devastating heat and glare, the blathering, humming afternoon light of a Midwestern summer day: a familiar furnace.

We walked along the street, past the large, silent houses, set, each one, in hard, pure light. You could not look directly at anything; the glare, the reflections were too strong.

Then he lifted me in his arms—aloft.

He was carrying me to help me because the heat was bad—and worse near the sidewalk, which reflected it upward into my face—and because my legs were short and I was struggling, because he was in a hurry and because he liked carrying me, and because I was sour and blackmailed him with my unhappiness, and he was being kind with a certain—limited—mixture of exasperation-turning-into-a-degree-of-mortal-love.

O r i t w a s another time, really early in the morning, when the air was partly asleep, partly adance, but in veils, trembling with heavy moisture. Here and there, the air broke into a string of beads of pastel colors, pink, pale green, small rainbows, really small, and very narrow. Daddy walked rapidly. I bounced in his arms. My eyesight was unforced—it bounced, too. Things were more than merely present: they pressed against me: they had the aliveness of myth, of the beginning of an adventure when nothing is explained as yet.

All at once we were at the edge of a bankless river of yellow light. To be truthful, it was like a big, wooden beam of fresh, unweathered wood: but we entered it: and then it turned into light, cooler light than in the hot humming afternoon but full of bits of heat that stuck to me and then were blown away, a semiheat, not really friendly, yet reassuring: and very dimly sweaty; and it grew, it spread: this light turned into a knitted cap of light, fuzzy, warm, woven, itchy: it was pulled over my head, my hair, my forehead, my eyes, my nose, my mouth.

So I turned my face away from the sun—I turned it so it was pressed against my father's neck mostly—and then I knew, in a childish way, knew from the heat (of his neck, of his shirt collar), knew by childish deduction, that his face was unprotected from the luminousness all around us: and I looked; and it was so: his face, for the moment unembarrassedly, was caught in that light. In an accidental glory.

Puberty

SOMETIMES in New York, I can create a zone of amusement and doubt around me by saying I was a Boy Scout.

I am forty-four years old now, bearded—I suppose I have a certain personal ambience that makes Boy Scouthood unlikely.

I don't think it's my fault.

I WAS a Boy Scout in 1942. I was about five seven, newly grown from five two or three; I was temporarily deformed, with short squat legs and feet that were nearly square—the arches had grown but I still had a child's toes. I had other physical anomalies of that sort: big knees and stick-like thighs.

My balls had dropped; my prick had started to grow—it was about five inches, not particularly thin, large for a child's—it was still growing.

I was by some standards of measurement the smartest child in the state of Missouri. I was, am, Jewish and had been very ugly and was still, as well as deformed, but I was slowly turning, slowly showing a pale, transparent physical quality, which in the suburb where I lived at that time was called "cute"—it didn't mean cuddly: it meant interesting—I think. My ears stuck out: I had them pinned back when I was in college, grown tired of the problem posed when one's appearance lies about what one is like. My father had heart trouble and was something of an invalid; he dabbled in the black market—there was a war and rationing.

My mother was mentally unwell. I mention these things because they made up my social position.

The Boy Scout troops I knew about were, each one, attached to a church—or a temple; I don't believe synagogues bothered. Each troop had a social rank according to the social rank of the church or temple that founded it.

It cost money to belong to a Reform temple: you had to have that extra money and be willing to enter on the confused clashing of social climbing and Anglo-Saxon mimicry and personal loneliness and religion as a set of tenets and questions about the secular, the fate of Jews, and the nature of guilt—such things as that—in the Middle West, among the cornfields. We had Sunday school and confirmation—nothing Jewish except the rabbi's nose: it was the boniest, largest, most hooked nose I ever saw, ever in my life; he also used his hands a lot when he talked. He was reputed to be "a good speaker," but I believe it was his nose and hands, his physical status as a Jew—I don't remember him ever making a religious remark or showing any interest in anything to do with the spirit—that enabled him to force a salary of twenty-five thousand dollars a year, in 1942, from the Russo-Jewish magnates—well-tailored, quick-eyed, bad-tempered, secretive, restless, and clever—who ran the temple.

The rabbi was so jealous of a book called *Peace of Mind* written by a Boston rabbi, and which became a best seller, that he wrote a book called *Peace of Soul*—he wanted very much to be famous—and he had it printed privately and mailed to every member of the congregation in a plain brown wrapper with a bill enclosed: a married couple would be sent two copies and two bills, each bill being for three dollars.

We were members of the temple because my mother's brother was on the board of directors. He was rich by local standards, and I was smart; and either he had a dim sense of community duty or else his two sons irritated him: he did not think his sons were smart. I thought they were smart enough. One wanted to be an artist and tried the arts, each in turn, and he insisted he was unhappy, which made his father very restless. My uncle was skinny. His other son was a perfect Anglo-Saxon except for a nose shaped like a peanut: that, too, displeased my uncle although this son was brave and athletic and likable enough; he did drink and spend a lot of money, and he wracked up the family Cadillac twice, once by crashing into the gatehouse that guarded the entrance to the enclave where my uncle had his house. Of that son, his mother said,

"He's so brave: his jaw is wired shut and he never complains." My uncle said his son was meshuggeneh, and to irritate him and the other one as they irritated him, he would praise me and "do things" for me such as send me to Sunday school or finance my entry into the Boy Scouts: not only finance it but insist the troop pursue me since I didn't want to join. It seemed I owed it to Judaism and the war effort to be a Boy Scout.

The troop had a reputation for consisting of three types of boys—the refined, the would-be refined who would probably never get there (to refinement), and the wild ones, the crazy or tough ones, pugnacious or obsessive. I always thought refinement was a joke, all things considered, and do still, but some of those boys were very impressive, I thought: two of the older ones, who had remarkable, even tempers and never showed signs of cruelty or of pride except for expecting quietly to be dominant, spoke to each other only in Latin. Another boy knew entire Shakespearean plays by heart. And two of the boys would hum themes from a Brahms quintet—I couldn't do things like that. But I was famous locally, and they were not. I was powerful at school and could force a teacher to regive a test that was unfair or unclear: not for my sake—my grades were always high; my average was sometimes given as 101—but for the sake of my classmates. Then, too, because of my foul tongue and for other reasons, the working-class kids at school, a minority, accepted me: I was a point where the varying kinds of middle-class children, the few rich, and the slightly more numerous poor met. There were two or three other children of whom this was true (including two political girls), but they were fine children and had not read Thomas Mann. I was considered a fine child because of my parents' plight and the way I treated my parents, but there was something decidedly not fine about me, something anomalous and confusing; it is very unlikely but it is true that I was treated, on the whole, with respect; and so fineness was ascribed to me to resolve the anomaly and strangeness.

In those days, fine or "distinguished" families had a decided moral tone: social climbing had a moral cast to it—as in how much you gave to charity and how much charitable work you did—and this moral tone was refined: it included euphemisms such as "passed on" or "passed away." It was my opinion as a child unable sometimes to crack the grownups' code of talk that if someone will lie about what to call a fuck, they'll lie about anything. Also, if you remember, eleven and twelve pre- and during puberty are particularly nasty, intellectual, realpolitik ages— at least for some kids, male and female. I had, decidedly, a moral rank, a high one, but it was not based on the right things; however, people did not keep track, and they would have some vague sense that I *was* refined. Meanwhile the war blazed. I had enormous maps with flags; and I fretted over strategy, the quality of Allied war matériel and leadership—Churchill was a complete bust militarily—the problems of courage, and the daily and unremitting horror of what one translator of Proust calls "a bloody hedge of men constantly renewed."

If life were nice—well, nicer—one would have Einstein's katzenjammers, space and time for research, a number of anecdotes, nuances, but one is rushed. One has to forgo discussing the names of ranks in Boy Scouts, from Tenderfoot to Eagle Scout, and the Merit Badges, and the costume partly designed to mimic the uniforms developed by the British during the Boer War. There is the subject of Anglophilia—where *is* the Anglophilia of yesteryear?—and the equipment: where did those sleeping bags and axes and knives come from in wartime? Perhaps everyone had an older brother.

In small towns, social class is comparatively simple: the line is between respectability and the rest—if the small-town rich are not respectable, they are excluded. It's more complicated in a city. The Scouts from the beginning had an origin in social class but with a built-in ambiguity: there were to be troops for poor boys to give them a chance at purity and so on; but the main thrust, I think, was to keep the middle class or upper middle class trained in outdoorsmanship for leadership in the Boer War. It was a junior paramilitary outfit designed to teach skills for guerrilla warfare in open plains—maybe in the woods. It was not up-to-date: the Scouts in my time were still doing Morse code and stuff with semaphores; and the walkie-talkie was already in use, and slang instead of codes (or so the papers said). Besides that, one *knew* about the army and social class, that the poor and Southern rednecks made up the troops, and they shot incompetent, cruel, hysterical, or snobbish officers in the back in battle—or so *I* was told—and how could we practice leadership if we had no rednecks, farmers, or working-class boys in the troop? These things worried me. I was told that as Jews we wouldn't be given a chance to lead usually anyway, not even in the quartermaster corps. It seemed our refinement, as a troop, was slightly warped by competition toward other troops and was actually an exercise in self-righteousness expended in a vacuum.

I think a third of the boys in the troop were quite mad—some with unfocused adolescent rage, some with confusions, others with purity.

One boy, the son of an accountant and a very talkative mother, had a mania for Merit Badges, a silly giggle, acne on his back, large muscles from lifting weights, and a way of leaping from stillness into a walk like a two-legged horse that suggested to me considerable mental dislocation. Some boys were mad with slyness, some were already money mad, some were panic-stricken. There they were, lined up in the temple auditorium in their khakis, with axes in snap-on head holsters, or whatever, on their belts and sheathed knives and neckerchiefs and that damned sliding ring to hold the neckerchief.

I remember—not in great detail: this is not something I am going to present in the full panoply of reality—going on a fourteen-mile hike. Or was it a twelve-mile hike? I don't remember, but you had to do it to pass from some rank—Tenderfoot?—to another—Second Class? Maybe. (You had to pass other tests, too.) This hike came quite early in my brief Scouting career before I created the scandal and furor in the troop by insisting that for my outdoor-cooking test I be allowed to use premade biscuit dough from a can—like a real soldier. "Do you hate Scouting?" one of the men who ran the troop asked me. I don't think I did, but perhaps I did.

The hike had to be done within a certain length of time, and I think you had to run or jog twelve minutes and then walk twelve minutes, it was twelve somethings or other, twelve paces maybe (the injunction against self-abuse was on page four hundred and something of the manual). The route had been laid out on back roads in the country—roads built in the twenties for developments that weren't built because the Depression came. They were concrete, mostly, and cracked, and grass grew out of them in spots. I had a new pair of shoes paid for by the uncle whose doing all this was—Boy Scout shoes. A slightly older boy—he was thirteen, probably, with a patch of pimples on one cheek, an exacerbated triangle of them, and then a few single ones on his forehead and chin—was to lead us, instruct us, keep us from cheating. Quiet-voiced, he bore the look of someone planed down and cautious from the skirmishes grownups wage, often for the sake of social climbing or in the name of happiness, in order to enforce what purity they can on their young. He had not yet outgrown his freakishness: he was too broad and short-legged and long-necked; he was less freakish than I was—I think he took on the final physical shape for the duration of his youth when he was fifteen. This boy's eyes were extraordinarily blank, as if he had found childhood and youth to be a long, long wait.

I can almost count us—five or seven boys were to make the march. Ah, memory—or research. I think there were five of us. The leader made six. The idea of seven comes to me because the five of us doing the march for the first time, the Tenderfoots, were dwarfs. Two were still physically ten years old although they had turned twelve: they were bright and quick, brainy. No bodily growth dimmed their intellects or powers of vision.

Where did we gather? Someone's front lawn, I think. I remember we talked about how we were doing more than the statutory distance because of where we started. There were jokes about the humiliation of giving up. We clomped along. I don't remember the running—the alterations of running with walking: it seems to me some of the younger boys skipped; and we were of such different heights that we couldn't run with any order; and so we walked slowly for a while, and then faster, then slowly.

One boy had to give up or thought he did: he had a blister; he was one of the smaller boys—proud and temperamental, too. He didn't receive much sympathy, but he wasn't mocked, either—we stared at him; I don't know why we didn't mock him: either because this was Scouting or because we were well-bred Jews, you know, compassionate. It was one reason or the other. I remember him sitting by the side of the road in the weeds, an apple-cheeked kid small for his age. Do weeds survive pollution? Was he supposed to walk home or hitchhike: an occasional car did pass on this road but very occasionally. Hitchhiking wasn't considered dangerous in the county: you knew what a safe person looked like and smelled like; if they had the wrong eyes or smell, you said, "No, thank you," and if they persisted, you screamed. I don't remember grownups talking much about children being molested—we children spoke of it once in a while: it is strange to remember the essential panic and curiosity we felt day after day as we struggled to grow up.

Anyway, we left one child behind or was it two? Did we assign him a companion? We young ones did not know what was going on, and it would have been pushy, like usurping control of the hike, to figure things out. Our leader had no interest in leadership: he had been made a leader against his will, I think, and he found it dull and had no particular talent for it; he would stare off into the sky or into the branches of trees—this was latish autumn, chilly and damp, a gray day—if you asked him a question. I think he had an older brother he was pretty much dependent on—not that it matters now.

We didn't know how to walk distances. We discussed how to carry yourself—we put our shoulders back—we rose up on our toes—but none of our particular group was coordinated physically yet, not even our leader; and we progressed clumsily, in haphazard effort, muscular effort; at times, two boys—it was usually by twos—would find a rhythm, find a way of walking, hip joint, spine, ankle, knee, and foot; and they would sail along, sail ahead, ahead even of the leader, who clomped along at the side of the road, sad and dutiful. I had a nail in my shoe—I've never been lucky with equipment: I once had a pair of galoshes that leaked. The nail gouged my heel, and it was painful as all hell, but people were always worried about how sensitive I was—how much I noticed, what did I think of them, was I a sissy all in all, did intelligence make a coward of me: that sort of thing—and I was used to concealing pain: in this case I persuaded myself it was preparation for real war, but I hated the pain anyway as unnecessary and part of a fools' march.

The route was laid out like a rough figure eight, and when we came to where the two loops crossed, we saw some other boys coming down the far road at an angle to us. They were not dwarfs. We knew them, but I don't recall if they were from our troop or merely from the county somewhere. I think they were richer Jews—maybe merely older, with real legs, real hands. There was a twenty-mile hike, I think, for passing from some upper rank to one still higher; or maybe it was thirty miles.

The greetings echoed among the trees on that empty road. But they were not really good-natured. There was some discussion between our leader and their leader—the other leader was not bored and had on at least three lanyards: the ends were tucked into his pleated pocket, but I would imagine he had a whistle, a pocketknife, and maybe a compass. I suppose the ill nature of the greetings came from mutual suspicion: we were outcasts, prepubic; but the other group was crazed and low with Scouting. One forgets how satiric children are just before puberty, how harsh in judgment; and how strange the ones seem who after puberty are cheerful or enthusiastic and not gloomy and secretive.

The older Scouts were on a rigorous schedule, and yet two of them joined us. The mysteries accumulate and suggest to me the mysteries of that day as I lived it, of being on a road I did not know, doing a faintly foolish thing, among boys I did not know.

Because of my reputation, I was more or less suffered to ask more questions than most younger children were allowed to ask, but I was not in a mood to use my privilege: I was being one of the bunch. The

new boys were quite old and glamorous; one was skinny: in the end I
did gravitate to the older boys and to the leader—I felt older than my
age, and I was nosy, I believe. One of the newcomers noticed I was
limping and I told him about the nail, but he didn't believe me. An entire
lifetime of people saying *I don't believe you* suddenly weighs on me.
Sighing, I sat down on a stone alongside the road and took off my shoe
and showed him the blood on my sock; and then I took off my sock and
showed him the wound. There was talk of tetanus from the nail, but one
of the dwarfs said his father/was a doctor and the nail would have had
to have been exposed to manure to be dangerous. I had been told
swearing was lip filth, but I did it anyway. I said, "Well, I didn't shit
in my shoe, so I'm probably all right." This was considered pretty
charming and was looked on as revealing a real sense of humor—life was
simpler then—and it made the leader like me and the two older boys
and some of the dwarfs: I had magically become a nondwarf in the
course of the hike, a big shot. Liking led to talk of sex: the boys were
walking more or less in a circle around me—some of them walked
backward—and told me about fucking. I had heard before, frequently,
but I was one of the more latent boys: it had never really penetrated,
but now it did; I was disbelieving. "My parents wouldn't do that," I said.
They had to in order to have children, I was told. "Not my parents,"
I said, and then thought about my parents: "Well, they might do it in
a closet," I said. One of the older boys said, "Don't you masturbate?"
I did but wasn't sure how that related to sex, to fucking; the explanations
I was offered were unclear to me. An older boy said, "Didn't you ever
fool around with another boy?"

"What do you mean? We're fooling around now."

"It's called homosexuality," one of the younger boys said, "and it's
a phase."

"It's all right until you're about sixteen, and then it has to be girls."

"How come?" I said.

"Let's go in the woods and look at each other's pricks," one of the
younger boys said—one of the boys with no prick.

There was a sudden flurry of talk: did we have the time, and one boy
had promised his parents he would never do anything dirty; and then
we all went into the woods, the two newcomers, the older boys, leading
the way.

We crashed clumsily among twigs and bushes until we came to a
clearing, a mud-floored glade. The older boys and some of the younger

ones immediately took up positions showing experience—from summer camp or wherever—in a circle.

But there were two kinds of circle: clumped close together, the units, I mean, and more spread out. Somehow without voting we settled on a spread-out circle or oval—we were about an arm's length from each other. I believe one of the older boys counted and then we all unbuttoned; and some boys revealed themselves at once; but some didn't; and the older boy counted again, and at the count of three we all displayed ourselves.

It was very quiet. I thought it was all very interesting, but I was a little blank-headed, almost sleepy: I wasn't sure why it was so interesting: but it was clear from the silence, the way the boys breathed and stood, from the whole atmosphere, that this was more interesting than the hike itself, this curious introduction to genital destiny.

Then it was decided we should all try to come—I think how it went was someone asked if I could come, and I wasn't sure—I wasn't sure what he meant: I really had an enormous gift for latency.

Some boys didn't know how to masturbate and were shown the gesture. But before we began, there was a ceremony of touching each other's pricks. No one in that glade was fully developed. The absence of cruelty became silently, by implication, an odd sort of stilled and limited tenderness.

Then the circle was re-formed—in the silent glade—and we all began to pull rhythmically: perhaps it was like rubbing at Aladdin's lamp; perhaps we are at the threshold of the reign of magic and death. The glade was shadowy and smelled vinegary—it also smelled of earth. A few boys came—a drop or two. We cleaned ourselves with leaves and with a Kleenex one boy divvied up.

The leader looked at his watch and said we were ten minutes behind schedule.

S o   t h e n we hurried—we left the woods and went on with the hike.

There is no time for the rest of what I want to tell about the Boy Scouts.

Bibliographical Note

The stories in this book originally appeared, some of them in significantly different form, in the following publications:

"The Abundant Dreamer"	*The New Yorker*, November 23, 1963
"On the Waves"	*The New Yorker*, September 4, 1965
"Bookkeeping"	*The New Yorker*, April 27, 1968
"Hofstedt and Jean— and Others"	*The New Yorker*, January 25, 1969
"The Shooting Range"	*The New Yorker*, September 13, 1969
"Innocence"	*American Review*, 16, February 1973
"Play"	*American Review*, 17, May 1973
"A Story in an Almost Classical Mode"	*The New Yorker*, September 17, 1973
"His Son, in His Arms, in Light, Aloft"	*Esquire*, August 1975
"Puberty"	*Esquire*, December 1975